THE
SWEET-SCENTED
MANUSCRIPT

TITO PERDUE # THE
SWEET-SCENTED
MANUSCRIPT

ARKTOS
LONDON 2019

ISBN   978-1-912975-37-2 (Paperback)
                      978-1-912975-38-9 (Hardback)
                      978-1-912975-39-6 (Ebook)

PROOFREADING   John Bruce Leonard

COVER & LAYOUT   Tor Westman

🌐 Arktos.com   ◉ fb.com/Arktos   🐦 @arktosmedia   ◎ arktosmedia

I

ONE

SOMETHING *WAS* HAPPENING; there was no sound anywhere. These faces moreover, which turned away whenever he looked at them, they seemed unusually pale. He saw a middle-aged woman who had not slept in days apparently, and yet was able to smile back bravely through her make-up.

Quickly they passed through town. Here inside, the bus was loftier than ever he had imagined; it seemed to promise an unsteady voyage. That he was going away, that he was never coming back... Suddenly, an automobile came up and then was gone, leaving him with the memory of a blue glazed face that began to break up even as he meditated on it. Came next a girl, a mere long-haired child sitting by the roadbed while talking to herself bitterly in autumn. Next to him, someone coughed twice, a polite sound followed up by low conversation with many long pauses.

When they broke into the adjoining county, Lee saw that all was as had been foretold: a lake that sparkled redly for an instant and then shifted back to blue. He clove to the window; it dizzied him, how that the world could be as extensive as it was, with numerous counties, each with its hue, all sitting shoulder to shoulder year after year and each with a long and unguessable history of its own. Now came a village, noiseless behind glass. Everywhere he looked — campaign posters on behalf of Eisenhower. Here, too, something had happened once, something that had reduced to silence the six petrified old men sitting out in front of one of the stores. Lee looked for, and found, the inevitable sleeping hound with missing tail.

The bus slowed, clambered across a wooden bridge, and then began running again over open country. He spied pumpkin fields and browned orchards with apples decaying forgottenly on the stem. No doubt about it, the world was plaid-colored in September, and never had the farms been more picture-worthy, with pastel roosters posturing on every gable. Any moment now he expected to read the name of this county (as if on a map) engraved in mile-high characters across the rather complicated terrain. Meanwhile, in the East, a long row of clouds was scraping at the hill whileas for the peasants, (and he could see numbers of them), they were altogether too intent upon their hoeing to stand upright and plunge their heads into the stuff.

They were riding upon a city, a grand one with tall buildings heaped up one on top of another with birds wheeling about the spires. Next to them, stride for stride, Lee identified a bald-headed truck driver in opaque glasses who seemed to be lunging forward hungrily toward a fascinating death. In front, two of the women had taken out their combs, their rouge and equipment, and were assisting each other in their haste. Suddenly, Lee grabbed for his wallet, finding it intact. What his own future might be, whether startling or not, or whether purchased at huge suffering, he could not rightly say. Just now he felt nothing but envy for the little grey man two rows in front who had finished with all that and who kept glancing back at him in amusement while sucking all times upon his pipe.

The city itself, once they had come into the heart of it, astonished Lee so much that he lost the expression of perpetual boredom that he preferred to maintain. Pressing at the glass, he quickly singled out a girl in heels and merrily bouncing hair who had a certain optimistic gait. Young was she, lovely too, and yet, oddly, such as they were, with separate fates… Never would they meet, never. Came next an evil man, and behind him a fat woman floundering in his wake with packages and bags. A theater came up, and now Lee saw that it was showing a Marlon Brando film that he had seen but twice before. For one brief moment he was tempted to rise and go and see it again; instead, just then, he noted a boy of his own precise type, size and style lounging in one of the doorways. This boy, however, smoked cigarettes. They looked at each other, nodded, and glanced away.

The bus turned and entered now through an opening in the wall that immediately closed up behind them, like a camera shutter. At once Lee stood and began to fight his way to the front.

"Birmingham, right? Is this Birmingham? It is, isn't it?"

The driver turned slowly. Lee had seen his sort before, eyes like seeds, always searching through his inventory of withering things to say. Finally, able to stay no longer, Lee stepped down onto the platform and, moving backwards, was taken up by the crowd. Now it hit him, the unparalleled smell of the city. Lee grabbed for his wallet. But mostly it was the surprise of finding that the little grey man of ten minutes ago had somehow put himself at the head of the line.

Inside the station, the throng was greater than he could have imagined. He saw all manner of people, but especially he saw two cheap-looking girls in shorts and lipstick loitering around the pinball machine. He very much wished to use the rest room; however, there were far, far too many people coming in and out, testing their zippers with one hand while wearing starched faces. Instead, he went into the little green restaurant that smelled of perfume and cigars and, seating himself, ordered coffee in a bored voice. He had just begun to sip at it and to study some of the personalities in the room when, suddenly, mind reeling, he stood and dashed back to the open space where, as he saw with huge relief, the bus was just where he had left it, the driver munching on a sandwich.

"I forgot something," he said.

"Somehow that don't surprise me."

"Can I come in and get it?"

The man looked at him, apparently on the verge of that withering comment he wanted. Instead, he said:

"Pro-ceed, pro-ceed."

Lee leapt to it, finding his lunch bag and then reemerging slowly, lest the man try and trip him on the stairs. The cheap girls were still in place, one of them now bending over the pinball machine in her tight white shorts; girls did not dress in this fashion in the place he came from. He wanted to throw something at her, but instead turned in at the men's room which proved vacant now, apart from a pair of shoes, a briefcase, a half-empty bottle and Kewpie doll visible beneath the walls of one of the cells. Too, there was a well-dressed man gazing hypnotically in the mirror while slowly and patiently washing his already very clean hands. Himself, Lee went to the urinal and had almost finished with it when, suddenly, it came down on him in horror that he had left his suitcase behind. This time it required a major exertion of the Will to shut off what he was doing and then, flying down the hall and into the little green room, to get back his possession before another could claim it. And now he was calm, but the coffee had gone tepid on him. Suddenly, he dug for his billfold.

For ten minutes he sauntered here and there, nodding condescendingly to the merchants in their booths. Finally, he approached the cage where a shrunken-looking man in a yellow visor was studying his nails with a face of astuteness.

"Where?" he asked.

"Sir?"

"Where're you going!"

"College."

"What?"

"Ohio."

"Where in Ohio!"

Lee had to think. The man, who was uttering rapidly — Lee could decipher none of it — then threw down a sloppy volume with pages coming out and began splashing through it, his face reflecting anguish.

Lee could see this much, that while he was but an insignificant person, or anyway held but an insignificant position, yet did he wear a massive blood-red ring with a cobra on it. Lee paid, slipped the ticket into his pocket but then immediately took it out again and laid it away more carefully in the folds of his wallet. Next to him was a booth full of magazines and souvenirs, all of it presided over by a worried-looking Chinese in a baseball cap. For some moments, Lee stood examining the merchandise, his attention caught by a tray of little pink plastic mermaids dressed in brassieres.

"You want…?"

"Naw." Suddenly, without having thought about it, he added: "I'll have a pack of cigarettes however."

That someone was standing too close to him… Lee was acutely aware of it. Now, coming nearer, the man, who was full of whiskers, began to examine the left side of Lee's face at very close range.

"Reckon you're headed somewhere important with that there suitcase, real important. 'Wonder what he's got in there!' I said. Couldn't lend me a dime, could you?"

"Naw," said Lee. "I got a quarter though."

"Why… You're a damn good man! Damn good! You just wait right here, that's right, and I'll git your change for you, just wait right here, that's right." He turned and bumbled off hurriedly across the rotunda. Suddenly, Lee plunged for his wallet, which still was there. An orderly came by, a mordant-looking black man pushing a little hill of dirt with a long-handled broom.

Full five minutes he had waited, his mind benumbed with noise and sights, when came the summons by a huge God-like voice so slurred and cloudy that no matter how cogently Lee listened or how near he drew up to the speaker, he could make out no word of it. Again, he plunged. The ticket itself was long, thin, rose-colored, and bore the picture of a bus on it. It was only then that he realized that the man in the cage had been yelling at him.

"Hey! aren't you supposed to be on that bus?"

Lee could not but smile. "Naw. I've still got a couple of minutes."

"You've got about two seconds, is what you've got!"

"But what about my change?"

"Go! Go!"

Mind reeling, he gathered the suitcase and fled. This time the driver was an elderly man; Lee could see that he was debating as whether to open or not.

"I had to wait for my change."

"'Change.'"

"I didn't get it."

"Goddamn it, I'm late already, and now... I don't know what it is with you people!"

Lee entered, doing it with dignity. Inside, he found thirty upturned faces all straining to see what sort of person it was. His preferred place, the bench in the extreme rear, was taken already by a plump red-faced woman who plainly wanted him to come no further. The only other vacant space would have placed him next to a child who, even as they looked at one another, began to drool. Under the circumstances, Lee went and squeezed in next to the woman.

Night did come. Cars ran forward to meet them, their drivers missing, while in the far distance he could see random dots of light indicating where some people were willing to reside on the very edge of the world itself. The bus meanwhile was slicing into the substance, hurrying toward Tennessee and other points that he had never seen before. Half a mile in front, a lemur turned and fired back at them with amber eyes. These were empty lands, these, so much so that he began to suspect that they were being conducted, not through modern times, but ancient Assyria, or Persia perhaps, or rather through some giant coiled mind capable of having dreamt it all. The moon, too, had altered and was a frail thing now, brittle as lace and in danger of breaking apart. Taking a cigarette, he lit it with aplomb, (right away, his head began to feel despicable) and then glanced to the woman whose eye was upon him even while her face pointed straight ahead.

The match, still bright, was on the floor where at first he tried to spit on it. In the mirror, Lee now found the driver staring deeply into the future with eyes agog, his expression having taken on an evil cast.

They came to a town, slowed, and then went on noiselessly for a distance before turning into an avenue bordered on both sides with stores and churches in perfect preservation. The station itself gleamed in the distance, an aquarium as it seemed, with curious life forms pressing at the windows.

He left the bus, picking up a wad of gum on the sole of his shoe the moment he touched down. The waiting room was full of souls all hungering for rest, for respite, and final destinations. He saw a young pale girl with two large babies, one of them crying desultorily and the other frantic. A fat man, his shirt torn, himself unclean, was continually hanging around the pay phones with his finger in the slot. Having made his tour, Lee ducked into the toilet where some dozen men were dancing adroitly to keep from stepping into a large golden pond snaking toward the door.

He went outside, loitered for a time, and then cut behind the building. Was it Tennessee? The moon was large enough, while further away on the horizon, the cloud blots looked like so many little boats bobbing cheerfully out to eternity. The night was mild and had a blueness to it that made him want to run and jump, pushing aside the molecules. Suddenly, that moment, three hundred crickets chimed in with one voice, a tremendous noise that caused at least one light to come on in the upstairs window.

He strolled to the front of the building. He was smoking well, enjoying it even through the headache when, to his absolute amazement, he saw that the other passengers were on board already and waiting for him, all of them highly displeased. He jumped to it, never looking at the driver, and then padded on down to his bench where, as he realized at once, someone had sat upon the bag that was supposed to hold his lunch. Again, the bus lurched forward, gathering speed and then joining the highway amid a flurry of bright yellow signs with instructions on them.

It was the finest of hours, between one and three, when his own system was at its utmost and others were at their most defenseless. Indeed, those in front could scarcely hold their heads up, as if they had nothing but the mandate of the sun to keep them going, or rather as if they could think of nothing to do when there was nothing that had to be done. He considered flipping his burnt-out cigarette in amongst them, but then changed his mind and let it fly out the window instead. Already the first infinitesimal break of day was visible in the far distance, exposing itself through a fissure where the clouds were thin. They were running over dead-level country now, through a region without qualities where no one had chosen to live. Had he, without knowing, passed over into the North? Such was his knowledge of geography. He did see one ruined house with a curled tin roof, and out front a long-headed mule keeping strange vigil in the night.

He took a cigarette, considered it, returned it, and then probed around for his lunch bag. Inside was a sandwich (much flattened), an exploded banana, and some other material in wax paper. The sandwich itself held four excellent slices of broiled chicken straight off the breast and dotted with black pepper, all of it spread on a page of lettuce. He preferred it this way, when the meat was cold and had lain for a great or lesser time in mayonnaise and mustard. Suddenly he began wolfing it down, making so much noise that the man in front, without actually coming awake, pricked up both ears. The wax paper held four, (hitherto the number had never been more than three) cookies, all now reduced to rubble.

When came dawn, Lee awoke, stretched, took his first view of the undoubted North and then immediately closed his eyes again. He had expected a pulsating city scene with whores; what he got was a long level field of sorghum. He grabbed for his wallet. Down the aisle, a woman was listing dangerously with mouth agape, while the driver himself, in morning light, now turned out to be a poor ashen figure of a man such that Lee could hardly believe him to be the same as had guided them safely through the foregoing black night.

There was a strangeness to it, of having resituated from his own region to this new one, of which he knew virtually nothing. He saw a man who, apparently, had been trying to get home when a cold front had moved across; he stood now in the sorghum field, frozen forever with one foot off the ground. Further still, he saw a radio tower, immensely tall as it was, with three blinking lanterns marking where once a civilization had risen and fell.

He stood, inadvertently yanking out a handkerchief that he had never seen before, a big square item that unfolded slowly like a flag. Four rows in front, a bulky woman had set her thick stockinged leg in preparation to rise. Looking at her, and the leg, he tried to deduce from this whether she was of the college or not, and therefore whether highly intelligent or not. The town itself, which had come up around them, seemed unexceptional at first, until he spotted a very tall boy dressed in a black beard and sandals hunching along with the weight of the world on him. Lee was stricken — he knew great intelligence when he saw it. And then he saw a girl in stringy hair and glasses carrying two books and a violin case. Yesterday, he had been but a boy, a pecan gatherer dithering in culverts and gulches, and now he had broken into a pocket of thought and art that, just as he had always suspected, had been abiding here in secret all these years. Heart booming, knee caps trembling, he stood, put on a bored expression, sat again, stood, and then, (suitcase with him) rushed to the door and tumbled out onto a platform with a roof over it.

He was alone. Moreover, he had lost his cap somewhere along the way. He had expected to be put down among students and brick buildings overwhelmed with vines; the only building here of any size lay well off the road and seemed designed for poultry.

He moved hurriedly, covering the three blocks to the center of the village. There was a dress shop and then a theater, (small) a vegetable stall and, next, a vacant building used as an art gallery. He had intended to proceed straight to his room and to stay there, instead, with his face and nerves, his accent and the preposterous handkerchief hanging out, he saw that he must return at once to Alabama, either that or hold out in the woods for a few days and wait for a moonless night.

He went on more slowly, trekking past a shoe repair, a tinsmith's shop and then, next to that, where the city came to an end, a darkened café in which he could make out a tiny number of little tables with candles on them. From here he could look out over a tundra, as it were, waste land with but few houses on it; it led, he knew, to Springfield and beyond. Now again he heard that libelous voice telling him that his real destiny was not college so much as that he ought to go traveling, traveling forever, traveling to Springfield and beyond. Indeed, bending forward, he thought that he could make out the very path to start him on his way.

He turned, trudging eastwardly, (he was not good, not yet, at walking on cobblestone) and then, with the suitcase beginning to drag at him, set foot on a placid-looking street decorated with old homes and painted trees losing their leaves already. This was the street, he knew, that led on down to campus.

TWO

HAVING ASKED FOR HIS ROOM, he went straight to it, glancing neither to right nor left. Four flights he climbed, into a stark region that lay under darkness and smoke. Here, bag in hand, he stood looking down a row of cells where a tapering swatch of light washed against the wall. Twice he tested the floor before venturing forward into an area invested with the smell of coffee and mildew and where two shafts of sunlight had broken through to illuminate particles of dust dancing in suspension. Music was playing, very far away. It was while he was standing, his suitcase in one hand and wallet the other, that a boy burst out of one of the cells, stopped, and then came closer.

"We have to go to the President's home. Who are you?"

"Leland."

"From Alabama?"

"Right."

"Gloomy-looking bastard! How long you been standing there? We have to go to the President's home."

"Where is it?"

"Hell, I don't know."

They stood looking at one another. The other boy was shorter than Lee, but more aptly built. His was a handsome face, lightly speckled and set on a loaf-shaped head. Moreover, he wore a suit.

"Maybe we could find it?"

"The President's home? I don't know Leland. Finding is tough."

(Lee looked off, humming. The boy inched nearer.)

"Are you able to find things? Not me. O.K., tell me what it's like, O.K.? In Alabama, I mean."

"We could ask somebody."

"Ask somebody? But who could know better than you? Alabama, I mean."

"No, ask about the President's home."

"President, Fresident, who cares about that?"

Lee looked off. The boy came nearer, inspecting him from six inches below.

"Tall son-of-a-bitch. Girls like you?"

"I don't think so."

"He doesn't think so. He doesn't know, he just doesn't think so."

Lee now looked off into the other direction, his gaze running into the picture of a nude pinned to the wall.

"You like that? Oh, I know exactly what you're looking at, because I put it there! My name's Luke."

They shook, doing it in a more or less friendly fashion. Having satisfied himself on one side, the boy now began to examine Lee from the other.

"I don't know. And yet, I used to think that I might like the South. Come on, let's go find the President."

They marched to the stairs, the boy nudging him forward and then, suddenly, whipping out a tiny harmonica and beginning to toot on it. Outside, a crowd of girls had mustered in the yard and formed up in line, a long procession of pilgrims, as they seemed, all of them dressed in gloves, hats, stockings, and demure white dresses.

"Gosh! Look at all that material, Leland! Must be a hundred of 'em!"

Lee nodded slowly

"Which one do you like? You can tell me."

"I'm not sure."

"How about the surly one? Christ, she'd just as soon stick a knife in you as to…"

"The skinny one, you mean?"

"Leland! There's no such thing as 'skinny,' not with girls."

"What are you saying!"

"Oh sure, I like 'em skinny. You should too. Skinny and in black leather jackets. Christ."

"Yeah, but…"

"No, no, I can tell what you're looking at — the one with the bosoms! O.K., you can have her. Or them, I mean."

They moved on, trying not to outpace the girls with whom they were marching in parallel. Up front, the President's home had come into view, a stately-looking place, two stories high with a yard full of flowers. The day itself was bright and clear, "picnic weather," one might have said. And yet, already, the faint strange summons of autumn cast a sadness over town and lawn and garden, over the girls sitting in the grass with white dresses spread out around them, and yes, over the President and his wife waiting in the doorway to greet each new student. At once Luke strode up to the man, took out his harmonica, tooted, and put it back.

"Luke," he said. "but you can call me Lucien. I'm Jewish. No! I used to be but now I'm a Taoist." And then, as an afterthought: "What's *your* philosophy?"

They looked at him, man and wife, in a sort of amazed surprise. The President seemed to be a decent-enough-looking individual dressed in shoes and a rouge-colored tie. "Good, good," he said finally, "very good," and then handed them off to his wife, a woman without beauty or figure and dressed far too glamorously for the self-effacing type that she seemed actually to be. Her hand now came forward to Lee, who had the greatest difficulty in accepting it owing to the suitcase that had bonded to his paw.

"He brought his suitcase," Luke explained.

"I see."

"I knew he would. He's nervous."

They shunted forward, toward a mile-long table laden with pink punch, cake, and pastel napkins set out like a hundred tiny tents. Wearing his bored expression, Lee stood back while Luke poured a drink for himself, consumed it, poured another, consumed most of it as well, and then plucked up one of the brightly colored napkins and folded it away in the breast pocket of his rich suit where in truth it made an elegant display. Lee knew so little of Jews; until now, he had assumed them to be but one more Baptist sect. Finally, looking sleepy, the boy came back and then slowly and carefully and without asking, extracted a cigarette from out of Lee's vest. He had a lazy way of smoking. The used-up match he returned to Lee.

"And so, you plan on standing there all day, is that what it is? Well, maybe that's just the way it's done in Mississippi, I don't know. Goodbye."

Lee watched him move out into the garden where he stood for a time gazing up at the sky and nodding with approval. It was a clear day, bright and brilliant to a major degree. Next, Lee saw him go up to a crowd of girls, speak, and then disappear into their circle.

Lee had one serving only of punch, a pastry with frosting on it, and then stepped to the President's home and entered along with a small smattering of other quests. He moved past a mirror in a golden frame that proved he still possessed the hat he had thought to be lost. Behind him, a bearded man (no tie, one foot on the arm of the couch), was debating earnestly with three students, (two bearded, one not) whilst at the same time gesticulating with a soiled hand that looked as if he had been digging in the garden with it. He was unclean, unshaven, brilliant probably. Lee came nearer. In fact, he came *too* close; the man looked up at him.

"Hm? How about you, you ever heard so much nonsense?"

"I only heard a little bit!"

"Good man! You didn't miss a thing."

Lee wandered on. The house was huge; he did not, however, attempt to go upstairs. Already in the east wing he had discerned a numerous library arrayed in enameled shelving that reached all the distance to the ceiling, ten feet high. Now, seeing that the room was free, he went to it.

It was indeed a goodly collection, even if someone had left a half-finished cup of coffee in the worst of all possible places, where it might easily spill and contaminate the book that it was sitting on. Lee moved it and then, using his height, brought down an intriguing-looking volume in glassine covers. At nose level were half a dozen white plaster busts of the composers, Germans mostly, together with one uncomfortable Italian. Uncomfortable also were the chairs, albeit covered in a bright polished fabric that bore the picture of yet further books. Indeed, all things were pristine and clean, but especially so the sun (very finely granulated on this day), that poured in through the half-opened doors and bestowed a pool of wisdom on the floor.

He was reading, reading well (the chairs were not altogether uncomfortable), when came Luke, bringing the suitcase with him.

"Christ, I have to follow you around, is that what it is? So's you don't forget your teeth?"

Lee blushed.

"You're nervous."

"Not me."

"No, it's alright. I'd probably be nervous, too, if I'd just crawled out of the swamps of Mississippi."

"Alabama."

"That too. You like these books?"

Lee muttered something; no one could hear it.

"You muttered something just now, but no one could hear it. Tell me, have you read a lot of these books?"

"Some."

"'Some,' he says. Well how about that one, have you…? No, no, not *that* one! Christ! Anybody could read that one. Have you read" — he touched it — "*this* one?"

Lee took it down. "As a matter of fact…"

"He *has* read it! Son-of-a-bitch. Knew it, soon as I saw him I knew it."

Lee looked down at him, at his calm oval eyes and cerebral forehead.

"Are you…?"

"Yes?"

"You said you're from Rhode Island?"

"That's right, yes. But I was conceived in Minneapolis."

"Good Lord."

"Want to be my roommate?"

"I reckon not."

"'Reckon,' he says. I've got a huge I.Q., Lee; you'd like that. I could have gone to Harvard, anywhere. They wanted me to."

"I doubt if your I.Q. is any bigger than mine."

"How big is yours?"

But here Lee hushed; a girl had come into the room, the two boys waiting for her to go away. Finally:

"I have to tell you this, Lee: I'm going to be a doctor. They want me to."

Lee nodded and pulled down a book, a fat thing seemingly in Latin.

"You could be a doctor. Christ, we could even practice together, I'll take care of everything above the waist, while you…"

"No, no, I…"

"Yes? You can tell me."

Lee looked off. In order to return the green volume, which was heavy, he had needed to stand on his suitcase, which was teetering.

"Going to be a farmer, right? So you can lynch Negroes in your spare time — is that what it is?"

"No! Good Lord, all I said was…"

"Yes?"

"I'm going back to the dorm now."

"Why? You won't find any Negroes there."

"Aw, good Lord, all I ever…"

"Hold it! There's one. Big, too. I'd just like to see you try and lynch *him*." He hurried to a tall lanky boy, taller yet than Lee, who stood with his punch while gazing out the window in misery. Lee exited the place and passed speedily through yet another garden equipped with a sundial and birds and a bench on which a boy and girl had found each other on this the first day — their smaller fingers were entwined — and were looking rapturously into each other's eyes. It was a bright day, clear and clean. He had but three hundred yards to travel. And that, of course, was when Luke came chasing up behind, the suitcase dragging after him.

Alone in his room, Lee took out the most interesting of his new textbooks and read a full chapter of it. Finally, toward twilight, he got up, paced about, and then looked out cautiously where, two doors down, Luke, still in his good clothes, was sitting on top his desk while listening with no great interest to the conversation that had been going on all day. Lee slipped past quietly, thence to the fire escape and the four stories to the ground.

The evening was cool, clear as water, and the sun a mere far-away pebble, its strength all gone. But mostly it was that lavender-blue of the late pre-autumn weather — never yet had Lee been able to catch a specimen of it between finger and thumb.

He was tall, uncouth, and had a lumbering gait; nor did he try and follow when a girl strolled by in tattered shorts. In front of the library, two boys were playing chess in an accelerating hurry to beat the dark, one of them in a beard and the other wearing steel glasses that bestowed a peculiarly intelligent look. Suddenly, that moment, one of the girls strolled over and placed a kiss on the neck of the bearded boy who never so much as looked up from his work.

Inside, Lee had intended to examine the books, but instead contented himself in the knowledge that there were in truth a great number of them. One girl was reading, reading and chewing and had a fine brown well-oiled leg up on the table itself. He saw others, too, none of them bothering with lipstick nor shoes nor smiles, while as for the boys they all seemed to resemble revolutionaries, chess players, Marxians and the sort. Finally, seating himself, he reached for the nearest magazine and sat for quarter of an hour pretending that he was reading. In this position, he could see much.

It was full black when he left, the moon high and luring. A boy came toward him, a Marxian with his face half in shadow. There was also an adult of some kind, possibly a professor out walking with his child, while in the gloaming Lee was able to make out two silent figures holding each other urgently. He continued on tiptoes; people were embracing in doorways while others sat in groups on the darkling grass speaking of literature and theater and the rest. All this was as nothing, however, when compared to what he found in the cafeteria.

He purchased a cup of coffee and went and sat in the corner. He saw much and among it all a group of four girls — a pile of lips, breasts and hips — four girls crowded about a thin bearded boy who seemed to be going down for the third time and who (Lee later learned) had had a story published in a magazine. Nearer, he saw a fat girl sitting in someone's lap. These were anarchists, some of them (he learned later), while nearby he had already seen two existentialists, another Marxian, some Jews, and then a table full of artists' models, Romanians and whatnot, dark girls with cigarettes and shaven eyebrows, some of them cynical beyond belief and bored past endurance. He saw a black girl, but not the sort of black girl he was accustomed to seeing in the place from which he had come. Music was playing, the Five Satins singing their insidious song.

He came out, aimed for the dormitory, but then changed his mind and continued to the corner. Here he found himself in a narrow-cobbled street lined with canted houses whose upper stories hung out over the road. All was silence, moon, shadow, smoke. However famous it might be, however lofty the turrets of Antioch Hall, this was a tiny demesne, a capsule, as it were, a parcel upon the platter of the world and very hard would it prove to find a way *out* once he had found a way *in*. And yet the village wall, as ancient as the centuries, had worn down very badly and the gate itself had not merely been left ajar but taken off its hinges. Behind, the five towers were wavering and dissolving and correcting themselves in what looked like sea and fog, but in fact was simply an Ohio evening.

He stood, looking down into the abandoned town. He could have gone all the way to the edge of the settlement, there to press upon the invisible barrier dividing off the tundra that led to Springfield and beyond. Instead, taking out a cigarette, he went ten paces only, up to a neon sign blinking mysteriously in one of the stores.

THREE

UNTIL NOW, he knew nothing of those quartered with him, not until he saw them posing for a photograph in their best suits among rays of moonlight from the fourth-story windows.

First, Martin, his assigned roommate, a small man, very serious and with an air of leadership to him; he, too, had come down from out of that same New York City of which Lee had heard so much. And yet, his suitcase was the very poorest, its contents the most meager; inside (and the boy had been reluctant to open it), Lee spotted a few mere pairs of socks and not much else. They nodded, one to the other, his roommate announcing in his well-spoken voice: "Lee! Put your tie on; we're going to visit the girls."

Lee reeled. No doubt these were northern girls of which the boy was speaking. Lee had heard about them.

"Naw. I'll just stay here. Read."

"Not a chance," said Martin.

"Afraid?" asked Sal.

"Afraid? Ha!" (It gave him his chance to turn and look at Sal, a grinning monster with a beer in each hand. Impossible to look at him without also grinning.)

"Now these girls…"

"They won't hurt you! Not if you don't resist too much," Reed promised. This was a calm and detached sort of overweight person with a pipe and the scientific objectivity of a psychiatrist. He liked to *observe*, gathering evidence, and then follow it up by blowing on his pipe.

There were many others as well, all standing in line with Martin in the leadership. Lee could not very well make out their faces however, not with the hall as smoky as it was. Suddenly, that moment, clouds passed under the moon, shutting off the last source of light. Lee ran around to the other side, there where he could get a better look at Martin.

"These girls…"

At first, the boy said nothing. His profile was that of a keen and ravenous bird, while as for his eyes (well-hooded), they could not be seen at all. Normally, they had a darting quality.

"These girls now, they…"

Now the boy answered, doing it in a quiet voice that the others would not hear.

"These are *nice* girls, Lee. Trust me. Look, you can always leave, if you don't like it."

It was true. Luke had come out of his room and, looking sleepy, was hoisting up his pants. He had forgotten the comb lodged in his hair.

They clopped downstairs in a herd and set forth into the evening with Martin scouting out ahead to verify the path. The campus itself was lovely and leaf-bestrewn and profited from the faint far-away elucidation of rotting apples and dogs hallooing from hill to hill — it promised to be an autumn unlike any in a thousand years. To left, they passed the outdoor Shakespearean stage where some dozen students were rehearsing in their roles. What was it about this part of Ohio? He saw a boy playing on a flute. A land of art and music, with scholarship betimes and loveliness withal? Suddenly, Lee ran forward, putting himself near the head of the line.

They went down into a long narrow basement decorated equally with crepe paper and colored leaves pasted to the wall. The girls themselves, plentiful in number, were lined up behind a table on which nuts and eatables were spread out in generous array. One girl suddenly pushed forward a bowl of fruit, but then quickly drew it back again. At once Martin stepped forward to negotiate with their leader, the tallest of them, an ungainly girl whose shirt was too long, reaching nearly to the floor. Already Luke had made a tour of the place and now was standing, hands in pockets, looking frankly into the pickings.

"Christ. O.K., what's *your* philosophy?"

"Me?"

"Sure. Or that one standing next to you."

"We have cookies."

One girl continued to face the wall, refusing to let herself be seen. Lee realized that he, too, was making a graceless picture, his two plowman's hands hanging down. Suddenly he stepped forward to the table and, putting on his bored expression, collected his punch and wafers. Two new girls had just come into the vestibule and were taking off their coats.

Lee now saw something, something that made him stagger and cough and set down his cup and ignite a cigarette and turn away. It was a mute scene that now passed before him — two girls in the vestibule, one of them plain-looking and the other…

He suffered. It seemed to him that he should depart at once, return straightway to his room and pack his things. Taking the train, he might move on to some other school, or even venture forward into one or another of those giant northern cities — New York — where he might take up in a tenement, doing work on behalf of the poor. Later, he might visit Alabama again and the places he had known as a child. He felt so old. During the past thirty seconds he had even taken on some of the limping and scowling characteristics of his late garrulous grandfather. Or, he might go straight to Paris itself. That was when he saw that three other boys had converged upon the …*thing* and were dripping on her, as it were.

Lee groaned. A red-headed boy — already Lee had come to dislike him — had moved up to within but inches and was marveling at the

girl, very like unto one peering 'neath the hood of a splendid car. Lee
could feel his gorge rising; soon there'd be nothing left of her but a few
tatters of a once-white sweater, a few threads of her red, red ribbon.
The other girls were displeased. Suddenly, he ran around to the other
side.

He would have said that she was short, shorter than usual, and had
wide blinking eyes that looked about in some alarm at all this attention pressing in upon her. As to the face itself, and the figure... Again,
Lee groaned, very loudly. It was too late, Paris not far enough, and
now, functioning under dictates that were not his own, he ran forward
and bounced but then immediately got up again and forced first his
arm, and then his whole person, through a cranny that had opened up
between two of the boys.

She was a phenomenon, the loveliest that ever he had seen.
However, she was far too baffled by all the attention to pay any notice
to him. Lee cleared his throat and spoke, using his most peremptory
tone.

"Hi! Alright now, let's you and me — that's right! — lets you and me
just go over here, that's right," (he took her hand), "where we can talk."

A moan went up from the crowd. Meanwhile, the red-headed boy
was trying, with no success whatsoever, to break Lee's grasp upon the
girl's arm. Would she go with him? She had no choice and moreover,
he was stronger.

He led her quickly to one side but then changed his mind and,
leading her back through the same crowd (it had refused to disperse),
bundled her off into an alcove with a sofa and several vacant chairs.
His hallmates continued in a knot, glaring back at him with the most
profound disapproval. His gaze met Martin's and then, next, turned to
Reed, who stood as on the deck of a ship (feet planted far apart) while
studying Lee in the calm, meditative, pipe-smoking objectivity of one
who had an especially keen interest in erratic behavior.

Lee sat next to the thing. Mercifully, his nerves had waited until
this moment before turning to milk.

"I could see that they were pestering you," he said chivalrously, voice cracking, southern accent revealed.

She turned and looked at him.

"Me, I'm from Alabama. It's hard! Of course, there aren't many of us here, people from Alabama. Birmingham has lots of 'em. Luke, he's from… I started to say Minneapolis!" He laughed uproariously, laughing alone. "I don't know if I ever told you this, but I have a huge…" He stopped. Never had he spoken to so pretty a girl. That was when he recognized that he was still clutching her tightly about the wrist.

"Alabama?"

"Right. Yes, it is."

"I've never been out of the city, before I came here."

That voice! It was a full octave deeper than he had looked for, and seemed deeper still in consideration of her small size. He was absolutely delighted with it. Always he had been partial to short girls, whereas this one had in addition a dark voice and a figure so stunning that his own chest began to ache. One might search throughout the Western world and never find such another sweater, so white, and with such unfair demands being put upon it.

"Which 'city'?"

"New York."

Lee reeled. "Yes, I'm not surprised. Me, I'm from Alabama. However, things are getting better down there." Suddenly his glasses tumbled out, hitting the floor. At once he scooped them up. "I just use 'em for reading, that's all. Want to dance? Naw, you don't have to."

He led her out onto the floor, the foremost girl of his generation; she came up only to his chin. Again, it was brought home to him — the amazing privileges that dancing confers; never would he have dared hold her like this in the open street. Her figure burned holes in him. He counted four boys in the four corners of the room, three of them looking back with great displeasure. Luke, however, was grinning. Now the record ended whereupon another immediately came on. Someone, apparently, had come up with a collection of old music dating back to the Romantic Period:

Beware, my foolish heart,
her lips are much too close to mine.

Lee reeled. How calm she was, her cheek resting on his shoulder. He
had left home not thirty hours ago. And how many times, time out of
mind, had she not been dancing in New York with others? He waited
in dread for the next record, lest it send him falling and spinning
back with more emotion than he could bear into those earlier 1950s,
reminding him of when he was eleven, and in love for the first time:

Take away the breath of flowers,
It would surely be a sin.

It hurt him. He had in his arms a golden swan, a piece of pastry with
frosting on it. Moreover, small as she was and as compact and perhaps
a little sleepy, she rested on his chest with more trust than he could
have expected. He knew this, that no matter if all of Ohio tried to
launch an attack on her, still he would know how to protect her. Came
now another record, this time the final straw:

Mona Lisa, Mona Lisa,
Men have named you.
You're so like the lovely lady
With the mystic smile.

Lovely lady! he wanted to expire. Mystic smile! Suddenly she moved,
draping one cool arm lightly about his neck. He suffered. Her perfume
was having a cumulative effect and he no longer knew whether he was
on the verge of anger, or whether he wanted to cry. Now came a boy,
the coarse one, wanting to take her away.

"No," said Lee. (He was quite prepared to fight about it, if it came
to that.) "Hell, no."

The coarse one blushed and then stomped away with a hot expression on his face. Came now the following record:

If they made me a king,
I'd be but a slave to you.

If I had everything,
I'd give it all to you.

Two times the girl drew back to look at him — the very last he wanted was that she might see the sort of emotionality he suffered from. At the fireplace, meanwhile, some of the hallmates had built up a conflagration and were beginning to toast marshmallows. The girl drew back to look at it.

"Would you like…?"

She nodded enthusiastically. No doubt about it, the smell of fire, leaves and apples, together with a crackling sound, was having its effect upon them all. He was given a wand with a marshmallow on it. Luke, still in his good suit, was perched up on the table, his eye upon a certain wan girl sitting off by herself. For some time now, Lee had been aware of this person, and aware, too, that she had been watching all evening as if she took more pleasure in what others were doing than in having any doings of her own.

The room was silent, all of them gazing with horrible fascination into the flames. Next to him, the foremost girl of his generation had fallen into a study; it gave him the opportunity to look at her more closely. In fact, she was sitting in the way a child sits, her shoes pointing straight up toward the ceiling like two simple utterances, such as "May I have another marshmallow?" or "See where the fire is green!" Looking at her, he could not but grin.

"Alright! What's so funny?" she asked, watching him suspiciously. The fire was failing and no one making any effort to save it. Behind, two of the girls were folding up the tablecloth. This whole evening was coming down to an end. He saw Luke hop down from his table and go at last to the wan girl, who flinched back in alarm. Lee heard this much of it:

"… Taoist."

(The girl said nothing.)

"But I used to be a Jew. Lee" (he pointed) "is *not* a Jew. And yet he is circumcised however. Strange." He took out his harmonica. The girl was trying to edge away. Lee heard further: "Are you from Alabama, too? Hard to tell, since you don't say anything."

"No, no."

"'No,' she says. Hey! Where're you going?"

Outside, the weather was clear and cool, a very great many white shiny bright stars having chosen *this* night to attend to west-central Ohio. Likewise, Lee could not but contrast *his* girl, who was tidy and beautiful and, with her tight white sweater and red collar, was like a swan, could not but contrast her with the other girls who by comparison were like so many barnyard hens. Accordingly, he led her up under a tree, allowing Luke — they nodded to each other — and Luke's girl, to pass them by. He could hear whispering on all sides. Amazingly, some of his own hallmates had actually fallen for some of these same hens and at least one pair of them had gotten into a kiss. Looking at them, and then at his own girl… Already he had achieved so much; nevertheless, so huge was his folly, he turned the girl and forced her to face him. At once an arm came up, a bar of steel, her expression showing how disappointed she was.

"I'm sorry."

"It's alright."

"I won't do it again."

"I know."

They stepped away from each other whereon she turned and walked back to the building. Head spinning, Lee plunged off down the walk where Martin and the others were waiting.

"Great Scot!" said one. "That's the prettiest girl in the world. How'd you do it?"

"What's her name?"

"It was rude, I thought, not to let anyone dance with her."

"Her *name*, what is it?"

"What?"

"Her name, man. What's her *name*?"

FOUR

NO SLEEP. Instead, toward midnight, he slipped down past Martin on the lower bunk, dressed, and then tiptoed out into the hall. In his own room, Luke was sleeping, sleeping well, but doing it in his suit. Lee used the fire escape, a four-flight drop to the ground.

Fleeing from autumn and the winter that must follow, the last of the summer clouds sped past overhead. If by placing himself under one certain cloud and staying in its shade... In this way, he thought, one might cross the entire campus without ever being seen at all. And yet, there were rooms in all the buildings, and in one room in particular the silhouette of a girl at desk studying in the hours of the night. Lovely was the moon, and grander in size than Ohio and Alabama both; all the bottom part of it, however, had been nibbled away by moths.

He went into the woods, catching and then passing a very late-night couple who, apparently, had been hit by love while on the trail and who were now embracing in the vines. The leaves were in flood, or soon would be, and although one could not divine all the colors in the dark, it was clear that they had hardly cooled at all since the middle of the day. He climbed past an enormous tree bending to earth, the result of an acorn spilled eight hundred years ago by medieval travelers pilgrimaging to the following valley. Below, he could also make out the ruins of the antique wall that had defended the town before that bad day so many years ago when the masonry had failed to hold.

Now again all was abandoned, or so it seemed in the little bit of light provided by the gnawed-away moon. He saw a light go on in Antioch Hall, there were some of last century's students, unwilling to leave the place, continued to gather. He knew furthermore that the town had bookstores in it, taverns and wine merchants, theaters and cafés. More than that, he could see a scattering of apartments where even now some of the faculty were worriedly preparing the next day's lessons. He did so love it, already he did, the possibility that he might someday be made to leave it awakening just then a great resentment in him. There was also the girl. It was too much, he too young, the night too green, too clear, too far, too many leaves. Down below a light came on and remained until someone blew it out. Lee got to his feet. The town was darkening, no doubt about it, and unless he hurried, he might run past it in the night.

FIVE

AN ODD STRUCTURE, Antioch Hall; one could run five times all around the circumference without ever divining its authentic form. Inside, the floor was rickety and swayed whenever one moved too far from the joists. And then, too, it was suffused with the uncanny odor of deceased students who once had come crowding into the place wearing the haunted looks of nineteenth-century photographs.

Lee stopped; the floor was weak. And that was when he saw the wan girl of last night, a gawky creature who flitted toward him in stiff-legged fashion, oblivious to the floor and its dangers. Today, she was grinning broadly, even irrationally, it seemed to him. People turned to look at her.

"Greetings!" she said. "I approve."

"Good." (He started to move away.)

"You and Judy! Oh God, do you want my help or not?"

"You…"

"We're roommates!"

"We are?"

"Not *you*! God. Judy!"

"'Judy.'"

"The girl you were with last night! God."

Lee reeled. This then was Judy's roommate and Judy was her roommate's name. Moreover, she was carrying two thin volumes, one of them frayed and in a pale lemony jacket with penciled notes on it. Her clothes were drab and long; indeed, she seemed to have come forth herself from out of one of those nineteenth-century photographs that lined the walls.

"You're Judy's roommate."

"God. How quick you are!"

"Judy is…"

"The girl you were with! That's right. And I approve."

"And now you're in the same French class with me."

"Apparently, yes. I do hope you don't object?"

Lee looked at her. Was this in truth the same wan and striated girl of last night?

"You weren't feeling well last night, probably."

She blushed deeply. "No, no, no; I'm mentally ill, if you must know."

"Oh."

"I have a syndrome."

"Naw, that doesn't matter."

"But today I'm fine."

It was true. "And what is that yellow book you're carrying around? It looks like someone has written all over the covers!" Then: "You're from down south, too, right?"

"Baudelaire. I have to translate it."

"You have to?"

"Well, somebody has to. Yes, yes, North Carolina."

"It's already been translated. I know because I've read it! North Carolina? That's where Thomas Wolfe came from."

"Then you read a very poor translation. Oh, Wolfe!"

"And that blue one, what is that?"

"'Wolfe,' you can do better than that. This? Rimbaud, of course."

They went in, the room was open. Lee took up next to a tall cloudy window where one bad move would have sent him tumbling down onto the outdoor stage where for the past nights a Shakespearean troupe had been performing. Sitting next to the girl, her hands were in view, big ones, as big as his own, her nails chewed down to nothing. On all sides they were surrounded by highly gifted students, some of them barefooted, others in scarves and braids and long, long hair. One girl was wearing tattered shorts that were unweaving and in peril of falling apart. Among such a crowd as this, all one's resources would be needed in order to compete. Lee bent toward Judy's roommate, whispering:

"I forgot to ask your name."

She whispered back:

"That's why I didn't give it."

"What is it?" (He was whispering still.)

"Phyllis."

The teacher entered, a busy man, frowning, dressed in jeans, a beard, no socks. Lee could see why this was the teacher—he was far the grubbiest man in the room—and all the rest were merely students. Just then a breeze nudged in, bringing with it the smells of leaves and fungus and new-cut hay. Down below, children were playing and a dog was running with a stick. Lee could see where the blue-tip mountains, one behind the other, ran on down to the edge of the world before stepping out to sea. Far from harkening to the teacher, Phyllis had taken out her ink pot and was toiling happily, grinningly even, with head bent deeply over her translation. Lee's eye was upon the girl in front of him, an intellectual whose neck however was amazingly thin and covered with the most innocent growth of cilia ever seen. He groaned. Life was in tide and lapping, lapping at the base of the building itself. It would break him someday—life, hills, cilia. Far away a flute was playing, its music insidious beyond belief. Phyllis paused, giving thoughtful heed to her translation while Lee squirmed, exchanging glances with a girl. Outside the fields were broad and apt for running, and now the dog of two minutes ago was barking at a kite. All might still have been well—it was not too late—had he not then laid eyes upon a certain Judy trundling forward across the yard in a red collar and sweater as white as the pages of a mint-new book. Well-shod was she, in two tiny neat shoes. All might still have been well, had not then the sun opted to glint upon her high luminous forehead. That broke him; he sickened, withered, and perished. Down below, she had come to a stop and was bending forward, conversing with a bird. Love had him in its grip. Now, slowly and reluctantly, he took out a sheet and carefully noted down the exact date and hour, his age and, insofar as he was able to do so, a brief comment upon his own spiritual condition at the time.

They gathered that night in the hall, Martin and the others and Luke sitting on the table in his suit. Himself, Lee had selected the floor, choosing a place direct across from Reed who was pulling continuously on his pipe and then ever and anon taking it out again in order to blow bubbles into the already very cloudy atmosphere. He was a calm person, extraordinarily mature; he liked to pass his time observing the immaturities of others.

"Hey, Reed! What time is it?"

Reed took out his pipe. "Why do you ask?"

Martin, meantime, had put on the coffee and now was moving fussily through the group filling every cup. Four others had squeezed onto the sofa and were facing forward, like riders in a space machine. So many were smoking that a layer of the stuff had cumulated beneath the ceiling and was beginning to weigh on them. Suddenly, that moment, an alien boy from one of the lower halls popped up at the head of the stairs and, shielding his eyes, peered down curiously at them through the obscurity.

"Jesus!"

"Get the shit out of here!"

They rose in a group; the boy fled. Now Luke came over and while looking directly and worriedly into Lee's face from five inches away, slowly and carefully, one after the other, extracted three cigarettes. A radio was playing lowly, mixed with static. And all this time, the voice of Martin going on in a grim and determined tone, speaking of women and girls.

It was toward midnight that Lee stood and went to fetch a book of matches. Outside, a mighty fog had settled in at just below window level and was lapping at the pane; one sole figure could be seen struggling to pull himself along the sidewalk and now he, too, disappeared. Sal had fallen off to sleep while still staring up at the light with open eyes. The phone rang, Martin hastening over to make it quiet again. In addition to the percolator, the radio, and the sound of snoring, a dead voice could be heard intoning endlessly in some distant part of the building. Finally:

"You have to know your own strength, that's all. Me, I think he's going to get hurt."

"So what? So, what if he gets hurt? That's life."

"He's already hurt," Luke said. "Look at him."

"Hurts me, too. You see the sweater she was wearing?"

"Those who don't know their own strength, or lack thereof..."

"You've already said that, shut up. Sit down."

"Or rather, don't know their own capacity for self-delusion..."

Reed raised his hand. "May I...?"

"Yes, yes."

"She comes to us without any attachments—is that what you believe? No one back home waiting for her? Think about it, man!"

There was a long, deep and profound silence.

"He's right."

"It was rude, I thought, not to let anyone dance with her. Can you hear me, Lee? Rude."

"Now don't go jumping on Lee. He's from Louisiana remember."

But here Keith, the nicest boy in the hall, had to object. "No, actually it's Alabama."

"Same shit. But what I want to know is... Goddamn it, would you kindly get your fucking elbow out of my fucking face!"

"But those who can judge accurately, understanding their own strengths and weaknesses..."

"Aw, shit. Hit him, would you?"

"...cognizant of what they can reasonably expect to accomplish..."

They stopped. Ray had been out drinking again and again had come home late, this time without a shirt.

"Good, good, oh good. Well I guess he'll be up vomiting all night. How about it Keith, you going to be the one to clean up after him?"

"Probably."

"May I...?"

"Yes, yes; say it."

"Think about it like this: 'Am I discouraging his bad behavior, or actually encouraging it?'"

"Reed?"

"Yes?"

"Fuck you."

By two-thirty the fog had climbed higher, effectively shutting them off from the outside world. One pale glow, miles away, showed where someone had elected to wait it out in the library. Reed, who had not moved nor spoken in several hours, was drawing on his pipe while reflecting calmly about the end of life on earth. Himself, Luke had gone off some time ago and taken a nap; now, looking fresh and combed, stepping between the bodies, he came back. Martin was slumping and seemed to be reading the floor. It was his silhouette (dark, alert, highly vulpine) that was still looking straight ahead. The radio had long ago ended to be replaced by a soft furry static that no one bothered to shut off. Now, after fighting in vain for a share of the sofa, Luke came over and flopped down on the carpet.

"It's mad, staying up all night. So why are we doing it?"

"Duty."

"Oh, yeah. Want to be my roommate? I hate to say it, Lee: those other shits haven't read nearly as many books as you."

Lee looked at him. In his dark suit (greatly disheveled now) and with the three rivulets of black hair running down over his forehead, his recent aplomb seemed blown away.

"Gnawing over that girl?" he asked.

Lee blushed. Across the way, Martin's shade was bending nearer. Meanwhile, two of the boys had gotten down flat on the floor in hopes of recovering in what was a slightly less unhealthy layer of air. No moon tonight; the fog didn't permit it. Suddenly, a woman's voice was heard over the radio, apparently the station's janitress dithering with the microphone. Sal stepped past tugging on his blanket, a candle in one hand and beer in the other.

"Gnawing over that girl — it's not good, Lee."

"Did you see her?"

"Skinny girls, Lee, you know that. I like skinny girls."

"In black leather jackets."

They laughed, both. Martin bent nearer.

"Gnawing, that's right. What a riot. Yesterday he was picking up pecans in Alabama and now... Hold it, I got to write this down."

And in fact, he actually did get up and go to his room, coming back a moment later with a little stub of a pencil and a sheet of tablet paper.

"I'm thinking of becoming a writer, too, Lee."

"Too? I didn't say I wanted..."

"Oh sure, I knew it right away. It's alright. See those shits over there? They're writers, too."

Lee looked into the group, most of them having trouble staying awake. "All of them?"

"Sure, except that pale bastard." He pointed to a pudgy boy who, with his short hair and tidy dress, didn't look like he belonged to Antioch in the first place. Came now Larry again, who had come and gone a dozen times, this time carrying the empty mayonnaise jar he used as a chamber pot. Slowly and carefully, all times watching Lee's face for indications of displeasure, Luke now removed the last of the cigarettes.

"I have to tell you, Lee, I'm thinking about romancing Judy's roommate. See? So, we ought to be roommates, too."

"Yeah. Her name's Phyllis."

"Phyllis! That's a tough name, Lee. Wait, I got to write that down."

"She's…"

"I know."

They looked at each other.

"Nobody else is going to be romancing her, that's for sure. Want to be roommates?"

"Alright."

"You do? O.K., I'll think about it. I'm going to be studying Hinduism. You'll like that."

"Good Lord, I thought you were a Taoist!"

"Oh. Now I see how it is with you — a person has to be all one thing or all another. You ever read Hesse?"

"Not yet. You ever listened to Shostakovich?"

"Oh sure. Taoists don't care for him."

"Why not?"

"Umm."

By five, the meeting had dwindled down to a mere residue of those who, night after night, had proved the most determined. Tommy had slumbered off an hour ago, his huge face even more optimistic in sleep than in life. Horribly, Martin's shade had soaked into the masonry itself, while in the other direction, Luke was on the floor, his pencil at the ready.

SIX

AFTER TWO WEEKS OF IT, he began speaking to himself, especially when he went splashing through leaves of vellum dripping seemingly with paint. Even here, there still sometimes came to him the smell of smoke and kudzu and passion flower blooms drifting all the way from the ruined hills of Alabama. Above, brain-clouds were seething past, Lee gazing up at them delightedly until a huge yellow leaf came and fastened to his face. These days of September! Using his abnormal memory, he took a photograph that he would be able to call up in future years when autumn came and he would feel that he had to get his things together and be off to school again.

Inside, two hundred students were scattered among the tables. At once Lee snatched off his glasses, replacing them with a bored expression. Today, the existentialists had gone off into the corner where the hardest of them remained barefooted in spite of the weather. Lee was enthralled by them; nor did he venture any closer to their tables than he as yet deserved. One of the girls had suffered unbelievably, judging from her, and moreover had a baby that she carried in a shawl. Among such people, there was not a one of them who did not carry two or three mellow-looking volumes showing cigarette burns and coffee stains and holding pessimistic contents.

Lee too. Taking a cigarette, he let it dangle from the lip while squinting through the smoke itself. Suddenly, he tossed the hair out of his eyes, discovering for the first time that Phyllis was just two tables away. Today she seemed constrained and shy and in a great hurry to be done with things, as if she, too, were experiencing that sense of unreality that also afflicted him when he was in a noisy place and watching, as it were, through walls of glass. And that was when he saw Judy.

He hurt. She was alone, dressed in a starched white uniform and sitting on a high stool with a spade-like instrument in her lap. The truth crashed in upon him when he saw a boy go up and utter something and when the girl herself climbed down from her tall perch and began to dig into a large ice cream container with her tiny shovel. He saw her take the coins, saw her unleash one of her man-slaughtering smiles upon the wretch, and then saw her turn and climb back to the top of her tower where she sat blinking and thinking, a look of wide-eyed seriousness on her face. He saw her glance down sadly at her own depleted ice cream and then, a gesture that destroyed him, steal a quick look at her watch.

He let two minutes go by while she served both from the chocolate and the peach ice cream. And when the two minutes were over, he rose mechanically and waited in line. "Judy," he wanted to say to her. "Judy, Judy, Judy." In actual fact, what he said was:

"Hi."

"Oh, hi! Is that you?"

"I think so." He touched himself on the face. "It *feels* like me."

She laughed, a dark laugh deep and low that could not possibly have come out of so short a person. And then, too, all the time, she filled out her demure white uniform in such a way as to make him refuse to think about it.

"I don't know if I ever told you this, but... Hey! Want to go out tonight? Naw, you don't have to."

"I can't."

"Tomorrow night?"

"Alright."

There was at this time a certain man on campus, a tall one with a leached-out face and dark woolen coat; oftentimes they saw him moving to and from the library with a neatly tied-up bundle of superseded newspapers which, purportedly, he was carrying home for further study. Not only was he lean and shabby, not only a leached-out face, not merely a genius, he had also two or more great hands that hung out of his coat for a great distance, powerful enough for strangling bourgeois people.

"Who is that!"

"Oh, sure. That's Bernie Krestinsky. He graduated twenty years ago but doesn't want to leave."

"Good Lord."

"And is he ever clever, too! The brainiest guy you'd ever want to meet."

"I can tell."

"Someday you'll look like that, Lee; I'm confident of it. Want to meet him?"

"What!"

"Oh, sure. Tonight?"

Lee ran to all his classes, learning very little owing to his mood. Finally, toward four, he dashed to the cafeteria to find that Judy had been replaced by a plain-looking girl who had no real affinity for the work and who, moreover, was continually dropping hairpins into the stuff. He was now much more able to look unflinchingly into the whores and artists' models, including a new one who sat so carelessly. Phyllis, he saw, had come in for afternoon tea and was sitting far apart. She wrote like a child — it was her way — with her nose close to the paper and her hair hiding the translation.

They set off at dusk, moving through the gate and then past the smith's, the cobbler and tinker, the pastry-maker and rose merchant's down to where Bernie dwelt. Lee was nervous; Luke, by contrast, was utterly at ease, even at one point taking out his harmonica and piping on it.

It was a chill night, saved only by the neon signs from being chillier still. Almost all the flower boxes that sat throughout the day along the sidewalk had now been carried inside. They passed the tavern where some dozen artists were gathered around a candle for warmth. The bookstore came up, the interior made yet more dark by the quantity of dark volumes.

They came to a stairway, very narrow, that led up sharply from the street itself. At the top, a pair of massive shoes, completely fur-lined, had been set out to dry. Luke knocked once, tenderly, the door opening almost at once upon an unusual-looking girl with freckles big as dimes and carrot-colored hair braided into cables held with red ribbons.

"Oh, please come in!" she said. "You're welcome to our house!" (Behind her, another girl came out of one of the rooms, looked, and then went back in.) "Can I get you something to drink?"

"Naw," said Lee.

"Sure," said Luke. "What do you have?"

"Coffee?"

"Sounds good."

"We have sausage, too."

"Christ."

She turned and hurried away, her two naked feet just barely vis-ible beneath the long peasant's shirt she was wearing. A third woman had come out meantime, this one middle-aged and with a great deal of Aztec jewelry about her neck. Whether these were wives, or mistresses, or socialists… He wasn't sure. Somewhere a child's voice was calling, and from elsewhere came the sound of someone reading aloud in hollow tones.

They sat. The apartment was long, very long, but also narrow and with hardly space enough for the sofa that was itself a rather abbreviated piece of furniture. In the middle there sat a giant spool, formerly used for telephone wire but now turned into a table with antique lace on it and, on top of that, an assortment of magazines in foreign languages. It was loaded with books, the whole apartment, even in the kitchen, the bedroom, and lined up on every window sill. Luke went forward to the nearest bookcase and, while making small sounds on his harmonica, began to inspect the very impressive array of heavy volumes, of years-worth of journals put neatly away and fattened notebooks with clippings peeping out. He took one, the fattest of them; it dealt with the industrial situation in Czechoslovakia. And how many times had not this same Bernie, how many times had he not lain awake all night pouring over just such stuff?

The girl came, bearing a tray that she tried at first to set on the table but then ended up leaving on the floor. She was a happy-looking sort of person, very busy with her tasks, her freckles, her ink-smudged hands. Concerning the other people in the house, Lee could say nothing.

"Try now the coffee!" she said, and then came to do the pouring herself. Of sugar, being boycotted, there was none. She did have four little brown cakes with icing on them.

They ate with genuine enthusiasm, both seated upon a paper-thin carpet that had shriveled so much over the years that it covered only perhaps one-third the area.

"Is Bernie coming?"

"Oh!" (She looked at the clock.) "He *might* come. But you don't have to wait, no; no, you could start the discussion right now!"

They looked at each other, Luke suddenly clapping his hand over his mouth.

"Now if he *does* come, will he...?"

She was gone, stooping through the doorway and then vanishing at once into those more distant parts of the building whence music could be heard. Five minutes went by, Luke pondering up at the ceiling in an effort to come up with a proper discussion topic. Lee had gone to look at the collection of mounted photographs of men in suits — nineteenth-century labor leaders, as they looked to him. Here, through old curtains (also of lace) he could spy down into the moistened street almost deserted now but for the wee figure of the little lame balloon man still shouting his wares. A child drove by swiftly on his bicycle, chased by a small mechanical dog. Across the way, a blood-red neon sign was pulsing with liquid noises, flinging "drops," as it were, into the road and apartment both. A student came out of the tavern and then, after looking about, opted to go back in. By now there was but one single delicacy left upon the platter, Lee taking the icing and Luke the cake. That was when Bernie blew in.

He was a big man who wore, seemingly, boxes instead of the shoes they had contained. Moreover, he carried a vast bag of groceries in which a bottle and loaf could be seen sticking out at angles.

"So!" he said. "We meet again." And then: "Two of you!" He continued to unpack the bag, a difficult operation since he must at all times take care not to brush the ceiling with his head. To Lee, he reeked of danger, intellect, and ten thousand cigarettes. Luke, meantime, had retreated deeper into the room where he could be seen sitting in a kind of simple dignity. Now, fetching a cup for himself, the man came and took a seat, not in the remaining chair, but on a three-legged stool so brief that it threw his knees up higher than his chin.

"Good!" (He stirred slowly in his coffee, examining the currents that such stirring made.) "I had hoped that Jan and Marty might come too, but… so be it! Now your name is…?"

Luke gave his name.

"I know you?"

"Sure. Well, not literally."

"And you?"

"No, sir. But you might have seen me around. I'm around quite a lot."

"Deep south — is that what I hear?"

"Yes, sir. Alabama."

"Alabama." (He pronounced the word slowly, stirring still. The voice was hoarse, as of one who smoked too much. At the same time, he was often stroking his thick whiskers, each whisker as thick as pencil lead — it produced a rasping sound.) "You know Alvin Sanders?"

"No, sir. Actually…"

"Doesn't matter, never mind. Big Al is doing good work, working out of Birmingham. Steel mills. I'd like to see the two of you get to know each other." He lifted the cup, a tiny article that looked like an acorn in his massive hand. "You'd make a good team," he said, looking into Lee with penetration.

Lee looked off into the distance.

"And you?"

Luke jumped. "Rhode Island. It's very small actually." He pushed back more deeply into the shadows where soon after Lee could see him carrying out a small repair on his harmonica.

"Very good!" said Bernie. "Now how do you suggest we bring in more people like you, umm? Luke?"

"I think you're on the right track already."

"Oh? How so?"

"Well, you managed to get *us*."

"Yes! Ha! So, I did!" He laughed merrily. "Excellent!"

The girl came in, saw that they were debating productively, and then stood beaming down proudly at them.

"What's lacking, of course, is the sort of organizational talent, not to mention sheer grit, that Wilson and his miners have been displaying. Isn't it always so, umm? Miners?"

"Wilson is tough."

A cat, an orange one of giant size came and leapt into the man's lap. He looked at it studiously and without actually seeming to see it, began massaging the thing tenderly about the ears. "Wilson is tough," he said softly, the last syllables falling away into dreams and thoughts. Stationed where he was, his white hairless legs looked like two trees from which the bark had all been stripped away. Both trees wore big flat slippers. "And have you never considered, Luke, how that the only true distinction of modern society is its denial of any real, honest-to-goodness female earth deity? Um?"

Luke, blinking, nodded four times, thoughtfully.

"No wonder the Spanish go on holding out, turning their backs on it — mercy in the one case and morality in the other."

"I agree about the Spanish."

"Yes, I think you can fully expect it, any day now, to see that Science has finally organized itself into that priesthood the masses so seem to demand, oh yes. Votaries emerging on holidays in scarlet robes, etc., all of it. I suppose they'll be resurrecting the dead for a fact by then, willy-nilly, whished-for or no." Suddenly he snorted and then laughed out loud, caught unexpectedly by the humor of it. "No, no, no, no, don't let it happen to you. And yet... Consider this, that if it be truly a deterministic world after all, and if..." (He stopped, thinking yet more deeply than before. He had taken the cat's ear between thumb and finger and was trying astutely to measure its thin meaning.) "Old Düring, damn his eyes! So, don't be surprised, Leeward, if things begin to happen quite suddenly, water coming to a boil, quantity into quality. You read me?"

"Yes, sir." Outside the moon was down, leaving the room in darkness save for the three cigarettes and one weak bulb sputtering in the alcove. Listening to the man, midnight coming on, it seemed to Lee that he had broken into the very house and headquarters of world intelligence. Here was nothing but silence, a few pictures on the wall, and in front, the man's disembodied face reflecting one by one the hues of neon, each hue a separate thought. Never had Lee heard so much brilliance so brilliantly put. He concentrated, trying to assimilate what he could. At the same time, part of him could not but wonder about the other inhabitants reading themselves off to sleep by candlelight in far-away parts of the complex building. Finally, he stood and found his way to the bathroom where, here once again, large numbers of books were housed, some of them stored in the little green cabinet along with the medicines. Also, a painting on the wall showing a winter hunt with hounds. And six giant-sized maroon socks hanging out to dry.

They had found their way to the seat of world intelligence, yielding themselves to a man whose very description would have given their parents a thrill of horror. It was late, Lee was smoking, in Luke he had a friend who was beginning to treat him with the sort of regard that he demanded in friends of his. And there was Antioch itself, and autumn, and the fact that more and more everyday he was looking like a tramp. He knew this: let him but have the girl and happiness would be more than could be endured.

Two full hours before they were allowed to depart, both of them loaded down with pamphlets, frosted cakes, and a newspaper article authored by the man himself. The hamlet was abandoned at this hour, save only for the baker, flour up to his elbows, getting a long start on the day to come. Luke was tired; nevertheless, Lee led him on for another thirty steps down to the edge of town and the tundra stretching north to Springfield and beyond. Two faint lights were riding out to sea, as it were, farmsteads bobbing on the current.

"Soon I'll be heading off," said Lee. "Wandering aimlessly. I always knew that's what it would come to."

"Sure. Then you could reappear years later, eaten-up with corruption and experience." (He lifted the harmonica and played mournfully.)

"Two or three years — that's all I want. Chatterton was seventeen."

"Bullshit. My guess is that you'll still be here when you're forty."

Suddenly it began to rain, a ferocious downpour that had given no warning. They ran, moving at first out onto the steppes before remembering that it led, not to college, but Springfield and beyond. Itself, the town was small; they were able to flit past the baker's, the barber's and the shoe repair and then get onto their own proper ground — the gate was open — before the deluge became impossible. Already it was too late for the cakes; the frosting was gone.

"Lee!"

"What?"

"Why are we running?"

"Well…"

"We can't get any wetter."

That was true. They slowed. At that moment, Luke tackled him, a neat movement that sent both of them rolling into the shadow of the second-tallest tower of Antioch Hall. Lee turned and grappled with him, finally pinning him to the ground even while the boy continued to wheeze on his tiny harmonica.

"I'm stronger than you."

"Possibly. But I, on the other hand, am better-looking."

That was true.

"I've read more books."

"But Lee! I've done more traveling," — he pointed, east and west — "than you can imagine."

"I'm taller."

"Only from the shoulders up. And consider this: my father makes fifty dollars an hour."

"And I've caught more fish than you'll *ever* catch."

"Yes, you'll go far, Lee. The girls will love you for it."

Impossible not to laugh. Again, Lee lunged, throwing him back smartly into a half-foot puddle with a newspaper floating on top. The rain was so terrible, the globules so preternaturally large and coming, as it seemed, from so high above… The college itself had washed away, leaving them in a blue void, as in times before cities and civilization. It was Luke who had the shoe and now was pounding Leeward about the back and hips.

"Bastard!"

"All those grits! No Lee, I have to say it: you're just no good."

"Whereas *you*…" Lee hushed. He had found that his mouth was full of a clot of earth, Luke having very kindly just placed it there. They rolled, etc., etc.

SEVEN

HE CAME OUT and dropped down the stairs. Day by day, he was looking more and more like a tramp, and now for this occasion he had put on a broad yellow tie bearing an image of the smiling Christ. Outside, it was dappled weather in full autumn flood, while high above, he spied a solitary bird propelling itself in a southerly direction while emitting cries of woe. Already the dark moon — or was it one of the balloon man's wares? — had snared in the branches. Lee now lit a cigarette and, throwing the hair out of his eyes, allowed the fumes to be drawn off romantically toward the stars.

He knocked twice, waited, and then entered a narrow vestibule furnished with a table, couch and paraffin lamp. At once Judy came to the door, smiled and said something — he was paralyzed by the looks of her — and then drew back inside again.

He waited. No doubt about it, there was a certain furtive and busyness going on behind that door — a drawer being opened and closed, a telephone, someone complaining in a whining voice. He could envision a full dozen of them standing about cynically in nail polish and little bits of underwear. A minute went past. And then Judy came out.

"Ready?"

Lee was shocked. He had never before seen her like this, in stockings and heels, make-up and pearls. Probably he allowed a strange look to come across his face. In any case, she could not possibly fail to realize how stunning she was.

"Good Lord."

"You like?"

"'Like'? Holy Toledo, Jesus. Oh!"

She stood, neatly shod in her tiny shoes, partly embarrassed and partly pleased. Lee sweated. Finally, it was the girl who nudged him to the door and closed it behind them. As always when under great stress, he could hear nothing, not until the sound registered on him of her high heels tapping briskly down the walk. Never had he had a possession like this in his keeping, a tiny adult, serious and wide-eyed, a phenomenon wrapped around a soul.

He called it "a date with Judy." Quickly they moved through the shadows and then down a line of trees to an outdoor stage where some twenty rows of seats were set out in semi-circle. Suddenly, he grabbed for his billfold. From his position, he could see at least three boys casting jealous looks at his possession. Just then a small black dog (the thing seemed to be sharing in the joke) leapt up onto the empty stage and grinned down at the audience.

"'It is from studying the facial expressions on dogs that I first learned of the essential unity of all life' — that's what Bernie says."

"Are you going to be good tonight?" (For his hand had been resting rather too close to her nearer knee.)

"I'm certainly going to try."

"That's very good."

The play was the thing, the first few minutes of it holding their attention by reason of the costumes and the wonderful strangeness of a performance in the open air. They were much too close to the stage to be taken in by the story however. He locked glances with one of the players, a frightened-looking student no older than himself who, moreover, was fitted out in tights and a deal of red rouge. Lee lit a cigarette, but then had immediately to put it out when someone began hissing at him. Finally, he shifted to get a better look at the girl's ankle, which was not as thick as his wrist and culminated in a foot smaller than his hand.

The play came down to its close, the actors one after another falling dead at various corners of the stage. The audience exploded, some of them leaping to their feet to call out in a kind of baleful approval.

"Did you like it?" she asked happily.

"Naw. But I used to, when I was a kid. Now I like Marlowe better."

They strolled away, threading through the students, the professors and their wives, and the smattering of townspeople who were permitted on these occasions to set foot on campus.

"Can you stay out a while?"

She looked up at him, the least little bit of suspicion still showing in her eyes. "For a little while."

He reached for her hand, but then changed his mind and took a cigarette instead. They drifted, covering the two hundred steps to the village without further talk. The theater came up, the ticket-seller having closed for the night and gone away. Upstairs, in the second-story window, Bernie's window was aglow. They moved past the tavern, which is to say until Lee stopped and turned and then led her back slowly in front of the window in order that the people inside might view her and see who it was that was with her, and whom *she* was with.

"Like a cup of coffee?"

The café was narrow, dim, and even here, too, there was a cabinet full of books and on top of that a phonograph playing some of the new music of the Five Satins, or Four Platters — he wasn't sure. Instead of coffee, he sat staring at the girl.

"What do you see?" she asked.

"High forehead."

She touched her forehead. It was high, high and luminous. Moreover, given her short size and taking into account her deep dark voice...

"Judy, Judy, Judy."

"Yes?"

"Wish I'd never seen you."

She understood him and looked away. Then:

"Do you like your classes?"

"Don't know. Don't go anymore."

"You don't go to your classes?"

"Naw. Anybody could make good grades that way. I consider it a form of cheating."

"But what about the money your parents have to spend? And what about your career?"

That voice! As for the face, he was lost in it, floating helplessly. Her neck was joined to a superb head which itself had two eyes with very heavy lashes, each lash the same precise length. The nose was blunt; Lee looked at it.

"Career! That's one thing I don't have to worry about."

"But why?"

"Why? Because I don't plan to live that long."

She blinked, three times. "How long will you live?"

"I don't know. Twenty-two or three. James Dean was twenty-four."

"But you'll be nearly that old when you graduate."

"Graduate? Aw, good Lord, I can't waste that kind of time just to graduate!"

"But…"

"Anybody can graduate. Dostoevsky — where did *he* graduate from? See?"

"But where will you go?"

"I don't know. India, Sweden."

She thought about it, eyes blinking seriously.

"Anyway, there's nothing here for a person like me. I wouldn't be surprised if the goddamn scientists turned into a priesthood, started wearing scarlet robes around — that's the way I remember it."

"Remember?"

"Previous life. Million years ago." He lit a cigarette and tossed the hair out of his eyes. It was his good luck that just then music came on, a song from out of the South called *Now and Then There's a Fool Such As I*; it let him look at her tragically through the smoke. She seemed fascinated, confused, interested, uncomfortable.

"And now it's late, I suppose, for someone like you. I'll take you home."

They went in silence, past the bookstore with one or two late-night intellectuals in it, then the confectioner's and pipe shop and the balloon man wending homeward muttering to himself. His three hours were almost over; having now brought her to her doorstep, he stood, watching as she continued to blink thoughtfully at all she had heard.

"But…"

"Naw, you'll have forgotten me by then. Well, I'll say goodnight now." He stood for five seconds, looking off toward the distant hills. "Try to remember me… tolerantly, if you can."

Suddenly he was off, gone, having cut through the bushes and then down behind a row of houses.

EIGHT

HE WOKE, realizing with an increasing sense of disappointment that he had been sleeping all night on the toilet. Sal came in and stood grinning down at him. Lee hobbled back to bed and got inside.

When, toward noon, he was himself again, it was Luke sitting at the small wooden desk squeezed in between bed and sink. For some minutes, Lee watched quietly while the boy laboriously wrote out two or three lines and then, as often as not, came back and scratched them out again. Suddenly, Lee leapt up. The closet, too, was full of very different contents than of last night, nor was it Martin at the desk.

"But…"

"We're roommates now, Lee." (He held out his hand for shaking.) "It's what Martin wants, too."

"Does he? I see."

"Yeah. He seems to think you're going to pot."

"I see."

"Disintegrating."

They looked at each other and then, of a sudden, broke out laughing both.

"No damn good! Never have been and… "

"Never will be!"

They smoked. On the desk was a weak lamp, a harmonica, a pencil stub and a hefty pile of manuscript crowded with odd-looking writ. Lee was not allowed to gaze at it however; Luke covered it with his handkerchief.

"What in the…?"

"It's hard, Lee! We're correcting some of Pound's translations."

"Correcting? 'We'?"

"Yeah, Syl and me. It's a tough nut, too, Lee, all that Chinese."

"You aren't fixing to tell me that she can read *Chinese*!"

"Sure. Well, not exactly. But you can tell a lot by looking at it!"

"Bullshit."

"She can, Lee."

"Nope."

Now, for the first time in their acquaintanceship, Luke began to bristle. "She's smart, Lee."

"Not that smart."

"She's the cleverest of all girls. You should listen to her."

"I do listen to her! And sometimes I *don't* listen to her."

"Always listen to her, Lee; you should."

"Anyway, there's lots of smart girls here. I saw one — no brasière, no lipstick, not even shoes."

"How could you tell?"

"I could see 'em! She had nail polish on her toes."

"No, I mean the brassière."

"I can tell. They do it on purpose, too."

Luke thought about it, plucking at his chin. "Yeah, me too, I can tell, too." Then: "How do *you* tell?"

"No make-up. Hadn't combed her hair in years."

"I still say Syl is smart. Hey! maybe you could help us."

They stepped hastily across the yard, pulling themselves through the yard-deep deposit of red and yellow leaves. In these last days, autumn had gone to extremes, so much so indeed that the girls in their sweaters seemed miffed by the rivalry of such weather. For his part, Lee was bearing up well under it — until a breeze came along.

"Oh!"

"It's the season, Lee. Don't think about it."

"Maybe…"

"No, no, no, Syl's waiting. Later you can roll around in it all you want."

They went on, Lee casting backward glances. Luke, still in his suit, had done all that he could to press his black straw hair into a somewhat less startling shape. Mysteriously, he seemed to have forgotten the science of getting dressed; one of his cuffs had come undone and now he was treading on it at every step.

They pounded at the door and then, getting nothing, ran around to the window where Phyllis could be seen standing in the corner of her darkened room. It was a bad moment — the girl had put on her long maroon dress that scraped the floor and was standing with both arms hanging down. She had not used her tube of lipstick, although she continued to hold it in her large hand.

A certain strange silence followed, the three of them looking at each other. Finally, very delicately, Luke climbed in through the window, went to the desk and began to work. For Lee, it was the first time he had viewed the place where Judy lived, a room in disorder with combs, pencils, scarves, little mirrors, purses and socks, all of it taking up every available surface. There was also an easel with the beginnings of a canvas on it, and on the floor a wooden crate full of half-used tubes of paint. Now, going to the bookcase, Lee got down in front of it. Judy's books were easily to be identified; she had wrapped them all in bright covers and written her name in a cheerful script that was as clear and honest as the girl herself. Far more numerous was Phyllis' collection, some thirty or more volumes of Proust and Rimbaud, Pound and Verlaine, and down below, a hoard of Latin authors of whom Lee had only very faintly heard mention of before. He took one of them, a thin item in a mustard-colored jacket, a crushed flower inside, and copious notes in the margins written in a microscopic hand.

Luke called it "a date with Phyllis," although the girl herself was in bad condition. Finally, after an infinity, with Luke working steadily and Lee standing deferentially in the further corner, she moved, bringing the lipstick up to her mouth where, however, she seemed unable to use it. Clearly, her syndrome was in force and they had come upon her at the worst of times. Meanwhile Lee had much to do, if he wished to memorize the room and all the things that might be Judy's. He was sickened to see the photograph of a boy, a New York boy as it seemed to him, with his arm about the waist of a sixteen- or, possibly, a seventeen-year-old Judy caught by the camera just before she had ripened into her present-day perfection of eighteen. Looking at this, his condition deteriorated even as Phyllis' improved. The girl had by now put on her lipstick and was beginning to chat in her gay way by throwing her arm about and then stepping here and there like a stork while she gathered up her things.

"God!" she said. "What, is he going to help, too? He doesn't even like Pound!"

"I used to," said Lee. "When I was a kid. Which bed is Judy's?"

"Oh God. Well at least he can transcribe."

"No, Pound is tough, Lee."

They went out, Phyllis talking, Lee sulking, Luke dragging his cuff. Of literature and art, of books and music, the girl had an endless number of things to say. She made such long strides, however, the others had trouble keeping even with her. And then, too, she had a way of grinning inappropriately, such that people turned to look at her. Just now she was talking of the atonalists.

"But it can't be *sung*! Oh yes, yes, yes, I know about *Berg*, don't tell me about Berg."

"I won't."

"What, is Judy writing letters to that character, the one in the photograph?"

"I'm not saying it's *invalid*, Berg, no. It's just…"

"I understand," said Luke.

That moment a girl came by on a bicycle peddling with delight. The day was full of smells and sun and of leaves scuttling off to die; it caused Phyllis to smile and then to twist her head to one side, as if listening to faint distant music from beyond the hill. "The Pristine," as Luke was to call her. They could read her face and knew what she was thinking.

"You'll never see that again, that same girl on that same bicycle at this same time of day. Autumn is ending."

Phyl said nothing. That was her style, when she agreed.

The chill was perfect for coffee and hot chocolate, wherefore large numbers of intellectuals had come together in the cafeteria in the middle of day. Lee saw one of the more advanced girls, this one some twenty years or more in age, but comely still. Never would he get used it, this wealth of brains and bosoms, chess and beards. That was when he spotted Judy atop her perch with the pathetic little shovel resting in her lap. At once Lee ripped off his glasses — too late — and put on his bored expression. Already Phyllis had set out her materials, including the massive Chinese-and-English dictionary and, bending near, had begun to work. This day *was* lovely, the very fulcrum of summer and winter; it flirted with perfection in degree of clarity and the size of its outrageous leaves. Outside meantime, the eight towers of Antioch Hall were weaving in the breeze, each spire flying a long coiling pennant with an armorial device on it. And eight times Lee turned to spy on Judy, sometimes catching her looking back, and sometimes blinking, and once he found her counting out the coins to a customer whose gaze was fixed upon her person.

He was consumed with hunger, with wanting, with autumn. But mostly it was Judy, Judy, Judy — Judy in her white starched uniform and serious ways.

"Now does Judy — no, don't look at her! — does she go to bed early, or late? And what does she wear? No, I'd just like to know."

"God. And I thought we were here to work!"

"Pajamas probably. Or nightgown, maybe? I wouldn't know."

They laughed, whereon Lee stood, sat, put on a bored expression, and then went to retrieve another cup of coffee. The music was loud but good, that same *In the Still of The Night* that seemed to represent both this whole decade and his own philosophic position within it.

NINE

FOUR DAYS LATER IN EARLY NOVEMBER, just moments before autumn was to achieve its crescendo, the two boys went lumping
off across campus toward a certain run-down building that sat off by
itself at no great distance from the barn and stable. Twice Luke took
out his harmonica, both times putting it back without making music.
Lee was glum, having been two nights without sleep. Luke, on the
other hand, had been seven weeks in one suit.

The building was open. Furthermore, there were any number of
little cells up and down the corridor, each containing a professor or
administrator or, in one case, a scientist working ecstatically amid
flames and glassware. It was the secretaries who had the hauteur; they
had a way of looking out with disapproval at everyone who passed.

Luke went first. His counselor was a fastidious man, largely bald,
with a mustache fixed to his face and on his lapel two tiny awards of
some sort. Following in Luke's wake, Lee went and stood quietly in the
corner. The man looked at him.

"Ahhh… Generally, we like to conduct these interviews in private."

Lee nodded and closed the door. It was a thin dossier that lay
on the table, hardly enough to hold a photograph and fingerprints.
Nevertheless, the man now opened it and began reading, his fingers
at all times tapping and testing the contours of his own forehead. Lee
smoked.

"So! Lucien. And are we still thinking in terms of Medical School?"

"No, no, no," said Lee. "We've been through all that. Luke's going to be a writer."

There was a long, very long silence while the man took off his glasses and began kneading the narrow of his already rather narrow nose. He seemed tired, exhausted, a headache bothering him. Finally:

"I was thinking more of his long-range plans."

"They *are* long-range! He's writing a novel *right now*."

"Two volumes," said Luke. (He appeared to be pleased, happy to have so many friends around him.)

"Your parents…"

"Right. They're in the novel, too. Tell him."

"Sure," said Luke.

"And no doubt you're helping with it — did I get that right?"

"Naw. Luke? He doesn't need help."

"Lee's going to be a writer, too."

"It follows."

"If he lives. Right now, he's not writing anything yet."

"Yes, we have a number of people like that. However, I think that you will find that even the greatest of writers still had to earn their way. Tolstoy? A doctor."

"No, actually it was Chekhov."

"Shakespeare? You've perhaps heard of *him*? A professional actor."

"O. K., Luke, tell him you want to be an actor."

"No, Lee, he's right. Maybe I could write on week-ends, but then during the week itself…"

"No, no, no, no, no, Jesus! We've *talked* about it and *talked* about it. Do you know how long it takes to be a doctor? We'll be dead by then!"

"He's right."

"And think about Phyllis, too. What, is she supposed to just wait around while you're cutting up corpses? See? You have to think about these things, all the time."

"This is true."

"Phyllis'?" the professor asked. "Is she the one who…?"

"Naw, she's alright."

"And so, we have you two and Phyllis as well — I see. She writes, I presume."

"Essays," said Luke. "And poetry."

"Translates, too."

"Translates essays and poetry?"

"And philosophy, too, sometimes."

"Goodness. We seem to be entering a new Golden Age here. And yet all the same…"

"Paints, too."

"Three writers and a painter! I'm impressed. Now! My recommendation to you, Lucien, is that…"

"Plays the harp, too. 'Course now, it may not sound like music, not to people who…"

"Not to people not on medication? Good! Now Lucien, I did want to advise you that…"

"And next year we plan to collaborate on an opera."

"Certainly. Let me see now: Phyllis will write the music, yes?"

"Right."

And you, you'll…"

"Libretto! I can do it, too. You should see my I.Q."

The man looked at him for a long while and then let out a groan followed by smiles and outright laughter and a facial tic they hadn't seen before. Finally, he took off his glasses, laid them flat and began to squeeze his nose.

They had to hasten — Lee's interview was next. In this case however the man was an historian, his office laden with a larger number of books than ever had been seen brought together into so tight a space. There was also a dog, a fugue-state asthmatic who constantly wheezed and snuffled and, from time to time, made as if he intended to launch an attack upon Luke, whom plainly he abhorred. The historian himself was in slippers, trousers (no belt), and whiskers three days old. A cup of last year's coffee had been shunted off to one side, detritus floating on the surface.

"Leland, yes indeed; been wanting to see you. Who's this?"

"Luke."

"Of Biblical fame? Heal thyself! No, no, ignore me, ignore me." He yawned and then, suddenly, snatched up a newspaper and spent some seconds scanning down the columns. "Old Leland Pefley from Alabama and his northeastern friend. It happens. I have your dossier. No, no, his, not *yours*. You've had *your* interview. 'Course now if you want another... You know what Treitschke said about that, don't you?"

Lee nodded.

"What did he say?

"You already know."

"O.K., I'll let that pass. Now why are we here? I've forgotten."

"Interview."

"That youth knows nothing of the impossibility of happiness — *that's* what he said. Or was it Ranke?"

"Possibly," said Luke. (His instrument had become clogged with tobacco and he was working feverishly with his pencil to make it right.)

"Ranke, yes. The little shit! And now, Leward, we need to consider what you'll be doing next quarter."

"New York," said Lee. (In truth, he had been trying to put it out of mind, how that soon he'd be expected to forsake campus and, as part of his program, to take up a two-month job in some part of the country.)

"New York! No, no, those jobs have been taken long ago. You're a little behindhand in all of this you realize."

"He's been busy."

"So I've been given to understand." Then: "Too much ice cream, perchance?"

"Europe then," said Lee.

"'Europe.' I have it; let's approach it this way — what does he plan to do, once he's finished with school?"

"Finish? Ha!"

"Actually, he doesn't plan on living that long."

"I see! No wonder he's pestering that poor little girl so strenuously."

"It's now or never."

"Yes! And I understand we have about forty other boys here who feel the same way about her."

Lee sickened. The man had a way of grabbing up his paper every half-minute and reading therefrom. The dog was growing bolder.

"Lee's going to be a writer."

"Well, I should certainly hope so. But with so little time to do it in! I don't know. Now Leland, what if it should come down to a choice between the girl and the... "

"Girl," Luke said.

"Wise. You're both so wise I don't know what to say." (He grabbed up the paper, there where History was taking place in front of his nose.) "Now Lee, we have a job opening in Toledo — you'll like it — a job in journalism. Think you'd like that?"

"I doubt it. I'd rather just stay here."

"I see. And are you really so wedded to the place as all that?"

"Yes, sir."

"Really! And will he feel the same way in four years from now, I wonder."

"Four years? He would have been twenty-two by then."

"Careful, Lee; you'll end up like Bernie Krestinsky. Hanging around campus."

"He seems happy."

"Well, he's not. And besides, who said you're supposed to be happy? Happiness is something you can expect about fifteen minutes of in a lifetime."

"He's already had more than that! Twice as much probably. "

"Oh? Doesn't have much to look forward to then, does he?"

"No, sir. Couple of years."

This man too seemed to have contracted a headache. Finally, he said: "Now about that job in journalism…"

"Journalism, fumbalism. He's not interested in writing editorials, stuff like that."

"Actually, we were thinking in terms of a copyboy."

"Cop…!" Lee stood. "Good Lord! Look, I did not fall to earth in order… "

"'Fall to earth'?"

"… to be a copyboy!" He could feel his gorge rising. Luke, too, was frowning deeply.

"Yes, but that's the way it is fellow. You go on up to Toledo, Lee, and be the very best copyboy you can!"

"Jesus. Sounds like a bourgeois town to me."

But by now, the man had gone back to his paper, folding and re-folding it with such great noise as to show that the interview was over.

TEN

HE WAS WALKING toward the library with the finest of intentions when suddenly, having stopped, he saw that today's weather was superior even to yesterday's. It was a golden crust, the world, and when he saw how the leaves rained upon him of their own volition... Lee dropped his books and forty seconds later was at Judy's place.

"Come on out and play!"

She leapt. She had been sitting in the window gazing out in wonder.

"I can't, Lee; I just can't! I have to study *sometime*."

"What are you saying! You see how it is out here."

"I know."

"And that it's going to be winter soon?"

"I have to."

"And then we die — is that what you want?"

He lifted her down from the window, both arms about her waist. She had a marvelous density to her, nor did he turn loose of her all at once. Her blouse was white but just as full of riches, and meanwhile her shorts told him all that he immediately needed to know about that.

"Oh God in heaven."

"What?"

"Your perfume — it smells of lavender and rue."

"I know! Larry gave it to me."

They took any direction, talking, laughing, insulting one another. At one moment, he was in process of tying his shoe when she actually pushed him over into the leaves and ran away chortling. He chased, astonished at how ineffectively she ran, like unto a pony whose hooves clashed and chimed against the cobbles. Lee caught sight of an old grey professor, the spell of death upon him, watching delightedly from his window.

It did not need long to run her down, to lift her, to force her down into the leaves. It needed even less to remove her shoe and begin tickling her foot, a peculiar-looking part that was quite square and had the thinness of a duck's   he looked for but never found any actual webbing between the toes. The girl meanwhile was fighting earnestly, her eyes squeezed shut by virtue of the great effort she was making to pull out a full handful of his hair. He experienced waves of involuntary anger mixed with acute lust. Two boys moved in to get a better view. Never had they heard such braying, so deep and so baleful, from so short a person.

They went on, working down the slope and into the glen. The place had aged shockingly since his last visit, every corner and every glade having mellowed down to the sort of gold found sometimes on the fore edges of valuable old books. The brook, previously so lassitudinous, was running in a panic now. The girl had seen something in the stream and — and all things seemed to surprise her — was watching it worriedly.

"He's trying to get out!"

"Who?"

"A little lobster!"

"Oh, no! Run!"

She fled, going thirty yards before she stopped. Seeing her, her wide-eyed face peering from the foliage... He knew this much, that someday someone sometime would be the one to take her and to have her, to carry her off and yes put her to bed. A goodly bed, too, with quilts and fresh starched sheets, a fire going and books on the shelf.

They crossed and began to climb the hill. Behind them, the five burnt-out minarets of Antioch Hall emerged slowly above the trees. Here, autumn seemed to be taking place in an aquarium, or rather, the more he looked at it, as if it marked the last phase of that most autumnal of all known epochs, the lovely Cenozoic itself. Looking back, he could see the very window in which Luke would be laboring at his desk. In truth, this whole province had been laid out in precise accord with the instructions he himself would have given — the library and village, the cobbler's and vegetable mart, the shoe repair and pastry maker, the tavern and rose-seller and place where Bernie dwelt. And now, just in front of him, Judy's face, a moon-swept lake. He studied her in seriousness, the girl waiting on his verdict.

"What do you see?"

"Judy, Judy. 'Thy beauty is to me like those Nicæan barks of yore, that gently o'er a perfumed sea...'"

"Bark? Alright for you!" Then: "And *now* what do you see?"

"Not what I wanted."

"And what was that?"

"That she loves him."

She laughed, partly to taunt him and partly as to change the topic.

"Maybe if I were to bang your head up against that tree..."

"Nope; that won't do it."

"What then?"

"Wait and see." She laughed and then, seeing that he would kiss her, put one arm about his neck. At first, he kissed only briefly, but then soon came back for more. Good were her lips, but what affected him most was the arm about his neck and her fingers running excitedly in his hair.

"You ruin my life."

"I didn't mean to."

"I could have been..."

"I know, I know. You still can!"

"I don't want to anymore."

"Please, Lee."

"It's like I've got a 'Judy' in my head, and... "

"Please no, Lee."

"It's killing me of course — just hope you realize that."

"No. Oh look, there's a squirrel!"

"I have it: you go stand over there, and when you turn around, why then I'll be dead."

"No! Alright, I'm not going to talk to you anymore."

She moved off, going only a short distance however before she stopped and retrieved something off the ground, a leaf or nut. Lee stood, watching quietly. Time, dread Time, it was nudging both of them closer and closer to eternity, night closing in, leaves falling. And sometimes it seemed to him they had but moments, parts of moments, and then must go tumbling forever among the stars.

ELEVEN

FULL TWO DAYS he spent in the library. Situated beneath ground, it had dark reaches well-insulated with books, the one place where he could get some sleep. And when he emerged, believing it was day… In fact, he found that it was absolute night again and the sidewalk crowded with girls shuffling on toward his own dormitory where — he had forgotten about it — a party had been scheduled to celebrate the achievements of the past two months.

He raced forward, passing through the girls and then bolting up the stairs where Luke had come to a standing position while still bending over his desk. They were accustomed to it, how that the boy made some of his best poetry thinking on his feet.

"The girls are coming!"

No answer. He was writing with a pencil that was so used-up that it could not be seen within his fist. And then, too, there were any number of giant dust bunnies proliferating beneath the furniture and in the corners, too. Better to leave them in peace. Instead, Lee chose to get into his scarlet shirt, his sunglasses and cigarettes.

Moments later, the girls were clattering in the hall. Luke also turned to take a look, but only to get held up at the last second at his desk. Opening narrowly, Lee could descry a thin one (smiling) and then a great one clutching at a big white purse. Clearly, this latter person was intimidated by the music and the dim, and that the only illumination was comprised of a single blood-red lamp glowing evilly in the rear.

"Whose girls are they?" Sal asked, hissing across the hall.

"Reed's."

"Both of 'em?"

"No, no; the great one."

Lee ducked back in. He had decided at the last minute to change over into his satin shirt, a green item that scintillated in the dark and zippered diagonally across the chest. He was smoking so much these days, he had learned to see clearly through the haze while keeping his own face invisible. Outside, meanwhile, someone had put on *Love Is Strange*, the strangest indeed of all the new music of this strangest year. But he preferred to wait for *The Man with The Golden Arm* before making his own appearance in the hall.

He did wait, counting up to thirty before opening the door very slightly and peering into the murk. Judy, she *had* come; he knew it at once by the way she took one step forward, stopped, and then looked about in some confusion at the extreme dark, the beer, the red haze and insidious music. She was looking for him, he was sure of it, and yet, that moment, one of the alien boys who had somehow inveigled an invitation and who knew nothing of the story between himself and Judy, this boy went forward and tried to take her hand. Lee pushed off at once, exposing himself before *The Man with The Golden Arm* had played even once. The boy, as it proved, was rather small and had, moreover, a weak face.

"You're trespassing," said Lee.

"He wasn't doing anything."

"That is his very good fortune."

She was in one of her sweaters, a famous one. Her figure was blinding, even in the dark, and formed such a contrast with her wide blinking eyes and high forehead.

"You don't have to be so mean."

"Judy, Judy, Judy. You're going to be the death of me."

She waited patiently to see what else he might say.

"I'd like to bite your head off."

"That might hurt."

"Oh, I'll hurt you alright."

Came then a spate of loud music sung by a new singer, a notorious individual from the deepest South whose clothing fashion might almost have been modeled after Lee's. Lee harkened to it, staring into the girl, waiting for that section of the music that sorted best with his own personal style — satin, sunglasses, and cigarette.

"Dance with me."

"Alright."

"Pretend like you're in love."

And did so, even drawing up tightly against him and floating one weightless arm about his neck. It was good, the top of her head slipping in precisely under his chin. Slowly and slowly, hopelessly and hopelessly, he was growing more and more addicted to her, her blunt nose and womanly bosoms, so much so that he could no longer be happy all those times he was not being scorched by her chest. Dim as it was, he saw Martin drifted past in the arms of one of the tiniest of girls, no doubt a prize from the local high school who, even as they twirled about, went on happily chewing gum. Ray came up, drunk already.

"You're always with *him*," he said. "Damn! And now he's got that fucking shirt on, too!"

Impossibly not to laugh. Sal came next, the most irresponsible boy in the hall but as yet only half-drunk. His gaze fell on Judy's sweater, make-up, and ribbon and stayed there.

"Whew! Want to swap girls?"

"Not really. Who is that real tiny girl with Martin?"

"From the village. She only weighs eighty pounds." (This last said in great amazement.)

The record had finished but someone with taste had put it back on again. Lee took a cigarette, lit it, and then on an inspiration offered one to Judy as well. At first, she was startled by it. Lee had to admire the way she recovered, as if to say there was nothing he could do that she wouldn't be able to follow.

"Beer?"

"Alright."

He led her back and then, while she stood smoking amateurishly, drew off a mug for her. Robert, the twenty-year-old Hall Adviser, the one purportedly supervising the affair, had retreated off into his own room and was to be seen sitting on his bed reading a newspaper. Lee tapped once, politely, causing the man to look up in surprise.

"Robert, I'd like to introduce Judy."

"Yes? Goodness, such a pretty girl, Lee!"

"I know."

They moved in hesitantly, both a little in awe of the man's sophisticated ways. It was a tidy room, full of books and pictures, fine objects and a carpet with an eschatological design.

"Welcome to Bedlam, Judy." Then: "Tell me, what do you see in this fellow?"

"He's funny."

"And such a pretty girl, Lee! No wonder they hate you."

"Robert's graduating," said Lee. "And then he's going on to college for another two or three years. That's on top of what he's already done."

"Where...?"

"Paris." (They could discern an involuntary little note of pride.)

"Paris!"

"Bernie's been to Paris."

The boy laughed merrily. "I expect he has!"

"Paris. How'd you do it?"

"Well! There's a fund. For Negro students."

Lee blushed. Never had he heard that word from out of a Negro himself.

"Well, we'd better get back. Dance."

"Right."

They took a last look at the cozy little chamber with its pictures and bright quilt. A very good thing it was, living in a place where one could visit any sort of personality according to one's mood; already Lee had read so many nude magazines in Sal's room that he had, as it were, earned a preemption both on the journals themselves and the niche where they were stored.

"You'll go to Paris, too, someday," said Judy.

"Probably. It's a pretty good place to die, I guess." And then: "We're not like these other shits, Luke and me."

"I know that." She had been pulling at him to dance and now, with one glass arm resting lightly on his shoulder and she herself slipping in precisely under his chin, it was the most comfortable moment in the week, the bounty of all his studies since the last time he had held her. And that, of course, was when Lloyd broke in upon them and took her away.

The boy was of about his own size, but strong-looking and craggy-faced; Lee elected not to get into a fight with him all at once. And now they were playing *Earth Angel*, but this time Judy was no longer in his arms. He had known from the beginning that something of this sort would happen someday. Accordingly, he sauntered down to the beer and stood drinking carelessly without removing the cigarette. Outside, a fog had come up, a blue one that was beginning to pour through the chinks of the antique building. That was when he noted a girl, a lonely one in no way attractive who for lack of better to do had taken over the phonograph. Lee went to her.

"I believe we have the same taste in music," he said charmingly. Suddenly, reaching forward, he brushed back a curl of her hair that was out-of-place. He divined three things about her at once, namely that she was not pretty, that she had never before been touched by a male, and finally that Judy might, or might not, be looking.

"Are you... the way you talk?"

"Don't really know anymore where I'm from, been drifting so much."

"Drifting?"

"You know: Mexico and whatnot. Jail. Want to dance?"

He led her out and held her in what was an almost illegal fashion. Across the way, Judy had just now unleashed one of her man-slaughtering smiles upon her partner, the same sort of smile that had so blighted his own life, shortening it. Love, apparently, meant nothing to her, not so long as she had those on whom to exercise her spells. Lee maneuvered closer, until he could read the numbers on the watch that was on the wrist of the arm that was draped about the neck of the most ignoble boy in the hall. One brief moment, he was in danger of vomiting. Instead, the music having finished, he dropped the girl and headed back to his own room where Luke and Phyllis were working in weak light amid a clutter of coffee cups, notebooks and dictionaries.

"Well, that's it. She's dancing with Lloyd now."

Phyl looked up smiling gaily, an inappropriate response, as it seemed to Lee.

"Love means nothing to her, I guess."

"Aw, Christ. Those shits out there, they don't matter, Lee. Five hundred years from now and nobody will know they ever existed."

That was true. Lee slipped off his shirt, got into bed and lit a cigarette. The music was louder; it mixed with the sound of Luke's half-inch pencil scratching away at the translation, the pile of manuscript getting higher and higher. Down below in the fog meanwhile, a solitary intellectual was coming back from the library, arms laden with books.

Lee slept twenty minutes, hardly more, and then woke to find that Phyllis had gone into her other mode during his absence and now was sitting on the carpet, her two bamboo legs (sores on them) jutting out across the floor. Lee jumped up.

"It's a bad moment, Lee."

"It's not normal, is what it is."

"I'm alright! God."

"Get Judy."

"*I* can't get her — she hates me. *You* get her."

"Then you watch Syl."

Lee nodded and pulled up a chair. The girl was in a bad state; coming nearer, he saw that her flesh had a whiteness and was stretched too tightly over her skull, making its cornices too prominent. At moments like these, there was nothing about her that was pretty. And yet her mind was intact.

"How goes the translation?" Lee asked.

"Oh! You never cared about that."

"I do! I did. But I've been busy."

"I think you should go back to the party now."

"Soon."

"Oh God. I'm not going to hurt myself."

Judy came in, very worried-looking, and rushed to the girl. Lee had seen this before, how she resonated with sick persons, with dogs and the squirrels that clambered into her lap, the whole animal world.

"Oh, this is not so bad," she said. "It's alright; just go back to what you were doing."

They left, Lee and Luke, one for the men's room, the other to the beer. That moment, Lee's dancing partner jumped into his path.

"Alright now! Something's going on in that room" — she pointed to it — "and I have a pretty good idea of what it is, too!"

"No, no; it has to do with my roommate."

"Oh."

He led her out and danced, conscious at all times that she simply was not made from the same sort of stuff as Judy — the distinction between butter and gold. This girl was very nearly ready to take off her clothes for him, if he but asked.

"What did you mean, Mexico?"

"Doesn't matter. It didn't work out anyway."

"What didn't work?"

"Revolution." He saw Judy come out and Luke go back in. It was the time to be dancing as lewdly as the girl would permit. Certainly, the music was pernicious enough, that same *In the Still of the Night* that expressed the sort of person he could have been had he chosen girls for his main career. Tonight, his aplomb was especially great; moreover, he had on a dark green shirt that shimmered in the haze.

"And what did you mean, jail?"

"You don't want to hear about all that. Please!" He held her closer. As squat as she was, albeit heavy, he could go on dancing while he smoked. Judy meanwhile had taken up with Martin, who was dancing in dignity while at the same time trying to impress her with his sophistication, as if he thought to win her with such materials at that. She did listen, but not so intently that her eyes couldn't lock with Lee's.

Those eyes could smolder. Lee prayed for, but was not vouchsafed, his own personal theme from *Man with the Golden Arm*; instead, someone put on *Earth Angel* again. Sal had drawn off into one of the darkened rooms with Martin's high school girl who, however, appeared to be bored by it all. Just then a terrific commotion broke out at the head of the hall where two boys and three girls were struggling to ward off an intrusion by two other boys from another dorm. Beer was being spilled; Lee saw one girl go flying. He used it to retreat into Robert's room.

The boy had gone to bed wearing a blindfold of some kind; now, suddenly, he sat up with an expression of horror on his face.

"Dancing with Lloyd. We both know what *he* is."

Robert said nothing. And now Lee saw that he had swatches of cotton in his ears.

"She's out there with Martin right now."

"What?"

"Judy. You've got a blindfold on. Phyl is sick."

"Lee?"

"Right."

"What time is it?"

"I don't know. Fog's getting worse."

"Good grief. Well... Want some coffee?"

"Love, apparently, means nothing to her. She'll dance with anybody."

"Oh boy." He rose painfully and put on his robe. His was the great privilege of a room of his own, a "T"-shaped affair with carpet and quilt. Lee went and plopped down in the crossbar of the "T."

"Cream and sugar?"

"You saw the sweater she was wearing."

"Let's hope she's still wearing it. Cream? Sugar?"

"You're supposed to be an adviser. I'm ready."

"It's easy to advise you, Leland. I mean if you only have a year or two in which to live. So, if I were you, why I'd just go on back out there and... You read me?"

The man was wise; Lee nodded and gave back the coffee. In the adjoining room, the boy called Gil had gotten naked and was going through his yogi positions — he looked at Lee in unfriendly style. Robert, meanwhile, had slipped back to bed, robe and all, and was adjusting the cotton and blindfold.

Lee went direct to his room — Luke was reading out loud to Phyllis — and changed shirts, the green one having become exhausted by now, with beer stains on it. The sunglasses he left behind. For some time now, the music had been deteriorating, until at last someone put on *Little Darlin'*, playing it twice. Lee moved forward to the rickety fire escape where Grady, supported by three others, was vomiting down on the pedestrians far below. Further, the seven spindly towers of Antioch Hall were bending in the breeze.

He had to probe deeply, pushing the haze out of his way before he found Judy sitting on the couch with the shyest person in the hall, called Phil. The boy had seized upon her hand, was holding it and, by the looks of him, had rather die than let it go. Lee sat on her other side, saying nothing at first. Finally:

"Yes, you've had yourself quite an evening, haven't you? Goddamn it! Of all the people — Lloyd. Makes me sick!"

"Oh? Oh? And what about *you*! You were *feeling* of her!"

"'Her'?"

"That floozy!"

"Well, I can see you just don't understand anything. You're not in love with me whereas I *am* in love with you — that's the difference. So, there's nothing more to be said." He stood, took two steps and then turned and came back. "You really don't understand, do you? You're supposed to love just *one* person, not a whole bunch. *I* love just one person."

"I will."

"When? When? Can't answer, can you?"

"She doesn't have to answer," Phil reminded him.

"Goddamn it! You sit there. She'll drive you crazy, too, just wait; she likes it. Oh well, it's only for a year or two and then I'll be dead."

"Oh, you will not."

"I'll do it myself, if I have to. Hey! Want to watch?"

"I'm not going to talk to you anymore."

Came now the floozy, her face flushed, eyes bulging with anger; she positioned herself squarely in front of Judy.

"I think it's just *stinking*, the way you won't leave him alone!"

Lee nodded. Phil, meanwhile, had brought Judy's hand up yet closer where, so it seemed, he might be thinking of kissing it.

"I'm going home."

"Ha! In *this* fog? Wait, I'll go with you."

In fact, the fog had lifted somewhat, giving them just less than five feet of clearance. The girl was five feet two.

"And when you *love* somebody, no I mean *really love…*"

"I'm tired, Lee."

"No, it changes your whole life. Look, I didn't ask for it to happen."

"I have a test in…" (she looked at her watch) "six hours!"

"Six. We could be dead by then."

"Well, thank you for walking this far."

"Right. And I'll take you the rest of the way, too."

"Me, too," said Phil, "I'm taking her, too."

"Look at that moon!"

It was indeed the loveliest in years, yet also the most sinister. As for the lovely aspect, it was in token of the very lovely autumn, now all finished. The other aspect, the sinister, it had to do with winter coming in.

TWELVE

HE WOKE, looked for the moon but couldn't find it, and then went back to sleep again. Suddenly, he leapt out of bed.

Already there were four or five cars in the road, also a truck with its bay full of luggage. Lee went direct to the proper window and climbed inside, finding a very fretful Judy standing among her things — boxes and bags and at least two giant-sized suitcases that were full and more than full.

"I don't have time!" she said. "And I don't have space!"

"Calm, calm. Remember, you can't *think* straight if your *stuff* isn't straight. It's natural. My stuff is always straight." Suddenly, he perceived two boys standing in the same room with them, including a large one wearing a fine coat with a velvet collar of some sort.

"These are not Antiochians!"

"Oberlin," said the lesser one, who held out his hand to be shaken.

"Oberlin has never produced a great writer in its whole existence," Lee described.

Phyllis breezed in, thrilled by the tremendous confusion everywhere. She breezed out again. Now Lee caught his first view of Judy's open suitcase, an unorganized affair with a large pine cone floating on top. Her purse, a modest-looking thing paid for with ice cream earnings, was full of sweet gum balls.

"Oberlin might have produced some scientists or government officials, people like that. I say *might*. Where does this go?"

"Wherever you can find a place."

"There isn't any place."

"Then put it anywhere."

"There are no anywheres, not anywhere."

She was close to getting mad at him. Looking at her, her in her white sweater, his more urgent desire just then was to take a bite from her neck, there where it ran down into the sweater itself. He looked at it.

"Are you going to help? Or just criticize? I need to know."

"Help." (The two boys from Oberlin had gone out into the hall where they were jittering back and forth and smoking and plainly growing impatient.) Lee hissed at her:

"Who are *those* types?"

"They're taking me to New York."

"Oh, good. No, that's wonderful. She had to go home, therefore she chose a couple of shits from Oberlin. I see."

"I'm going to hit you."

Again, Phyllis dashed in, the easel under her arm. Her hand, a masculine instrument, was full of a book and two paint brushes. She dashed back out again. They had a fleeting view of Luke sprinting past the door, the boy having changed into a mint-new suit that he would use and use till came the time to trade it for another.

Lee now set to work in earnest. First, he stripped off the pillowcase and filled it with some of the short girl's assortment of jars and whatnot, vials of various kind, many of them empty. He found at least a dozen nail files in worn condition, a pound of pencils, several acorns, (someone had painted a face on one of them), lipstick, an odd rock, loose stamps, hairpins, a bundle of letters, a flashlight (it didn't work), and two clocks, one without a dial and one without a cord. Referring to the letters, Lee said:

"Me, I use a letter opener. Instead of just ripping them open."

"Oh, shut up." She continued to sit upon the suitcase, as if it might at last give in to the fine sort of person she was and agree to close. He daren't recommend that she throw away the pine cone, knowing as he did of their rarity in Manhattan. Instead, by sheer chance, he had plunged his hand into the very box that held her brassieres. She had a black one, too, full of snaps and hooks; he could feel a tremendous headache coming on. Outside, the Oberlinians had retreated to their rather expensive-looking car in which a third boy of the same general type was slumbering in the back seat. Judy had meantime fallen into a trance and was staring toward the woods, the same woods where she had collected her acorns and cones.

"Oh, Tweedy, Tweedy. Will you write me?"

She nodded.

"But don't write Phil, O.K.?"

"No, no." She laughed merrily. "But will you write *me*?"

"Naw, I doubt it. I'll be too depressed all the time." Holding her, he gave a quick kiss to that spot on her neck that had been such a nuisance to him. She was small but solid, her shoulder blade an extremely thin component that he with his usual perversity could envision as moldering in the ground someday, evidence for those insouciant archeologists of the future who might, or might not, consider it worth saving. History need blink but once in order to melt her down into an old woman; two blinks and she was gone. He could see her, wide-eyed, blinking, fretting with her hands whilst she went tumbling head over heels forever among the stars. Lee now lifted her and set her in the window, the better to see her more objectively. She waited to learn what his verdict might be.

"Hmm. You appear to be wearing that same sweater and little red collar as on that night. Doing it on purpose, too. O Judy! I don't want you to leave!"

"I know, I know."

"It hurts! All the time."

"I know." She was Love and Beauty, and yet she had a little fortress at the core with high walls and archers on call. More than anything, he hated to relinquish her just now when she was a little off balance and, conceivably, teetering on the verge of love.

"I'll be thinking about Judy, Judy, Judy all the time."

"When you can't sleep?"

"Right."

"And it's going to be even worse now?"

"Much worse. I expect pure hell from now on out."

"Oh, God." Her chin was trembling. Now, once more, he came forward, kissing and memorizing her for posterity's sake.

II

THIRTEEN

HE TRAVELED FAR, running by bus into further and further reaches of the cold North. Nowadays when he smoked, he did it for warmth. And if he had the entire bus to himself, as very nearly he did, yet the outside landscape was largely worthless. He passed what might once have been a farm, reduced now to briars and scrub. Finally, at just after seven, he stood and went down to the driver.

"Never had a whole bus just to myself before!" he said.

The man turned slowly. He was able to drive with one eye while looking at Lee with the other. Lee had been wrong, quite wrong, to imagine that just because the man was plump, he must also be jolly.

"Well, think of it like this: that it wern't for you, I could be home with my wife."

"Oh."

"And kids."

Lee went back. Impossible to read, the lights from Springfield having long ago faded away to nothing. Instead, he took out the photograph of the girl and then, lying at full length, held it up in the little bit of illumination emitted by the moon, by his cigarette, and by certain roadside signs bearing sparkling script. She seemed to be smiling back at him from light years away, and he had no better hope of holding her again than if she had lived and died in ancient times. They plunged into a tunnel, or perhaps the moon was down; in any case, it darkened out the picture and sent Lee fumbling for his matches. There was no shortage of stars certainly; he could see great ones and small ones and some that were jagged, could see them littered across a sky that had gone from blue to purple and had then proceeded on to some new color that he could not recall having ever seen before. As to the moon, formerly his own special favorite, the thing had taken up in the window across the aisle and for Lee's sake was riding mile for mile with him to northern Ohio and beyond.

His mind drifted. Where, then, were Luke and the others? He imagined them as giant-sized playing cards in the sky, queens and knaves with faces composed of stars. Came now a car with lights bright enough to let him see the photograph. Lee groaned, stood, hummed and then, with the driver squinting unfavorably at him in the mirror, began to rove up and down the bus, searching for a better nesting place.

They hit Toledo at a little after eleven, the third largest city (outside of Birmingham) that ever he had seen. They halted in front of a typical building where, to his amazement, a stowaway in the form of a little old woman in a shawl leapt up quickly and squirted off the bus in front of him. He followed with difficulty, owing to the flood of people coming on board. He found himself in a strength contest with one of them, a grim-looking Latin-American-type woman backed up by a numerous family. Just then he turned, Lee, and rushed back for his suitcase.

He wandered, going he knew not where. Itself, the city was ablaze with neon and endless strings of cars lined up and blasting at one another. He had expected a bourgeois situation whereas in fact he could hardly recall having ever seen so many bars and taverns pushed together into so crowded a space. Of whores, he had seen just one by now, judging by her. Suddenly, that moment, a police car leapt out of line and, putting on its enormous siren, went chasing down the block. Lee trod forward, wending a way through whorls of red and yellow neon extruding from the stores and street lights. Not very many pedestrians in the street itself though he saw great numbers of them barricaded in the bars and taverns whence strange music came to his ears. Lee put on a bored expression. He preferred to skip past the mouths of the alleys, moving quite speedily in spite of the suitcase and books.

He was smoking on the march. Finally, after certain blocks, he came into what really was a bourgeois situation — twenty homes well-zippered for the night. One small child he saw, a tiny one peeping out worriedly from a roost beneath the eves. Here Lee stopped, availing himself of the street lamp in order to read his map, a primitive one composed by Sal on a paper napkin. A dog barked and then, seeing Lee's expression, broached nearer.

He returned to the neon zone. Never had he been more at a northerly point than here, here where the chill was chillier than was good and where the city was shoulder-to-shoulder in evil-looking bars. He came to a tavern wherein a grey-headed man, drunk possibly (his eyes were extinct), turned on his stool and grinned at him. If only the dog could leave off following! For only then might he have passed safely through this district without calling down any further attention to himself. It was not until he came to a furniture store with a mirror in it that he saw that he was still in his cap and that the bill was pointing off to one side.

His apartment was nearby. For two minutes he stood fronting the building, estimating its age and history, and the fact that while it was narrower than most, yet also was it taller. He viewed the chimney and ambient swallows, saw a woman at her ironing board, and several other things as well. He knew so little of big cities. A car came by, slowing when it saw the kind of person he was. (Apart from his books, he had no weapons of any sort.) And when he looked again, the swallows had flown and, in their place, he found a giant-sized placard in the sky of his late beloved grandmother smiling down sweetly upon this, his current adventure.

It was not an "apartment," but rather a single room that awaited him. Lee gasped; seldom had he seen so much austerity in respect of furnishings and "drapes," and such a carpet with unambiguous holes in it. True, the previous tenant had left a jar with flowers in it, the petals having browned very badly by now. He crossed to the window and looked down upon the automobile that had been following him but had now come to a complete halt and — and nothing surprised him anymore — where the driver had come out and was peering up at approximately the window whence he himself was looking down. His first impulse, Leland's, was to bolt the door, a task made impossible both by the lack of any such bolt, as well as by the dog's absolute re fusal to stand aside. Nor did the "apartment" hold any sort of weapon, not even so much as a kitchen knife.

He tried to sleep. The sheets were stained and the room had a medicinal smell of urine and camphor that had soaked into the very walls and lathing. Unfortunately, the mattress, though firm, rested on two different levels; he exclaimed aloud when, rising and drawing back the mattress, he found that it was supported in part by a disused automobile tire and in another part by a soft drink bottle. Sitting upright, he tried to read. The mirror itself was weak; coming nearer, he found it so blackened by age that it no longer functioned anymore. Just then, someone coughed in the next room. Lee knew the sound of old men spitting sputum; *this* old man was not eighteen inches away. Suddenly his own quilt (it had the picture of a rooster on it) gave off a further burst of the same odor with which the room was already so invested.

He knew this, that there was a golden seething city scene with whores on every corner, not quarter of a mile from where he lay. With no other option, he rose, peed, got into his lavender shirt and jacket and made his way beneath street lamps into a more domestic area that lay over against the downtown city itself. The homes here had a gelatinous quality struggling to stabilize in the silence of the night. Glancing upwards, he spied the moon ascending in great haste.

Already three strobe lights had sprung up out of nowhere and were raking excitedly across the remains of yesterday's clouds.

Two blocks further, he passed into still another realm of bars and restaurants where the advertisements put out a granular haze that got into his eyes. There came the sound of jukeboxes from many quarters at once, blatant music cumulating like water before spilling out into the road. He moved cautiously. A couple was waltzing in a hotel lobby — a mere boy, as it looked to Lee, together with what he estimated to be the second prostitute since he had come to town. A taxi pulled up, releasing two girls in heels and glitter who ran giggling and squealing into what at first looked like a normal dwelling with an out-of-date Christmas wreath on the door. That was when Lee spotted an unforgettable face looking out with a pleading expression from a parked taxicab, as of one who had only just now recognized that she was doomed or diseased, lost or dying; they looked at each other for the space of maybe three seconds. This, then, was what he had always expected from Ohio and of the North generally. A couple blew out of one of the bars and came toward him, the girl a withered exhibit with sharply-pointed nipples in a tight sweater but hardly any actual breasts.

He passed a stairwell in which an elderly woman sat dreaming, material enough for a dozen books, if only he knew how to produce them. At this junction, people were crossing back and forth in a frenzy, determined to visit every tavern (and there were many of them) before they died. His one disappointment: that the music was not as vile nor as insidious as some he could have mentioned. In fact, they were simply playing country music that he thought only the people of his own region ever listened to.

He went on. It was a mixed group at the corner, including a grandmotherly woman pulling a little red wagon stacked with newspapers. Also, two youths, ardent for evil, who continued to stare down hungrily into the smoke and neon that filled all the lower part of the city. That was when Lee saw something in the alley, a street cat swollen to six times normal size and comprised, as it seemed to him, of cotton candy. For all that he knew, the world was full of such things, this being the first to let itself be seen.

He went one block deeper, past another rash of bars and eating places in which more than one person had fallen asleep upon the stool. He had been wrong — this was no bourgeois town, not altogether. A car came past, chauffeur-driven, offering a glimpse of a beautiful girl in earrings, make-up and a black velvet jacket with the collar up.

He began to drop into the lower city, past boarded-up warehouses and a bridge that spanned a railway track. Three soldiers were bending to speak with someone in a car while across the road, a lone figure in a raincoat had his eye fastened on Lee. Lee went on, passing a storefront that might have been thought empty but for traces of music leaking under the door. In front, two derelicts in beards and flowing white hair were leaning up against one another, both of them watching cordially as Lee came on. He was about to cross when one of them spoke up in a calm, reasonable, and even a distinguished voice: "Hey, pussy-doll; c'mere a minute, will ya?"

Lee was stunned, the more so when he saw that the man had his hand in his pants. The next building, a ten and fifteen-cent store, had a policeman hiding in the doorway. Lee took only a fleeting glimpse of the man's face peering out coldly from under the bill of his hat. Three doors further, a numerous family of gypsies had taken up in a deserted furniture store wherein Lee was able to see a candle, someone sitting at a table, and someone else lying on a mattress.

He pushed on. A theater came up, the showcase holding shiny black-and-white photographs of women almost nude. It appalled him, seeing such pictures as these hung out to dry. But what bothered him most was the poster of a blond girl looking back over her shoulder with a scandalized expression, her military uniform not coming down quite far enough to hide all that it should. Lee nodded in a friendly way to the ticket-seller, a pessimistic-looking woman knitting in her booth.

He had made a decision and yet he could not quite envision himself actually going up to the woman, of looking into her face and of pushing in the money. A minute went by, Lee humming.

He did do it. He thought that she was about to offer him some advice (seeing how young he was); instead, she sighed deeply and sat shaking her head. It looked to him an infant's costume she was knitting, with bows and tassels. Meantime at home, all the lights went on, his parents sitting up suddenly in bed.

He entered quickly. The foyer, smelling of urine and perfume, held a plump man with a cigar and swollen fingers staring back at Lee in dead seriousness. Lee nodded, moving at once down into the audience (very thin at this late hour), that had grouped about the stage. On the stage itself — again, he was horrified — was an almost naked woman performing to the sound of saxophone music. Excitement flooded him, followed by a sense of rising indignation. Women simply did not behave in this fashion, not where he came from. He got into his glasses. Of the woman herself, she had come down to a few mere patches of green silk, a cowboy hat and a diamond lariat. Her breasts were grand and made, seemingly, out of jelly with marmalade nipples. Voices called out. On one side, Lee had a farmer in overalls and on the other, a sixty- or seventy-year old with long grey hair frozen in aspic and oil.

"She ain't going to take it off!" someone yelled.

"She might," said someone else in a small voice.

Lee looked to the saxophone, a vile and egregious instrument in the hands of a bald-headed man who was himself conspicuously egregious and vile. The woman was so white — or did it have to do with the floodlights? — and so tender about the thighs… He was too young, was Lee, too excitable, too nervous for such displays. He *was* able to put on his bored expression. Just a few hours earlier, he had been in an academic environment among people who carried books wherever they went.

"Take it off?" she inquired. "But it's all I've got!" Her voice was cheerful and never had he thought to hear her speaking from the stage. Not far away, he detected three hard-looking women who, for all that he could understand, must have wandered in by accident. Just then, even while the girl was on the very instant of altogether uncovering her breasts, that was when the house fell dark. At first, Lee thought she had passed out and was perhaps lying on the floor. But when the lights did come on and the music started up again, he saw with bitterness that the girl had actually in fact just left the stage.

Two comics strolled out, one of them that same fat man he had seen in the foyer. The skit, which relied upon a confusion of good words with obscene ones, was only faintly amusing; even so, Lee laughed along with the others. His mind was upon the girl and whether she was not even now escaping out the rear and going home. Or would she come back again?

What followed was bad — a woman considerably older and heavier and with an appendix scar. Lee thought at first, they had interlarded a dance recital into the program. A minute went by while she swept from side to side of the stage with a spiritual expression. Someone did finally yell up at her, forcing her to expose the great lumpy orthopedic brassiere she was wearing.

"Aw, Jesus, look at that," someone said. The three black women were gleeful, actually throwing up remarks at her and slapping themselves on the knee with delight. The woman herself had gotten into a squat and was struggling to get to her feet again. The crowd roared, including even the little boy in the balcony whom Lee had identified as perhaps her son. The audience was given a view of her mouth opened in horror when for a moment it seemed that she might actually topple over into the orchestra.

The woman left, it fell dark, the saxophonist played and then, just as he had wished, the girl came back again. Gorgeous was she, young, too, and pretty, and although she started off simply by grinning at them, his headache had returned with even greater force than earlier.

FOURTEEN

ON HIS FIRST DAY, he reported to work straight from the burlesque house. Seventy-two hours without sleep, he made his appearance in a bright scarlet shirt that had laces instead of buttons.

"Hi," he said. "Well, I reckon I'm ready to go to work now."

"Leland Pefley?"

"Right."

"From Alabama?"

"Absolutely."

"Good. But I think Mr. Arbuthnot wants to see you."

Lee followed. Clearly, this was a much larger operation than he had expected, judging by the employees, the typewriters, the noise, and the number of little glassed-in offices that, some of them, sat out in the middle of a vast room that had at least two score of desks in it. Lee put on his bored expression, especially so when a tall unkempt man who had a bored expression of his own tossed a paper airplane at him. Three nights without sleep and he was by no means certain that any of this was actually happening.

He was made to stand at attention while Arbuthnot, one of the smallest such persons that Lee had recently seen — he looked to Lee as if he had been sawed off at the ribs and his trunk set up in a chair — while the man went on thundering over the telephone in a voice that was deep and hollow and that seemed to come up out of the earth itself. Very few books; Lee spotted perhaps a dozen in all. And because the books were canted (leaning up against one another), Lee had also to cant if he hoped to see the titles. Suddenly, the man threw down the phone.

"You come in here… What's your name boy?"

Lee gave it.

"Alabama, is it?"

"Yes, sir."

"Manure! Don't you fellows know how to dress for work? Hey, Kurt! Come here, look at this. My, my. So, tell me this: you ever read *The Birmingham News*?"

"I used to. When I was a kid."

"So, who's the city editor there?"

Lee thought. Kurt, he believed, was cheering for him. The light fixture seemed to have a paper airplane on it.

"Don't remember."

"My goddamn brother-in-law, that's who!"

"Right."

"And so, my advice is to keep away from it. Hey! You listening to me boy?"

"Yes, sir."

"Those are *my* books."

The phone rang, the man lifting it half an inch and then slamming it down again. Outside, beyond the glass office, Lee could see where one of the reporters had gathered up his typewriter and was making as if to crash his neighbor over the head with it.

"I don't know why you want to go into journalism, I sure don't," Arbuthnot revealed. "Great God Almighty, if I was young as you, I'd be President by now. Look at me."

"Yes, sir."

"I tell you the squat truth boy, if I was to do it over again, I'd go into the military. Kill people."

"Yes, sir. I used to read *The Birmingham News* on Sundays."

"Sundays?"

"Yes, sir."

"I do my drinking on Sundays. You drink, boy?"

"Not much. Beer."

"Then you're in the goddamn wrong profession! Out, out, get out of here, go on!"

The man had gone back to work. Kurt now took Leland gently by the shoulder and nudged him back to the corridor. With difficulty, they worked their way through a gathering of reporters, typists and ink-smeared men struggling at the counter for sweet rolls and coffee. Lee had assumed that it was for lack of sleep; instead, it came to him that the building really was trembling, the windows rattling, pencils rolling about on the desks. Kurt smiled.

"No, no, that's just the two-star edition, all that noise."

"Two."

"It's coming off now."

Lee put on his bored expression.

"And tomorrow you can wear your *white* shirt. And tie."

They had come to the typesetters' room, a bad place full of clatter where two rows of men, all of them fat and all (save one) wearing blue visors, were punching away irritably at huge loom-like machines that gave off a crashing sound. His guide took him to the fattest of them and made an introduction, whereupon the man simply turned and snarled. The next one, him with the yellow visor, was typing with one hand while holding a sweet roll in the other with the result that his one paw was heavy with frosting and the other smirched with ink.

In truth, the personnel were proving less and less cultivated the deeper they went. Two men, naked to the waist, were rooting about in a pile of metal type while striving to load the stuff into a little wheelbarrow. It was here that Kurt turned back, unwilling to go further.

"Good. Just keep going, that's right. You'll be alright."

They shook. Ahead, Lee saw fog and the dim outlines of a gigantic machine that had always been the source both of the two-star edition and the extreme irritability apparent on every face. No coffee, no roll, no sleep — he was too discombobulated to feel fear. In any case, the pressmen greeted him, so to speak, with open arms.

"Now what do *you* want? Shit-head. Hey Tony, look here what we got."

"Hi," said Lee.

Tony came up. He was not a large man; he was, however, one of the very hardest-looking persons that Lee had yet seen. More than that, he had as much hair on his chest alone as the average person possesses altogether.

"Hi."

"'Hi'? What, you some kind of fruit cake?"

"Naw."

"Aw, man. What you want here, um?"

"Nothing."

"Nothing? I think you're nothing. I tell you what, you get your butt on back upstairs, O.K.? And then you and me, we'll get along real fine."

"I was planning on going back upstairs anyway."

"That's it! You're thinking real good now, keep it up."

Lee turned and trundled back, expecting at any moment, and without worrying overmuch about it, to have a folded newspaper, or shoe, or perhaps a paper airplane to come smashing into the back of his head. He was flattered that Kurt had waited for him.

"How was it?" (He grinned.)

"It's the two-star edition alright. It's coming off real smooth, too."

"Smart! Damned if you aren't. Want some coffee?"

The cafeteria was small enough but had the advantage of letting them look down, and into, the many little glassed-in offices. Unfortunately, the best of the sweet rolls were gone.

"I used to be the Managing Editor myself," said Kurt, once they had settled.

"What happened?"

"This is what I am now."

Lee looked at him. He was a depleted person, unhealthy-looking and endowed with an extravagant tic that made it seem that he was smiling and then unsmiling at each and every moment. Just now, he was pointing with a finger that was short, blunt, inked, and none too steady.

"Arbuthnot — he's mean. Well, not *real* mean. But he sure doesn't like young people."

"I could tell."

"Now you see those fellows there? Hee! They don't have any notion that we're watching 'em. They do the editorials."

Lee perked up.

"Me, I used to do 'em. Now, you see that lump there? Sour fellow? He's the music critic. He'll soon be inviting you to dinner — how old are you? — about eighteen? — but don't you go. Not unless you go in for that sort of thing."

"No, no."

"Smart. Now, over there you got the sports writers."

Lee looked. They were a beefy people, uncomfortable in suits. One man had a golf ball enshrined in a golden claw.

"You'll be alright with them, particularly if you can help with spelling." He laughed, a wheezing sound that came to an abrupt end when suddenly he opened his mouth and with his forefinger and thumb began testing one of his teeth. "Good. Now you see that woman over there in that dress? I bought it for her. We used to be married back in the old days. I guess she's just about the smartest cookie in the whole place."

"Married?"

"Long time ago. She's with Arbuthnot now. You look sleepy."

"Naw." Lee took out the picture of Judy and passed it over to him. "And I used to go with this girl. Now I'm here."

"Gracious."

"Love means nothing to her of course. Right now, she's in New York."

"Oh, dear. I used to go with a New York girl."

"So, if I'm sleepy, it's because of her. That's just the way it is."

"I used to sleep real well myself." And then, gazing at Lee's pastry: "Boy howdy, I sure wouldn't be eating that thing, not if I was you. The ink."

They went out, feeling their way down a long, narrow, poorly lit corridor featured on both sides with tiny offices full of noise and ongoing typewriters. The janitor, an enormous individual with a giant's girth, stopped short when he saw them and darted into one of the doorways. The "wire room" proved to be a cave with twenty rattling machines extruding long, sometimes very long yellow tongues of paper. Immediately, the attendant came over, an earnest type explaining in earnestness just how matters stood. The more impossible it was to hear him, the more agitated he became. "Urgent!" Lee heard him say, and then: "… late, too late!"

"Who watches over these things at night?"

"What?"

"Night."

The man smiled, nodded and then, having heard none of it, tapped shrewdly at his brain.

They moved on, even to the art department where an untidy man welcomed them with a friendliness carried to extreme.

"Polly! I knew you'd come back, just knew it."

Lee saw something else — a heap of well-made paper airplanes and, next to that, a drawing in blue ink of an excellent nude entwined in a boa constrictor, all of it having apparently been done by a smiling eighty-year-old who looked back at Lee in wickedness. The third artist had taken off his shoes and was snoozing, his feet on the radiator.

They went back, Lee and his guide, and began to circle about a tall wooden table piled nearly to the ceiling with bundles of unopened mail. Here Kurt stopped and turned to him.

"See this table? Probably you've noticed that I haven't said anything about it yet."

"Yes, sir."

"I thought so. Incidentally, you don't have to call me 'sir,' not anymore."

"What *is* all this stuff actually?" Lee asked. "Looks like mail to me!"

"Well…" He blushed. "Not to put too fine a point on it, we used to have another copyboy before you came along."

"And now you've got me."

"Quick! You really are quick, aren't you?"

"A little bit."

"It's not so bad. We only ask that you sort it out, all this shit, and then pass it along to the proper people, as it were. We don't expect you to get it all done in one day! Lord no."

"How will I know who the proper people are?"

The man looked hurt. "Well, I've just introduced you to some of them, haven't I? That's what I do now."

Lee agreed. The pile was enormous, larger than the world. He saw what looked like a pair of well-packaged tennis racquets or possibly snowshoes sticking out of the pile. Kurt went on talking:

"And someday you may come across a certain blue envelope, long and narrow. When that happens, you will have a choice: either you can just hand it over to me or — and I won't hold it against you — or you can open it yourself."

"What is it?"

"You ask. Alright, you should know that we used to have a movie critic on our staff."

"What happened?"

"No one knows. Anyway, they keep on sending us these free passes."

They smiled, one to the other. Lee now saw that the whole left side of the man's face was trembling wildly, overmastering the tic.

"We could share them," Lee proposed.

"Quick! Damn, you're quick! No, we're going to do beautifully, you and me. And now…"

"Time to get to work?"

He nodded sadly, blushing about it.

FIFTEEN

NIGHT DID COME, the fourth of its series without sleep. A long time he sat on the edge of his bed, even while admitting that he had no real chance of falling off to sleep in a position like that. It was because Judy's photograph was propped on the window sill. Of the bed itself, he preferred the lower level, there where it was more solidly supported on a used automobile tire. Finally, half an hour passing without result, he got up and began his search for that deceased cat that, it alone, could have filled the room with so awful an odor.

Outside, it was a black season holding ten thousand little square homes in which the bourgeoisie was locked away for the night. On the other side, he could see the dying sun experiencing a hero's death amid buntings of lilac and gold. Night was coming on, no doubt about it, a night comprised of billions of black dots like punctuation marks. Moths and butterflies had gathered for warmth about one of the street lamps where, however, a bat was feeding.

He found a restaurant almost at once but, dark as it was, he could not think that it was actually doing business until he drew up near enough to discern three unlike faces peering out between the red and yellow neon lettering. He entered quietly and, with no one paying notice to him, moved by instinct to that furthest and most private of the booths that for the next ten weeks was to be held in escrow, as it were, for him alone. It provided a delicious feeling, that of being in a cock-pit, so to speak, that was moist, dark, and anonymous, and whence he could study others at leisure without himself being seen at all. Outside, meanwhile, pedestrians were streaming past, all of them inscribed on death's agenda and all highly resolved not to be late. Among them, he saw a grandmother of many, a woman in a shawl. And where, pray, was she so hastily going just now, she whom no one visited anymore? That moment, someone at the bar ignited a match, waiting a brief two seconds (which was all that Lee needed) before blowing it out again. He could hear a voice, a low resentful sound that could have come from any of the half dozen hulking silhouettes ranged along the wall.

He took his pen and, bending near, began now to sketch out a letter to Luke that went well at first but then soon enough turned to boasting. What he wanted — he admitted it — was to be admired within his own circle, as of someone engaged constantly in hair-raising adventures. In fact, the letter already had three lies in it, and him not ninety hours away from school. Finally, reluctantly, he plucked out the picture of the girl and set it up in front of him. He groaned.

"Oh!" quoth the waitress. "I didn't know anybody was over here! That you, Tinker?"

"Naw, somebody else."

She hurried off to fetch the menu, a folio-sized affair whose two pages were gummed together with a substance of some kind. Holding it in front of him, his privacy was restored. Only now did he realize how terribly hungry he was.

"Pork chops," he said, "two," and then went on to enumerate many other things as well, all of which she wrote down as adequately as she could considering the dimness, which seemed to give great trouble with the calligraphy.

The food was good, pretty good, and the coffee excellent. Leaving behind an above-average tip for the standard waitress, he exited into the Toledo night and turned toward the slum. A good thing, that he owned a jacket such as he did: dark blue leather, two zippers, much fleece, and considerable numbers of steel buttons. And when he smoked, he resembled the sort of person whom no one in right mind would wish to provoke. It was, of course, the moon that made him so powerful, his own favorite star. Now was the time to be at Antioch, there where the faster he ran and the louder he screamed, the more he wanted to scream and run. Here, by contrast, a tricycle had been left out on the sidewalk; he sailed over it effortlessly. He could not draw in sufficient oxygen that was cold enough nor sharp enough for his winter liking. In front, a woman got quickly out of his way. Tonight, he felt, he could run forever, across the whole of Ohio and down to where Judy was dwelling.

In this way he went six blocks, bursting into the slum with his shirttail flying. He had planned to visit all four movie houses; instead, threading through the derelicts and footpads and confused-looking country folk who, apparently, had blundered into town by accident and knew not how to get out again, instead of that he felt a great urge to go into one of the bars and find whether anything was happening that he might wish to write about someday. In front of him, a woman came up out of the dark, an atrabilious individual dressed in the fashions of fifty years ago. Lee photographed her and put her away in his head. He spotted a little old man breaking for home with a bottle and loaf of bread, and decided to follow.

The next blocks went past very quickly, the man checking over his shoulder at every three steps before finally choosing to make a run for it. Lee chuckled, allowing him to go his way. Of people that needed to be followed, there were many that were more interesting than this. Suddenly, teetering badly (he had been a hundred hours without sleep), he turned, went back, and then entered a tavern with the sign of a green crow hanging out over the doorway.

With boredom showing in his face, he began to move crab-wise between the clients, hostile-looking, most of them, and the bar. He went gingerly, even on tiptoes, direct to a miniature booth in the very back which seemed to have been saving for him all these years.

This venturesome nature of his would be his death someday; he knew it and so, too, did the crowd of ruffians at the bar, hard-looking types more than a little surprised to see someone of his type in their special place. Bored, he opened his book, set it up on the table, and began reading. The music was so bad and so loud that he could not even with the best of intentions hide the displeasure on his face. He smoked. Slowly and slowly, the people seemed already ready to let him stay. Came the waitress, an ungainly woman carrying on her head a large bundle of caramel colored hair.

"Could I have a glass of beer?"

"Are you twenty-one?"

"Ha!"

"Seventeen, *maybe*. Maybe not even that much." She smiled however and then strode away with her clicking heels and jangling bracelet. She was thirty years old or older but from the rear she was still somewhat attractive as he was willing to admit. Except for her, there were but three other women in the whole place, one of them not really so much a whore as simply tired and, in any case, too old for whoring.

The beer came in a tall, narrow, well-frosted mug with the image of a crow on it. He drank once and then, holding the stuff up to the light, descried what looked to him like toy galaxies or little tiny amoebae tumbling head over heels in the stuff. It felt to him that he had been a regular here for years and now was well on the way, like James Dean, to becoming a burnt-out case before he was nineteen. Two tables away, a suspicious man had wormed his arm around the waist of the oldest of the three women and was whispering vilely in her ear. These were not the best grade of people. The bits of conversation that came to him between the music, it was always about money, Negroes, women, or automobiles. But mostly he fixed upon the man in a sailor's hat with a nonsymmetrical face; indeed, the two halves seemed to have been taken from different people. Lee forced himself to look at it — a tableau with holes in it.

He was tempted to depart; instead, he took out the two photographs he carried at all times and propped them up against the novel. Again, he felt the grief of it — that he was in love with her, she who was not in love with him. Yes, her letters were full of affection and a warmth that he had no use for, that she could just as well give to someone else. What he did want, and he wanted it utterly, was to see her twisting with the same hunger that twisted him — that or nothing at all.

He now tore open the first of today's letters and, with the trash at the bar watching studiously, read through it at high speed. The handwriting was cheerful of course and smacked perfectly of the sort of girl that in fact she was. He read it through again, lingering over certain words. He was not entirely unhappy. For if he had asked for éclairs and wine, he had at least been given a helping of some decent vegetables.

He drank. In the next booth, a man came up suddenly for air, allowing himself to be seen for the first time. They looked at each other, Lee and the man, both sharing the intelligence that life was old and death just outside the door. The jukebox, ignorant as it was, yet it harkened him back to Alabama and to his own incredible career that had played itself out to just such songs. Yes, it was the Past once again tossing up memories whether he wanted to look at them or no. And sometimes it seemed to him that he could not go on much longer, seizure to seizure, memory to memory. So much he wanted the girl, the tip of his nose was hurting.

Lee now forced open the earlier of the letters to find that her traveling companions, nice boys from Oberlin, had stopped to fuel the car and she was writing from a coffee shop in West Virginia. Never, insofar as he knew, never had that state produced a fine writer, not in its whole existence. He could see it all — coffee shop, mountains and sea, and then the girl herself setting down the words one by one in her clear fashion with, perhaps, her chin trembling slightly as she attached the stamp. He would not be answering it of course, neither this nor any other letter that was not suffused with passion and longing and everything else to full degree.

He paid, went outside, and then stood looking down into the pullulating vista of green and yellow neon that persisted as far as he could see. His heroic blue jacket now seemed too big for him and with a great deal of left-over room for his rickety chest to rattle about within. The crowd had thinned, leaving only the actual criminals, the true whores and, across the road, a certifiable ghoul in his cloak, or robe, or, possibly, it was simply a blanket the man was wearing. Taking a cigarette, Lee put on a rugged expression. An airplane moved overhead.

He pushed on, moving by rote along the same trail he had cleared the night before. He moved past the evangelical mission, this time filled with a new shift of contrite people dipping silently into their bowls of gruel. Two doors further, a western movie was showing, the posters featuring a black-headed woman of great beauty looking off dramatically at some danger on the horizon. He saw a herd of cattle and then, in diminutive perspective, two men firing at each other in front of a saloon.

He had not thought to visit the burlesque again, not until he found himself once more squinting in painfully at the ticket-seller who sat humming inside her box with a Bible. The text itself remained mostly hidden beneath a pile of recent knitting.

"What time does Monique come on?" Leland inquired.

"I wouldn't know."

"Has she been on yet?"

"I wouldn't know that either."

Lee bent nearer; the cell was dark.

"Well, how many times will she come on tonight?"

The woman stopped, sighed deeply, put down her needles, and stared at him for a long time. Lee blushed, grinned, paid, and then ran inside.

SIXTEEN

IT NEEDED ALL HIS STRENGTH, youth and determination to get out of bed. The moon was gone, replaced by the loathsome morning sun.

The bed had collapsed during the night, requiring him a full half-hour to build it back up again. He was pleased that the apartment had come with a radio, even were it but a mere pile of components without a housing; hardly had he turned it on before the woman next door began pounding on the wall. He did so abhor it — morning, sun, light, and noise of traffic. And now he must put aside his likable clothes and get into…

His suit. Lee took it down and looked at it. For the life of him, he could not understand how so many centuries of authors and great men could have agreed to the routine use of costumes designed originally for funeral wear. Not brave enough to use his tie with the smiling Jesus on it, he got into a different sort of thing and then put on his shoes, doing one thing at a time and resting up between.

He hiked straight to the building, straight upstairs, and thence straight to the mountain of undistributed mail that had grown only the taller during the course of the night. All times, he had his eye open for narrow blue envelopes. As to the journalists, they had returned to their same desks of yesterday, these forty- and fifty-year-old men with cynicism embedded in their faces. In the cafeteria, three of them had come together for breakfast and, with mouths besmirched, were eating with knives from out of the same jar of jelly. One man had wasted so many years here that he had actually worn through the linoleum beneath his desk. Lee locked eyes with him for a moment, the man putting on an apologetic look, smiling weakly, asking toleration. Lee watched coldly at first, but then ended up nodding back at him after all.

There was much to be done, and many other duties apart from the mail. Lee, however, worked only very briefly before, first, going for his sweet roll and then, secondly, vanishing into the men's room where he could eat at leisure. He did not make a good appearance in the mirror, not in a suit, and never in the morning. Coming nearer, he could make out where a certain aging process was already perceptible in the lineaments of his face. And that, of course, was when he began to have the hideous feeling that came to him each time he looked too long in the mirror, the feeling namely it was *himself* encased in that anonymous skull. The spell was broken when one of the journalists, his face averted, darted into the room and dashed for the nearest cell where, almost immediately thereafter, Lee could hear him yelping out in pain.

Of all the day to come, only twenty minutes had gone past. He knew this, that he had not come to earth in order to fritter away his precious days in a men's room in upper Ohio. A reporter entered, a tall bristling individual in unclean shirt and trousers with the prescribed urine stains. They nodded, the man finally coming out in a nasal voice that sounded like a child's:

"You're the new boy." (He was looking with incipient dismay into the same mirror that had dismayed Lee.) "So, how do you like Toledo? Grubby enough for you?"

"Yes, sir."

"Yes, you like it, or yes it's grubby enough?"

"Both."

He laughed merrily, revealing a flash of silver and gold. "Don't tell me you want to be a newspaperman!"

"No, sir."

"No. No, I see you more as a trumpet player, something like that. What do you plan to do?"

Lee tossed the hair out of his eyes. "I don't have to worry about stuff like that."

"Really! Well I wouldn't worry too much about that, not having to worry. I'm sure you'll find something. And if not now, then later. You'll have to come visit us sometime."

"Sir?"

"Bring your trumpet. Good God! who *is* that in there making all that noise? Claude? That's right, bring your trumpet, and my wife will make you a spaghetti supper. Looks to me like you haven't been feeding properly."

"Spaghetti?"

"Oh, it doesn't have to be that." (Suddenly, he pulled out four paper towels in quick succession and crashed them noisily.) "We live in that blue house. On the corner. Motorcycle on the porch."

Lee nodded. There *was* a blue house, and he had noticed a motorcycle as well. "I could come tonight."

"Gawd! Alright, alright, make it tonight. Blue, remember."

He exited, leaving behind a mess of litter, puddles, and a broken bar of soap. Claude, meanwhile, had disappeared. Lee had just time enough to wolf down the last of his breakfast before three further journalists came and, laughing and snorting with tremendous noise, seated themselves around the table and began dealing out the cards.

Not enough that he must sort the mail, he had also to be running back and forth at all times, a mere messenger indeed. Finally, after three hours of it, he drew off into the cafeteria and began mapping out a letter of protest, heavy with sarcasm, for Arbuthnot's eyes. But had made only small headway before a group of press operators came inside, the leader of them motioning for Lee to depart at once.

He went outside and thence into the clear blue open air where no journalists were to be seen anywhere. He strolled past a dress shop, out front a pale farm woman staring in hungrily at a certain yellow frock while plucking thoughtfully at her chin. The sun today was smaller than usual, weaker, too, a tiny red seed retreating further and further as winter came on. He passed a pawnshop, stopped, came back. It was a wonder to him, how that every such place as this seemed to have the exact same offering of merchandise, as if it were a traveling exhibition following him from town to town.

He pressed at the window. Someone had sold his own family album of photographs — it lay open upon a happy scene of the dog, the family, and a brand-new car. Coming as near as he could, he was actually able to make out the photographer himself (who bore also the family features) reflected in the windshield of the brand-new car. Next, he saw a collection of baby clothes, tiny shirts and trousers, all of a pale, pale blue, and all tucked away very tidily upon the topmost shelf just next to a display of open knives. Of the knives, some were gorgeous and, in one special case, had a forest scene graven on the blade. Another possessed a barb and was deep enough to transfix a full-grown man at the level of his belt. That moment, he chanced to look up, catching the proprietor, a thin, grim, undertaker of a man smiling down upon him falsely.

Lee moved on. The wind was chill; it pushed him to the corner and spun him around. He had been wrong to imagine there were no journalists in the outside world; he now saw two of them, fat men sitting side by side in the very restaurant he had wanted for himself. These were hard men, their clothes filthy, hard faces, too, but soft bodies, soft as dough; they had taken out a little flask of whiskey, placing it on the counter, and were continually chafing each other at elbow and shoulder every time they turned on their stools to smile sweetly into one another's face.

He crossed and sliced into the crowd. He felt as if he were in a sandstorm of peoples, with thousands upon thousands of lips, ears and eyes that had been painted, as it were, upon balloons the size of human heads. He knew this much, that they were none of them in love, or at any rate not seriously so, and that for them life had come to an end on that day when things were not exciting anymore. A locksmith's shop made its appearance, a giant emblematic key hanging out over the walk. The following building traded in used books — Lee stopped immediately — and had a few decrepit-looking volumes set out proudly on display.

He entered but then had to loiter about for a time, tapping one foot impatiently as he waited for his eyes to adjust. It was a barn-like domain, dense with the smell of lanolin and desiccated leather. He halted in front of a table that supported an immense collection of magazines and brightly colored comic books of the sort he had once depended upon for his education. Having chosen one of the things at hazard, he opened it and then right away began grinning with all sorts of memories. And how well he did remember! a red spaceship with faces in all the portholes, a journey to the huge yellow moon. Suddenly, he glanced over at the shopkeeper, a bald-headed gnome toiling fastidiously at a roll-top desk.

The books themselves — and there was a much greater quantity of them than the sampling in the window could have suggested — were stacked in numbers up and down the four walls and eight windows, reaching everywhere from floor to ceiling and to the stove where Lee now for the first time identified two cats taking their leisure on the rose-colored carpet that itself had a pattern on it portraying yet further cats and books. Having been blinded by the magazines, Lee now turned and cautiously approached the shelves. All the wisdom in the world was here, precisely where it was least likely to be disturbed. He turned and shot a glance at the man, who immediately looked away.

He took down a thin, ochre-colored volume and against weak resistance, forced it open upon a poetry that had an attenuated quality.

Next, was a two-volume edition of Bede bound in membrane and offering a massive apparatus of scholarship in microscopic print. For two minutes, he stood fingering it and staring down astutely into the text, as if he might break the cipher of those days when the very hills had been soaked in blood and every page had some remarkable individual on it of whom he had never heard before.

He edged forward, coming of a sudden upon the man just as he was in process of transferring a sum of coins from what seemed to be a leathern pouch to what appeared to be a cigar box. They looked at each other, Lee recognizing with a rush of horror that the man's head was small, far, far too small, a mere fragment of what it should have been, and that it featured two crowded eyes that touched each other and, glittering brightly, fixed on Lee. Lee paid, waiting while the man, whose pale blue hand seemed ordained for just such work as this, dropped Leland's money partly in the box and partly in the pouch. Clearly, he was loath to let the Bede get away. He coughed. A bundle passed between them.

It had fallen colder in his absence. Ahead, a humpback woman was bending into the wind while holding tightly to the roof of her head. From somewhere, a starveling dog came up, sniffed hopefully at Lee's fingers and bundle, and then looked up to check his face. Lee put on his bored expression.

His inclinations being what they were, he found that he had worked his way back to the slum again. No neon, not at this hour. And yet, if anything, it was more dangerous here by day than at dark. A car pulled up, letting out a woman whose long dainty leg made a lengthy appearance before being followed up by the person herself. He passed an eatery, the smell of potatoes and grease drawing him inside.

The place was as long as a boxcar but yet had very few customers in it. The booth he wanted had been taken by a large dreamy-looking man who seemed to be studying the ceiling. Lee scowled at him and then, finding that he refused to leave, stepped past in indignation to

a table littered still with platters and soiled napkins and two unclean
tumblers bearing lipstick smudges in purple and red. There was a bit
of left-over meat, pork it looked, frozen upright in a pool of grease;
Lee watched as it arched slowly and then fell over in agony onto its
back. Finally, he noted the waitress moving in his direction, a big-
boned woman whose solemn face put him in mind of all those other
gaunt women from his grandmother's time.

He waited as she gathered up the plates, her bony arm passing
in front of his eyes. She might have strangled him easily with her
strength, doing the job solemnly and with a hopeless expression on
her paper-white face. Her apron was as ghastly and splattered as a sur-
geon's. He knew her, and knew her kind — capitalism's waste material;
she, too, had been singled out for poverty in the same way that certain
people come into the world with a designated career lying in wait. In
any case, according to his theory as it then stood, systems were not to
be judged on their economic results, but their spiritual. On this showing, the system had something to recommend it. The woman drew out
her pad and pencil and then backed off a few inches for him to make
up his mind.

Somewhere far away, a conversation was continually going on, but
apart from that, the place was silent, the few customers not wishing
to give away their location to the people streaming unawares past
the window. Lee observed that special stink of onions, urine and un-
washed clothes that had come to represent for him the very signature
of poverty — urine on linoleum and the chalky faces of that fifteen
per-cent on whom had fallen the dignity of being cheated instead of
cheating. He wanted no contact with them of course and yet, oddly,
he was never more at peace than when in their midst. Suddenly he
blushed, realizing belatedly that he had again been speaking out loud.

When the woman came back, she had a tray in one hand, the other
hand hanging down uselessly. Lee set upon the potatoes at first, wolfing them down at speed along with the butter and grease. The meat
was full of gristle and yet did have a good flavor to it; he could feel

himself rejuvenating even as he sucked upon it. Across from him, a fat woman was sitting with a stunned expression, knees far apart. No one loved her, no one ever had, and now she no longer thought about it anymore. Outside, a tramp drifted past, his face revealing that it had only just now occurred to him that this was to be his last winter on earth.

It was deep into the afternoon, the street almost bereft of people when Lee stood at last and shook the crumbs out of his lap. He had pondered on it at length; now, finally, he took out a full dollar bill, a crisp one picturing the ruthless smile of a certain well-known dignitary, and then folding it twice, nudged it beneath the saucer rim. His plan was to dash around to the window and wait, there to witness the joy that must surely be seen on his pale waitress' face.

SEVENTEEN

THAT NIGHT, in obedience to his promise, he stopped at the blue house and knocked three times politely. A woman came.

"Hi," said Lee. "I'm Lee."

"Yes?"

The house was preternaturally dim. Probably he would have left, had he not then seen within the room a piece of furniture well-laden with books.

"My name is Lee."

"I believe you. What can I do for you?"

Now, finally, came the man. Lee was taken aback to see him dressed in jeans, as opposed to journalists' garb.

"Leland?"

"Right!"

"Come on in, come on in, that's right. Want something to eat?"

"I already have."

"Want some more?"

He was left in the middle of a tall, dark and damp room of his favorite kind, with wallpaper that had soaked through. The pair had returned to the kitchen where Lee could hear them dining together very lustily. After a minute of it, with nothing else to do, he went and peeped into the adjoining room. They had had a night of it, apparently, and had left their bed in absolute disarray. Lee could feel his indignation rising. Marriage! a transparent excuse permitting people to do anything they wanted. He raced back to the couch, arriving there just in time before the man came out with three glasses and a fancy decanter holding a golden fluid.

"Drink it. It's brandy."

Lee obeyed. The stuff was sweet but also uncanny, quite unlike anything in Alabama. Again, he could hear the two of them in the kitchen speaking in the abbreviated language of people who have been friends for very long. They had done all they could with the meal — the man would eat no fat and the woman wanted nothing to do with lean   and now they were loading dishes into the sink with much clatter, as if they were tossing them in from a distance. Finally, the woman came out, smiling at him sympathetically. No one could say that she was lovely; she did however have two womanly buttocks of his own favorite sort, one of them slightly more womanly than the other. The man now brought forth yet another odd-shaped bottle, this one holding a fund of what looked like, but almost certainly wasn't, water.

"Leland wants to be a newspaperman."

"Really! Well I think that's wonderful."

"No, ma'am. Actually, I never even wanted to come up here."

"Oh? You didn't want to leave all your girlfriends behind — is that how it was?" They grinned at each other, husband and wife. Lee could see that they really were friends and not just contractuals to a husband-and-wife document — they were able to communicate with eye beams alone. Lee drank, lit a cigarette, and then took out the girl's photograph and passed it over.

"Gracious!"

"Oh, boy. Yi, yi, yi. And where is she now?"

"New York."

"Oh, boy."

They laughed, both. Lee could feel himself feeling more wretched than he had felt in days.

"Well? Aren't you going to tell us about her?"

"She's short."

"Yes?"

"But love means nothing to her."

"I see! Whereas you, on the other hand…?"

Lee looked off. He had not asked about *their* love.

"Well, of course he loves her!" said the woman. "Anybody would. Look at her."

"Yeah; and it's those 'anybodies' that worry him. Right, Lee? Come on, drink up!"

He drank, drinking bitter dregs. He knew this much, that the man had had three glasses already and was into his fourth.

"Keep away from newspapers, Lee — that's my advice."

"I plan to."

"Find some other way to make a living."

"Yes, sir. But that's one thing I don't have to worry about."

"What, you rich?"

"Ha! No, no, I just…"

"Say it."

"Well. I'm already eighteen. Chatterton was seventeen."

"And?"

"Jimmy Dean, he…"

"We know about him."

"… was twenty-four. Heck, I'd settle for that."

"You're not ill? Oh Lee, I hope not."

Lee turned and looked at her, embarrassed to see how concerned she seemed to be. The man, too — he had never intended to render them as morose as this.

"With me," said the journalist, "it's cancer. Oh, yes! However, I still have about two years left. Or so they tell me."

Lee was stunned, appalled, horrified. And if here before he had had qualms about the man, now he felt a great kinship with him.

Between the three of them, it was the woman who seemed the most stricken; she sat staring down at the floor.

"Shoot, you can do a lot in two years," said Lee. "Shoot, you've probably already done a lot. Me now, what can a person do in twenty-three years?"

"I want him to resign," said the woman. "But, oh no. Why, he's never even been to Europe!"

"*I'll* never see Europe, that's for sure."

"No children," said the man. "I suppose that's my one regret."

"Oh! So, you have no regrets about me? And what am *I* supposed to do, pray?"

"Judy'll know what to do. Boy, will she!"

"When I think… Oh, I don't know. I just don't."

"Keats too — twenty-four. Of course, they didn't keep real good records back then."

"Saving and scrimping, scrimping and saving. What for? Don't you do that, Lee."

"Don't worry! I plan to give all my royalties to the poor. *I* certainly won't need 'em."

"Yes, it's strange: you work in a place for twenty years and bang! You can't leave it."

"People talk about Poe. Ha. He was *forty*."

"I don't know, I just don't."

They drank. Outside, such was the propinquity of the slum, the sound of screaming could be heard. It seemed to sort so well with the bursts of red and yellow neon that streaked the window pane. The woman had come back with a shoe box full of rollers and pins and was calmly and slowly and in his presence doing up her hair with the same immemorial comb strokes that dated back to Penelope and earlier. The man himself was slumping badly, half-drunk. And although he was growling on at length, Lee could pick up only that small part of it that referred to Claude and to the paper, and how that this time they were endorsing not the man Eisenhower, but rather his rival. "Madness!" Lee heard him say. And then: "Ah, well."

Lee woke and climbed to his feet, but then had to stumble about for some while before he remembered where he was. Not only had they put him to bed, they had also left the brandy out. Suddenly, he grabbed for Judy's most recent letter, opened the envelope and tore the message out by its roots. Too dark — he couldn't begin to read it, not even when he took off his glasses, struck a match, and held it up to the strongest of his two eyes.

He sat smoking in the dark. According to his theory he was in the south-southwestern part of the building where it was exposed to the neon blasts coming from the lower city. It must be very late indeed, judging by how the slum, too, was for the most part dark. One grainy green light remained, the evilest in the world, and the hulking figure of a man who had tried to camouflage himself within it. Suddenly, springing to the window and grasping at the bars, Lee almost called aloud, amazed to see that it had snowed while he was sleeping. (Dew, he knew, was never like this.) He wanted to rouse the neighbors and warn them — until he recollected that this was by no means an uncommon phenomenon in the land to which he had come. Snow! Could anything be more strange? It stifled the slum, lending it an innocence that was unwonted and unwanted. He saw a bird standing on one leg, much peeved at this new hindrance.

He came back, drank, and then began to make a cursory search of this room and the one adjoining it. The house had books, good ones; unfortunately, they were not organized according to any scheme that he could understand. And the man himself? Lee concentrated, trying to divine in which quadrant of the house the journalist and his wife even now would be staring up at the ceiling with nothing left to say.

Lee dressed and then, taking the bottle, the letter, the cigarettes and the book, stepped out into the snow. The night had a sanctity to it, while the sky itself was of a shade of dark royal blue with a very great many bright shiny white stars in it. Everything pleased him, especially when he entered the slum proper and observed the confusion of those who ordinarily would have been drunk by now. They stood, hands hanging down, crowding at the corners. Of whores, (and there were some) they were hard to identify in their umbrellas and cloaks. Lee passed between them. He must make haste if he planned to get back to his own apartment before the sun would come and melt them all away.

EIGHTEEN

THUNDER IN THE WEST, the sound of it coming closer. One man, drunk already, stumbled out into the road and stood looking up at the noise. Lee pushed forward hurriedly, straight back into the blue district. All day and all night, and now it seemed as if this storm might prove more than the city in its current moral condition could endure. He saw a derelict grinning weakly, the whites of his eyes showing, while above him, on the second story, a woman had brought her chair out onto the balcony itself where she sat rocking and humming and sometimes breaking out into a religious song.

He found himself looking down into the notorious "Heaven-On-Earth," so-called, a marshy district where the clay houses, igloo-like, rested higgledy-piggledy with their entrances pointing off in all directions. That instant, a bolt of lightning smashed down on Fulton Street followed very soon by yet another that was so much closer that he could all but seize it by the wrist. Exhilarated, Lee scampered to the top of the hill and opened his shirt, making himself available to the best of all possible endings — death by lightning strike. Two minutes went by. Down below a train, frantic to get back into open country, shrieked horribly, thrashing through the stews.

Reluctantly, slowly, casting many a backward glance, he climbed to the top floor where, as always, the Night Editor sat in the cockpit of his horseshoe-shaped desk. This one Lee liked, a manly man who had a way of checking through his proofs with quick decisive strokes of a red pencil that permitted no appeal. They nodded, one to the other, night-lovers both. The man had many other red pencils, too, twenty in a mug, their sharp, sharp noses all pointing to the ceiling.

Lee found four reporters cleaving to the four corners of the enormous room — reading, typing, smoking, and sometimes whispering lewdly into the telephone. All feared the Night Editor, fearing him just as someday Lee hoped that men would fear *him* on account of the sort of person he expected to become. Entered now two others who, spotting the editor, moved quietly to their desks.

Outside it was snowing powerfully, driving away the few late-night pedestrians whom in normal times he was able to study from his perch. He heard the foghorn; apparently it was snowing out on Lake Erie as well. The illumination was just sufficient to let him see that the vacant building next door was in process of trying to crawl away. Meanwhile, a fire had broken out in the hills, too far indeed for the screaming to be heard and yet not so far that he couldn't feature tens of little human figures jumping up and down in wild distress. Again, there came three blasts from the foghorn and in between them the truly horrendous sound of an ape, or orangutan — (and he would read about it next day in the paper) — liberated by the storm.

He toiled for perhaps an hour, his mind partly on Judy and partly on her photograph. She seemed to be looking back at him through the centuries, her smile warm and yet full of rue. Would that he could have miniaturized himself down to mite-size and leapt into her eye! Judy! But not for him. It was the Devil had brought her on stage and then, having allowed him to gaze upon her, led her off again.

When, toward one, he went to check on the teletype room, he found the machines sending out cries for help, as it were, from the more excitable parts of the world. Something was afoot in Montevideo; lifting up the three-yard coil of paper, he saw where a conference had taken place. One machine had actually gone dead in the middle of a story, as if the originating journalist had realized that it wasn't really worth reporting about. He read part of it and then, fetching his shears, began to harvest the many yellow coils of paper worming about on the floor. The phone rang, Lee picking it up to hear a moribund voice that seemed to be reading from a list of numbers — it needed a full minute before he recognized it was a recording. This *was* strange: the man behind the voice had no doubt gone away hours ago and gotten into bed, leaving behind a tale of numbers that meant nothing whatsoever to anyone likely to hear it. Nevertheless, Lee listened dutifully, five minutes of it, before gently letting the receiver down.

The cafeteria was open, a black woman presiding with folded arms. Lee handed in his order, getting, in addition to sausage and gravy, a long sigh and a look of undisguised disapproval.

"What you up so late for? Um?"

"I like it! Peace and quiet."

"You ain't even 'sposed to be here! *I* know why you had to leave home. They know it, too."

Lee blushed.

"You ain't got no business, a place like this. How old is you anyhow?"

"I like it like this."

"No, you don't."

He took his cup and platter (she had given him a generous helping) and headed for his place by the window. Now, instead of the naked lights that used to burn all night, he could make out two or three dim glimmerings where someone was waiting it out, quite alone, while listening to the bombardment on the roof. Judy, lodged as she was in a different time zone (he could see her, ensnared in the matrix), had been sleeping for eight hours, doing it quietly while taking up very little space. Strangest of all was that she, too, must someday perish, and someday slip out of mind and memory of the last person to have remembered her while she was yet alive. His job therefore was to take her quickly, before the sun should stop and world grow cold. As for the arid little affairs of others, reasonable types with careers lying in wait… Lee snorted and tossed the hair out of his eyes.

This time the machines were talking all at once. One indeed had exhausted its paper and was gossiping away happily on the spool itself. Finally, he got down and opened the thing, a soulless-looking mechanism that immediately began to gobble away with an avidity that nauseated him. As for the story itself—and he would never understand this adult fascination with taxes and legislation, or why the editor was waiting for it—the story was no good and no one, he thought, would ever miss it.

An hour passed, the snow never ending. It was late, he was tired, the fire gone, and yet he knew very well that he would not be able to sleep, not even if he were laid out in darkness in a casket full of petals. Across from him, the Night Editor had turned the radio low and was listening presciently with one ear pressed to the speaker. Lee saw him grin, halt, utter, and then break out into a most happy smile, the man having no doubt picked up some very fine news from elsewhere in the matrix of the world.

NINETEEN

SATURDAY WAS FOR READING; instead, having slept away the day, Lee got up and strode around the room. His compartment had the intensifying odor of something that had gotten beneath the flooring. It dawned on him that someone had been in his room and had blackened out the teeth on his James Dean posters while leaving the nudes alone. Ten minutes went by accompanied by the noise of an airplane driving overhead. The stars had a brilliance certainly which, however, tended to break down into colors the moment they touched the glass.

He strolled through a winter scene in which every pole and post was wearing a risible little hat composed of snow. As to how the opossums and crows and the raccoons, as to how they were making out in weather like this... It didn't bear thinking about. He passed a succession of dark houses, great foreboding structures from the Age of Integrity — they seemed to be deteriorating even as he gazed upon them. Somewhere, sometime, somehow, he had seen them all before. However, even if his *déjà vu* was better than most people's, he could never be altogether certain of what was going to happen next.

He had forgotten about Christmas. He saw a tree decorated entirely in strings of light, each bulb as blue and chilly as the depths of a frozen lake. By contrast, the next home had a big, sloppy, unbalanced tree loaded down with fruits and gifts and even a cardboard skeleton left over from Halloween. The journalist's house, it, too, had a cheery look. Lee need only tap once to bring them to the door and so receive his due meed of sympathy and brandy; instead, he went on, pulled helplessly toward the slum.

He followed a vagrant for several blocks, in and out of the hotel lobby where the man checked the ashtrays for leftover cigarettes and each table for uncollected tips before returning despondently to the street. Suddenly Lee spun around, embarrassed to find that a small boy, a soiled type with bad teeth, had been following him for... Minutes? Hours?

Lee was never at his best when among crowds but now, with the unremitting flow of faces gliding up to meet him, he began to feel truly ill. Across the way, a blond woman in a fur coat was observing two men yelling at each other. He caught sight of an elderly woman beaming at him, as if she knew him very well. In truth, the city was full of people continually mixing him up with their own stray children. And all this time, he was being persecuted by the most unpleasant of sensations, namely that he was being chased by a void, and that the sidewalk and everything else along with it was being eaten away behind him.

He ran forward. The drugstore had a prostitute out front, the town's most handsome (she had a lofty look), while inside, the honest pharmaceuticalist himself stood proudly amongst his potions and vials. Ahead, lay the bleak zone. Lee crossed quickly, entering his own personal neon garden that had never yet failed, no matter his spiritual state, to set his pulse to beating. Someday, some night rather, he would wander in and never come out again. Two frightened policemen came by with their sticks at the ready — they never went anywhere but in pairs. Someone had vomited here recently, the stink of it mixing with the music that, to Lee, was very like vomit, too. And yet, he approved of everything; it accorded with his philosophy that good things should be far, far better than they were, and the bad worse, and never to avoid an extreme.

In the next block, the Salvation Army had set out its kettle and tripod, assigning a bony woman to clang away all night on an iron bell. Lee moved past, only at the last instant edging near enough to peer into the pot. His first notion was to laugh out loud — he saw three pennies, nothing more. In a sudden access of kindness, he came back and contributed four or five of his own coins, big ones, some of them, and then went off a distance to watch whether she would be pleased or not. It was while he was waiting that yet another woman came tumbling out upon him from one of the saloons, a fifty- or sixty-year-old wearing a formal suit and corsage. Lee waited patiently as she picked herself up and then, retching, ran back in. Nothing surprised him anymore, least of all that the boy with the bad teeth had picked up following again.

He went two blocks, crossed, and then stepped into the slip between the display windows of an abandoned store. With no breeze here, he could light his cigarette and at the same time keep watch on the street. It was the most secure of places, the best that he could ask for. And that, of course, was when the door came open behind him. At first, he imagined it was a final customer heading homeward.

"Hey, boy."

(Gypsies! Lee froze. The city had many of these.)

"Hey boy, I see you. What you want, hey?"

He could have fled, it would have been easy, but for the onus that lay upon him (and which he would have been very glad to have outgrown by now), of never running away from a new experience. In the room itself, he could discern a man and three children sitting on a cot, all of them looking back at him wonderingly.

"You want?"

"What?"

"Sure. You want fuck?"

Never had he heard that word in a woman's mouth.

"What?"

"Sure. Five dollar, you got?"

(The man now rose to his feet and began to usher the children from the room.)

"Sure, you got money, lots. Right… here!"

In fact, she had plucked out his wallet and was turning it in her hand. Viewing her up close, with the putrefaction in her eyes, her nostrils two perfect holes, her malarial breath, he thought he might actually vomit,

"You want magic trick?"

"Hold it. I'm not running away, not exactly. It's just that…"

But now she had taken out a handful of bills, two weeks of wages, and was flashing them in front of his eyes. He grabbed, taking them back before they disappeared. No longer, he observed, was she speaking of acts of sex.

"Give me some money," she said finally, coming out with it. "A little bit."

He looked at her, at the whey in her eyes. A huge guilt now came down on him, that he had insisted upon her going through her humiliating part before he would turn loose of anything.

"How much?"

"Five dollar."

He gave, his hand trembling. She took it, too, but then stayed to give him a look of rue that he felt he deserved. A new party had meanwhile come into the niche and threatened to block off his escape. Lee ran.

Vast was the city, vast; he could go on for years, never exhausting this exhibition of souls, not when there were always new ones coming in each day from the outlying countryside. Some things were contrary to nature, a truth that he had only come to realize once he had gotten out of normal Alabama and far away.

Chinese restaurant! he had seen it before. He stepped inside and proceeded more or less calmly to a table whence he could keep his eye both on the door in front and the door in back. There was but one other customer in the place, a Chinese in a suit eating slowly with extreme seriousness. Lee smoked. His table had a blue paper lantern showing a junk, they called it, gliding under the moon. Suddenly, he glanced up to see a ghastly-looking person stride past outside with a face that was as narrow and as ferocious as a hawk's. This, too, Lee approved. Night had him in thrall, his bones growing softer, his eyes abnormally large. Difficult for him to remember that once he had abided in a place of great orderliness, a brown and gold domain in which people went about with books hugged excitedly to their breasts. But most of all he remembered it as where a notorious love affair had had its start.

His plan now was to move on into yet greater slums, leaving behind a last letter to Judy to make it impossible for her to marry. Or, if she did so, make it impossible for her to be carried to bed without his own baleful shade leaping up and down in the corner. Or, he might reappear years later, his face caked over with absolute corruption, and then to drift nonchalantly across campus while people he barely remembered whispered excitedly behind his back.

Came now the inscrutable waiter, a nervous man who proffered the menu with so much courtesy and from so far away that Lee had trouble getting hold of it. It surprised him that the thing was in Chinese hieroglyphics, as if the succulents that lay in store for him were simply beyond translation. He went down the list anyway, hoping to make some resemblance between the curious little runes and the dishes they represented. For all that he could be certain, he was reading a message from the kitchen, a warning that he ought to rise and leave the place at once.

"Do you speak English? Naw, it's alright."

The man looked down, twisting in his clothes; never had Lee exercised so much influence over an adult. Finally, he pointed to what he wanted, a word, or pictograph rather in black, black ink. Judging by the face on the waiter, he had chosen wisely after all.

Lee had no time to smoke; the man was back immediately with a goblet holding perhaps ten milliliters of a slowly rotating fluid that smelled like ambergris. Lee looked at it, electing momentarily to leave it alone. Instead, he whipped out Luke's letter and quickly read it through. The churl had been reading, reading widely and reporting back on it — nothing worried Lee more than that his friend might leap out ahead of him in maturity, vision, and development. Next, he took out a letter from Luke's mother, a short inquiry in which she asked for Luke's address. Lastly, he opened a letter from his parents. His messages had been so cheerful of late, and so full of respect, plainly they were getting suspicious. He read it halfway through, a tired and weary feeling overtaking him as he got down to the unfavorable part.

The waiter laid out his meal with trembling hands before then backing off toward the kitchen where Lee caught a momentary view of half a dozen coolies in their underwear. What he saw in front of him (it shocked him) were four tiny squid (at first, he thought they were actually swimming) in a bowl of broth. Lee put on his glasses and then, slowly, using his pencil in lieu of a chopstick, turned the biggest of them on its back.

He drifted, encountering those other squid of the night, pale people, rays and skates and awed, primordial-looking types who loomed briefly before moving in closer to look him over. Gazing up, he saw strands of hair, or weed rather, waving in the current. Another two weeks — he knew it — and he would be too in love with it, in love with misery and the thousand faces that were beginning to take a permanent place in his mind and memory. Three doors down, the second-most interesting prostitute was on duty, the first time he had seen her in this locale. Tonight, her face was cold; it reminded him of a certain third-grade teacher from an earlier period in his career.

He smoked, tossing the hair out of his eyes, his old arrogance returning in proportion as night drew on. With full nine hours of sleep to his credit, he could have strolled all the way to the edge of the world and back, filling his notebook with thoughts and original impressions. Truth was, he had construed of himself the nexus of a tiny slum-civilization of his own, with threads running out to Luke, Phyllis, and the girl called Judy. Meanwhile, the most exhilarating theories, those the authorities most wanted to quash, were taking place in the most unlikely cranny in the world, where no one knew to find them.

Because it was Christmastide, the town was full and busy. Departing from the crowd, he entered a shop heaped up high with the same sort of artifacts that once had driven him to thieving — yo-yos, ping-pong balls, rubber knives. The puerile psychology of children — what was it? In front, he saw two suffering girls, their eyes dead and hollow from staring in hungrily at a bin of grinning little dolls in diapers. Next to them, he passed a tall bedraggled boy aiming a pellet gun here and there while dreaming he was killing someone. Another was going through the jelly beans (choosing out the red ones), while his smaller brother sat weeping on the floor. Lee pushed on, past an old woman holding to the column and trying to store up as many pictures as she could of her last Christmas on earth. Lee began to feel seasick again. At the door, a giant Santa stood looking straight at him with loathing showing through his uproarious laugh.

There were two theaters in this district, one of them a tiny place that specialized in foreign films. Here Lee halted and offered up one of his last free passes. There was a vestibule, inside it some thirty artistic-looking people drinking black coffee out of acorn-size cups. Two languorous women, sophisticated types, were chatting insouciantly at one side. Though twice his age, he could not for anything keep from gazing upon their four well-holstered legs. So long had the semen been cumulating in him, now it was lapping at his brain. He took up one of the tiny cups of coffee and sipped at it.

At last they filed in, some carrying their cups and saucers with them. He admired all forms of late-night activity, so much so indeed that he could not imagine why adult people in their freedom were not any more happy than they seemed to be. Or was it that life's newness was bound to wear away, and nothing was amazing anymore?

The film began, a love story out of Sweden that took him by surprise. The girl was ethereally beautiful and possessed some of Judy's golden-brown hair. Halfway through with it, he began to weep secretly with a bored expression. Truth being what it was, he was simply too unstable to be attending so many fine movies. Across the aisle, the woman was smiling patronizingly and meanwhile he had to struggle to keep from bawling out loud.

He went outside, turned, and headed back to town. The crowd was thin. And then, too, it might rain. And that, of course, was when he spotted a humpback creature, a hulking animal very like the escaped ape discussed in the newspaper, a big one fleeing down the alley.

TWENTY

IT WAS THE SUN that made him sleepy; three times, listing badly, he almost fell off the stool. This was the authentic North — new snow covered the parked cars and even the adjoining roof where a squat chimney with doleful mouth went on emitting little puffs of smoke shaped like animals. Suddenly, Lee snapped to attention. A big man in greasy trousers was striding down the aisle, his grey-and-black hair full of lubricants and oil. Lee looked again — there was yet another person following hard behind, this one fatter still and with an even grander belly that ventured well out in front of the person himself. Lee put on his bored expression; he knew, of course, that there was yet a third person moving toward him, this one the absolute king of them all, fat beyond belief and with pants more unsanitary than any yet seen. In every case, their bellies were bigger than their chests. This person stopped, turned with difficulty, and spoke wheezingly:

"You're supposed to be tending to the teletype aren't you!"

"Yes, sir."

"Well hop to it then! Jesus!"

Lee yearned to kick him in the belly, save that it might probably explode. He trundled off toward the room where yet another of the editors, a man he had rather liked heretofore, was searching irritably through a long yellow scroll of the stuff.

"I thought you was looking after this shit! Good God Almighty, would you look at all this stuff! Dulles is flying in to Berlin and what we got is a mess on the floor."

Lee looked at it.

"And while we're on the subject, where were you yesterday actually? We could have used a little help, know what I mean? I don't know; you seem to come and go at random for Pete's sakes. You're supposed to be in this building" — he pointed to it — "all day long!"

"Yeah, but I never even wanted to come here in the first place. If it wasn't for the money, I could be at Antioch right now."

"I wish you were!"

It was dark when he left, the white moon dawning. The bus arrived, halted, and then opened with a gasp. Here, just as on every other day of his life, he found the same party of exhausted people sitting in their accustomed places with their same coagulated faces looking off into nothing. Today, however, one man was wearing a Santa hat pulled low over his suspicious eyes. Lee saw a defunct woman, at one time a beauty no doubt; now, she sat with two swollen legs wrapped in brown gauze dangling several inches off the floor. Lee moved closer. She was studying a grocery advertisement in her newspaper and had discovered a bargain on lettuce, circling it several times. Suddenly she stopped, looking at him over her glasses and warning him away.

Lee sat on the edge of his bed. The room was small, musty, the wallpaper fading even as he used his Will upon it. Above the line of distant buildings, he could see the radio tower blinking more frantically than ever, its six blue signals racing up and down the spine, broadcasting lies. Meanwhile, down in the street, a good little man in a hat was being led on gullibly by a small black dog on a string. Finally, Lee summoned the strength to rise and repair the bed, but succeeded primarily in stirring up a cloud of ill-smelling smoke.

He went out, drawn irresistibly to the slum. He passed a church, a noble-looking structure doing big business ever since bad weather had begun coming in. How well he knew them! And knew, too, that whereas primitive people had a primitive god, these had a god whose respect for private property was large. The drugstore came next, inside it the resolute-looking pharmacist who had learned to function all day in a continual swoon, enveloped as he was in the smell of so many medicaments and powders — Lee could envision him coming back each night in order to tide himself over with the contents of one or another of the little brown vials of which he had so many.

He went on. A cold wind was up. He harkened to the eleven-o'clock train, a sound that proceeded, as it seemed to him, from out of a reptile's mouth. Strangers came up to meet him, a lost people, mere boys some of them, drawn forth out of the countryside by the allure of neon and mystery. He acknowledged his first whore of the night, this one young and amazed and perhaps even horrified to realize what she had let herself in for. A hundred years would have to go by before he'd have the courage actually to go up to such a person and hear about the activities she was offering. Ten years anyway. He followed for half a block, also keeping his eye upon the store windows and their contents. He moved past an old-fashioned hardware no longer much patronized, inside it a little grey man bedding down for the night on a pallet. The Baptist Mission was next, crowded this night with a new shift of contrite old men singing hymns. The whore had gotten away.

He traveled far, once more into the awful section. No one molested him — he ascribed it to his Alabama upbringing and that he might, or might not, be carrying a knife. His arrogance increased. The slum people, some of them, now nodded to him out of sheer familiarity. It seemed to him indeed that he might yet have a career in this place, here where the streets had become extensions of his own mind and imagination.

He arrived at last in front of the ticket seller. All this time, he had believed that she was knitting a scarf; now he saw in fact that it was a coverlet of some kind with a Navaho design.

"Has Monique come on yet?"

She put the coverlet aside. "Monique's gone."

"What!"

"Oh, yes. Gone, gone, gone!" (She was extremely happy.) "So *now* what are you going to do?"

Cold night — he dressed for warmth. Adorning himself in a business shirt and two pair of socks, he slipped cautiously beneath the quilt. His was a sputtering lamp, yielding just enough brightness to let him read. The corners of the room had shadows in them; they bent and groaned like ghosts in pain. He recalled the country nights of long ago, with real fires going, wind howling, the quilts imbrued with camphor and antique dust. Truth was, he could admire anything if only it were old enough, including even this brown-and-ochre wallpaper that had faded down into the delicacy of hundred-year-old postage stamps. Taking the radio, he turned it to low volume and drew it into bed with him. He had respect for radios, just as for photographs and books and all things that conveyed information from long ago or from distances far away. And then, too, the radio gave some warmth.

He had three volumes within easy reach. Taking the first of them, he opened it and stared for a long time at the print itself on milk-white pages. He admitted it: he would have been a lover of books even had he been incapable of reading. And in fact, he wasn't reading now, not with his mind forever reverting to Alabama and to the fire and quilt and the sound of his own people playing dominoes in the next room while uttering seriously in low tones, far into the night.

He tried the radio, locating voices that came, some of them, from within the city, and others from beyond Ohio itself. A woman was going on at length in the Spanish tongue. He moved on, using the dial to crash through time and space. A chorus was singing, followed shortly by an advertisement for cough medicine. He gave attention to it before then losing the voice amid a barrage of static that, the more he gave heed to it, the more it made him think that it might be a recondite code of some type. If so, he couldn't break it.

All around him, the city was bedding down for the night; he knew this from the silence and dark and from the number of individuals who already had retreated off into blackened rooms to lie agog for certain hours until the sun might consent to come back again. But of all the shadows that he could see, one in particular gave him especial concern. That second, he heard something indeed — three gunshots that came from within the building itself, a tremendous noise followed by a silence as cold and remorseless as outer space.

TWENTY-ONE

IT WORRIED HIM, specifically that he might either expire too soon or, worse, find that he had grown even worse than he knew. Finally, toward noon, the man called him in and, before sending him off on a final errand, offered his farewell.

"Are you going to be with us again?"

"I don't know. Maybe! If they want me to."

"Well. We can always use fellows like you."

Lee was shocked — the man was sincere. He could feel his whole philosophy crumbling and, in its place a strange new world-wide pity for this and for every other old man who had worked himself to death for nothing.

"Yes, sir. It's been quite an experience."

"I bet it has, I bet it has. Especially the places where you go, right? Whew!"

They laughed, both. And when Lee realized the man was winking at him, he winked, too.

By afternoon, the journalists had not only left off working, but had gone down in a group to link up with the artists. Phones rang, no one taking notice. Across the way, the Man of Reduced Status was kowtowing to his former wife, the smartest on the staff. Finally, Arbuthnot himself came out in a Santa suit and began to distribute little bottles

of his favorite *liqueur*. Some were drunk already. Lee expected next to
see the whole bunch of them break out into the street and go dancing;
instead, even as he watched, the party began to fall apart and those
who only a moment ago had done the most whooping, now they
were slinking back to desk and office, there to wait another full twelve
months among ink and trousers, till came the time to rise and die.

Lee had brought his suitcase with him. He had done well, he
thought, to have reduced the pile of unopened mail down to where he
could see over it. Finally, just before noon, he got up and paced to the
cafeteria where the black woman stood waiting with folded arms.

"Well. Goodbye!" he said. He held out his hand.

"I come up North for the wages. I don't know what *you* come for."

Lee blushed. The leader of the press operators was looking at him
warningly. The sweet rolls were gone.

Never had the time passed so slowly. He was standing, looking out
over the mail pile with one eye while searching with the other for one
last blue envelope when, suddenly, the tone struck five. At once he
lurched forward wearing his bored expression. Two of the secretaries
were dawdling; he simply strode through the middle of them, washing
both of them up against the wall.

"Crumb!"

"I forgot my suitcase."

"Serves you right!"

The Toledo Bus Station — he found it swarming with refugees,
including at least one person he remembered from his initial voyage out from Alabama. He fell in behind a large woman in several
coats who turned and looked at him indignantly, as if she expected
him to try and make off with one or another of the half-dozen bags
she was shepherding across the floor. At the other side was a black
man, exhausted-looking, eyes extinct, the sort who had been through
all the worst that could happen to a person and who now was picking with a match stick in his golden teeth. An announcement came
on, a wild blur of noise that brought the congregation to its feet. Lee

witnessed a distinguished-looking older man in a black suit carrying a murderous-looking cane in one hand and a Greek-language text in the other. They looked at each other. Behind that person came a Mexican girl with two babies, a big one and a small, both clamoring for the same, and presumably more productive, breast. Lee noted how the driver, a cadaverous man, allowed nothing but outright optimism to show in his face.

The vehicle itself was of the older type, a coal burner, stodgy both in appearance and performance alike. Holding the suitcase well out in front of him, Lee edged down the aisle. One of the seats had a head on it, unattached seemingly to any visible body. And all this time, the woman behind him was pressing and pressing, pressing him forward insistently with her breasts, elbows, and nose.

Somehow, he managed to move forward, at one point having to step over a small tremulous animal that he had at first thought to be a dog. Suddenly, he grabbed for his wallet. The rearmost bench, of course, was taken — it never failed — and he must instead squeeze in next to a gigantic human being whose face was in the clouds, so to speak. From this position, he could watch with amusement as the new passengers came forward one by one, hopeful at first, until they saw how dark and unfriendly it was. Lee smoked, refusing to turn and read the face of the colossus next to him whose powerful elbow continued to chime against his own. The man just in front, meanwhile, had turned and was peeping back over the top of his seat with the aid of what appeared to be a jeweler's eyepiece. The bus shuddered, rolled, came back, and then sprang forward into the town's awful section. Lee was to remember seeing a gaunt man standing on the corner with the dead hollow eyes of one who wasn't going anywhere. Finally, he turned, Lee, appalled to find his neighbor glaring down at him with two bulging eyes of cotton atop a cardboard nose. Also, to his amazement and absolute shock, he just that moment recognized that someone was actually lying in the aisle, eyes open, both arms trussed-up. Herebefore, he had generally thought of himself as a connoisseur in the matter of buses and night travel, but never had he sampled the like of this. He wanted a flashlight, except that it were perhaps better after all not to have one. Someone lit a cigarette, cupping the flame in a hand that looked like an old garden glove that after many years had been retrieved out of the soil. Feeble though it was, Lee's match made a painful impression on the salesman across the aisle who stirred and groaned, finally bawling out "Oh God, why hast thee?" before twisting over and settling down to sleep again.

They broke into open country, the bus bobbing merrily between the brown fields and cattle. Up front (held by the bourgeoisie), a woman coughed twice, doing it sedately. Lee begged for rain, the last touch before he could be completely depths. He thought he had a chance of gliding home in peace and languor — until he saw Judy's face showing up in the heavens as a giant-sized poster comprised of stars.

Toledo was far behind. In his absence, he envisioned it breaking into photos of taverns and urine. He might almost have been able to set up a mathematical expression for the forces that repulsed and attracted him, provided it also account for the persistent pull of Antioch as well. Now, soon, he would have drawn in close enough to free-fall the rest of the way, like a fly sucked helplessly to the immense yellow wall of the moon.

He understood of course, that he taken on the tincture of corruption that Luke and the others would immediately observe. The others, his dormmates at school, they looked upon youth as upon an untoward probation during which they were not yet earning significant money. Himself, he cared nothing for life after such time as life had cooled down. Just now in fact, he was observing a middle-aged woman trying with increasing panic to get into a satisfactory position, her dilapidated body no longer a comfortable fit. And still her decline had not come to an end — far from it! Lee watched cruelly. For while she might yet possess the general shape of a woman, it was but as something for Time to do its work upon. He knew what it would come to — age and shapelessness, and nothing left but a book of adored, ancient photographs.

They moved on, deep into the carbon night. Toledo now figured as a mere episode, something to snort about and put behind him; indeed, he questioned whether such a place had ever existed. Antioch was in front, and the promise that even now certain favored persons were converging upon the place. Suddenly, he realized that he had been speaking out loud for the last minute and that the man next to him, as also the person on the floor, were both losing patience with him.

They entered a small town, moving noiselessly down a row of shops where a rim of light was burning around the edges of a certain yellow window shade. A grocery came up, inside it a bald man holding death at bay with a broom. Moments later, they were in the country again, slicing into a woods so dense that it was difficult to see how anything larger than a cat could gain entrance to it. Lee caught his first real view of the driver, a tired person with lids propped open with toothpicks and thread.

They went on, crossing a jammed river stopped with new-cut logs. The moon was with them, mile for mile; compared with this, daytime was like someone's inexperienced nephew — good enough but to hold a job and marry a church-going girl. They passed a farmhouse, the lanky man inside it with his nose pressed against the glass. Lee saw a dozen cattle sitting out piously in a black paisley field. Others of them were crossing the road with extreme delicacy, each carrying her cargo of precious milk. In the bottoms, he spied yet another of the rivers of Ohio, this one as narrow and jagged as lightning the color of red.

They entered Yellow Springs at just after one, Lee awakening in time to catch Bernie's place with the same dim lamp glowing in the window. Heart pounding, Leland grabbed for his suitcase and wallet. The man next to him had absented himself at some point, leaving behind, apart from the person on the floor, a quantity of trash and watermelon rinds. Came now the tavern into view. He saw a solitary figure, a haunted type in a shabby coat who bore all the earmarks of this place, including one cigarette and two books. Lee would travel no further. The driver, only half awake, tarried a very long while, as it seemed to Lee, before popping open the door. Now, finding himself *in* it, which is to say the night, Lee turned in each of the four directions and, putting on a bored expression, smelled deeply of it.

He stepped quickly to the cafe, his eye lingering upon that same little table in the rear where once he had explained to the girl about his nature and destiny. The bookshop was next, Lee immediately identifying where some of the volumes were missing, or perhaps just rearranged. The next block was all residences, three- and four-story cliff dwellings, as it were, with here and there a light showing where someone was reading in the off-season. The minarets loomed into view, a few degrees off course from where he thought he had remembered them. It was his theory that he would never be fully and truly at home until he had gone up to his room and then come down again and rubbed his forehead against Antioch Hall. It bore in upon him that he was fast approaching the quadrant where he had been wont to lie out in the weather and allow the leaves to cover him up. He hurried, hoping to touch down on native ground before the bullet that had been chasing him all his life, before it could... He jumped, panting and laughing at himself, and then tossing his suitcase across the interval and scrambling after it onto the grass.

III

TWENTY-TWO

AFTER A CERTAIN TIME, he rose and pressed forward. Ahead, the school itself comprised a moonlit ruin of which it was hard to remember that ever it had held so many vociferating students. He paced on until the bill of his cap touched the wall and then stood for a time waiting in vain for someone to open for him. Finally, he began the arduous work of climbing all four flights of the fire escape while carrying thirty pounds of luggage on his back. From this vantage, he could stand on a level with Antioch Hall itself and, peering clear through it, find Christmas lights sparkling in the valley. He might have paused here and done some reading — he had the books for it and it was bright enough. Instead, he preferred to go on, even to the top where, after a good deal of further work, he was able to throw both himself and the suitcase into Robert's room.

At first, he simply lay in a heap. That he was home, he knew it from a certain residuum of beer and perfume and from the general obscurity that never left these upper halls. His own dear room was in excellent condition, far more so than when he had abandoned it ten weeks earlier. But for one of Luke's stubby pencils, no one could have known that this was where two such persons once had lived.

Now that the place was back in his possession… Suddenly, he heard a noise overhead. He knew, of course, that there were no apartments higher than his own. He waited, smoking at 2:00 in the morning, the sheets pulled high. He felt that someone was reaching out mentally that very moment across the miles, past clouds, moon, and planets, from light-years away. Nor was it to be wondered at, that of all the billions of uncataloged souls scattered among the nebulae, nothing strange in it that one such soul might be questioning just now as to whether someone else was questioning, too. He concentrated, doing his best to launch into the cosmos a few disconnected thoughts that, however, traveled inches only before slopping back into his face again.

He tried the radio, his next-favorite source of information. There was a man's voice, an unctuous type speaking in lewd tones about a certain preparation for dry hair. The next station was delivering the weather; Lee loved it, when urgent voices warned of bad conditions, the prospect of damaging winds and squalls regaling him with reports about the way things were in other places. And was it raining in Toledo? He had his way and it were night always, and always raining.

When he woke, it was snowing, snowing slowly from a ceiling of clouds that looked like intestines. Again, the radio sputtered, a last desperate cry before the program went off forever. Groaning loudly, Lee tossed one leg out of bed and then wasted a minute before then trying to throw the other out after it. He hopped about — it was cold — finally catching sight in the mirror, not of the romantic creature he fancied, but of a naked Hindu dressed in a diaper.

Such was the intrinsic nature of snow, he felt he was strolling along a bright radiant beach in summer. He went slowly, in his fashion, his meager chest rattling audibly within his heroic blue leather jacket full of zippers and buttons. A woman came up, a person from the town to judge by her galoshes, her indignation and blood-shot face. Lee bowed theatrically, even sweepingly, getting in return a look of annoyance followed by a snort.

He turned toward town. The homes were abandoned, save that here and there he detected little glyphs of chimney smoke rising listlessly to heaven. A woman was monitoring him from behind a curtain — Lee turned to face her, bowing deeply and taking off his cap. He had very nearly stepped on a child, a small one bundled to the teeth in coats and jackets who went on glaring back at him silently. At the restaurant, it delighted him to find his own special table free and available and with parts of yesterday's newspaper on it. The waitress, his favorite, was a bosomy woman but already some thirty or forty years into her age. He did not object to it if she also wore that slightly amused expression that ordinarily he so resented in adults.

"Yes, sir?" she asked, turning the last word into an irony.

"Could I have some breakfast?"

"No, honey; not after eleven. What do you need?"

"Eggs."

"Aw. Does him need some eggs?"

He nodded. Her breast, which was of his precise favorite size, was not five inches from his eye.

"No baby, that ain't no egg. How many does he need?"

"Two," he said, but then quickly changed to "four."

"Scrambled?"

"Absolutely."

"Bacon?"

"Alright. Yes."

"Coffee?"

"Sure!"

"Toast?"

"O.K."

"Jelly?"

"Please. And grits."

"Say again?"

He watched her move away, doing it indolently, the same way she chewed her gum. It was rare in his experience to come within range of a woman with such credentials and the hips to go with them, all of it superbly packaged in a tight white uniform that smelled of flowers. With such a figure, he could imagine her undressing exultantly in her privacy, spending hours over so many buttons and snaps and… Hooks.

The food came quickly, the woman needing three trips to bring it all. As to the eggs, four in number, they constituted a golden hill of notable size that caused the customers to turn and wonder. Leland, in his enthusiasm, went first for the toast, injuring his hinge and getting jelly on his nose. Once again it struck him as to how odd it was, especially eggs, which seemed far too personal to be treated in this way. Bacon! once the very pith of some poor creature's actual person. Nevertheless, he chomped on it, the flavor mixing perfectly with the coffee, eggs, and toast, the four fundamentals of an Ohio morning.

Again, the waitress came by, her first-class buttocks competing for space in what was almost surely a pair of tight white panties. He liked her — Lee put on a bored expression — liked her all the better for being ripe and for having already done so many of the things that women were for doing. Indeed, once her day was over, he would have gone very willingly into the back room with her and willingly assisted with all those buttons and snaps and… Hooks.

It was pleasant — life in restaurants; just now, he was having his second coffee while looking out over a snowbound waste with grackles and cows. Two black hounds came bounding out of the woods, grinning creatures who immediately set about filling the field with prints. Lee smoked. The fire was warm; it kept the cider bubbling and made the apples turn. No doubt about it, he must have spent at least one of his iterations in the Middle Ages, and even now he still sometimes felt the urge to rise and go to the barn to check upon his ewes and swine.

Truth was, he longed for world disasters, and that these modern people might once again find themselves pressured by Franks and Goths and again sent scrambling back to the countryside and life on the farm. Now, donning his glasses, he focused on a true farmer sitting alone at the counter, his face all wrinkles and sunburn. Must there not also be a used-up truck out front with its bay full of tools? Coming to his feet, Lee verified that the truck was worse than he had thought, the hood tied down with a cord and in the cab, the very sort of wife he had expected, a dry woman, very patient, who continued all times to stare straight ahead.

The waitress flitted by, glancing at Lee's barren plate; he had five minutes, no more, before using up more of her affection than he had paid for. He looked to the farmer who at once turned away. Clearly, he wanted no one to be looking into his underdeveloped mind. And yet, Lee knew the fellow had suffered and had wisdom of a certain sort and, moreover, derived from ancestors who had carried the world safely through the pitiless ordeal of the Middle Ages. Again, Lee shot a glance in his direction, the man ducking down behind his newspaper. Lee relented and looked instead to the field. The hounds, of course, had gone, displaced by an evil-looking grackle joyously tossing up handfuls of snow.

He went outside and strolled thirty yards in the direction of Springfield. Above, in Bernie's room, the green lamp was dimmed with rime. Lee now regretted that he had not more availed himself of the man's knowledge, so arduously brought together over so many years, and which Lee had so much trouble understanding.

He passed an antique shop in which the grey-headed proprietress stood proudly among her objects, waiting for that day when a customer might come along. Lee went to the window as if deeply interested, not in the woman herself, but the antique typewriter on display. Suddenly, she scooped up her cat and brought it up close to her with a burst of wild affection. Lee had seen this before, Judy having many times seized up his hand in the same impulsive fashion. There could be no doubt — this old person had some of the same hormones as activated Judy, asterisk-shaped things that flowed in the blood like stars and burrs.

He shambled on, reading the cobbles. Curious, how he had come to be possessed by these few acres. Below him in the valley, he saw a woman come out with a broom and go chasing after a dog. In the other direction, a score of unspeaking birds was wheeling slowly around the towers of Antioch Hall where six bright pennants were furling in the breeze. Always this vision put him in mind of the summons of scholarship, and of the years in front of him for theorizing as dangerously as he wanted and with no responsibility — so he thought — for the way things were in the outside world. Young was he, and not the attenuated youngness of nineteen or twenty, but young to the bone, and endowed with youth's sublime equipment that could carry out any procedure he wanted. Arrogant was he, and confident that biographers were watching from behind every corner. His one great obligation: to be such a sort of person as to warn off future readers from imagining that they could be like him.

TWENTY-THREE

THREE DAYS, Christmas having come and gone while he held out on the top story of a hundred-year-old building. Gradually, he had become aware of a second person, a sandy-headed boy who had taken up on the floor below him.

"Your old man throw you out, too?" the boy asked on the one occasion they stopped to speak.

"Naw, I go to school here."

"School?" He made a pained expression, and then turned and moved back deeper into the hall.

By the end of the week some students did begin to show up at various points on campus and downtown where he found them standing about staring noncommittally into the night. One, a fifth-year boy famous for having had a story published, made an appearance at the cafeteria at a time when Lee and others were sitting at separate tables in sullenness and despair. Lee studied him, not greatly impressed until, suddenly, the boy whipped out a pencil and began to lay out a new story on the tablecloth itself. There was silence in the room; Lee saw one of the existentialist girls training on the boy with hungry eyes, her mouth hanging open in envy and desire.

The tavern was doing business, inside it two coarse-looking townsmen sipping the beer of ignorance. Lee moved on, passing the girls' dormitory where already a few silhouettes could be seen passing back and forth in the windows. Strangely, he could see more of what was transpiring in that building than could the dwellers themselves. One, a tall person, was standing uselessly, her hands hanging down. Previously, he used to wait for one or another of them to undress in full view, but now, with his philosophy crumbling day by day, he experienced a pity for all the unexceptional girls in their lipstick and beauty-efforts, all of them having been sent forward under strict sentence of inspiring in someone, anyone, some glimmering of love. Especially he sympathized with the fat ones, two of them having just now and with some difficulty crowded into the same cell.

He turned to his own dormitory and climbed the steps. No longer did the place belong to him alone; on the contrary, a caucus seemed to be going on in Martin's room. Lee swore. These voices had all the quick urgency of New York in them, although nothing urgent was going on. He dashed to his own room and grabbed up a book.

"Lee!" (It was Martin.) "When did *you* get back?"

"Back? He never left."

"How was Toledo?"

"Bad," said Lee. "Kafka. You wouldn't like it, don't go. Bad."

"I saw Judy," said Reed.

"Nothing surprises me anymore."

"I saw her, too." (Sal.)

"They've got these 'journalists' there… "

"And she was doing real well, too. At a party."

Lee sickened. "Judy? Oh, I expect she's married by now or something. Right?"

"I wouldn't say she was married exactly."

"Engaged. I see. Nothing surprises me, not anymore." He turned away and hummed while the others—and he did not know why—while they laughed. That there was palpably a perfume in the room and that it derived, not from the crowded marketplaces of Asia but rather… He turned. It hit him in the eye, far too late to take off his reading glasses now.

"Oh!" he said, but then immediately followed it up with: "Hi."

TWENTY-FOUR

HE CERTAINLY DID TAKE HER HAND and did carry her off into the adjoining room where someone lay snoring in bed. They were not accustomed to each other. Would the top of her head slip in as precisely as before beneath his chin? After all, it was *her* person and not his own that he now tried to force up against him. She was somewhat yielding, even if not altogether ready to look him in the eye.

"Oh, baby."

"You didn't write."

"Baby, baby." (Had she seen the corruption in his face?)

"Not even one letter."

"Oh baby. I didn't know whether you were coming back or going to parties and everything."

"You never even wrote a single letter."

"Didn't have a real bed. Just a goddamn tire."

"You could have called."

"No! I wanted you to see what it's like — suffering all the time. Did you?"

She nodded, the sight of it dizzying him with exultation. "I wanted to see if you'd forget me."

"You wanted to ruin my life."

"Why not? You've already ruined mine."

"Not on purpose."

"So, what does *that* matter? I'm ruined anyway. See anything in my face?"

"Oh!"

Now, finally, she kissed him, even to running her fingers through his hair. It worried him still, the procedures she might have picked up in New York, things done in full calm while smiling at the recollection of his backwardness. Moreover, she had modified her hair and make-up, doing it in wanton indifference to the effect she must have known it would have on him and others. Finally, still holding, they sat, the boy in bed making space for them rather grudgingly, it seemed to Lee.

"And did it seem at any time as if you were starting to fall in love with me?"

She thought about it in her serious way, blinking. "Did Phyllis say that I was in love with you?"

"No! 'Later on,' she said. 'Maybe.'"

"What did you say?"

"That I would just keep on trying."

"How long will you try?"

"I don't know. Till I'm twenty-three."

"Then what will you do?"

"I don't know. Go back to Toledo, I guess. A person could disappear in there and never come out."

"Don't, Lee."

"Didn't have a real bed. However, I couldn't sleep anyway."

"Why?"

"Oh! You know why."

"Oh, you poor thing!" She bent over him, her soft bosom, (swollen with pity) raking his chest. He did so love it when she took the initiative in these matters; indeed, he could have spent months in such activity, day after day while she embalmed him in kisses. And now, he would have liked to rise and flee away with her at once, looting Antioch of her presence and bundling her off down to harbor and to ship with Martin and the others chasing along behind.

"Why don't we just go somewhere? Get some peace and quiet."

She kissed him on the neck, hitting a certain spot. "Where do you want to go?"

"I don't know. Venice."

Having identified the spot, she kissed it again. "What about Luke and Phyllis?"

"Shoot, we'll take them, too!"

"Luke might go, but she won't."

Always, always, there were reasons for not doing something. It put him in a panic, how that life was flying. And now she had pushed his collar to one side and was nibbling at him with her small white teeth.

"You couldn't sleep at all?"

"Absolutely not! It was Judy, Judy, Judy all the time. That's all I ever think about."

"You poor thing!" She had a tear in one eye. Again, they kissed. That was when Luke walked in.

"Christ. I come home and here they are."

"See anything in my face?"

"Lipstick? You should have been with me Lee — carrying out bedpans in a dingy old hospital while you two were sitting here smooching. I have to say it, Lee: hospitals are tough." (He did look smaller and more unkempt, even if his suit was new. He had a guitar over his shoulder and carried two giant suitcases.)

"Didn't have a bed to sleep in — just a tire. And by the way, she still doesn't love me. Just thought you might want to know."

"I like him. Lots."

"Yeah, but shit, he could be dead by the time you make up your mind."

"Oh, he will not. We're only eighteen!"

"Yeah, but he's read a lot more than most people. Besides, I'm *seven*teen."

"What!"

"Sure. It's the I.Q., Lee. And, of course, you have to grow up quick, when you're a Jew. You could be a Jew." He flicked his cigarette with a haughty gesture and then settled the two large suitcases on top the boy still trying to sleep, "I have to tell you, Lee: my father got his Ph.D. when he was twenty." And then: "What about your father? Judy?"

She squirmed uncomfortably. Her voice, already very deep, grew deeper still. "He's a skilled laborer."

Lee reeled; it seemed almost more than he could hope for, that in addition to her other qualities, she might be destitute as well. They sat, watching her jealously. It was cloudy outside and the chamber in near-darkness.

"Christ. Other people talk about being poor; Judy really is. 'She came into the world poor, and so now she has to sell ice cream.' Want me to play something on my harmonica?"

"Not necessarily."

The blackguard was good and getting better. After two months of practice, he could now play certain snatches from the classical repertory.

"Dvorak," he explained.

TWENTY-FIVE

LEE WOKE, groaned, rolled, and then hobbled on down to the facility and urinated at such tedious length that his gorge began to rise. And when he returned, Luke was in place, a pile of manuscript rising at his side. Lee looked at him. The boy's suit, to be sure, was rich, but sorted very oddly with the hair that had been allowed to go to weed. Clearly, his ten weeks of working in a hospital, the boy had taken it hard.

"There was an old man, Lee. They kept sawing the top of his head off."

"What!"

"To fix him. But all he wanted was to die."

"Not your fault."

"And he did die. I know, because I was holding him."

"Nothing surprises me anymore. However, if it wasn't for such things as that, suffering and so forth, then there wouldn't be any beauty in the world."

"Beauty? I can do without it."

"Not me."

"I snap my fingers at your 'beauty.'" (And did so.) "Christ, what a load of shit!"

"Yes, actually we should aim for a great increase in human suffering."

"That sounds like you. I have to say it, Lee: you make me want to puke sometimes. Know what I mean?"

They sat, glowering at each other. Nor could Lee have specified what it was that drove him on to the tormenting of the best man he knew. He said:

"Well. We can discuss these matters later on."

Now that he was in his clothes, true clothes, including the broad yellow tie with the Christ on it, he could feel his strength returning by leaps. The moon, formerly his own special star, was mustardly tonight, with ants on it. And though he might be somewhat more corrupted than before, nevertheless he was still able to gaze out romantically through smoke and haze, his vision never slowing until it hit the far distant mountains lined up one behind another, all the way to Virginia before stepping out to sea.

He was home, he knew it from the sort of people that filled the cafeteria. He went and retrieved his coffee and then sat next to where the philosophy professor and three of his pupils were slumped in despair. Up until this moment, he had resolutely refused to glance toward the ice cream perch where Judy might, or perhaps might not, as in the old days, be blinking and thinking and looking out over the crowd with the pathetic little shovel in her lap. Instead, he allowed himself only to look toward the window and at the reflection that must, or perhaps must not, be there. They looked at each other. And now indeed he saw the shovel, saw the uniform, saw the girl, saw her blinking and thinking and, suddenly, also saw her break out into one of her manslaughtering smiles that traveled across the room and smote the window and smited *him*.

TWENTY-SIX

NOW HE WAS HOME, he had to start in at the very beginning and, once more, get into the practice of sleeping until noon. Finally, at two in the afternoon ("morning," he called it), he was standing out in the yard when Phyllis came running up.

"Greetings!" she said. (Her face had some color in it and was almost pretty.) "I approve."

"What?"

"Yes, I've thought it over and I've decided it's alright. You and Judy, I mean."

"Good." (Sometimes, it seemed to him that she took more delight in their affair than in her own.) And then, too, she had a patronizing way, as if she had herself long ago passed all through the Age of Romance and come out safely on the other side. In fact, she was practicing up to be a spinster, experimenting with long drab coats and somber dresses with nineteenth-century lace.

"Well, tell me this," said Lee. "How long before she'll…?"

"Surrender? Ah. You must journey to Delphi, Mr. Pefley, if you would know that."

"That's hard."

"It's supposed to be hard! However, if you want something that's easy…"

"No, no."

They went on. She walked speedily, like a goose. Moreover, she was forever grinning irrationally, so much so that he was not always keen on being seen with her. Finally, because he thought he should say something, he asked:

"Are you doing any translations these days?"

"Oh! You don't care about that."

"I care a little bit."

"There's so much to be done! I can't do it all — how could I? — and I don't even know all the languages either! You won't help. And Luke! Well, he tries. Oh, God."

Lee looked at her. She was growing desperate and walking too fast.

"Where are we going?"

"God. I thought *you* knew."

They stopped. Lee's inclination was to travel west, there where the cafeteria seemed to be burnishing, as it were, in the morning sun. But for her, her inclination was eastward, toward the woods.

"Well..."

"Yes, yes. Goodbye!"

Evening came on. Lee, who was quite willing that this be Phyllis' chapter and not his own, had gone three times to the cafeteria and now was back again speculating between the sheets. Far away on the other side of the snowfield, he saw the three lilac lights of the radio tower blinking perfunctorily, as if warning that there the earth came to an end. The phone rang. Judy.

"Phyl's been eating aspirin again! A whole bottle full!"

He raced back and reported it to Luke, who was on his feet and out the door before Lee could finish telling it. They flew down the four flights, running through the huge shadow of Antioch Hall. And who now would Judy live with? He could envision her holding out alone, blinking, wide-eyed, trying to coordinate her own possessions of pine cones and the like with what was left over from Phyllis' poor thin books and drab dresses. He knew her, of course, and knew, too, that she would certainly do all her best to complete any unfinished canvases that Phyllis had left on the easel.

They entered by the window. Phyllis was not dead; on the contrary, she was sitting in a chair.

"Oh, God. I'm perfectly alright!"

"Make her vomit — she's got to vomit."

"No, make her walk."

"How many did she take?"

"All! All of them, she took all of them!"

Luke lifted her by the waist. Thin as she was, he was nevertheless having trouble prying her out of the chair.

"I'm alright! God!"

"You going to help? Or not?"

Lee came forward slowly. He did not feel that he ought to be handling her, so much did her figure remind him of a boy's.

"Make her vomit, make her!"

"This is what I ask: why would she take a whole bottle when we know she took twenty of them last night?"

"She won't open her goddamn mouth!"

Two girls came down to look in upon them, one of them a bird-like personality whom Lee had never before seen without her make-up. Staring at her, he almost forgot what he was supposed to be doing.

"I'm alright!"

"This is what I think: someday she'll succeed."

But now Luke had forced her open and, using his physician's skill, soon would have her vomiting again. Lee didn't care to see it. And all the while, a succession of girls coming by to have a look, and looking, and wandering off.

TWENTY-SEVEN

WINTER, HAVING ONCE MOVED IN... However, he was resigned to it, and to these blank, cold, milky days that reminded him of long-ago Toledo when he used to go for weeks so enraptured in his theories that he hardly bothered to speak.

He got into his robe, stumbled down the four flights and out into the yard. Students flowed past, girls, some of them, some of them giggling at him. Above, it was cold, cold weather with innumerable clouds fleeing past on the current. He saw one cloud in particular (giraffe-shaped) that he had first observed some fifteen years earlier on a day somewhat warmer than this. Chased by winds, the thing had traveled all around the world and now was loping home again.

He went back and searched the hall for a cigarette, finally having to purloin it from the adjoining room. Six hours more and it might be dark, provided he could wait that long. Luke was absent, his very pencil missing as well. Without his roommate on guard, Lee had a horror of his enemies stealing up on him when his eyes were shut.

He did sleep, a solid nine hours of it that satisfied and more than satisfied his quota. He did so enjoy the view from this vantage, comprising, as it did, not only the ten thousand lights of campus but also the two radio towers currently giving off conflicting signals. Luke was back. Instead of rolling off to sleep again, Lee spoke up loud and clear:

"Read to me. That stuff you're writing."

The boy grinned bulbously, nodded twice, and drew on his ciga-rette. His stack of manuscript, it was getting higher.

"You aren't ready for that. Besides, you have to go out in twenty minutes."

"Read, read."

The boy groaned but then did finally arise and go to their common bookcase. Lee did not much care what the material was, so much did he enjoy the boy's slow pleasant voice dawdling over sentences and sometimes stopping altogether to allow the significance to sink in. Under these conditions, Lee was able to sleep a few minutes more, awakening when he detected Luke sobbing over his favorite story about the little Match Stick Girl who had frozen while trying to sell her wares.

"It's a ridiculous situation, Lee. I'd appreciate it if you didn't tell people... "

"Ain't *nobody* going to tell *anything* to *anybody*. I'll beat the shit out of 'em — want me to?"

"No, no."

"I'm ready! *Anybody, anytime* — remember that."

"I'll write it down."

Having agreed, Lee dressed and dropped to the ground, danc-ing down the hundred steps by rote. It was a night of winds and fog; moreover, Luke had loaned him a black coat that, while it was a foot too short, nevertheless was also far shabbier than anything he himself could lay claim to. Tonight, he could have faced down anyone in the world, whether in a matter of mind, spirit, or fist. A boy walked by, a third-rate type who glanced at him in alarm and then hastened to get inside.

Lee moved on, his face hidden in the high black collar — he adored traveling portentously in extreme slowness, a cigarette dangling from his pair of lips still smeared with lipstick. His arrogance increased. He tossed the hair out of his eyes. Two girls merged out of the darkness, both falling silent when they saw the sort of person he was. Wise of them, he thought, always to go in fear of the Male.

He came forward and rapped twice at the parlor door. A girl opened, one of the rectitudinous and high-principled types that hated the sight of him.

"Tell Judy I'm here," he ordered.

She looked at him, made a clicking sound, and then shut the door in his face. There was not the least chance in the world that she would actually do what he wanted. Again, he knocked, this time getting a shy girl who opened cautiously and peeped out through the crack.

"Tell Judy I'm here. Right now."

She came at once, dressed in her beret. Lee reeled. Moreover, she wore a certain golden locket he had acquired at great expense from a certain pawnshop in Toledo. No doubt about it, every other girl on campus had been cheated, all beauty-proceeds flowing directly to this one girl alone who, apart from her beret and pert ways, seemed almost indifferent to the effects she caused.

"Judy, Judy, Judy."

"What's the matter!"

"We have time — you want a cup of coffee, you and me?"

It was his great good fortune — their same table of old times was free and available. This time, Lee lit the candle himself.

"Well, you're probably wise not to love me," he said. "It *is* good coffee though."

She sat, stirring her cup sadly. In her beret and with her high luminous forehead… It was her looks and her height and her sweater and beret that went straight to the brain centers of his mind.

"We're alone, right?"

She nodded.

"Very well then! And now you can tell me."

"Tell you what?"

"Why, anything you want. For example: 'Am I beginning to fall in love with Lee?'"

She laughed merrily. "And I thought we were here to talk about books and literature."

"O.K., talk about that."

"No! *You* talk. I'll listen."

"No, I only want to talk about Judy."

"Alright, I'll listen about Judy."

He lit a cigarette. He had opted to concentrate upon just one of her eyes, brown and clean, and to go swimming in it.

"Judy is…"

"Yes?"

"Stubborn. Very stubborn."

"Oh, I am not."

"She used to be in love with me, but not now, oh no. Now she just sits there."

"What do you mean, 'used to'?"

"Million years ago. That's right! I can remember, even if you can't."

"What was it like, so long ago?"

"Those were strange times, Judy, in the late Cenozoic. We used to go out walking in it."

"Strange times." (She had put on a far-away look and seemed to be drifting.)

"Yes, Judy, strange and strange. Flowers big as trees. And how the colors washed and swirled around us! Perpetual evenings. Of course, we had to be careful, with the world as thin as it was in those days."

"Did we have a dog?"

"Certainly. Well, it wasn't a 'dog' exactly."

"And a house made of gingerbread?"

"You do remember! Well, basalt actually."

"What else?"

"Everything you want. And after another million years, you'll be thinking back on how it was tonight in this coffee shop when you fell in love with Lee again. And so, my advice is that you pay special attention and try to store up as many memories as you can. That's what *I* always do."

She nodded and began to look about at the furniture and the scholars, the pictures on the wall and the vision of snow dropping ever so slowly past the window. Lee came nearer, bending over the table. He whispered:

"There was never a time when you were not in love with Lee, never."

She thought about it.

"There's no escape, none."

(He grew hoarse, his mind beginning to spin and tumble with hope made new. She seemed to him very weak at just this moment.)

"Never a time?"

"Never, never, never. Judy! it doesn't do any good, being stubborn; I know it and you know it." (He came close.) "And someday, we'll be two mountains, miles high, standing side by side in…"

"Please, Lee."

"Side by side. Judy!"

"I want to go home now."

He carried her home, saying nothing, and then stood back while she climbed in through the window and dropped out of sight. A full minute he waited, hoping she might yet change her mind and elect to come back out again. Was she angry with him? Impossible to say and in any case, he thought he knew how to absolve himself later on. But because the night was young, he turned back to town and the coffee still waiting for him.

He was sleeping, sleeping well, when he became suddenly aware that Luke was bending over him. In the dim, the boy had taken on the look of a giant mantis probing cautiously.

"Ahhh… Lee? It has to do with Judy."

Lee leapt up. "Dead!"

"No! Christ."

"Aspirin then."

"No, no, not at all. Actually, it has to do with something else."

They dropped downstairs and flew across the watery two-o'clock shadow of Antioch Hall. One single boy was observed at this hour, a vague-looking individual who seemed not in the least surprised to see Lee racing past in a robe followed by Luke in no shirt. At the parlor, they rapped loudly and then, recognizing that no one would admit them at this hour, dashed around to the window. The light was on, the curtain closed.

"Judy!"

No answer.

"Phyllis!"

Luke came up. Lee was aghast that the boy could have selected this moment for his harmonica.

"Judy? Alright, I'm *ordering* you to open this window!"

Now, finally, the curtain did move slightly, Phyllis at last opening and then sticking her head out.

"Who is it?"

"Us! Goddamn it."

"Oh yes. I can see you now."

"What's the story with Judy?"

"What? I can't see you."

"Judy! What's the story?" (Suddenly he grabbed, almost snatching away the harmonica before Luke could jump back out of his way.)

"What?"

"What's wrong with Judy!"

"Oh, God." (Upstairs, two lights came on.) "Is that Lucien with you?"

"Judy, we're talking about Judy! I want to see her."

"You can't."

"But why! Why!"

"You're not dressed properly. Besides, I... Oh, God, wait a minute, just wait."

They waited. Lee continued to lift one foot and then the other to prevent them from adhering to the ground. Luke meantime had taken a seat and was playing woefully on the larger of his two instruments. Lee now saw numerous heads protruding from numerous windows, near and far.

"She doesn't want to talk to you," said Phyllis. "Nor can I blame her."

"But why! Why! That's what I ask."

"She wants to talk to Luke."

To show his location, Luke raised his hand.

"God. Alright now, Luke, you go to the corner and wait. Not you! She wants to talk to him, not to you."

"Very well," said Luke. "I am now moving toward the corner."

"Good. But not Lee. Lee stays."

"We understand."

"What?"

"Lee."

"No! He stays."

"I *am* staying. Goddamn it!" (He had hoped to catch a view of the girl Judy; instead, Luke simply hoisted himself to the sill and through the curtains. Five minutes went by, time enough for one of the bright little January stars to blink and falter and then go out forever. One by one, slowly, all the lovely heads had drawn back in where, presumably, they were sleeping lovely sleep. Two minutes more went by. Finally:

"What the hell's going on in there?"

Phyllis came. "Oh, forgot about you — sorry. You can go away now; they left a long time ago."

"What!"

"Oh, God. She wanted to talk to Luke — is that so difficult? Even for you?"

"Goddamn, that makes my dander rise. And now I'm *telling* you..."

"Goodnight."

To his amazement, the window closed in front of his eyes and the curtain, too. He cursed, he could not, however, get it open again, not unless he was ready to break the glass. He heard a liquid sound, one of the upstairs girls having missed him entirely with her pan of water. How well he knew them! And knew, too, that yet other kettles even now were warming on the stove.

He ran around — his feet were tender — until he found himself fronting the building that held neither Judy nor his friend. His bitterness increased. Next, he ran to the chapel and searched it thoroughly, but found only that same sandy-headed boy whose father had tossed him out. In this area, the avenues were lined on both sides with noble-looking homes, the domiciles of professors and their wives. Himself, he had come away without books, shoes, glasses or money. And if but recently, the bright little white January stars had been highly visible, now a huge black cloud had come to cover them up.

Half an hour he searched and called, sometimes breaking out into curses. According to his theory, he had a counterpart on the moon, the sole person in all the universe who knew both where he was and what he was suffering. But was anyone writing it down? Lee knew this much, that if he must freeze, he preferred to do it next to the Horace Mann memorial where it would be seen that he had tried (even if not succeeded) to achieve some victory for mankind before he died.

And if he slept, it was only briefly, for the stars had not budged from their positions. He thought he could divide the true stars from the false, and both of these, in turn, from the appalling void of space itself. That was when he observed Luke coming toward him across the shadows. The boy was tired-looking and had switched to the smaller of his two harmonicas. Like a giant insect he came, probing at Lee with one foot. Side by side they sat in the shadow of the Horace Mann crypt.

"Well," said Luke. "I just hope this has been a lesson for you."

Lee nodded. "It has."

"I haven't slept in two nights, and now this."

"Right."

"I've got a test, too."

"I know."

"Chemistry. And is he ever a hard ass, too."

Lee nodded. Himself, he had kept away from chemistry.

"So now what are you going to do?"

"I don't know. Toledo, I guess."

"Christ. No, I mean now that you've got what you want? Start deteriorating, I suppose."

"What I want?"

"That's the way of it: get what you want and right away you'll start deteriorating. Oh sure, you'll soon be like all these other shits." (He motioned around at the campus where some few lights were beginning to show up in various locations.)

"Not me," said Lee. "I won't be living long enough to do any real deteriorating. What did you mean: 'what I want'?"

"I have to say it, Lee — you're deteriorating even as I look at you."

"Naw, it's just the sun. It'll be here any moment now. What, was she drunk?"

"Oh, sure. She'd have to be, to be in love with the likes of you."

"In love."

"Sure. 'Two mountains, higher than the sky'? Idiot. 'One million years ago'? Well, it worked."

"Good Lord." Lee stood.

"So how does it feel?"

Lee sat. "I don't know." He stood.

"You stand there, mouth hanging out. Me, I've got a test."

"God!"

"Sit, sit."

"Oh! Oh! Oh!"

"Idiot. Hey, there it is!"

Lee turned in time to catch the sun's upper rim, enormous beyond belief, breaking above the distant hills. It urged him to fall on his knees and pray to it. Instead, he saluted only, but then turned to watch as one grand ray, moving with hideous slowness, came and revealed that he had by no means been the only lover camping out that night.

TWENTY-EIGHT

HE WOKE — his arrogance had increased. The day itself was brilliant and bright, snow on the ground, and the calico sun giving off shades of lavender and grey.

He dressed quickly, gathered his books and, his joy building, hurried downstairs. He knew this much about himself, namely that he had come out of nowhere equipped with nothing and yet, against all reason, had carried off all the best that life and world could offer.

The first to congratulate him was one of the rectitudinous girls who had always loathed the sight of him.

"Well, you did it." She smiled, to his astonishment, and shook hands with him. "You better be good to her."

"I will."

"You better."

Lee went on, hopping and skipping and then finally breaking out into a loud hum to match his bored expression. Three boys were waiting at the corner.

"Son-of-a-bitch."

Lee grinned.

"How'd you do it?"

"Talent, I guess."

"Bastard." (They, too, shook hands — Lee was touched. On this morning, apparently, the whole world was ready to forgive all his trespasses of the last five months.)

"You come out of nowhere. She was the only one on campus, and now *you* got her."

Lee grinned.

"He's grinning. What, you going to take her back down to Mississippi with you?"

Lee shrugged and then looked off, his gaze promptly running into Steve, twenty years old, who was known to have had a serious interest in the same girl; they looked at each other. Indeed, this day was particularly brilliant and had a haze that hinted where purple hills ran across the surface of the sun itself. He was looking at it, dreaming while in the midst of people. That was when a crowd of girls came running up.

"He did it. I don't know how."

"How does it feel?" Beth asked.

"And now that you've got her, what are you going to do with her?"

"Oh, he'll think of something," said Linda.

Lee shook hands with each of them, saving Judy until last. Between the girls, the sun, and his bored expression, he was beginning to wish that he could have gone on living somewhat past the age of twenty-three in spite of all. Now Carol came up, the same Carol that had so many times tried to drown him in boiling water.

"It won't last," she said. "He's so smug."

"It *might* last," Linda said. "You can't always tell. And besides, he's tall, and she's so…"

"Short."

"It might last."

Lee nodded lazily. For him, it was a rare thing to be surrounded by five girls. But mostly, he worshipped the sight of Steve glowering in the doorway. He smoked and then, squinting with ruggedness, focused on the sun, it's shining fields and general strangeness on this his day.

TWENTY-NINE

THE DAY DID PASS, followed by others. At this time, he wanted nothing to do with the girl. Nor she him, to judge by how she turned and galloped away each time they set eyes on each other. Finally, with January running out, he telephoned Phyllis, catching her in one of her moods. She listened with impatience, sighing constantly and then hanging up on him in the middle of a sentence. Lee marked the time, giving her exactly one hour and thirty minutes before trying again. This time, her mood was cheerful in the extreme, indeed rather too much so, to his thinking.

"Will Judy go out with me tonight?"

"Will Judy go out with him tonight? God. She's right here!"

"No! You ask her."

He could hear snickering coming, as it were, from far.

"Yes, Mr. Pefley, she'd be charmed. God!"

His suit, the same he had left home in, fit poorly now. Luke looked at him, saying nothing.

He waded across campus, moving against the crowd. It embittered him that his affair was no longer the chief topic of discussion in the community. One girl did smile and wave, whereupon Lee nodded back to her. At Judy's place, he had to knock three times, but when she did come, she came forth quickly, refusing either to say anything or even to look at him. In this way they marched side by side all the way to town. Dressed as she was in one of Phyllis' long drab coats, she wasn't precisely the Judy of three days earlier. The moon, too, or what remained of it, looked like a mere daub of paint and was giving off a questionable light.

"Now according to Luke, you love me. Is that right?"

They sped up. The town was so small, soon they were back on campus again.

"If he said so."

"He did say so!"

"And now I suppose your 'arrogance' will be 'increasing' again."

"But what about later on? When I get old?"

"That's one thing we don't have to worry about. Besides, don't you think I'll get old, too?"

He did not. "But what about when I start getting disgusting and everything?"

"You already are."

"Sometimes, maybe. But not all the time. Anyway, you have to start doing what I say now, if we're going to be in love."

"I know that."

"For example, if I were to say: 'Alright, take off all your clothes…'"

"I *knew* that would be the first thing! I *knew* it!"

"Or, if I were to say: 'O.K., we're going to Paris.' Would you go?"

"If that's what you want."

"Or…"

"Oh, be quiet. Just don't talk, alright?"

Her voice! It was darker when she was in love. Just then he realized that the campus gate was in process of being closed by three upper-class boys pushing on it. They must hurry, or else be locked out for the night.

They went straightway to the gymnasium where already some two dozen couples were dancing in the dark. The music was insidious and the girls, many of them, were wearing cosmetics. Lee could not but notice how people stepped aside for him, owing to his sudden prestige. They were waiting for him to unveil the girl.

"I'll take your coat now, alright?" he said. She gave it over, revealing the authentic girl underneath. Lee reeled. Not only was she in black, not only heels, hose, jewels, earrings and all of it, not only that but she was also in a gown that, if folded rightly, he could have slipped into his wallet.

"Good Lord!" he said, moving back a few inches. "You want to go to jail?"

"I know! I feel like I'm about to come out of it."

"Ohhhhh!" His famousness increased. He looked for, and found, Steve glowering from the bar.

"Come," he said. "Let's just go over there."

"No. You just want everybody to see me."

"Not me." He ran around to the other side, studied her for a moment, and then came back. "Oh, Tweedy! You'll never be more beautiful than at..." (he checked his watch) "... nine forty-six in January, nineteen hundred and fifty-seven."

She thought about it, blinked, and then checked her own watch, a dime-sized affair that once had been her grandmother's.

"It's nine forty-nine."

"See? We have even less time than I thought. Dance with me."

She obeyed. That it was Judy and not an impostor sent forward by Steve or Martin or some genius of New York evil, he knew it from the way she slipped in precisely under his chin.

"Oh, Tweedy."

"I know, I know."

The music was good, the lights low. Again, he resorted to the punch bowl and poured himself a drink that stood deep in the goblet that held it. He realized that this was not merely a girl in his arms but rather a tinted pearl in human form with lovely long brown hair holding glints of gold. Sal came up and, in his immense stupidity, tried three times to intrude upon them.

"Leave us," said Lee.

"He wasn't doing anything," said Judy.

"I'll kill him. Kill 'em all."

"No, no. Hush."

They danced. Or rather, they stood in one place. And now that they were in love, he with her and she him, he wanted to get down into her past history and, as it were, recapitulate the whole of it.

"Remember when the war ended?"

"Oh yes; we went for a drive."

"And they were shooting off fireworks?"

She nodded uncertainly.

"O.K., what were you thinking about at that particular moment? I know what *I* was thinking."

"About me?"

"No, I didn't know about you. When did you know about me?"

"Always! I had a doll like you."

"What!"

"A long skinny doll. His ears stuck out, too."

"I think *you* stick out. That's why you wore that dress."

"Of course. I wanted to see you squirm."

Lee dizzied. Across the way, Martin was bending forward astutely, his face hooded; Lee had the feeling the boy could hear all that was being said.

"I love thee, Tweedy."

"I love thee."

"Oh God, I never thought I'd hear you say that."

"Love you, love you, love you." (She was watching closely, taking pleasure from the way her words made his eyes cloud up.) "My dearest darling, my beloved."

"Oh! 'Darling!'"

"Darling, dearest, adorable."

"Ohhh! Stop!"

"I know, I know." She was compassionate, and willing to stop. "Darling, dearest." All his life he had asked but for this — to have one perfect moment and then extend it to perpetuity. An odd thought now came to him: how that he would very much like to come back in fifty years and look in upon the two of them whispering excitedly to one another at this very instant when life was at its brightest. The 1950s! He had started out in it as a tiny boy and now the era was coming down to a close.

"I had rather be young now, in this decade, than rich and immortal later on." (Something of the sort he said.)

"Me, too. I think so, too."

"They won't believe it! They'll think we're exaggerating."

"They'll be jealous."

"But don't feel sorry for them. Remember, they did it to themselves."

Sal came back, bringing in tow a confused-looking little girl of fifteen possibly who wanted to go home.

"I'm drunk."

"Not me," said Lee. "I might be getting a little bit intoxicated however."

"Yes. You've had too much already," Judy said, striving to take the glass over into her own possession.

"More, bring more. More punch."

She sighed, but then did turn and go off for it after it.

"So now she waits on *you*. Damn! I don't see why she likes you — you aren't anything in this world but a little country shit, green behind the ears."

"Oh? Oh? I reckon as how I can handle you most any time. Want to?"

They glared. Judy came back, leaving a trail of turned heads and mouths hanging open. She had fetched a cup that was even less than half full. Lee could not but smile.

"See? She doesn't want me to get drunk. More, bring more!"

"No, Lee; it's not good for you."

"Look, I can even drink even while I'm dancing."

And did so. It mattered little to him whether music was playing. However, he did wish that Sal would go away instead of following along with his eye glued indecently on Judy. Lee now whispered into her ear:

"Say: I love thee altogether."

"Altogether."

"Adore you."

"Adore."

"Say: I would do anything for you."

"Anything."

He almost fainted. She had a way of whispering that went direct to the dizziness centers of his brain.

"Say: I would take off all my clothes for you."

"All my clothes. But not while you're drunk."

"Now say: Darling, darling, darling, and so forth, until I tell you to stop."

"Darling, darling… Oh! Am I boring you?"

"Actually, he always looks like that," Sal reported.

"Punch, more punch!"

He watched her file away, her hosiery and heels flashing in the dim. He was only distantly aware that the better part of his mind had gone dead. He danced, a long time passing, so it seemed to him, before he saw her again.)

"Judy, Judy."

"I'm here. Do you want to go home now?"

"Absolutely not! Didn't have a real bed, just a goddamn tire."

Her eyes were full of sympathy and yet he also thought he saw a bit of amusement in them, too.

"You don't love me."

"Lee!"

"Punch, more punch."

"No! Do you want me to get Luke? I will."

"Why bother? No, he hates me, too." He smoked with one hand and drank with the other and then, suddenly, burst out blubbering.

"Lee! No, no, no, it's alright, no, baby."

Far away, he saw her vanish into the crowd. This feeling, it resembled certain dreams that he had had. And when he reached for the cup, lo, he beheld that all its contents were gone.

Luke, when he came, came with the impatient look of one who had been torn away all too unwillingly from his lamp and desk.

"Christ. You're looking a little peaked, Lee. Want to go home?"

"Absolutely not! Punch is what I want. No, I *demand* it. And Judy."

"I'm here."

"And punch."

"No, I think you ought to go home Lee. Everybody's tired of you. And that includes me."

More distantly than ever, he realized that he was being stuffed into the wrong coat and then shunted outside where, it seemed to him, Ray was leaning up against a tree and vomiting on the ground. Ray's girl… Lee saw her standing off at a distance wringing her hands.

"Judy!"

"I'm here."

He woke, rolled, tried to sit up. The lamp itself was weak and gave off a grainy sort of light. Luke stopped, set down his pencil, and then turned and studied him calmly. "It's three o'clock in the morning, Lee. Everybody's long since gone home by now, long ago."

"Judy…"

"She's fine."

"Is she asleep?"

"I wouldn't know. Shut up."

Lee looked at him, meditating on his words. "You'd go get her, if you wanted to."

"Shit. Christ. Fuck."

They entered, Luke in his suit and pajama tops and Judy wrapped in a coat. Of all that he loved about her, mostly he loved the way she bent over him, filling the sky with her two brown eyes that seemed miles apart.

"Judy!"

They kissed violently.

"Judy! were you serious? What you said?"

"Well of course! What?"

"'Darling'?"

"Darling, darling, darling, darling."

(Luke had gone back to his place and, pen in hand, was making all efforts to ignore them.)

"And would you hate everybody else in the world if I asked you to?"

"Of course."

"Even your parents?"

She blinked twice, and then came down and kissed him.

"And Luke, would you hate Luke?"

"Luke is good."

"Would you?"

"Alright."

Now he was willing to let her go, he could sleep now. He had only a faint memory of the two of them moving out into the hall and far away.

THIRTY

HE WOKE with the most despicable feeling in his head. Luke was gone.

The second time he awoke (and his head was no better), the sky was red. Painfully, he hobbled on down to the toilet and began micturating so slowly and at such great length that in his exasperation he at last called a halt to it and left the place. That was when he heard the cry:

"Cookie lady!"

He scrambled into his clothes. It was but the second time he had met her, a sad little woman in too many scarves and sweaters. Her nose had a wart on it and her glasses were as cloudy as milk.

"What do you have today Connie?"

"Have?" (She was not fully normal, neither in hearing nor in intelligence.)

"What kind of cookies?"

She thought about it for full seven seconds and then began rifling into the pumpkin-shaped basket that hung from her neck. To Lee, she seemed a perfect medieval type, a vendor of cookies given special permission to occupy a room in the basement of Antioch Hall.

"Oatmeal," she said finally in morose voice, having first selected of the things and bringing it up close to her eye. "Where's Lucien?"

The boys pressed forward, thrusting money upon her. Her famous bags of cookies, they all traded for the same price and yet varied enormously in size and grade. Lee was satisfied to come away with but one single cookie, big as a pie. He went to look in on Ray.

"Still have your hangover?" (Three other boys, one of them from another dormitory altogether, had also chosen this room for their recovery.)

"Want a cookie?"

"No, I don't want a cookie! Go! Nobody asked you to come in here!"

Lee chose to return to his own place. He had been wrong about Luke — in fact the boy was sleeping in the top bunk, his noble head buried in a chemistry text. Looking at him, Lee once more felt a wave of exasperation for his peculiar sleeping methods, the bed freighted with books, bedclothes, toothbrushes, and harmonicas that lay heaped-up in widely separated piles.

"If you can't think *logically,*" Lee said, "and if your bed isn't logical, you'll never really be able to achieve anything."

"What?"

"Logic."

"Goddamn it! I don't wake you when *you* want to sleep."

"I'm not well." (He pointed to his still-intoxicated head.)

"Good. Hey! Connie's been here."

Cookies in hand, he dropped from the upper bunk. Lee watched darkly while he set about brushing his teeth. His bed was a mess, his suit falling apart; his teeth, however, were in peerless condition.

"And I suppose you'll be spending the whole week-end — what? Studying?"

"You should, too."

"There's a whole world out there!"

"I just woke up Lee."

"Someday, you'll be on your deathbed: 'Oh dear, what did I do with my life?'"

"Haven't even had any coffee yet."

"It's like Poe said — that he never could kiss a woman without being aware of the skull behind the face."

Luke turned angrily. "That kind of thing is bad, Lee; I don't like that kind of shit. Poe? I'd like to step on him."

"Think about it."

"I don't want to think about it! *You* think about it."

"I do. All the time."

"Well, count me out." He went to his desk, leaving Lee to stare at the back of his head.

"Just going to sit there, right? All week-end?"

"I'm waiting to hear what you've got in mind. Haven't heard anything yet. Except for a bunch of shit."

"We could go somewhere."

"Go somewhere. I see."

"Go to New York."

"That's real good, Lee."

"We could hitch-hike."

The boy listened.

"Take five dollars, no more."

"What a riot."

"New York and return, middle of the winter, five dollars and no more — think!"

"Christ." They looked at each other wildly. Life was returning — he could feel it. Running to the phone, he called Judy and then, realizing his great error, spent the next half-hour explaining why she couldn't come, too.

They strode to the East, their faces set against a rosy-fingered dawn from out of Grecian literature. Already, Luke was out in front, moving into the sun while piping fearlessly upon his alto harmonica. In honor of his instrument, the boy had put on his grizzled sweater and travel boots and never had Lee seen him more fit and healthy-looking and never more hopeful. He was, in short, the very perfect person to go traveling with. Himself, Lee was holding to his head (hangover) with one hand, and carrying in the other a long-crooked staff of considerable girth.

They cut behind the women's dorm, Lee striving by force of Will to bring Judy to the window where she might have a look at him in his aspect as prodigal and traveler and with a paperbound volume of seventeenth-century pastoral verse in his knapsack.

The town itself lay under winter's curse — silent, abandoned, disfigured with hills of unclean snow. They passed beneath Bernie's place, both going on tiptoe lest they be summoned upstairs to hear more of the man's wisdom, so hard to understand. The bookshop came up, inside it the same canny-looking cashier, the best-read boy in town. Today, his volume was enormous, and he must hold it in both hands.

Here, the town ended. It gave Lee the greatest queasiness to step off of, and down from, the one square-mile in all the world where he was in control and where Judy abided; his headache worsened the moment he crossed the line. Luke, meantime, had taken off his jacket and rolled his sleeves and, in his effort to pick up a ride, was showing a particularly wholesome and naïve face that Lee had not seen in him before. Ahead, nothing but waste. And when he looked behind... The village had become a seventeenth-century scene, a burnt ruin with hogs running at freedom and here and there a few blips of smoke lifting ever so slowly to paradise.

A car came, slowed, hesitated, the driver taking a long cautious look at the pleasantly smiling boy and his foot-long harmonica.

"I'm only going to Springfield," the driver said.

"Every little bit helps — I have to say it."

"Where're you headed?"

"New York."

"New York my ass!" He turned, catching his first view, an unfavorable one, of Lee sitting in the back. They proceeded forward in silence, Luke nodding approvingly at the shaven fields, the wan sun, and the occasional peasant's shack where, sometimes, the peasant himself could be seen singing to sleep in a rocking chair. The hounds, invariably thin, searched the fields in vain. Luke now turned and studied the driver at great length, an examination that went on for a full two minutes.

"So, what's your philosophy?"

"I'm in the distribution business."

"Sounds good. You happy?"

"You fellows from the college?"

"Oh, sure. We're going to be writers. Write about life and stuff."

"I guess there's some pretty strange people at that place — that's what I've heard."

"Oh sure. I'm going with a strange girl right now."

"Your friend doesn't have much to say."

"Not in the daytime. Anyway, there's something very grim about him."

"Why is he carrying that stick?"

"I wouldn't even pay any attention to that. He's in love, you have to realize." And then: "He's still a virgin however. Kind of funny, isn't it? How about you — do *you* have any little children?"

Lee listened. Slowly and slowly, he was coming to realize that his friend could not possibly get through life with his present methods. He did, however, have a good way of smoking; Lee had seen him put a cigarette away in his pocket and then draw it out an hour later still smoldering. Lee had visions of the two of them hiking forever, summer and autumn, youth everlasting, mind out of memory, until time to do it again. Very strange was it — knowing that whereas most people in overwhelming numbers had long ago been shoveled into the ground, yet he himself, and Luke, they were whizzing at high speed over the surface of the brown and lovely, extraordinary earth.

"This is good," Luke said suddenly, apropos of nothing. "You'll have to write about this someday Lee."

"Depend upon it."

"And Phyl can write a play." (The thought seemed to gratify him. Lee watched as the boy now settled back and then, allowing the cigarette to smolder on interminably without any of its substance being lost, put on a satisfied expression because of Phyllis' play.)

They rolled into the outskirts of Springfield, an impoverished district. During the last mile, they had fallen into a serious quarrel that had both of them now reaching for Lee's cane.

"'There are more things in heaven and earth,' dear Lucien, than your little philosophy ever thinks about."

"I know that!" (The man had pulled over some minutes ago and was waiting nervously for them to get out.)

"'The moving finger writes, and having writ, not all your tears can wash out the least bit of it.'"

"Christ!"

Suddenly, Lee swung out of the car, slamming the door with such force that it bounced open again. Now once more, he found himself facing a bleak grey city full of the sort of people who… Too late to go back.

"Lee!"

He slowed.

"I'm hungry."

"We just started!"

"I didn't have any breakfast."

"Breakfast? I haven't eaten in two days!"

"Yeah, but you're funny that way. Me, I'm eating."

"Soft! Soft!"

"A cheeseburger, O.K.?" (His face had an earnest look.)

"Half a cheeseburger for each of us."

"And coffee?"

"Yes, yes. Soft!"

The boy prowled forward, turning almost at once into a dilapidated eatery full of smells where a haunted-looking woman with a spatula, an apron, and a chin full of warts, seemed to have been expecting them. Her gaze settled maternally on Luke who, in his disheveled hair and his face of a ten-year-old…

"And may I have mustard on my half?" he asked.

"And coffee."

The cup was small, a mere dram when compared to what was needed.

"We'd better stock up on cigarettes, too," Luke whispered.

"Can't afford it."

"Yes, you do have a certain hardness, Lee, I admit it. That's why people hate you."

Lee looked off, toward distant hills.

"And so, you plan on getting harder and harder, is that what it is? Winter in the soul? I snap my fingers at it."

And did so. Meanwhile, the woman had shoveled up the meat and was trying very diligently to keep the mustard from running over the mark.

"Are you boys really that hard up? One burger for both of you?"

Lee noticed a calendar on the wall behind her that showed two wolves looking down from a hilltop in winter upon a sleeping village. Without knowing why, the scene, all in blue, impressed itself upon his memory forever.

"Yes, ma'am. Couldn't give us a job, could you?"

"Well…" (They could see perfectly well that she was preparing yet another patty of meat, this one clearly to be handed over to them free of charge.) "Well, things is kind of tight just now," she said. "What sort of work you fellows looking for?"

"Writing novels."

She looked at them. "It's a sin, to make fun of people." Lee found himself gazing upon her red elbows and grey hair piled up in the fashion of thirty years ago. Luke went on:

"What sort of things did you do when *you* were young?"

"Why, we behaved ourselves!" She looked back in exasperation and gave a little snort.

"Your children ever visit you?"

She turned, handing over her gift of a very fine-looking hamburger indeed, a thick one with beads of juice on top.

"Christ, you've got to write this down, Lee: 'She had no customers, and so she gave her food away to bums.'"

Lee nodded and then, seeing that they were waiting for him, took out his pen and composed a sentence on the napkin. The food was good, inordinately so. His headache was waning.

"We have to leave a tip, Lee, we have to," said Luke, once more whispering.

"A nickel."

"No, Lee. A dime."

They paid, hiding the coin modestly beneath the saucer rim. Luke was loath to leave. Finally, at the door, he turned and bawled out loudly, astonishing the woman and frightening away the approaching customer who choose now not to enter after all:

"I hardly ever visit my parents, but that doesn't mean I don't love 'em!"

Springfield was preternaturally silent. It was that time of day when people prefer to go off into little rooms to think about sleep and death. They strode past an old-fashioned grocery, and then a filling station where a black man was just getting into his car. At once, Luke stepped forward and peered inside the vehicle.

"Hi."

The man looked at him worriedly.

"I have to ask it — do you know the best way to New York?"

"New York?"

"Right. We've only got $4.65. Each, I mean."

The car moved forward a few inches. "Which road you looking for?"

"The best one."

"New York?"

"Right. We're hitch-hiking."

"You can't get to New York first. You got to get to some *other* place first. *Then* you get to New York."

"Sounds good. Which place?"

Again, the car rolled forward a brief distance.

"Well, come on, get on in here and we'll look at that map then. Lord, Lord."

In fact, the car was full of tools and lengths of pipe, a paint can and two pair of old trousers. Already, Luke had spotted something on the map and was pointing to it.

"Hold on, now just hold on; you don't know if that's it. Lord!" The man now took out a pair of golden glasses, unfolded them slowly and slowly put them on. From the back, the man's head had a tragic cast.

"You gots to go to Columbus first. See here?"

"Sounds good."

"But you got to get to the highway first. This here," (he pointed to it), "this here is *not* the highway. You got to get to *it* first."

"We'll walk."

"Hold it! I said I'd take you. Lord, Lord, Lord." He removed the glasses, laid them away delicately in cloth of chamois and then, suddenly, lurched out into the road at a speed that, from the looks of him, no one could have expected.

"Christ!"

"I don't like folks smoking in my car, no sir, I... Great God A'mighty, I didn't say you had to put it in your pocket!"

"Is it tough, being a Negro in this town? No, I have to ask." He plucked out the smaller of his two harmonicas. It was a desolate country they were passing, a mere shamble of warehouses, filling stations, and acreages of used cars. Soon enough they were at the broad highway itself, with cars zipping past. They all got out and looked in both directions.

"Now you want to go *that* way," the man said, jabbing with a finger that had one joint too few. "Not this way, *that* way. This way is wrong. Lord, you might end up in California!"

They laughed, all of them. Lee could see in him two teeth of gold and another of platinum along with several others filled with less costly stuff. A half-minute went past. Then:

"Well? You hitching, or not? Do it! Lord, Lord." Suddenly he stepped forward and threw up a thumb that, it too, lacked some distance of being what it should. Lee ascribed it to a life of using some of the perilous tools that he had seen in the car.

Luke followed. With his thumb and with the blast of traffic being what it was… Lee had little faith. Twenty cars flew past. The drivers, a bourgeois people all, pretended not to see them. Lee did spot one small boy offering a nasty face. Far behind, the man was yelling at them and making signals with his hat to show how displeased he was with their technique.

"You try it," said Luke. (He had been wearing a huge vacant smile for the people and now was having trouble getting rid of it.) Lee, on the other hand, had begun to question whether it was for this purpose that he had fallen to earth — to be caught in a supplicating position with his thumb in the air.

"Smile!" Luke called. "You can do it!"

Far behind, the black man had returned to his car and was sitting at the wheel shaking his head. One of the oncoming cars did actually slow, leaving them with the memory of a woman who wore a pitying expression.

"Christ. I have to say it, Lee — I think you ought to hide. It's that stick. They don't like things like that, and neither do I."

"Anything to make you happy." The weeds were tall enough — he hid. At once, a certain blue car, long and expensive, pulled over and opened for them. Or rather, opened for Luke.

"Howdy! Where're you headed?"

"New York."

"New York my foot! Well, get in, get in. Hey!"

"He's with me."

"Oh. But I still don't see why he has to bring that stick. Where're you from?"

"Antioch."

"Antioch! Not a couple of communists, are you? Naw, I'm just kidding. I go to Ohio State myself."

"Oh, yeah? How's the football team doing this year?"

He beamed. "Won the Rose Bowl."

"Hey, Lee! They won the Rose Bowl."

"Good."

"Does your fraternity go to all the games?"

"Sure! Well… not all the out-of-town ones."

"What!"

"Well hell, they go all over the country."

"Hey, Lee! They don't even go to all the games."

"A question of loyalty, I guess."

"Well, hell! Can't go to *all* of them."

"It's up to you." Lee now made himself comfortable, pushing aside the two books and the slide rule in its leathern holster. The light was failing, a familiar process they were abetting by running on at full tilt toward the dark side of the world. Up front, the driver was sulky. By contrast, Luke was looking forward with satisfaction, turning from time to time to stare into the face of any driver who happened to be riding abreast of them.

"Hey, Lee! Now *there's* a tough face. Look at it."

"I've heard a lot about Antioch," the driver said.

"Oh sure. That's why we're going to New York — so we can link up with some communists and Jews."

The oncoming cars, most of them, had switched on their headlights and were streaming westward in a caravan extending from the Atlantic Coast. This was the hour, Lee knew, when Judy would have just left her room and would be padding in her duck-like gait to the cafeteria where she must climb aboard her stool, there to sit full three hours with a tiny shovel in her lap. Suddenly, he realized that Luke was looking back at him wisely, his eyes narrowed to all-knowing slits.

"Judy, right?"

Lee nodded.

"Christ."

"What, is he missing his girl-friend?"

"Oh, he misses her alright. You've never seen a case like this one."

To Lee's chagrin, the driver smiled and giggled. The other boy was playing a sad tune on his reserve harmonica.

They came to Columbus — a bourgeois town — and proceeded straight to the University. Here, Lee saw all manner of people, all of them closely resembling the driver. They shook, Luke and the driver. Lee did not shake. It was Luke who remembered to go back for the staff.

It needed another hour — the sun was gone — before they could return to the highway and then find a car willing to stop for them. This time, it was a battered DeSoto with smoke coming out its tail. Lee ran forward in joy and yanked open the door to uncover three little boys in army uniforms sitting side by side.

"Watch it, shit!"

"Can you give us a ride?"

"Maybe not. Where're you headed?"

"New York."

"New York my prick!"

"But we'd be happy just to get to the next town."

"I don't know." (Lee judged him at twelve, perhaps thirteen years of age.) "Well, piss, git on in, shit, we can't set here all night."

The three boys moved, freeing just enough space for two more to squeeze inside. The car bolted, stopped, and then began moving very slowly, a great clanging noise striking up precisely under Lee's left foot. For some minutes they went on, no one speaking. Next to him, the smallest of the three boys was smoking constantly, holding the cigarette in his extreme fingertips. Lee saw him lift out a bottle (its smell reminiscent of medicine) and take two swigs.

"Gimme some of that shit," the driver said, sticking out his hand for the bottle.

The boy gave, belched, and then sat back with his mouth full of liquor and smoke.

"How far are you going?" Luke asked.

No reply. Lee was beginning to wonder if any of this was happening. He could feel his hangover coming back. It was the second-smallest of the boys, the palest and the most covered with freckles, who turned and, with their noses almost touching, searched Lee's face. He had bad teeth and wore a permanent grimace, as of one who suffered from gas.

"How far we going?"

"Shit, I don't know. Ask him."

"How far?" Lee called up to the driver.

"What?"

"How far?"

"Goddamn it, that's the second time you've hit me with that fucking stick!"

"Certainly, *I* never wanted to bring it," Luke said. "However, I, too, have been wondering…"

"What?"

"… wondering where we're going."

"Shit, I don't know. Ask *him.*"

Lee turned to the man seated next to the driver, an enormous individual whose head — and Lee could see it only from the rear — looked like a bowling ball set on top of a cotton bale.

"How far are we going? Naw, I'm not worried about it."

"What?"

"Where were you headed, so to speak, before you stopped for us? That's what we were wondering."

"What did he say?"

The boy took a swig and handed it to Lee.

"Got any money?"

"Ha! No, no, we just…"

"What did he say?"

"No money, they don't got no money."

"Well shit, that's alright. We don't got any either."

"We got a car."

"That's right. 'Course, we had to steal it to git it."

They laughed, Lee too, and Luke as well, although somewhat less confidently.

"Are you fellows in the Army?"

"Shit, no. Used to be. Show 'em."

The smallest of them now opened his pants, drew down his shorts and showed a vivid scar, jagged as lightning, that originated at belt level and then ran out of sight.

"He served his country, he sure did. That's why he looks that way."

"I wouldn't have thought…"

"Huh?"

"… that he was old enough."

"Yeah, but he used to be lots older. Before that goddamn fucking son-of-a-bitch… Before he got cut up."

Lee nodded. The largest of the three small boys had curled up in the corner and was asleep with his good eye even while his bad one, the one that had filmed over, focused on Lee.

"Might as well just let us out at the next town," Luke said cheerfully. "Anyway, who wants to go to New York?"

"What?"

"I snap my fingers at it." Suddenly, he pulled out his harmonica, creating such a gleam in the dark that two of the three little boys grabbed instinctively for weapons of their own.

"Shit!" (He offered Luke the bottle.) "You ought to be more careful, shit like that. You could git yoreself shot."

"Not me."

"And you, you hit me *one more time* with that fucking stick and…"

"Sorry."

"It's alright. Got any money?"

"Ha! Couple of dollars. At most."

"Couple of dollars ain't going to do you any good."

"Hey! Maybe we could git some more for 'em."

"No, no, you've already done quite a lot already."

Again, the bottle came to Lee, he who required it of himself never to refuse a new experience. The stuff was bad. He followed it up by offering it to the giant man in front.

"Oh, Holy God, don't let him have any of that shit! Goddamn! God Almighty!"

Lee withdrew it at once — the man groaned. It provided the only view that either of them were to have of the person's face, which was highly generalized and perhaps lacked the full number of features.

"God Almighty, don't *ever* let him have any of that shit!"

"Sorry."

"Sorry won't do you no good. You ever seen him drunk? That's the first thing you got to learn, if you're going to be with us."

"Or, you could just let us out right here. What do we care?"

Up front, the driver had turned on the radio and was fuddling with it in a certain slow patience that Lee found to be exasperating. The weather report came on, the voice hoarse with urgency. Lee had no fear of squalls, not at this speed; they were outracing the climate and radio signals both. Akron came on in the person of a dapper man speaking with an exaggerated calmness that might easily lead to sleep. As for the Ohio landscape, they had crashed into a blank zone devoid of homes, agriculture, or even other cars. Music came on, romantic material that caused the giant man to sit up and take notice. Lee saw him tilt his massive head to one side.

"Oh shit, that's *Earth Angel*," the smallest boy said. "Better let him hear it, I guess."

"Right."

"Unless you want him getting all upset again."

They went faster, pulled by radio beams that, this time, were emanating from further east. This very black night, it resembled a solid substance in which first a cat and then an opossum could be seen posturing at the edge of the unfolding highway. A sign came into view.

"Hold it! We got to go back."

"We do?"

"*You* don't got to go back. *We* do. 'Cause we ain't too popular — know what I mean? — in fucking Guernsey County."

"Guernsey? I snap my fingers at 'em."

Luke got out first, Lee second. It was Luke who remembered to draw the staff out after them.

"Well, we certainly do appreciate it. And maybe someday *you'll* need a ride, and we…" (It surprised him that the three little boys, and the two large ones, that they were sticking out some six or seven hands in a last-minute effort to shake with himself and Luke.)

"Just keep on this road — know what I mean? — and it'll take you right to Wheeling."

Luke came back to shake more formally with the large one. Lee shook with the driver, the two of them searching deeply into one another's eyes for the underlying integrity.

"Now just keep on this road — I mean it! — or else you'll sure as hell git lost if you don't."

"Right." Lee shook. "And someday *you'll* need a ride, and…"

"And I shore wouldn't stay in Guernsey County neither, not any longer than you has to. Know what I mean?"

They shook.

"Hey!" said the middle-small one, "let me have one of them long cigarettes you been smoking. You can have two of mine."

They traded. Luke returned and shook with the small one. Himself, the driver reached back and again shook with Lee, a long, steady shake in which each could read the other's whole past and future.

"You'll make it, I got confidence."

"Me too," said the wounded one. "I got confidence, too."

They shook. The music had ended, leaving the giant gazing down sadly at the floor. Finally, the car turned and then, amid a gnashing of gears, began the long, slow, but accelerating travail toward safer ground.

"Christ!" Luke said.

"Naw, I know how to handle people like that. Alabama's full of 'em. What time you got?"

The boy brought his watch up to his eye and tapped at it two or three times. They were walking but without fully realizing just how drastically thin the traffic had now become. One vehicle came over the hill and turned its lights on bright.

"I'm hungry, Lee."

"Forget it. It *is* cold though."

"Certainly, it's cold. How's your headache?"

"I choose to ignore it."

"Yes, that's best. Ready to turn back?"

Lee gasped. In the dim the boy's face had taken on the look of a huge ant suffering from curiosity and hunger. Lee said: "Hell no, I'm not turning back, hell no. Turn back? That's not my style."

"Mine neither. Hell no!"

"The world's full of Guernsey Counties, so-called."

"Oh sure, I know that."

They went forward. The squalls were behind them, so Lee believed, though there might yet be others further up ahead. An unsleeping farm dog had picked them up from a mile away and was yapping untiringly. Lee's mind leapt ahead to the mountains, and then to Wheeling itself and points even further. Certainly, there were a great many bright white shiny stars above frisking in the cold.

"I'd never turn back," Luke was saying. "I try so hard to pursue The Four-Fold Way."

Lee said nothing.

"And the Five Reasonable Virtues."

"We could sleep out under those trees, if we had to."

"They have a dog, Lee."

"Or, we can keep going."

"I can go for days."

"And if it gets too cold…"

"Yes?"

"Socrates used to do some of his best thinking in the cold."

"I know that. It wasn't Ohio, of course."

They went on. Judy was without doubt ensconced in her bed just now, deep into dreams of sunflowers, birds, and he. That was when a car came up without noise and pulled over for them. Lee ran for it, chortling happily, until he saw the insignia on the door.

"'Evening, gentlemen," the man said, employing the ironic tone that Lee could have predicted. "Now just what do we got here exactly — some kind of Mutt and Jeff act? It's a wee bit late, isn't it, to be out on the highway? This time of night?"

"It *is* late," said Luke. "There's no denying that." (Three times he tapped at his watch.)

"Where're you headed?"

"New York."

"New York my rear end! In the first place, you aren't even supposed to be hitching on this road. This is a *superhighway* boy — can't you see that?"

They looked at it.

"It is broad, certainly," Luke admitted. "From here to over there. How do we…?"

"Get off? Maybe you shouldn't ought to have never gotten *on*, hm?"

He did have a leathery look to him; his voice, however, lacked that utterly toneless quality affected by people in the highest authority.

"Well, we're almost out of Ohio, aren't we?"

"Not hardly, no sir. No, you're still in *my* territory."

"Good. We're looking for work actually and…"

"Going to New York to look for work?"

"Sure. I realize you've probably never seen two such people like us. And I wouldn't blame you." (He offered the man a cigarette.) "We've only got five dollars."

"You won't get far with that, not in New York. But what's the business with that stick?"

"Just the kind of person he is. He'd probably throw it away if you asked him."

He did not, however, Lee, throw it away, not when he was faced with a man who had two guns. More than that, there was also a rifle fixed to the dashboard and next to that a radio of tremendous complexity, with dials and buttons enough for a rocket ship. The man was continually putting forth his gloved hand and massaging with great love the leather-encased gear knob. His many rings, they must have been five sizes too large. For only in this way could he wear them *over the glove*. The other hand, the one he saved for his revolver, was housed in a holster of snake skin with fringe on it. Indeed, the entire cabin was imbrued with the smell of leather and lotion, ammunition and oil.

"This is an interesting car," said Luke. "One could practically live in here."

"I just about do."

"You like to work at night?"

"More action," said the man.

"I can understand that — action. You happy?"

That moment, the radio broke in with a static-ridden monologue uttered in a panicked voice. The man listened, his eyes darting.

Suddenly, he grabbed up the microphone and held it near to his lips, but could think of nothing to say.

"Just tell 'em you're on the case," said Luke. "Want *me* to tell 'em?"

Instead, after another minute of thought, the man pushed the button and spoke, producing a hollow sound full of static.

They crossed the line at high speed and shortly later butted up against Wheeling itself, a cantilevered town that floated on three different stages among sharp-pointed hills — Lee was enthralled.

"Alright now — hear me! — I don't want to catch you two hitchhiking out here ever again. Not while *I'm* on duty!"

"No, no."

"I'm not kidding!"

"I know you're not. I can tell."

"Alright then. Now you keep your noses clean, you got that?" (Clearly, he adored these last-minute admonitions. Lee would have said that he had a vocation for it.) "I mean it! And I'm not somebody you want to fool around with neither!"

"Whew! I never fool around, not anymore."

"Well alright then."

They shook — the man's glove was also oiled — and then moved out onto the bridge. Below was a black river, petroleum seemingly, on which a tiny boat was struggling upstream with what, at this hour, Lee divined to be a contraband of some type. He looked for, and found, an evil-looking oriental person standing in the bow under lantern light. Ahead were mountains, smoke coming off the summits, and higher still, the stillborn moon itself.

"Just think," said Lee. "Once over this bridge and there's no turning back."

"How do you mean, 'no turning back'?"

"Well! Not literally, of course."

"I'm very glad to hear it. You hungry?"

"Or, think of it like this, that this is only the first of the ten thousand such expeditions that we'll be taking, you and me."

They grinned. Luke's grin, however, had some uncertainty in it. "Those shits back at school, they wouldn't know what to make of it."

"Exactly. They can't stand up to it. We can."

They smoked. The bridge was high, the wind cold, the stars delighted.

"I feel like I could jump off this bridge just now and go flying."

"And fly? Don't do it, Lee."

"Why not! We'll never be this young again, never. Moreover…" (He had not seen that the boy was urinating, a tremendous drop of three hundred feet and more into the black river itself.)

"The moon's gone."

"Then we'll travel by starlight! That's the way it should be."

They crossed slowly, even into a hilly place dotted with little colored houses sitting at different levels. Lee noted especially a narrow home with turfen roof and teetering chimney, the very place where a jolly widow with infinite children might properly reside.

"But look at this one," Luke said, pointing to a house made out of fossils and decorated with broken glass. "What a funny place!"

They were stepping lightly, as not to awaken any of the dwarfs sleeping in beards and nightcaps behind candy walls. The moon had come back after all and now was sitting athwart the hill; it needed only someone with the temerity to go up straightway with a crayon and sketch in the requisite face. Next, he descried a wobbly house with either a vane or, possibly, a living cock posturing on the gable. Very easily could he envision the veteran or retired coal miner who lived inside, an old man in a robe who had selected this moment to get out of bed and again take down, the thousandth time he had done so, his hoard of old photographs.

Luke, meantime, had moved well out in front and was pushing face-first into the swirling night. Watching him, Lee could foresee how someday he must go falling over the edge of the world, feet still peddling forward while he tumbled ever so slowly through time and space with the same good-intentioned expression on his face. What

Lee did not know, and would not have credited, was that this boy's stay on earth was already nine-tenths over.

"Luke!"

They came into the heart of the town to find the shops closed and all lights extinguished. One single restaurant was open, and in it a tiny bald-headed man suffering either from boredom or extreme depression. Together, they filed in embarrassedly and settled at the nearest table.

"I figured I heared somebody out there, but I didn't know who it was!"

"You still don't."

The man stood and got into his apron. "What you boys going to have?"

"Cheeseburger!" said Luke. "Two of 'em. And could you put mustard on my two halves?"

The man wrote it all down at great length. Luke had begun to speak of the gift burger of yesterday and of the very good woman who had given it to them. The man listened to the end but made no such offer himself. Luke waited till he was gone before taking off his own watch, reading it, and then rapping violently with it across the table. By contrast, Lee was watching a faint pink blush in the sky where he thought the sun was likely to rise. A crashing sound came from the kitchen followed by a loud noise of coughing and cursing. Nor was it the real sun that now slowly came up over the mountains but only that "false dawn" of which he had read. It came and went, leaving it even blacker than before.

"What time is it?"

"January, Lee; that's all I can tell you. Nineteen and fifty-seven."

The man came. He had the burgers; unfortunately, one of them had fallen and been pieced back together with toothpicks driven in at various angles.

"You fellows aren't from around here, are you? I knew you wasn't."

"Because of the way we look? No, we're just traveling through. Trying to experience things, meet unusual people."

"Why?"

"So, Lee can write about them."

The man came forward into the light. "Well, you won't find anything like that going on around here. I run a *clean* place, decent."

"Yeah, but of course we can't just take peoples' word about stuff like that," said Lee, taking out a pencil and beginning to write a report on a paper napkin.

"Hey, what you boys up to! The state inspector was here just last month!"

"You happy?"

"Say what? I'm *always* happy. Look at me!"

Lee made a note.

"I'm happy. Hell, wait till *you're* sixty."

Dawn, with rosy-colored fingers… In fact, it remained black in the place where the sun ought long ago to have arisen. Luke, meanwhile, was humming cheerfully, smoking, bobbing up and down and, by dint of some odd physics that Lee could not much sympathize with, was making tree frog noises on his harmonica.

They found a road but had to cross two fields (pushing aside the cows) to get to it. With great relief Lee saw now that the sun *would* arise, and in the usual place. Suddenly, the first beam broke over the horizon and, traveling with inconceivable speed, went right past them and into the hills. Dogs yelled, roosters shrieked. The second beam, aiming lower, smashed into the silo with a shaft of light.

Night was over; Lee immediately began to feel sleepy. For five long minutes, the sun continued to tear away at the roots that held it to the horizon, a struggle that remained in doubt until finally it was able to float freely in space.

"Everything looks very differently now," said Luke, laughing and looking off across what proved to be, not the end of the world, but rather a long level meadow with a tower lying in ruins.

"It's differently over here, too," said Lee. (He could see a farmhouse materializing out of fog.) In this region, the highway had fallen into desuetude, with weeds punching through the crannies. So far as he could see, not one single countryman had consented as yet to rise from slumber and expose himself to a dawn as iridescent as this. Nor had night itself entirely left the stage, not while so many "tatters" of it continued flapping in the barren trees.

The first car of the day! In fact, it was a truck. Already Luke had taken off his jacket and rolled his sleeves and, putting on his most wholesome look, was standing in its path. The man slowed and squinted, striving to determine what nature of men these might be.

"Where y'all trying to git to?"

"New York," said Luke. "But we're *from* Antioch."

"I'll be jiggered. Well…" (He looked into the distance — he was shy — and rubbed his whiskers.) "I can take you to Pittsburgh."

Pittsburgh! Lee reeled. And this time, for Pittsburgh's sake, he took the seat in front.

"Do you like this?" Luke asked. "Morning time? No, it's really beautiful. You're a farmer, right? Tell me if I'm wrong."

"We have a little place."

"Little place! Aw, Christ, all my life I've wanted to be a little farmer. What, do you have a bunch of horses and ducks, things like that?"

The man looked at him.

"And your wife — what, does she wear one of those little bonnets all around? Boy!"

"She's with the gas company."

"And pigs! I have to ask: do you have one of those slop buckets?"

The man slowed. He appeared to be tired, needed a shave, and wore nonagricultural-looking glasses. "We raise beans mostly."

"'Raise.' Hear that, Lee? What else do you 'raise'?"

"Beans mostly. Soybeans."

"I should think you'd get tired of them."

The farmer began to speak, but then changed his mind.

"I'm surprised you haven't said anything about the way we look. Most people won't even stop for us."

"I seen it."

"Think *we* could be farmers?"

"You shore don't want to get into farming. No, sir."

"But I do! You ever read *Growth of the Soil*? That's what I'd like — be real simple and not afraid to walk around in the shit all day."

Silence. Luke looked at him. "You happy?"

As promised, they were carried all the way to modern Pittsburgh and then turned loose on a green sward that looked down, and into, a maze of shiny white buildings. To Lee, it was the biggest city he had ever seen.

"I'm not surprised," he said. Then: "The size of it!" And then: "It seems to be made out of crystal."

"Yes, yes, and now you've seen a big city. Ready to turn back?"

"It makes you wonder: how many great writers has this place produced? I just don't know."

"It's only a city, Lee. Christ, I was conceived in a city bigger than this one."

"And the women!"

"You've got a woman. Besides, these women would made mincemeat out of you."

"How do you get in?"

"Just go up and knock, I suppose. However, I don't recommend it."

But Lee was not listening. "There's even more things here than in Toledo — I can sense it."

"Yes. Evil things. Me, I'm going back." And in fact, he did take one step, immediately following it up with another.

"What are you doing!"

"I'm gone."

Lee caught him. "We're going to New York, Goddamn it! No, we're going even further than that!"

"I'm hungry, Lee. It's Sunday. We've only got three dollars! And you're a grim bastard, too. I've already been to New York. You like cities so much? There's one!" (He pointed to the city that was just in front of them.) "And tomorrow I have a test."

"Test? Test? God Almighty, we don't have time for tests! Sometimes... Aw, I don't know. Makes me mad!"

Luke grinned. Lee now suddenly for the first time observed that the boy was transporting a bundle under his belt, a full quire of very sloppy-looking manuscript held together in newspaper and twine.

"What...!"

"It's my epic, Lee. I wanted to try and peddle it to one of the great publishers in New York."

"Good." (He thought it might motivate the boy to go forward still; instead, he watched with horror as his roommate simply set the manuscript by the roadbed and walked away from it.)

"Maybe it'll serve as an inspiration to someone. A hobo or traveler."

"The wind's blowing it all away!"

"So? Let it inspire the wind."

They raced across campus, slowing only when they came within the shadow of Antioch Hall.

"These little bourgeois shits, they wouldn't have lasted ten minutes with us."

"Everything is so comfy in their little world."

"They just can't stand up to it, the things that we stand up to."

"Nobody can."

"And now, the girls."

They raced for it, arriving under the window just as the moon came out. Luke tapped twice, waited, and then drew out his harmonica.

Phyllis came first. "Oh God. Them."

Judy came second. "Lee! What happened!"

"Aw, it was horrible, Tweedy; we almost got killed."

"Oh, you poor thing!"

Abandoning the staff, both now climbed in through the opening. Phyllis, grinning irrationally, had gotten into her robe and gone back to reading. Judy made tea.

THIRTY-ONE

EVERY NIGHT HE ROSE AGAIN AS SOON AS DARKNESS FELL, and every night a lamp was glowing in the parlor. Night after night he knocked, until one or another of the girls came and slammed the door in his face or, as happened sometimes, actually went off to summon Judy for him.

Every night, drawn by habit, they drifted to the couch and then for the next hour kissed and whispered and gasped until the better part of her former lipstick was rather on him. Or, he might grab up one of her hands and look at it at close range. Outrageous, it seemed to him, that she had been pushed forward into life with such tiny equipment, as if she were not already in danger enough for being the open and wide-eyed person that in fact she was.

"Look at that hand. Now what can you expect to accomplish with something like that?"

She looked at it. "What's wrong with it?"

"Too small! You can't do anything with that."

"Never mind!" (She snatched it back.) "I can do very well."

They fought for it. He did so enjoy tickling her in his scientific fashion, until she was struggling and laughing and sputtering at the same time. They kissed. Two girls came in, observing it with great disgust.

"May I come to your room?" he asked, once they were alone.

"No!"

"Please."

"Alright."

They parted with formality, even to the extent of shaking hands in the doorway. Outside, he moved in dignity, and then suddenly turned and ran behind the building where she stood waiting at the window. They kissed. That was when he saw that Luke had arrived before him.

"Luke! Why aren't you at your desk?"

The boy lifted his head wearily, as if to ward away all such questions. "You're lucky," he said. "Judy loves you. But Phyllis here, she doesn't love anybody. And never will."

"I'm attached to you — isn't that enough?"

Lee looked at her. She was sitting in the corner and had her legs jutting out askew, mere sticks as they seemed, with sores and bruises on them.

"Now look," said Lee, "he didn't have to start romancing you — it was his choice."

"There's no feeling in her, Lee. Just a brain."

The girl turned slowly. Again, she was wearing her blond hair pulled back tightly, giving her a look of oriental cruelty. The face itself, with prominent nose and chin, was preternaturally serene.

"I never asked him to care about me."

Lee could feel his gorge rising.

"Look at this," said Luke, who turned and hit her a good blow on her thin upper arm. "See? It doesn't even register on her."

"*I* could register on her."

"Go ahead! Be my guest. She doesn't care."

Lee's gorge was high. The girl was lying awkwardly, her face pointed toward the ceiling. Suddenly — and he had never struck a girl before — he smote her in the ribs, a much harder blow that he had planned.

"Lee!"

"Christ!"

"I'll break her goddamn neck for her."

"Look at her. She doesn't care."

"It's not natural."

They sank down, all three, and studied her. She had two thin volumes, a pen, and a comb of antique ivory.

"Maybe if we threw a bowl of cold water in her face… "

"No." (Judy.)

"Maybe…"

"Yes?"

"If she were to get drunk…"

"Yeah!"

"Oh, God. I'm alright!"

"You're not, Phyl."

"Bobbie has whiskey. Lots."

Bobbie joined them but was content to sit at the desk and watch. Finally, after mixing the rum with water, Luke came forward with a steeping glass of the stuff and proffered it to the girl who had sunk yet deeper into her state. Judy, plainly very worried, continued to wring her hands.

"She won't open her goddamn mouth!" Luke noticed.

"Good Lord," said Lee. "You don't *ask* her to get drunk. You *make* her."

"No, wait," said Judy, taking the glass. "Now Phyl… Phyl! Can you hear me? It's good! See?" (She drank.)

"See? Judy likes it."

"God. I'm alright!"

"You're not, Phyl. Not really."

Bobbie moved closer.

"Maybe if we put a goddamn funnel in her mouth…"

"No, Lee. We must be shrewd about this."

"This is all very well," said Bobbie, "but I need to know who's paying for the liquor."

"Christ! She's trying to read again."

Indeed, the girl was reaching ever so slowly for one of the three little volumes. Her choice, apparently, was French poetry. Lee moved it out of reach.

"More whiskey. Show her, Judy."

Bobbie came closer. Two other girls had appeared in the doorway and were watching, one with indignation and the other with delight.

"Men in the dorm — that's against the rules."

"Oh, shut up. It's just Lee."

"Rules are rules."

Lee looked at her, his gorge acting up again.

"It's not as if I couldn't have had a real girlfriend," Luke said.

Bobbie came nearer.

"Show 'em, Judy."

"I'm counting to ten, and if there are still boys in this room… I'll just have to tell Edna about it."

"Look, I've already hit one girl tonight. Think about it."

"I've had girlfriends," said Luke, "more than you could count. And I'm about as good-looking as you could ever wish to see."

"You forgot to mention your I.Q. Watch it! she's going for the book again."

He saw Edna appear in the doorway, a tall, pinched, rectitudinous woman with her hair up in curlers. She wore two robes, one yellow and dirty, the other dirty and blue.

"You were right, Rita, it's men in the dorm alright." Suddenly she clapped hands, making an explosive sound. "Alright, out, out, out! Right now!"

Lee looked at her. His night of kissing had turned into a congestion of ugly-looking girls with no make-up, no jewelry, their coiffeurs in ruins. One indeed had a white cream on her face, a plaster mask with fissures in it.

"Gad."

Bobbie came nearer.

"Out! Out! Out! You too, Luke."

"Look, we're trying to do some good here, and now you come along and…"

"I'm counting to five. And if you two fellows are still here…"

"Five! Meg used to give us ten."

"… three… four… "

There was no help for it — she was older than the rest of them and invested with a certain authority that had come down to her. They left. But first, Lee, putting on his bored look, lit a cigarette, doing it slowly.

"… fourteen… fifteen…"

"I just hope you come down to *my* part of the country someday," Lee informed her. "This 'style' of yours, it just wouldn't work down there."

Now he left, leaving the words to echo in her ears.

He went straight to the cafeteria and, putting on his expression, sat at a table next to the existentialists. His clothes were as wretched as theirs, his hair as long. They, however, had passed into and through the age of love and had come out in cynicism on the other side. He observed one girl sitting so carelessly that he could have seen more than he wanted, had he wanted to see it. Instead, he tossed the hair out of his eyes and lit a cigarette. The fog was coming back; it made of Antioch Hall an undersea cathedral, its towers weaving in the current. He gave thanks to the music and thanks to the dim, thanks to the coffee and gratitude for having been set down amid a book-loving people, never mind how cynical.

He trudged homeward, stepping carefully amongst pools of molten snow. He had had his fill of it, winter, and nothing that he had seen or done could convince him otherwise than that this was essentially an uninhabitable part of the world, a nation of nose-blowers and snow-shoe manufactories; nor was he so certain whether those be mittens he saw on all sides, or whether an adaptive mutation. And how he longed for the companionship of crickets! — he could not sleep without them. But mostly, he longed for the supreme combination of Judy on one side and on the other, "moonlight through the pines."

Luke was at his desk, a long dark muffler wrapped three times about his neck.

"It's not a good situation, Lee. They've been kicked out of the dorm."

Lee stopped. "When you say 'kicked out'…"

"They think Phyl's going to kill herself. And so, they locked them out. Judy's drunk."

"I see, yes; nothing surprises me anymore. Goddamn it! Alright, I warned 'em, and now I'm going to kill *every last one of them!*" (He owned a shotgun; unfortunately, it was in Alabama. He wasted nine seconds searching for it in his Ohio closet.)

"It's true, Lee; they're living downtown now. In the church."

"When you say 'church'…"

"They took their things with them."

"Oh good. Goddamn it! What 'church'?"

The boy named it, whereupon Lee dropped downstairs, walked out into the yard and then, hitting the shadow of Antioch Hall, broke into a run.

The church was dark, old, soot-covered, and looked as if it had not been used in centuries. And when he opened, a certain volume of sanctified air escaped past him into the night.

Up front, he saw the altar where calves were sacrificed each Sunday — such was his aversion to such places — and their entrails interpreted. He inched forward, satisfying himself that the girls had not bedded down in the pews themselves. In a place like this, he could go on for days, probing deeper and deeper into the maze. He lit a cigarette, but then had to draw upon it constantly in order to produce even the smallest light. He saw a band of light showing beneath one of the doors. He called:

"Tweedy?"

No answer. The light went off.

"Phyllis?"

The light came back on. He could very definitely hear whispering behind the door. Finally:

"What do you want? Or rather: who are you?"

"Is that you, Phyl?"

"Why do you ask?"

"It sounds like you."

The light went off.

"Enter."

And did so, catching sight, first, of Judy sitting in the corner. Her bottle was not yet half-empty and yet, judging from her, she seemed more than half-drunk.

"Hi!" she said. He determined that she was dressed in pajamas that bore a pattern of little brown bears, each bear dressed also in pajamas that showed yet further bears.

"We're going to bed now," Phyllis described. "And so, if you'll be so good as to leave…"

"They can't just kick you out of the dorm! Rules are rules."

"They took a vote. Besides, it's quieter here."

Lee looked at them. They had chosen the kindergarten for their new quarters with the result that they were surrounded by toys and giant-sized blocks with letters on them. Among it, Lee saw Phyllis' few poor possessions — three thin volumes, pen, a comb of antique ivory. The girl herself was crocheting happily and in no way resembled any sort of person that might wish to destroy herself. Lee went to Judy and, while Phyl looked away, gathered her up in his arms. She was soft and smelled of fennel and honeysuckle, she who smelled the way she ought and who came up no higher than she should.

"Oh, baby."

"I know, I know."

"Let's go for a walk, you and I. Spring, I think" — he looked at his watch — "is almost here."

They walked hurriedly down to where the town pressed upon the countryside and beyond. Lee pointed:

"That way lies Springfield," he said, "and points further."

She looked, shielding her eyes. By comparison with the moon, the stars were not especially bright tonight. "All the great writers of the past, that's where they've gathered."

"On the moon?"

"Just so."

She looked. As drunk as she was, and tilting so much to one side… Lee went on:

"You'll have to do as I say, of course, now that we're in love. Oh, I'm not saying it's fair."

She nodded sadly.

"However, it's only for a little while."

"Until you're twenty-three?"

"Right."

A dog came up out of the shadows, a small black and white animal with two vestigial wings (hardly more than stumps), that had no further utility of any kind. Judy, in her condition, saw nothing unusual in it.

"And now, soon, spring will be coming in."

"When, Lee?"

"Well! Look there, for example."

But first, they had to watch while a great horrible thing, awesome in size, crept past the moon in guise of a cloud. Spring followed hard upon. Looking at it, the girl brightened; Lee, on the other hand, was looking at the girl. Young was she, pretty, too, but he could never shut out the foreknowledge of the little old woman inside already practicing with shawl and high-button shoes. She grinned, offering up to him an eighteen-year-old face in which he could have wandered for years through gorgeous scenery, coming at last to stand at the edge of an inky pool under smoke with comets overhead.

THIRTY-TWO

TWENTY-FOUR HOURS LATER, winter came back again, the third time it had done so. Finally, on a Friday, all four of them went crowding into a tiny office situated on the top floor of what once had been a private home. Luke coughed once, doing it politely. Clearly, the woman was not pleased to see them.

"Now, this conference is between me and between Phyllis. You other people will have to leave." She had a northern style of speaking, abrupt and cold.

Luke held up his hand. "We promise to keep quiet."

"It's not your 'quiet' I want, but your absence."

Judy spoke up: "This is my roommate we're talking about!"

"And I don't permit smoking in my office."

"O.K., we promise not to smoke."

The woman sighed deeply and looked out over the lake where until yesterday an unruly squad of swan had been crisscrossing in pursuit of bream. Lee, who could not abide her, stared back unblinkingly with his "dead eyes" expression. As to Phyllis, this was by no means one of her better days; Lee looked for, and saw, that her nails had been chewed down to the bleeding point. And then, too, she had a way of abstracting herself out of her surroundings, leaving only a husk behind.

"How about it, Phyllis — should they go? Or stay? It's up to you."

No answer. She had put on an odd smile, as if she were seated at her easel.

"So be it then. And now, Phyllis, let's start by..." (She stopped, waiting until Luke had left off blowing and had returned the thing to his pocket.) "...start by discussing your grades. They're not terribly good, you know, not at all, no. And yet, you came to us with every recommendation. And your scores! You're so very talented, why aren't your grades any better than they are?"

"She's been busy," said Judy.

"And me," said Luke. "You should see my scores."

Lee continued staring. He had seen this type before — too weak to get into a dead eye contest with someone like himself.

"Phyllis?" (Her smile had not gone away.)

"If you don't like her grades, why not just come on out and say so? Want *me* to tell her?"

"Phyllis?"

"Anyway, she's doing something lots more important than grades. Five hundred years from now, nobody will care what grades she made."

The woman sighed. She had decorated her office, not with pictures and books, but certain brass plaques and athletic trophies.

"You've just got to pull yourself together Phyllis. We're patient, we're not patient forever."

"Patient? How many languages do *you* speak? She knows Italian better than English!"

"Because there are a great many other young men and women, Phyllis, who would just love to come to this institution. Phyllis? And I'm sure they'd strive to make good grades, if they had the opportunity you've had."

"Show me these 'men and women,'" said Luke. "I spit on 'em."

"Self-indulgence — it's no good, Phyllis. Buck up! You can do it. Phyllis?"

Lee moved slightly, there where his burning gaze fell full into the woman's face. She had been a champion softball player in her time and now came equipped with a man's watch and shoes and wore her hair shorter than Luke's.

"Well, this is going nowhere. And so, I… Would you kindly…!" (Luke put it back.) "And so, I think we're going to have to insist. Phyllis? Instead of going away next quarter to earn money, no, I think you should stay right here, that's right, and finish up your course work."

Phyllis grinned.

"See? *I* still have faith in you. Phyllis?"

"She's tired," said Judy.

"It's the weather," said Luke.

Lee moved. He hoped still for the woman to glance his way; instead, she sat with folded arms, quite muscular ones, her eye upon that place where the swans might, or might not, ever come back again.

Judy's interview, her first, took place three doors down. It was a merry woman, this one; she waved them all inside, even going so far as to catch Phyllis by the hand and drag her in as well.

"Phyllis and Judy too — I've heard so much! Which one is Lee?"

Lee stepped forward, smoking, his face painted over in arrogance — until he realized that she wanted only to congratulate him. They shook.

"Alabama?"

"Yes, ma'am."

"No, that's alright. But when's the wedding?"

They looked at each other — Luke, Judy, Lee, and the woman. Finally:

"No, ma'am; it wouldn't be fair to her, a wedding. I don't plan on being around — know what I mean? — for real long."

"'Die young and make a good-looking corpse'?"

"Hey! that's good, Lee. Write it down."

"James Dean, he…"

"Yes, I know about him. Good, good. But it's Judy I especially wanted to talk to."

Judy waited, her eyes narrowed in suspiciousness.

"So, you're Judy."

"Sure," said Luke. "Right there."

"I don't know why I asked. But it isn't that you're so beautiful really, is it?"

Lee stood.

"No, not beautiful. You may, however, be the *cutest* thing I've ever seen. Come here, child. Look at that!"

"I know," said Lee.

"Eighteen. No wonder they hate you. And now I'm going to give you something." She lifted her purse off the floor and began furrowing in it, finally taking out several larger coins before she came to what she wanted — a little broach with a picture of some scenery on it made from butterfly wing. "And now, if he's ever mean to you — but he won't be — why then just wear this pin and…"

Judy took it and immediately passed it over to Lee to whom indeed it seemed to have some of the same "lake-under-smoke-and-moon" loveliness of Judy herself.

"I'd *never* be mean to her. As long as she does what I say."

The woman laughed merrily. Clearly, this was the best of all possible advisers, she who had no advice to give. Moreover, as if that were not enough, she offered each of them a cup of coffee.

"And you're Luke."

"Sure."

"And you all defend one another — am I right? Stick up for each other?" (She laughed happily. Lee divined that at one time she had defended someone, and been defended in return.) "But I must tell you, the time will come when… Don't listen to me. When you'll have to do it on your own. No, no, no, not you, Lee; I realize you're here only temporarily. And so, we come back to Judy. Judy?"

Judy listened.

"Your grades…"

"I've been busy."

This time, the woman roared. "*Very* busy, *n'est-ce pas*? Well, you're all very charming. I wouldn't give a nickel for your futures however. Oh well, who cares about that? And now leave me, I think I'm going to be depressed."

They piled out, but then immediately after came back for Phyllis. Outside, winter was losing; Lee could see places where the grass was reviving even as he looked. But when he turned to Judy, thinking to speak, lo, he found her dressed in a butterfly broach.

THIRTY-THREE

HE HAD SEEN ANTIOCH in the fall and seen it in winter and now the breeze was scattering the topmost leaves of Luke's manuscript heap. Lee came nearer. The boy's hair looked like a garden of weeds in which a few particularly egregious things had shot up higher than the rest.

"It's time to go see the girls."

"I've got a test Lee."

"And yet, you can see as well as me the way things are out there."

"The weather? Best to ignore it Lee."

"Did you know that someday you're going to wake up and — 'Hey! I'm thirty years old!'"

"Aw, Christ."

"I'm counting: one… two… three…"

Judy was in her window, blinking. Lee looked for (but could not find) any pathetic little shovel that might be in her lap.

"Tweedy!"

She screamed, very nearly tumbling out into the field.

"Come on, hurry, hurry, hurry. Spring is here and 'the bird is on the wing.'"

"Good grief! What 'bird'?"

"Hurry! You see how it is out here."

"I have a test."

"So did he. Hurry! You want to wake up someday and: 'O dear me! Where did the time go?'"

"No."

"And now, Phyllis."

She was in her favorite of all places, propped-up in bed in semi-darkness, the infirmary's only patient.

"Hurry!"

"Oh God. I was fine, until you showed up."

"Hurry! You can't escape reality forever, not in spring."

"He's right, Phyl."

"I'm not budging."

Lee could feel his gorge begin to rise. "Goddamn it! Alright, listen to this."

> When in summer, everyday
> is like a drawing by a child.

"Oh God!" She looked to heaven, smiling in spite of herself.

"So hurry."

"She's sick, Lee!"

"Hurry, hurry, hurry, hurry."

They moved down the walk. Luke was leading while Phyllis, moving backwards, gazed about in delight at all the things that spring had wrought.

"It *is* lovely, I admit it." She recited:

> Let us take another expedition
> down the way a mile or two.
> For look, we are but minute creatures
> hurtling through light and space,
> and you see the hills are blue.

In front, two boys had come to a stop and were watching contemptuously.

"Ignore them. They probably think we're odd."

"We *are* odd."

"Beat the shit out of 'em! There's four of us."

"No, Lee. Five hundred years from now, nobody will know they ever existed."

They went on. Phyllis, with renewed good health, was stepping forward like a stork while picking up faint distant music that no one else could hear. In front, the glen seemed darker than usual, the result of its manifold new leaves. They went apart, Luke and Phyllis moving to the stream and across it, and then meandering down into their own special hollow. Lee led his girl to the crest of the hill, there where the five brightly painted pennants of Antioch Hall could be seen furling in the wind.

"I'm thinking you don't love me as much as yesterday."

"Oh! I love you so much my bones hurt."

"O.K., *why* do you love me?"

"You're good."

"Nope, that's not it."

They left the trail and then entered a wooded chamber carpeted with leaves. Beautiful was she, serene, too, and yet he could feel a sadness tugging at him — the certain knowledge that she was the last of her kind, the strain that had come down from his grandmother through Grecian Penelope and one or two others.

"I love thee." He lay next to her and then, propping his head, began to read in her eyes. "How does it feel, being Judy?"

"O, I don't know. Cloudy, I suppose."

"No! You seem very clarified to me. Look at those eyes."

"But how does it feel…?"

"To be Lee? You don't want to know."

"I do, too."

"Well… Bad. Like being in a dungeon."

"Oh, you poor thing!"

She clutched him, soothing him with little pats of her hand. "But now everything's going to be better."

Lee nodded. He especially loved to look into her brown eye, lucid beyond compare.

"What do you see in there?"

"The future. No! The past."

"Tell me."

"Mountain tops. Lake. Fields of fennel."

"'Fennel'? There's no such word."

"And the moon."

"His 'own special star'?"

"Exactly. And the oceans. Or rather the ocean as it was ten billion years ago, in the incredible Silurian Age."

"And Penelope?"

"That, too."

She shivered happily.

"And what about me — you see anything in there?"

She searched deeply, frowning into his eye. "I see a dog. Real sneaky-looking."

"What!"

"And dwarfs. And monkeys."

Lee groaned, rolled away and then, after watching the sun-wheel for a time, began reciting:

When in summer, everyday
is like a drawing by a child.
So, could we not, once more
before I go away,
lie upon this hill and watch
where bees are working in the field?

She sighed happily. Behind her (Lee had not wanted to say anything), a millipede was struggling valiantly to hold ten roistering centipedes at bay. Further, in the tree itself, a large green spider was slowly and despondently rolling up its web until next winter. Lee went on:

Now one last time
tell me how it was to be,
and then wish for me the courage of a child
setting out to sea.

She smiled. The sun being what it was, he could have slept for years in her lap.

"Will you visit me in Chicago?"

"Certainly. Shoot, I could practically walk there from Toledo."

"No, you won't visit and you won't write, and it will be like last time."

"Judy! Everything has changed since then. For example, you didn't call me 'darling' in those days."

"Darling, darling, dearest darling."

He reeled, and then pulled her down and kissed her avidly. "Just think — we'll soon be making love to each other!"

"When we're nineteen?"

"Maybe even sooner than that."

She thought about it, blinking.

"Naw, you don't have to worry, I've read about it. Look at that sun!"

"I know."

"And the next time it goes down…"

"No, Lee."

"… you'll be in Chicago."

"I can't stand it."

"And I'll be in Toledo once again."

IV

THIRTY-FOUR

JUDY AND THE CITY, enormous city, sun pouring through the window. And because she was in her woman's clothes (a light grey shirt, pearls, heels, hose and all of it), because of that, Lee had not yet found time to dash outside and take his first look at the town itself.

They were sitting across from each other in the Chicago train station in March, 1957, with sun pouring through the window. Lee looked at her, saying very little. The girl was smoking, and in her grey suit she looked like just such a one as might be seen stepping along smartly to a lecture or concert even. And in truth, Lee was intimidated; never had he seen her in her own native milieu, a city as big as this one. He turned, catching a prosperous-looking middle-aged man appraising her with an expert eye. Lee glared back, using his "eyes-on-stalks" expression, a procedure that seemed to have no effect whatsoever.

"Chicago!" he said. "I've read about this."

"Are there lots of great writers here?"

He thought. "Nelson Algren is in there" — he pointed — "somewhere. Hey! maybe we should go visit him!"

"No, Lee, please. He doesn't even know who we are." She watched with concern as he swaggered to the booth and, using his bored expression, began splashing through the pages of the directory. The name was there; Lee dialed, realizing only belatedly that he might actually be interrupting the man in the middle of a paragraph, an important one. Furthermore, another person had joined the prosperous-looking middle-aged man and both were obviously discussing Judy.

Lee came back. The girl was deep into her newspaper, a much more massive news medium than any of his own acquaintance.

"You have a little wrinkle," he said, "quite a small one really, right in the middle of your high luminous forehead."

"I'm trying to read."

"Those two men…"

"They won't do anything."

"Maybe if you could just face this other way…"

"I have it—why don't you go get some more coffee? And for me, too."

He sauntered off, moving between the tables. That this was a very big city indeed and not simply an ordinary one, he could read it in people's faces. One woman, dressed elegantly, might almost have been pretty but for the involuntary twitches that afflicted her about the chin and her left-hand side in general. The place was noisier than he liked, especially with so many trains coming in at every minute and parking with great clatter. And yet, the restaurant itself was enveloped in the wonderful smell of coffee and food. Always he had looked upon sausage as upon a rarity; here, they had hundreds of the things, thumb-sized articles stacked neatly under glass. He moved past an aluminum tray holding hundreds of fried eggs trembling with excitement, all of them staring up at the ceiling like so many horrified eyes.

"Y'all got any pi?" he asked, addressing a black-headed girl in makeup who likely had been a whore at one time.

"Any what?"

"Pi."

She was mad at him, already she was. Another woman had come up behind him meanwhile and was urging him forward by going through a great number of short, noisy steps. Lee looked at her.

"I'm going as fast as I can!" (He had seen how the coffee itself came out of a little "faucet," as if the city boasted an entire plumbing system filled with the stuff.) The whore, meanwhile, continued to wait and to stare.

"You want *what*?"

"Pi."

"Oh, boy. Hey, Rock! C'mere a minute."

Lee put on his bored face. This "Rock"... To Lee, he looked like one of those press workers at *The Toledo Paper*.

"What d'ya want!"

"Look, all I wanted was to purchase a piece of pi. Never mind."

"Piece of *what*?"

The woman behind him was losing patience and meanwhile the cashier was motioning angrily for him to leave the line altogether. He looked to Judy but found that she was lost in her newspaper.)

"'Pi.' We don't got none of that, O.K.?"

"O.K."

"Try across the street."

Lee nodded. He had seen the pies, and seen further that at least one was of his favorite kind, judging by the actual blueberries visible in the tranche. He pointed to it, but by now the whore had lost interest in him. gone away. And when he came to the coffee, he pointed to that, too, instead of trying to enunciate what he believed to be its name.

Judy, (he found her easily, using as a landmark the great jumble of newspaper cluttering her table) Judy had come up with a map from somewhere and was hovering over it.

"What do you see?"

"Hush! I'm looking."

Lee hushed. Half an hour had gone by and he knew no more about Chicago than if he were still at home in Alabama.

"This is where I'll be working," she said, pointing to a tiny location on the map. (Five minutes ago, the map had been in mint condition whileas now, between the coffee and the lipstick and the rouge, it looked as if it had been used to bind up wounds. The girl herself, of course, remained as fresh, as tidy and as integral as always.

"I do not understand how you can be as you are, so fresh and tidy at the same time as your *belongings*..."

"Hush. And here..." (She pointed to yet another location, this one marked by a hairpin plunged up to its neck in the paper) "here is where they have concerts."

"Concerts, I see. And so, you'll be hanging around concerts while I'm suffering in Toledo. It all fits."

She ignored him. Sunlight was pouring through the window and direct onto her vast map where he could identify at least three hairpins together with a special location in a circle of rouge.

"Look," she said, "at all these canals they have!"

"Judy, I wish you wouldn't bend over the table like that. Those men... Good Lord! aren't you even going to fold it up?"

No, she simply made a ball out of what once had been a lovely map. Lee watched as, first, she forced the thing down into her already very crowded purse and then pushed back her chair and shook the crumbs out of her lap.

"Ready?" she asked brightly. "Ready to see Chicago?"

He ran along at her side. It was bright but chilly and with a smell of salt coming off the sea. The buildings were simply immense, larger than the pyramids, nor was he able to understand how the canal-infested land could support such weights as theirs. As to the people — and there seemed to be an endless supply of them — he could not begin to read all their faces.

"How come they look like that?"

"They're in a hurry. You should be, too."

He found himself constrained to travel much more quickly than was normal or good. In front, two men in suits were striding forward like camels; looking at them, he grew dizzy, especially so when he saw that his own legs were in peril of getting mixed up with theirs. Meanwhile, a woman was darting in and out, apparently displeased with him for some reason. Lee could not take his eyes off a certain bad man, a moral weakling who seemed always on the verge of a smile — they looked at each other. Suddenly, that instant, it crashed down on him that he had lost the girl, lost her utterly, and that he had small chance of finding her again.

He turned, fighting against the tide. This one street had more people in it than all the Alabamas combined, nor did he see one single face that had the least sort of pleasantness in it. He had neglected to arrange a special cry between them for situations like this; nevertheless, he tried it anyway, calling, "caw, caw!" in one direction, but then electing not to try it any further when he saw the result it obtained. That was when the girl came up out of nowhere and seized his hand.

"You great loon! Now don't turn loose this time."

They went on. She seemed to be laughing at him even as she forced him to run along at her side. He simply did not care to move that fast. And as for the women, the greater part of them looked like whores. It was when they came to a book-and-magazine store that he dug in his heels.

"Look!"

"Later," she said. "Here's the subway."

Subway! he had read about it. And now she was leading him down, down and down, down into a hole in the ground where, almost at once, he found himself looking in at a gnome in a cage who, he too, seemed already to be mad at him.

"How many!"

"Two," called Judy, who handed over a full dollar. Instantaneously, two little brass-type discs came shooting back followed by an amount of change. He was examining the two little quoits, turning them over with curiosity when, suddenly, he saw that Judy was laughing again.

"You're holding up the line! Oh, God."

In fact, there were at least a dozen persons formed up behind him, all of them tilting back and forth as if they had an urgent need to urinate. Next, was a turnstile, Judy coaxing him to try it. He found himself on a cement platform amid a hundred or more persons staring about at everything except each other. Never had he seen so many people with so little to say to one another. One man had fallen asleep on the bench. Lee was debating whether to rouse him when the train came in, slowed and stopped.

"No, no!" cried Judy, laughing even as she tried to hold him back. "It's not ours."

He saw hundreds spilling out on all sides, all wearing dead expressions. An old woman careened into him violently, spun, and then went tottering off blindly in a new direction. Everything was pointing to a crisis. He took a cigarette, but only to have Judy pluck it from his lips and stick it in her purse. It was a less-than-average sort of people, apparently, those who lived below the city. He witnessed two black women taking up an entire bench that could have held five that were white.

He remembered being pushed out onto yet another platform. His one great hope: that the hand he was holding still belonged to Judy. And now he was *in* the crowd without however being *of* it. Someone was chasing this bunch with a pitchfork, to judge by the faces and the haste. And then at last, the sun once more, shocking in its power. It was Judy, her neat profile bobbing cheerfully, not along the red brick buildings of Antioch, Edessa, but a row of city storefronts.

"Well? Do you like it?"

"Sure! Big city."

"But do you like it?"

"Sure!"

"That's good."

A car was nudging at his rump. That the city was very good, he knew it from the option that the people had, and had refused, of living in the country. They crossed and then moved quickly down to stand in front of an official-looking structure, a bank perhaps, or Post Office, except that in this case it was an upper-class restaurant in which a bald-headed man sat supping in the window with bib and fork.

"This is where I'll be working!" she said proudly.

"Expensive-looking."

"It's supposed to be!"

"Let's go in."

"No!"

Lee could feel his gorge begin to rise. "Listen, if you can *work* there, you can *eat* there."

The door was tall, heavy, gilded with gold and brass; at once they found themselves bogged down in dense carpeting. Came now a well-dressed woman, a tall one who smiled so sweetly that Lee began to search his memory for someone he had known at one time.

"Just the two of you?"

Lee shrugged. He did not understand the gist of such a question.

"Yes," said Judy.

Again, she smiled, this time not quite so warmly. She began to stride away.

"Follow her," Judy said.

"How come?"

"Do it!"

They chased after her, running down past a sequence of tables with flowers on them and goblets positioned upside down. The woman, her smile exhausted, took them to the furthest table of all and then handed over the menu, a massive thing as tall as a newspaper. Between this and the flowers, he could barely see the girl.

"May I bring you something from the bar?"

"Sure," said Lee. "If you want to." He smoked. Judy, meantime, had come to her feet and was bending over the menu in order to read it.

He fully expected to see her take out her lipstick and begin marking it; instead, she simply hissed at him through the flowers.

"Prices! Prices!"

He looked. "Good Lord!"

"Let's leave."

"Can't. We'd never make it."

"Please, Lee."

"Naw. We've got to get *something*."

"I won't do it."

Lee looked at her — he had heard that tone before. "Me, I'm going to have some of that *pâté de foie et de porc en brioche*."

"Swell."

Someone somewhere, was playing a piano. Finally, taking his courage, he moved the flowers off to one side. The neighboring table, he saw, had two fat women who, although eating with the exaggerated politeness of their caste, nevertheless continued to get lipstick on their beans and potatoes alike. The place held as many as twenty business-men, half-bald, many of them. With one, possibly two exceptions, he could have whipped every man in sight. Their own waitress finally came, a much plainer sort of person than the hostess. Her smile was unconvincing and had constantly to be hoisted back into place, like falling trousers.

"I'd like that superb *pâté de foie et de porc en brioche*." (His French pronunciation was not terrible at that time.)

She wrote it down and then looked to Judy.

"Nothing," said Judy.

"Nothing at all?"

"No."

"We have salads."

"How much are they?"

She described the price.

"No."

He ate in haste, trying three times to pass something along to Judy who, however, would have nothing to do with it. Finally, he pushed back and lit a cigarette.

"Four hours, and then you'll be all alone in this big city."

"I know."

"Are you going to be alright?"

She looked around, her gaze coming to rest upon the hostess who stood off at a distance with an expression of the most sublime hauteur playing about her face. Soon enough, it would be this person giving orders to Judy.

"Yes, I expect you'll be doing lots of suffering here," said Lee. "And now you'll see what it's like."

Her chin trembled slightly.

"At least you'll have time now to read those books."

"Which books?"

"Aw, good Lord. I gave you the list!"

"Tell me again."

He groaned, and then had to wait while she emptied out her hairpins and compact, her combs and snail shells and the other equipment that stood in the way of the two dozen pens and pencils rolling about at hazard at the bottom of her purse.

"O. K., first is Schopenhauer."

"No Lee, please."

He groaned. Staring at her fine brown hair that spilled onto the table, her innocent neck and two small vertebrae, he was swept with love and panic that such a thing must grow old someday, and someday die. A minute went by. She was prepared to write — it was obvious from the way she had come down to within an inch of the fingernail-size shard of paper on which she proposed to write.

"O. K., read *Look Homeward, Angel*."

"Is it long?"

He groaned. The two women next to them had left off eating at last and would need no more feeding, not for another two hours at least. All these people were rich; he saw a crowd of businessmen in suits, and then, next, saw how one of the fat women had turned to gaze upon the gorgeous Judy with loathing and despair.

"O. K., read *Crime and Punishment*. Read *Martin Eden*. Read *The Scarlet and the Black*. All these books are about extraordinary young men."

"Like you?"

Lee shrugged. There might be something in what she said.

"Do you have any that are about young women?" (She was running out of space.) "Short ones?"

He groaned. How was it that he loved her most passionately the very times he was most exasperated? Her bell-shaped head was bent so earnestly over the list. And why would he wish to satisfy his most base urges upon such a one as had never done harm to him? He whipped out a cigarette and headed for the toilet.

This, too, angered him: that there was more of comfort and luxury here, here in a rich man's rest room, than could have been dreamt of by his own adored late grandfather who had toiled himself to death with mules. Lee made use of the place and then, after casting about for some sort of sabotage to perform, ended up by writing on the mirror with a bar of blue-green soap, well-perfumed.

The crowd had thinned, the few remaining pedestrians resembling souls who had been condemned to stand about and cast shadows for a certain duration. Half an hour, they wandered at random, sometimes looking up into a sky that had turned threatening. On Clark Street, the girl took out her map and looked at it.

"Dearborn Avenue."

"And where is that, pray?"

"We don't know."

"We could ask him." (He nodded toward a policeman, an enormous figure of a man who for the past minute had been watching them dubiously while tapping at the pavement with a short blunt wand that hung by a thong.)

"No, Lee."

They went on, going another full block before Lee turned and looked back toward the man.

"Is he still watching?"

"More than ever."

They crossed and then began climbing a bridge that spanned the canal. Lee looked for, but did not find, fishermen along the shores. The district began to deteriorate rapidly. They moved past a warehouse, out front two whiskered men sitting with their backs to the wall. Lee knew in advance that one of them was sure to stick out his leg at the last instant and make an obstacle of it. He climbed over it, Judy went around. A killed dog was lying in the gutter with an exploded stomach.

They moved on, intimidated by the ancientness of the place, the dour sky and great number of abnormal-looking persons. He thought it curious that a woman should be sitting outside in slippers and robe, until he saw that every flight of steps had at least one such person on constant guard. Judy stopped.

"This is it."

"No!"

It was a five-story building, old and rotten and so exceedingly narrow that it was owing only to the adjoining structures that it had not long ago toppled over into the canal. Compared to the city, this whole section seemed "out of plumb," as it were. Furthermore, *these* stairs had two women on them, both old and both with enormous shocks of disorganized hair. They had been ignoring each other for years apparently, and now Lee saw how the southward-gazing woman had a radio with her while the other, looking north, continued to pick lewdly at the blue foot cradled in her lap.

They climbed to the door and rang, producing a sound of chimes from deep within. That they were being watched, and especially so from certain fifth-story windows across the road... The blue-footed woman had turned meanwhile and was smiling up at them with sympathy and warmth. Lee rang again and then, finally, peeped through the frosted glass; he could pick up tremors of someone very definitely plodding forward toward the door.

It was a woman, a heavy type, very imperious, with a wig-like apparatus resembling a baby-blue bonnet. Across her bosom, she wore numerous military decorations mixed with jewelry.

"Yes?"

"Hi. We've come about that room."

"Yes? But it's a single room. For one person."

"No, we're just one person. I mean, it's for her." (He pointed to the girl.)

"Ah. And are you married?"

It was the last question he had expected. He looked to Judy, mind spinning, struggling for the answer that would at least allow him to visit from time to time.

"Sort of."

She sighed deeply and began to tap one foot. "Well. You may as well look at it."

They followed. The woman had started out energetically at first but then began to slow as they reached the second and third stories. Soon enough, she was struggling, her thick calves lifting one by one in front of his eyes. Here the odor was of mothballs, mildew, and drapery imbrued with dust.

"I'll just wait right here," she said finally. "Here in the corner where I can think." She smiled sweetly. "But you, you're young; you can go the rest of the way by yourselves!"

"The key... "

"No, no, you won't be needing any 'key,' not way up there. Certainly not."

They squeezed past her, mounting higher. The staircase itself was rickety in the extreme; moreover, after another twenty feet of it, the walls began to merge, forcing them to travel edgewise, so to speak. Nothing surprised him anymore, he who had done all things, having done them ten billion years ago, eons out of mind. He put on his bored expression.

"Lee!"

"Just keep going."

The flooring was discontinuous and there was an open place whence he could spy down upon a woman working in her kitchen. They proceeded more cautiously, climbing past yet another window sealed over with wadding and plywood. He had but few matches left, hardly enough to light them on their return trip. The girl — and this did surprise him — was good at seeing in the dark.

The room itself was positioned on the sixth landing. The door was of wood and had burnt marks on it. No need for a key, Lee pressed against it and then entered an elongated setup supplied both with functioning electricity within and neon from without. The room was remarkably narrow, but stretched on for an interminable distance where visible details were few and far apart.

"Oh, I feel sure we can find another room somewhere," the girl said.

The window itself, when they came to it, was devoid of glass.

"Look, you can see all the way to the lake and back!"

"Please, Lee."

"Hey, look where all those people are jumping up and down! And those pigeons on the roof. Dead."

There was a chest of drawers holding one drawer only. The mirror had grayed and had a film over it. On the floor above them, a toilet was being repeatedly flushed.

"So, this is Chicago then."

She nodded.

"Big son-of-a-bitch."

She had taken to bed and was sitting on it, her two box-like feet not quite touching the ground. She had fallen into a dreamy trance that he had seen in her once or twice before.

"You're going to be very lonely up here," he predicted.

Her chin quivered.

"However, you will get a lot of reading done."

"I'll never see you again — I'm sure of that."

"What! I'll be here every week-end, all the time!"

"No, you'll find a floozie somewhere — that's what you really want. Oh, I'm not saying you won't visit me in the beginning."

He had to go and hold her, a good two minutes of it before she began to brighten again. The bed was vast, quite unlike the one awaiting in Toledo. The girl was picking at her hands as if she had a million little splinters in them. But her brown hair, he remembered, was of an exceeding fineness, and had a way of catching up the light in glints of gold.

"Stay with me."

"You know I can't. I have to be at work in…" (he counted), "fourteen hours!"

"No, Lee."

"I can come on Friday."

"You promise?"

"Certainly."

"Say it."

He said it, the girl watching him suspiciously.

"Swear it."

He swore. She did brighten somewhat. That was when they remembered the woman.

"The woman! We've got to go back!"

They closed the door as well as they could — the thing did not fit properly in the frame — and then set foot on the highest rung of the staircase. At once, a man in an undershirt ran out of one of the cells. Seeing them, he appeared disappointed and turned sadly and went back in again. The downward trek was easier; Lee used just two matches to reach the window, and none at all thereafter.

The woman remained where they had left her. Not only was she slumbering in a standing position, she was dreaming dreams.

"How much for the room?" Lee asked loudly enough to rouse her.

"Ja?" Her eyes came open.

"The room. How much?"

"So. Finished already. That will be three dollars."

"But what about for a whole week?"

"All week long!" (She winked at him.) "Five dollars."

"Five." He paid, borrowing the sum from Judy. "I've noticed that the door doesn't want to close, however."

"Ah? Vell, maybe you shouldn't argue with him then." She laughed gaily, showing that her teeth were as long as a horse's and of a dazzling yellow. "He knows what he wants, the door do. Now, you sign this."

It was a contract, full of stipulations. Lee was taken by the looks of it, a highly legal-looking document with gilt running around the edges.

"It seems to be in German!"

"Ja? You too, both must sign."

Lee used his own pen. He was shrewd enough not to use his own name however, choosing instead one from British literature. Finally, they shook. Judy, who did not shake, had left already and was waiting outside.

"She knows we're not married!"

"She doesn't care."

"She cares a little bit."

"She'll just have to accept it. After all, we'll soon be making love up there."

They glanced at each other. With her peculiar nose, high forehead and big sloppy ribbon, she did not look old enough to cross the road by herself, far less to be studying love.

"And now, soon, you'll be alone."

"No, Lee."

They ran into each other's arms. Over her shoulder he could see the tiny red sun spinning slowly, apparently on the verge of failing. That moment, ten thousand lights came on in the enormous white building that faced out over the lake.

"Night's coming."

Lee agreed. A cafe came up and then, two doors further, a blind Negro standing in their path with cup and guitar. Lee saw a barge toiling upstream, truly a ship of evil with and one lone figure waving to it with a kerchief from the top of the bridge. He was glad to touch down on the more brightly lit shore where a more or less normal-looking people were scurrying homeward in a more or less cheerful manner. Some indeed were actually smiling from thoughts of roast beef and potatoes, hot ale, and a night between fresh sheets. One woman turned to grin at them, proving that she at least could recognize love and youth when she saw it. Lee was flattered and yet, at the same time, curious as to how it felt to be such a one as she, and to know that one's own good days are over. He envisioned her in fifteen years hence, dead and spinning head over heels through space in her little lace purse and odd-looking hat.

They found the station and raced downstairs to hunt about in some confusion for the locker in which they had stored their luggage. The girl's suitcase was a humble thing made of a material inferior to cardboard, both sides puffed out.

"Now just how do you plan on getting this back to your room? It's too heavy."

She tried it, lifting it twice with a generally optimistic display. "It's easy!"

"You wouldn't get two blocks! Take a taxi."

"Alright."

"You're not going to, are you?"

"Poo. La, la, la. You're going to miss your bus."

Lee lifted his own luggage. The bus was waiting, the driver taking tickets. Lee went to him.

"How much time do I have?"

This was a small man, doll-like in the neatness of his uniform and artificial mustache. For some seconds, he sought frantically but in vain, for something sarcastic to say. "You got a few minutes."

Lee ran back to the girl. "Very well now, I want you to take a taxi — I mean it! — and go straight to bed."

"It's only six-thirty!"

"O.K., you can stay up till eight. But no later!"

She agreed happily.

"And that will give you time to write me a letter."

"Tonight?"

"Yes, tonight! Jesus. Tonight, and every night."

She agreed. They looked at each other.

"I'll be gone in another minute."

"I know."

"Tweedy…"

"I know, I know."

He wanted to hold her, but also wanted to spend these last seconds gazing into her eyes. "Oh, baby."

Her chin trembled. Suddenly, she ducked into his jacket and began burrowing into him.

Insofar as he was able to claim the last bench, his favorite position for traveling, he considered himself lucky. Now, looking back, what he saw was a pale girl, smaller than the average, a short one picking at her fingers as she turned into a figment of movement and light.

THIRTY-FIVE

HOW WELL HE KNEW THIS BUS, the same in which he had escaped from Alabama. It had that certain reek and even some of the same people who were to abide with him always in some region of the mind. In front, a salesman yawned exuberantly, even throwing up both hands in a seeming effort to touch the ceiling. Spotting Lee, he turned full around and winked knowingly at him. In truth, Lee did not remember this one. From somewhere, a child was droning on endlessly in deep voice, explaining something complicated to someone with weak understanding.

The bus wended through town with what to Lee seemed an excessive cautiousness. At the corner, a man of quite abnormal height came out into the street itself and, standing on tiptoes, glared in upon the passengers with detestation. No doubt about it, it was only at night and only in big cities, that the adult human male could be seen for what in fact he was. Lee's mind turned back to Judy and her inevitable struggle with the suitcase when she reached the bridge. Next, he foresaw her lying in the enormous bed, her eight minuscule fingers and two thumbs looped over the covers that would themselves be pulled up under her chin. And now, instead of racing to her aid, the bus was actually carrying him back once more to that same exile and punishment that… He refused to think about it.

The bus slowed, turned with unneeded slowness (his contempt for the driver was increasing), and then began running through what was unquestionably the most gorgeous slum that ever it had been vouchsafed him to gaze upon. Indeed, it was rotting even as he looked at it, the entire purlieu, all of it owing to the "ooze," (he called it) exuding from the red, green, and yellow neon lighting. That was when he spotted his first certifiable Chicago whore, a fat one in a skirt. Lost in thought, Lee studied her closely, looking for resemblances with the girls of Antioch. It nonplussed him to see a boy of his own general size come up and speak nastily to her, and follow her away. Leland reeled, he who had never refused an experience. He had never done *this*.

It was not a good moment. Behind him, a powerful beacon had come on in Chicago and was sweeping the countryside from its high place. No mouse nor miscreant nor skittering creature could escape *that* gaze. And when it entered through the back of the bus, penetrating the dim, Lee put on a bored expression. Judy, no doubt about it, was still staring up at the ceiling from her gigantic bed. Could anything be more odd than that he, who only yesterday had been a chattel of his parents, that he should have been able so quickly to secret her away in Chicago for his sole use alone? The last true woman of the Late Modern West? His arrogance increased. She did so love him; never was he more conscious of it than when she was sending out adoring thoughts from the imagined privacy of her mind. And yet, she, too, someday, she too, was to be sent spinning off through space, head over heels tumbling, a small one blinking in the vortex.

It never failed; give him a dark green vile and bilious night aboard a doomed bus and it perforce made his head go spinning. In front, two dozen ordinary people, mental innocents, had settled in and were going through the usual mental petrifaction of their kind. And he knew what it would lead to — sleep, ignorance, stupor. Chicago, meanwhile, was going down behind the horizon for the third time, albeit in full blaze and with Judy trapped inside. He grabbed for his wallet. He had, moreover, an extra package of cigarettes, and in his vest, a paperbound volume of outstanding literary quality. He might even have been completely happy, but for the bourgeois woman sitting at the opposite window. He preferred the grizzled old man three benches in front, who continued to take sips out of a little brown flask held tremblingly in both hands. *This* was the company he liked — those who knew about life and wished only to be done with it as expeditiously as possible.

The woman stirred and shot a look at him, whereupon he blew yet another column of smoke in her direction. *This* was the company he abhorred — those who know what is good and what is not and have proudly chosen the former. Grinning toothlessly, Lee began adjusting his testicles. At once, she stood and tripped forward down the aisle, there to settle in a far country on the other side of the world. It left him with all the room he could ask for, room enough to lie and stretch. The moon was watching, now once again his own favorite star.

They came to a town, coasted for two blocks, and then slipped into berth. Immediately, there was a great stir among the passengers. A grey-headed woman stood and came forward eagerly, until she recognized that it was only a small town in Indiana and not at all the place in which she had grown up. The driver, meanwhile, had turned and was giving the usual warnings in an indecipherable voice that sounded as if he were speaking into a jar.

Lee trooped out in single file, walked a brief distance — the wind was cold — and then stepped into a cafeteria that smelled of gas, coffee, cigars, and winter clothes. At the counter were some dozen of the local people who turned on their stools with a curiosity that veered toward sympathy at first, but then soon changed to outright laughter. Lee hastened to the men's facility but then, seeing conditions there, immediately came out again and ordered coffee. The man next to him — Lee thought at first it was someone he had known at one time — turned slowly, glaring back at him with displeasure. Lee perceived how one certain passenger in particular, a distinguished-looking sort with a pipe and shoulder patches, how he had taken so well to the locals, and they to him, that he would not be traveling any further. Meanwhile, the driver had gone off to sit by himself in the leadership role. Crushed by responsibility, he had been sent forth without so much as a kiss, condemned to drift forever, time never ending.

Lee stood and again edged his way to the men's room, his heart leaping up in joy when he found the place was empty. Out *there*, in the restaurant proper, the males of all ages were having their tea and munching croissants, while in *here*, once out of view, they had not felt constrained enough even to flush the toilet.

He went back, his head buzzing with detestation. It was late, cold, too, he was tired, he had not used the rest room and now, on top of everything else, he saw that the driver had disappeared. It was a hideous feeling, that of being abandoned in a town that would not want him, and with winter coming back. This "driver," moreover, he was just the type to depart at the precise moment, leaving half the crew behind. Lee ran for it. Never yet had he been able to dismount a bus and then board it again without the whole affair turning into an emotional experience.

He tapped politely, but had to wait a long while before the man would snap open the door.

"May I come in?"

The man continued to stare straight ahead. "I *said* ten minutes. You heard me."

"I had to take a leak."

"We don't want to hear about that!"

"But I didn't."

"Gad! Get in, get in."

He went to his place and plopped down gratefully. Based upon the experiences he had shared with the other passengers, he was beginning to feel a significant liking for them. Judy came to mind, that wide-eyed phenomenon who even now would be sinking deeper and deeper into the folds of her enormous mattress. He had been insane to leave her, especially without lock and key and with danger threatening both from the rooms below and the further region of her extensive room. A city of twisted people — he could envision them encroaching up the stairs, one step at a time, pausing only when one of the paper-thin boards revealed their progress. This was the third recent instance of his mismanagement: he had abandoned her to criminals and vivisectionists, or to be burnt alive on the sixth floor of the worst place in Chicago.

Outside the snow, insidious in the beginning, was coming down in a panic, dashing itself to death on purpose. He had been wrong, quite wrong, always wrong when it came to judging northern weather. And in short, he looked upon it as a sort of retribution for the things carried out against the South during the last century. Already he was half-drunk on night and speed and glimpses of cabin lights glowing yellowly in distant woods; now, in addition to that, it had been given to him to ride headlong through perilous weather while at the same time sacrificing nothing of his privacy and warmth. Above all, he enjoyed pressing up to the window and permitting these billion flakes to take personal aim at him, and all quite in vain.

It was coming down hard now, the driver wearing a concerned look that revealed itself in the mirror. Disaster! *that* was what Lee continually wanted. Or, to come limping in to the next station to find it abandoned by everyone save one single old man who would enjoy telling of the catastrophe that had overtaken the earth.

It was the finest ride of his career; he was overwhelmed by sadness, knowing that it must end someday. Down along the aisle, three dark lights were glowing peculiarly — someone, a man in aluminum glasses, had smuggled a radio on board. Civilization was being entombed in snow, Lee's delight then turning to outright ecstasy when he saw a mob of wild dogs or hogs possibly, snapping at the tires. The bus had been losing speed steadily, though not solely on account of the hogs. It was the grandest night of the year, and Leland's luck to have a spineless driver. He could feel his dander rising. *Now was the time to be running on at full tilt into the chaos!* He changed to the opposite window. Until a moment ago, the radio had been bringing news from Gary; now, it was crackling dangerously and threatening to explode. Before, Lee had been impressed by how these signals knew how to slice through any sort of weather.

It was dawn when they hit Toledo; Lee clove to the window, the old sickness returning now that he was again face-to-face with the locus of his former ordeal. Above, a microscopic sun, a mere dot really, was blinking erratically and giving off a most obnoxious light. Suddenly, as if to welcome him, he caught sight of a drunk man who was bending and uttering and then, finally, touching down on all fours and vomiting in the snow. Another such person stayed hidden in the doorway looking out calmly from under the rim of a cowboy's hat. And then, too, there were another thirty or forty such people across the street (Lee recognized at least one of them) who had formed up in line and were pounding on the tavern door.

They turned and rolled slowly through the business section where already numbers of people were stepping off briskly to office and work. Another block and the bus came at last to harbor, where it sat and trembled for a time. His fellow passengers had turned pale during the trip and looked now like so many chastened refugees spilling out into a city that was more egregious than they could know. Himself, he cut through the lobby and came to the street before turning back and running for his suitcase. The crowd was thick. Of all the humiliations that northern people loved to inflict upon themselves, Lee awarded first place to their style of walking, which put him in mind of that spasmodic business seen in early films. Unfortunately, he had been caught up in the herd. A middle-aged woman (she had been walking stride for stride with him) sped up suddenly to shatter any delusion on his part that they might in any way be friends, or colleagues even.

He went straight to the newspaper, nodded once to the receptionist, and then climbed to the arena on the second floor. Here, six journalists, all of them fat and each greasier than the other, were sitting girth to girth while laughing happily into one another's face. Lee wanted to puke. He spotted a woman sleeping at a typewriter, her hair entangled in the keys. Next, he found The Man of Reduced Status, saw him come bounding out of the rest room, saw him stop, saw him blush, and then saw him go back inside to close his fly. The organization was known to have at least three hard-core recalcitrants in its employ, one of whom now was standing in the corner with his face to the wall guarded over by a cold looking youth in a black uniform.

THIRTY-SIX

STOPPING, CHECKING, LOOKING UP AND DOWN EACH HALL, he climbed slowly to his room. His first action was to get down in front of his door and make absolutely certain that the thread he had so ingeniously attached to the jamb, that it was as it should be. Even then, he opened slowly. There was a little hill of snow, fantastically configured, that had built up in the corner during the time he had been away. He peeped under the bed, depressed by what he found there.

His tendency was to dash about town in an uncoordinated way, visiting one scene after another of his former ordeal. He signaled to the man in the pharmacy who, judging from the signal he got in return, didn't seem to realize that he had ever been away. Lee did not, as before, bow sweepingly to the whore, not when two evil-looking men watching from a car. Instead, he continued on to his restaurant, entered, and was halfway to his own special booth before he realized they were playing *The Man with The Golden Arm*, the best salutation he could have asked for in recognition of his return.

He smoked. Two booths down, a couple in late middle age had been quarreling all night; now, suddenly, the man bent near and shook his fist at her. They had been fighting for years — Lee could read it as clearly as if it had been written — a struggle that dated back to

when they had both been young. They were not young now! least of
all the man who, with his watery eyes and flaking scalp, looked as if
he belonged to the local guild of alcoholics. As for the woman, she
was presentable enough, but dressed in the fashions of forty years ago.
Lee could not take his eyes away. And how many times had they not
betrayed one another, wending in and out of each other's life, sometimes disappearing for long periods only to reunite in this city or that,
or conferring at intervals in bus stations and doctors' offices, a more
stormy romance than his own? And now the woman was speaking
softly while gazing down into the ashtray, no longer the beauty for
whom thousands had at one time stopped and turned and caught
their breath.

The waitress came, bringing him a white oval platter with rolls,
rice, and two sheets of turkey straight off the breast.

"Where you been?"

"Mexico," he said.

"Yeah?"

Lee nodded. His long, corrupting travels — he was close to tears.
And meanwhile, all this time, the endless stream of monads drifting
past the window, never knowing they were being seen. Two booths
off, the stormy couple was at it again, the woman was taking the
strongest possible exception to whatever it was the man was saying.
Already, she had wasted two-thirds of her life on him, and now he was
back, promising, pleading, whining and threatening. This much Lee
knew: that the man would have his way in the end, and in due time,
they would bed down forever in each other's arms.

But he had also begun picking up bits of conversation from the
open-all-night drugstore on the other side of the wall. He had always
been suspicious of walls, closets, partitions, and how it was that
people who might normally despise each other in the open air, how
they could live so proximately, as it were, or even in each other's laps.
Just now, someone was speaking not twelve inches from his ear! Lee

listened keenly, apprehending very little of it however. Or was it a radio? That moment, the stormy man made a crashing sound and, his face splotched with anger, pounded with violence on the table. Lee knew what it was he liked about such people — that whereas the whole world was out for money, yet here was an old man still playing for love.

Lee paid, leaving a grandiose tip. Outside, the snow had fomented numerous tinted puddles with trash floating in them. A drunk came up and positioned himself indignantly in Lee's path. Two soldiers were next, both wearing looks of suppressed glee, as if in anticipation of the place to which they were going. He considered following them, and did so, making a game of it until after two blocks he tired of it and dropped off to look in at the pawnshop.

Of wedding rings, he saw more of them than on his last visit. A leather-bound photograph album had been opened to show one of the weddings itself, an over-exposed sixty-year-old photograph of a mule and buggy, a grinning groom and a terrified bride. Where were they now? Grinning still? Spinning through space? A little old woman, someone's grandmother, had inadvertently stepped into the photograph and was trying with embarrassment to get out. Where was she now? That day's cloud formation, only on paper now, never again would it be seen in the actual sky. Strange, old photographs; they made Lee dizzy. And that, of course, was when he spied the proprietor, a grim quantity in a double-breasted suit and colored vest. Lee was aghast to see him break slowly and deliberately into a smile that grew and grew until it was as big as the world. Rose-colored teeth he had, and a vermilion tongue. It intimidated Lee, even after the man, who had been playing with him evidently, laughed and waved and turned away.

Lee went on, stepping down into the lower slum. Hardened as he was, this district still gave him pause. A car moved past, the elderly driver giving Lee to understand that he was altogether welcome to come and sit next to him. A bar came up, inside it a crowd of post-graduate people playing the music of *his* generation — it made his gorge rise — instead of their own. Some were attempting to dance to it, doing it poorly.

The burlesque was just in front; he had been drawn back to it out of stagnant habit. Monique was gone, her place assumed by a corrupt-looking blond enacting the role of Cinderella. Lee reached for his wal-let, but then exclaimed out loud (a thrill of horror settling over him) when he saw how small his funds were. He cursed. He had not come forth into the world in order to be stymied at every turn by trivial considerations, small shortages, and the like. He went to the woman.

"How much is it?" Then: "I'm a quarter short."

She put down her knitting.

"May I go in anyway?"

"Certainly not."

He stamped twice, glared, and then turned and trudged away. It was clear to him now, how that of all the small-minded towns the earth over, *this* town's mind was smallest of all. He planted himself some ten feet away and glared back at her, though it had no real effect on the smug little face she was wearing. Again, the car came by, the same pleasantly smiling driver again slowing for him. Across the road, a Marlon Brando film was showing, and yet he lacked even the money for this as well. He approached the woman.

"Do y'all offer charge accounts here? I'll pay it back."

She put down her knitting. "Thought I'd seen the last of you. Did you know that you're the worst person I ever met?"

Her's was a tidy cell and to appearances, apparently quite warm. She had an arrangement of a hot plate, cup and saucer, and what he took to be a tube of bouillon cubes.

"Cold out here," he said. "My room even has a little hill of snow in it. But it'll go away I suppose."

"That won't work with me."

"Ma'am?"

"So, you might just as well turn around and go home."

Lee cursed. It was cold and he had far to go. No, he had even further than that, if he hoped to avoid the pleasantly smiling driver who had turned and come back.

THIRTY-SEVEN

IN THOSE DAYS, he used to come awake at six and, though he would have preferred to go on sleeping, spend the next half-hour going back mentally over his own past life and activities. This was the best of times to be peeping down into the city, a magical scene in which even the drunk people and lay-abouts left off what they were doing in order to gaze up at the brand-new sun striving in the sky. Summer had come and gone and winter had returned for the main purpose of introducing summer for the second time that year. Down below, he saw an indecisive cat caught out in the open by the light. Years might pass and still the animal would not be able to choose in which direction it wanted most to run. But all this was as nothing compared to the sun itself, an inexplicable thing huger than North America and offering the brightest of meadows, the most portentous glaciers, the most sparkling and yet at the same time darkest of stinging seas, the most cheerful of bathers (mothers and children) enjoying that other sun that gladdens this one. Let him have but an hour and he could have traveled to every district of that far-away sun, seeing all manner of things. No, he had to go to work.

How he did so abhor the entire method of the adult world! One must be wretched at every minute in order to go on living — was this the theory that lay behind it all? He glanced at his watch. Another ten minutes and he would have earned his right to retreat into the men's room for a short vacation. He chose to ignore the pile of undistributed mail that had grown up during his absence, so much so that he could detect little disturbances that from time to time agitated the heap. He was looking at it, even rolling up his sleeves when the Man of Reduced Status dashed up out of nowhere, grabbed something out of the pile and, chortling betimes, ran away with a blue envelope in his hand.

The men's room was full of card players. Lee waited until noon and then, hoping for an hour or two of privacy, went outside and took the bus for home. Two letters waiting for him, both bearing that guileless script she had acquired in second grade after weeks of effort with her face bent over the desk. Taking his place on the cantilevered bed, Lee opened the first of the letters and ran through it quickly.

She was suffering, was lonely, she feared someone was residing in the dark part of her room. A man had followed her from the restaurant, refusing to leave off until she had climbed aboard the trolley and had spent the next hour sitting behind the driver, only to end up far across town. Her supervisor had insulted her to her face. A frequent customer, accustomed to leaving big tips, had proposed to her. Finally, she asked to alter somewhat the order in which the books on her reading list were to be read.

Very different was the other letter, written in green ink. Here it was all kisses and heartfelt words, enough to make him reach out and brace himself against the wall. To so great a degree had she bound herself over to him, he held her as a prisoner, so to speak. Indeed, he had set aside a whole city, a grand one somewhat to the north-northwest, for just that purpose.

He always had the best of intentions; even so, he found that he had to stop off at the bookstore on his way back to work. He had a pre-dilection for the classics, Greeks especially, even if, at that date, he could read not one word of it in the original tongue. He spent half an hour dawdling over it, even going so far as to read one full page of Thucydides in a noble-looking edition bound in scarlet cloth. He stole it, or tried to, changing his mind when the clerk began to throw too many glances in his direction.

It was late when he returned. Two journalists, one in sports and the other an editorialist, were digging into the mail. It was the sports writer who was angriest. Lee's head was full of Thucydides and Judy. He was also humming.

"Goddamn it, Goddamn it. You know something — I got a twelve-year-old boy could do a better job than you!"

Lee looked back at him coolly. Even now, he was largely thinking of Judy. "I can't do everything!"

"Everything? You can't do anything!"

Lee could not but smile. And if ordinarily his gorge would have already begun to rise, today he felt inordinately calm. The editorialist, a dark man with hard opinions, continued to stare at him blackly. Lee said:

"I did not come to earth in order that…"

"Burns me up! Look at him."

(Lee had on his bored expression.)

"Yes," said the editorialist. "I'm disappointed. Truly."

THIRTY-EIGHT

IT WAS HIS DESTINY, his fate and his longing—to spend his youth riding on a bus. He knew this much, namely that in Chicago the tenants were growing bolder, and that already one or two of them had begun venturing up the staircase to Judy's room before losing heart each time and running back down. And the girl herself? She would be lying in bed, blinking, her two sawed-off feet, (in their box-like shoes) pointing toward the ceiling while she measured off the time for his arrival with her eye upon the clock.

It was a blue evening, with many little towns lying across his route. Never yet had he been able to take a trip by night without it turning into a spiritual experience. Tonight, he had decided to allow his mind to range freely over the whole of science, history, and human experience. The other riders, of course, were simply looking straight ahead in wonderment, like children being led on to an undisclosed destination. But tonight, Lee was ready to make an exception for the driver, a self-taught man who knew how to use the rear-view mirror without ever himself being seen at all.

They turned in at Elyria and parked, the passengers coming awake abruptly and looking about in stunned surprise. Day by day, he was growing increasingly pessimistic about ordinary people. Again, they formed up in line and then, given the command, entered the station in smart array as they passed in front of the locals. Lee aimed for the men's room, but only to find a pond of urine taking up the middle of the floor. Fifteen men had lined up in order of size and were jousting for the dry spots. The shoe shine boy, although perched well out of reach of the flood, seemed genuinely astonished that so many unwonted persons had suddenly come crowding into his unpleasant home.

Lee went back straightway to the bus and reclaimed his own special place and porthole. Up front, the driver, his face hidden behind a hand, possibly his own (it held a cigarette), was explaining something in a low modulated voice to someone whose own face was lost in the shadows of a wide brim hat. This then was how Lee wanted it on his final ride — drowsy night with stars, a modulated driver, and a radio that would start at the very beginning and play in sequence all his favorite songs.

He woke, gazing out in disbelief upon the enormous city that had come up around them while he was sleeping. They were homing in upon the very core of it, the engine making a masculine noise, like unto a horse flying to barn for fodder and the promise of a night without dreams. To break into the inner city (crashing through the gate, if need be) and then to link up with Judy would require an accuracy that only the most modern instruments could supply. Already, she would have left her room and even now, by his reckoning, she would be pushing forward in her duck-like gait, blinking, rushing on to meet him and not be late. In ten minutes, he would be looking into her very face, a small thing of but a few square inches which, however, took up nine-tenths of his mind. It seemed another modern miracle that things as small as that could ever be retrieved, when even the tiniest deviation on the part of the driver would have put them thousands of miles apart.

The bus ran forward, tumbling into the maze. They passed a row of miserable-looking apartments with sheets and towels flapping from the upper balconies. Horns sounded, screams, the bus plunging through an intersection while shouldering all the lesser traffic off to one side. He got a brief view of the search light that sat atop the tallest of the buildings, an all-seeing eye, as it seemed to him, that looked deep, deep into the outlying countryside with an intelligence quite devoid of pity. And now that they were within the true city, he saw everywhere examples of long-term residents, women mostly, serving out their terms with brooms. There was a man, too, Lee remembered, the expression on his face proving how he had been destined from the beginning to be there at that particular instant.

Suddenly, the bus dropped into a tunnel and began to spiral down into a hole in the ground. In front, the passengers had picked up moaning and cooing and swaying back and forth in contentment. He could see a platform where an appreciable crowd, all of them smiling and all waving handkerchiefs, were cheering the bus across the last few yards. He searched wildly, his eye scanning the faces. Could she have changed beyond all recognition, the result of her suffering? Was she still as pretty as he thought he remembered?

He gathered his jacket and putting on his rugged expression, proceeded out onto the platform. He would count to six and no higher, and if she had not come down to meet him… There was *always* Alabama. And that, of course, was when someone tapped him on the shoulder, either Judy herself or someone similarly shy. He turned slowly. Judy.

It always shocked him. That face, it had been designed in precise accord with that other, pre-existing face that was inherent in his mind.

"Hi."

They laughed, the girl putting one cool arm about his neck and then standing on tiptoes to give him a kiss.

"I didn't know if you were coming down to meet me," said Lee.

"Oh! And if I hadn't?"

"Well, I…"

"You would have gone right back down to the Confederacy! See? I *know* you."

"Oh, Judy. I almost went crazy."

"You? You? I almost went crazy, too!"

They flew into one another's arms. People were watching, including two who were smiling and one at least who was muttering in bitter disapproval.

"Let's go up to your huge room, want to?"

They hobbled off, striving to make progress through the crowd even while they continued clutching at one another. Compared to the bus station with its mobs, the street itself was placid, a few neon lights blinking desultorily in the shops. Across the way, a hobo was coughing endlessly, pausing only to spit against the wall. Lee had noticed this before, that whenever anyone (himself) was drawing happiness from life, it was always in balance with the misery of someone else.

"So, you've been lonely then?" he asked. "*Now* do you see what it's like?"

"Yes. Horrible."

"Life is trash. Can you finally understand that now?"

She nodded sadly. (He understood perfectly well, of course, that she did not fully subscribe to his trash theory.) Ahead, the bridge had a ruined look, with broken girders hanging out over the canal. They went to the rail and peeped down into the licorice-colored stream.

"Would you jump?" he asked. "If I wanted you to?"

She looked again, measuring the distance. "But I don't know what's down there."

"So what! So what? Me, I'd jump. You want me to?" (He could feel his gorge rising.) "See? That's the difference between me and you: 'He would jump, she would not.'"

She looked again. But this time she seemed to hang back even further from the rail. "But why do I have to jump?"

"Not now. Lord! Later. If I were to die or something."

"Oh."

They went on, doing it a little more sadly now. They were moving past an immensely long apartment house, five stories high, that looked like an escarpment with geologic layers in it (the poorest and most recent sediment deposited at the top). He caught sight of a comfortable-looking interior with a sofa, a colored glass lamp, and a grandmotherly woman rocking slowly with her eyes upon the clock. Here, the roofs had sentinels on them, dead men disguised as chimneys who continued to vigil over their widows down below. And though a radio was playing, yet the music itself was of the 1930s. He saw a hollow man in an overcoat who, it seemed, was waiting for them to be gone, that he might return to spying into his quondam home.

At Judy's building, they turned off and then climbed past two hunched-up figures sitting as far apart as possible on the stairs. Bringing her purse into the light, the girl began excavating in it, coming out triumphantly with several various objects before she hit upon the key itself. The door opened narrowly, showing a bare red carpet with thin places. The odor was old-fashioned — carbide and molasses.

"Hush!" (But he had made no sound.) He waited until she had reached the first landing before climbing after her. The staircase had three black and white engravings, now much faded, one of them picturing the death of General Wolfe at Quebec. Apparently, it had been put up at a time when the subject was still fresh in everyone's mind; he had seen the same image in his grandmother's house in Alabama far away. A door came open, followed by the sound of someone lumbering toward them. They looked at each other wildly. His first impulse was to turn and race all the way down again, his second — and this was the instinct he followed — to continue the upward climb. Below them, the sound waned and then fell away entirely.

"We're almost there!"

"I know."

"Hush!"

At the top, he stood looking with amazement at the two bales of straw used for blocking off the door. No key; she opened cautiously, checking around carefully before she would permit him to follow.

"That's where they are," she whispered, pointing to the dark part of the room. Lee went immediately into the area, even pulling open the closet and probing in it.

"There's not anybody here! See?"

She nodded. Her suspiciousness, however, did not go away. Looking at her, her ribbon now altogether undone, it struck him what a fortuity it was that they should both be in the same room at the same moment and both knowing each other's name. Far more likely it would have been to slip past each other in time and space, one of them turning up fifty years too late or too soon. He could well imagine it — Judy here all alone, blinking. Quickly, he stepped forward, his eye at the same time falling on the photograph of himself pinned up over the bed.

"Very glad am I" — (something like this he said) — "that *we*, at least, did not slip past each other in space and time."

She nodded. The top of her head fitted to perfection under his chin, the final proof that this was Judy. How strange it was, far from Antioch. They were in an apartment elevated high above this deadly serious city in which, as long as she paid her tariff, no one cared whether she be young and stunning and in love, or whether not in love, not young, and never stunning. And then, too, the room was so large and so musty; they could do whatever they wanted. All his life the adult world had arranged matters so that people like him, and people like her, so that they could never be alone for any considerable time. They were alone now, and in the most undiscoverable niche in the country.

"Just think: nobody knows we're up here."

"I know."

"Weird, isn't it?"

They grinned

"They don't trust us, people like them."

"I know."

"They probably think we're…"

She nodded. They looked at each other.

"O. K., take off all your clothes, O. K.?"

"What!"

"Sure. We both know it's inevitable."

"But, why?"

"Or, I could just leave. Pretty clear you don't like me anymore."

Her chin trembled. She fretted with her hands. Lee began gathering up his book and jacket.

"Would you promise not to look?"

"Just for a few seconds! Until you count to ten. Or, till *I* count to ten. Now certainly *that's* fair!"

"Five."

"Seven."

Up until now, he had been rather calm. It was when he saw her go up sadly to the closet and sadly step inside… He lit a cigarette. He feared the police. He could distinctly hear her moving about inside the closet, though he could not absolutely say what it was she was doing at every moment. And when she did come out… In fact, she had retained her slip, a long white garment that was worse than her actual dress.

"No, no, no; I want it *all* off. All!"

She returned to the closet. It boded ill, it seemed to him, that Chicago's all-night beacon chose that moment to brush past the window and to hesitate ever so slightly before moving away. He smoked, he hummed, figments of world literature passing through his head. Nothing, *nothing* could have prepared him for what followed.

"Tweedy!"

It destroyed his mind; he had read of this. Quickly, she ran to the bed and got inside. Nothing could have prepared her for what followed. It had been foretold, all of it, foretold in the adult world, namely that they need only to be left alone for twelve minutes in order for those activities foretold of in the adult world to be carried out. And now she had no defenses, none, no archers on call, no rectitudinous proctor to shoo him home. He thought of all the widows down below, their eyes upon the clock.

And Judy? Young, new, and trembling like a colt.

By the time he was himself again (after having gone back over his past memories to remember where he was and why), the girl was propped up next to him, beaming with admiration. She seemed to imagine the procedure that he had just carried out had required the highest degree of advanced education.

"Good Lord, I… "

"Don't talk."

"How come?"

"Because!"

Morning came; he recognized it from the size, the shape, the brightness and the location of the sun-wheel working so feverishly to burn a hole in the curtain. Even so, it did little damage to the darkness that clove to that room.

The girl had left a note, or rather a full-length letter in which she spoke more abundantly about love than ever she had done when they were face-to-face. Three times he read it through, dwelling upon certain phrases. She was sincere — one need only to glance at that handwriting to see the sort of person she was.

Lee now rose and made a more complete inspection of the place. Her possessions were few, and yet he could not say that they were terribly well organized in any sort of logical fashion. Her little mirror had a piece missing, no doubt the result of her strange habit of staring into it hypnotically for long periods. There was a book, one of those that he had assigned, and next to it a snapshot of her dog (lugubrious, pleading eyes) in a stand-up frame. She owned a radio and, parked under the table, two puffy brown shoes of an amazing heaviness.

He had defiled an elf. He was reminded of a rabbit he had shot in his youth, and of the way in which the thing had looked back at him ruefully in the moment before it died.

He dressed slowly, encased in guilt. This morning, the stairs were especially brittle and he had to cling to the wall to prevent the boards from yelping out loud. He had no rights in this building, none, and his very presence was a violation of numerous rules. Further, now that his face was ten times as corrupted as only yesterday... He stopped. Someone was coughing convulsively just on the other side of the wall while trying in desperation to call out between the explosions. On the next floor he darted down to the rest room and used it, even though such usage was not covered by Judy's rent.

The sun was bright. At times like this, in big northern cities, he liked to plow straight ahead, cigarette dangling, his very arrogance propelling him along at a clip. Across the street, he saw some three or four raw youths, simple virgins, as they looked to him. He wanted to puke. A man walked by, one who had done nothing that Lee had not also done, and this in spite of the other's thirty-five-year advantage. Leland snorted and went forward in such a way as to cause the man to get out of *his* way, instead of the other way around.

He had seen this before, his arrogance coming on so strongly that he had to stop and take hold of himself. To be sure, everything was owing to the girl. Even now, his pockets were full of the dimes and quarters (Judy's heard-earned tips) that he had borrowed from her bottom drawer.

The bridge was free. The slum dwellers, who perhaps knew something he did not, were unwilling to use it in broad daylight. On the crest, he stopped long enough to survey the ghetto, a place where thousands were struggling incompetently for happiness and finding not any. Here, the sun pressed down with weight, forcing the people to go about with lowered heads. In truth, the whole precinct was dipping sharply, a cake of brown manure in peril of slipping off into the lake.

He went on, entering the modern city. In a town like this, it was the plenitude of things, quantity on top of quantity, whether of books or slums or snotty-looking women. He passed a pawnshop, the richest he had seen, and with the greatest troves of coins and whatnot, including half a dozen saxophones and... He decided to pass it by. Next, he drifted past a window that was running over with mannequins, rich-looking and bored, save for one who wore a look of spiritual distress. The next window displayed a mannequin family, even down to the life-like cat. And all this time, to be assailed by smells — he counted two bakeries in one block, all of it backed up by a haughty-looking restaurant that flew the French flag. He did not stop, however, until he came to a bookstore, a grand one, where he put on his bored expression before going inside.

It had that smell of ink and paper that made him turn to thoughts of scholarship. His height was good enough to let him pluck a certain volume from the topmost shelf, a portly business in blue covers with the title and author in gold. As to the writer himself, he was one of those who had lived a hundred years ago, leaving behind a corpus of poetry so hard to understand that the better part of each several page had been given over to footnotes that themselves required still further explanation in an ever-tinier print that ran off the page altogether. Lee put on his glasses. Such a book, it seemed to him, comprised the perfect bedside companion, a box of wisdom, as it were, into which one could dip at times of emergency. Suddenly, he snatched down something that was a good deal more familiar to him — a decorated edition of the Rubáiyát, this one with metaphysical engravings of moon and stars and huge jesting faces in the sky.

He bought it, paying with quarters and dimes. According to his new style of life, his day's work was over now and he could go back home if he wanted, there to read or take a nap. Instead, he sauntered on, permitting the warm sun to nudge him withersoever it would.

At the restaurant, he knocked four times with increasing force until at last the hostess came and let him in. This time, she wore no smile at all.

"Judy's boyfriend, are you?"

"I can pay." (He made the coins to rattle in his pocket.)

The woman sighed deeply but then finally did lead him down to a table (no flowers on it) near the kitchen. Hardly had he settled before he saw Tweedy marching past in front of him wearing an odd little hat that was part of the uniform. She was blinking seriously, taking it hard. The covered dish she was carrying, apparently it had something very costly in it. Lee called to her.

"Good grief!" she reacted. "You're not supposed to be here!"

"I can pay. Besides, I wanted to bring your present."

He handed over the book with its stars and metaphysical drawings and watched while she fumbled with it, seemingly on the verge of tears. Suddenly, she turned and ran off. He waited, smoking in dignity until she had hidden the thing.

"Can we go to your room now? Briefly?"

"No!"

Lee looked at her and then, without being overly aware of what he was doing, reached out slowly for that part of her thigh that the uniform ingeniously exposed. The hostess was watching darkly from afar.

Lee now asked for his favorite of all meals, a sweet numble pie with farkleberry wine; instead, the girl brought him a dish of tiny ribs that had been taken from a particularly tasty little animal that had been larger than a mouse but yet smaller than a hen. The girl herself kept running back to check on him.

"It's good," said Lee. "Very good indeed."

"Want more?"

"Certainly."

She hurried away, her uniform and her legs drawing a great many glances from the rich people who had to move their flowers to one side. Came then the same two ladies of last week, both of them talking at the same time. And now, Lee must witness something that he did not at all enjoy looking at — the divine Judy hastening over to be of service of them. He knew it in advance, that no matter how speedily she worked, the two women would always be wearing little faces of perpetual discontent. He had to hold on to himself to keep from flying to their table and doing things to them. For already he had learned this much about the American society, namely that each time he came up against someone who more properly belonged in a penal colony, lo, the person was rich and wore a little face of perpetual discontent.

He supped for ten minutes and then, much refreshed, pushed back and lit a cigarette. And although his bill came to but little (Judy having no doubt falsified the amount), nevertheless he laid out a tremendous tip in quarters and dimes.

He squandered five hours walking up and down the city, looking into faces and even, at one point, descending for a distance into the subway before spurting back out again. He had no equipment; otherwise, he would have liked to go fishing in the Chicago canals. There was more than one bookstore in a city as big as this. And yet, it seemed to him there were actually fewer whores here, acre for acre, than in filthy Toledo to the east. He followed one of them for three blocks, taking notes, as it were, until he realized she was simply another office worker who liked to dress a certain way. It was when he got into a black neighborhood that he remembered to guard his tongue for fear his accent stand revealed. He saw males here, a hot-eyed people whom he would never in this world dare to out-stare, and never mind that he might have read a great many more books than they. Finally, he waded into a Slavic neighborhood of some sort where the advertisements were in a language that made him feel quite helpless. But all this was as nothing, a mere trifle really, when compared to the difficulty of finding in the big city a place where one could urinate without going up against the law.

At shortly after five, he went to meet her. Instead of her saucy uniform, she was again dressed in her Antioch clothes.

"I have to leave pretty soon," he said.

"I know."

"To catch my bus."

They flew into one another's arms, oblivious of the Chicagoans cutting around them on both sides.

"And then you'll be all alone again in your enormous room."

"No Lee, I can't stand it."

Across the road, the decaying sun left streaks upon a building so old and ruined, it looked like a relic of the Roman Age. But what was wrong with him, that he could not so much as hold his love without anticipations of death flooding through his head?

"Remember, Tweedy: twenty years from now someone else will be standing in this spot."

"No, Lee."

"And they'll be saying: 'Just imagine! Twenty years ago, someone else was standing here.'"

They went on, looking down at the pavement. He knew her fate, the same that had afflicted that long line of girls that had begun with Andromache and that Judy would bring to an end. And now she was tugging at him, trying to bring him back to the world.

"Are you going to be happy?"

"I *am* happy."

"Let me see."

He let her see.

"You're not!"

"Yes, I am." (Oddly, he really did feel himself turning optimistic again.)

"Do you want to go look at the lake?"

"Naw, I've seen stuff like that."

"Do you want to go up into the top of that building? You're always looking at it."

He did, in truth, now think of it as his own special tower. "Are buildings in New York as big as this?"

"Oh, yes. Bigger."

Lee looked at her, she with her buildings in the biggest of all cities. "But what did you *do* all those years — that's what I want to know. All those years in New York?"

She thought about it. "My father took us to the mountains once."

But here Lee held up his hand to stop her, amazed that she would again bring up the same little story of a small holiday at age five or six.

"Good Lord, I've been to the mountains many a time, the sea, too, and ocean as well. Want me to take you? No, I mean what did you do in New York *itself*?"

"How would you take me?"

"Easy! Everything is easy for people like me. Listen, I once spent three days out in the woods all by myself, when I was eleven."

"They must have been furious."

"They knew where I was."

"They let you?"

"'Let me'? They didn't have any choice! Listen, when you're the kind of person *I* am…" (He had drawn himself up to full height, the girl looking up at him admiringly.) "Nothing can harm you as long as I'm around. Remember that."

"And who's going to protect me from you?"

"Nobody."

She shivered. They had come to that place in Chicago where a dark, resentful-looking boy in a window, (flour up to his elbows) was preparing pizzas, tossing them up in the air for the benefit of tourists. Lee met his gaze, neither of them choosing to make a contest of it. A cafe came up next, Lee holding the door and then showing her to a tiny table with chairs made out of wire. She looked good, she did, in her sweater and beret.

"What are you thinking?"

"About you. What are *you* thinking?"

"The same."

"Thinking about you?"

"No! You."

"The 'sublime' Judy?"

"Right. 'Divine,' actually."

The waitress came, bringing tea and crumpets. These latter were hot things, with molten frosting. They waited while the woman lifted the lid and began mixing their tea for them.

"O, yes," (she said) "I knew it as soon as you came in. 'Yep, they're in love alright,' that's what I said. Ask *her* whether I said it or not."

They looked to the other woman, the one in the kitchen. She was nodding.

"How could you tell?"

"Anyone could tell. Ah, well, enjoy it while you can."

"No privacy!" said Judy, once they were left alone. And then, with the horror registering on her at last: "What else do they know? Oh!"

They moved down Clark Street holding hands and looking into the shops and marts. A pet store was open, three little puppies leaping up and down in the window. Judy, of course, had gone up straightway, had gotten down on both knees and was cooing at them. He had to drag her to the intersection and then down into the next block where a crowd of sullen-looking boys stood about in front of an arcade. Lee waded in amongst them, aware they were falling silent as Judy cut across their view. Now did he most sorely regret it — that she was not in her tightest sweater and highest heels, that he might stir up ever larger degrees of envy and hate. But what strange new pleasure was this, the joy of being hated? The girl herself wanted to cry.

"I wish I were old and ugly!"

He had heard it before.

"And lived on a farm!"

They had come to a section where vendors had set up on the sidewalk and were offering jewelry and souvenirs of various sorts.

Lee sidled to one of the tables, viewing the stuff with a critical eye. Already, the man had keened in on them.

"That pretty girl ought to have some earrings — what's the matter with you?" He stretched forth, holding the thing to her ear. "See?"

"How much is that…?"

"That? That's an *opal*, son — you've got real good judgment, I'll say that much. What, you used to be in the trade?"

"No, sir."

"You've made a study of it."

"No. I swear."

"O. K., for you it's three-fifty. I'm losing my shirt, you understand."

"I reckon not."

"Hold it! O. K., for you, three even. I'd like to see it go to somebody like you."

Lee paid, digging out the dimes and quarters one by one and then waiting while the man wrapped the thing in tissue and put it away tenderly in a tiny white box.

"You be careful with that now, you hear?"

"Yes, sir. I will." They moved off hurriedly, going a full block before he presented it to her with a certain formality.

"How does it look?"

"Perfect! It goes with the kind of person you are."

"What kind?"

"Opal."

They flew into one another's arms.

Judy, who knew the building much better than did he, led the way. Tonight, the landlady had left her door open and was sitting in a rocking chair with both eyes on the staircase. They moved past quickly, Lee in his bored expression. The cough that he had heard three weeks ago? The person was even sicker now. From somewhere, a toilet somewhere was churning over and over and gasping for air. They threw themselves into the room and secured the door. It gave him a wonderful feeling, knowing that this tenth-acre of space had been set aside for them at this particular moment in history, just when it was most needed. No one knew where they were. They might hold out forever, given a rifle and supplies of food.

"No one can find us here."

But the girl, sitting with her feet ten inches off the floor, had fallen into a reverie. "Soon, you'll be gone," she said.

"Will you cry?"

She nodded.

"How long do you cry? An hour?"

"Sometimes. Usually half an hour."

"Then what?"

"Then I go to sleep."

"And then cry again the following night?"

She nodded. "Unless I'm too tired."

It satisfied him. He watched while she took her book and her opal and made space for them next to her dog picture.

"I had to borrow some of your money."

"Do you have enough to get back to Toledo?"

"Maybe I could borrow it from you."

She came around, opened the bottom drawer, and took out a white sock full of quarters. He remained silent as she counted them out, nestling each coin momentarily in her miniature palm. He knew well the humiliating work they had cost her. Guilt crashed down over him, the most intense that he had known since that day he had massacred a rabbit who had done nothing to bring it on.

"I'll pay you back," he said, his voice catching.

"You don't have to."

"Judy, Judy." He brought her down and folded her up in his arms. And now he was spinning again, catching glimpses of her book and coins, her elfin shoes and small black dog trembling now with indignation.

THIRTY-NINE

BEHIND HIM, the quartz city grew further and further and smaller and smaller until at last it disappeared altogether, taking Judy down with it. There was something metaphysical about it, that whereas but a moment ago he had been in her arms and in her bed, now the entire city was no greater than a proton floating in a glass of milk.

Each journey had its flavor; this time, he felt he was riding down into a valley full of colored houses. Up front, five profiles could be seen, one of them in a hat that resembled a tea kettle with handle and spout. For some while, a motorcycle had been running mile for mile with them, caught helplessly in their wake. Crows, too, he saw, a long unsteady file of them flying off drunkenly to the immense yellow wall of the moon.

They came to Indiana and parked at a station in the north-northwestern corner of the state. It never failed: no matter what time of night or morning, there were always widows and grandmothers — Lee recognized two of them — slumbering among the benches. He went to his favorite booth only to find that someone had recently been there before him. There was a used cup with sediment in it, also a paper napkin blotted with a pair of huge red lips. How he loved it! the ugliness and poverty, the coffee and grease. The music, too, he loved that as well, though it stabbed him to the heart to know that someday it must be seen as something merely quaint, or in any case as having happened long ago.

It was not the first time that he had felt that he was himself obsolete already and that the very next bus might be bringing in a new boy, younger than himself, whose taste in music (as in other things) would be more up-to-date than any of his. And yet, he was not the sort to go through youth and then leave it behind, forgetting how it was as soon as it was over. He understood, of course, that he was simply a mid-century type, a transitional figure between the rough men of the past and the soft ones coming up. Death was everything, and even that required a long and tedious wait. *These* were his thoughts when, suddenly, he leapt up and raced for the gate.

He had to run alongside for a good twenty yards, pounding on the door. But this time, the driver turned out to be a jester who got joy by opening and then slamming the door in Lee's face before at last permitting him to squirt on board and take his place.

The next miles were stranger than the first. He remembered a river, a town, and then a train full of well-dressed persons traveling in parallel with the bus on the opposite shore. *They* were pushing into the future, *he* falling back into the past.

Presumably, he slept, awakening to detect a face hovering over him and someone poking him with a flashlight.

"O. K., fellow, this is it."

"It?"

"That's right. Come on, let's go."

He stumbled out, moved a few paces, and then ran back for his suitcase. Already a crowd was pressing at the bus, their anxiety to get out of town making him wonder if he had not come back at a bad time. Save for the three ticket-sellers peering out from niches in the wall, the city was abandoned. These three had faces so elongated and so thin, they were invisible when viewed straight on. Lee moved past hurriedly, hitting the street and then launching off by habit for the newspaper. A derelict floated up, a hard-looking man who glanced at Lee, debating whether to try and take his suitcase away.

Two blocks further, Lee sliced into the neon zone. He pushed through a yellow halo that looked like a dandelion gone to seed, and then came out safely on the other side. Next was an orange-colored sign melting onto the walk. He felt the very walls were built of chalk and ambergris, and that he could discern fragments breaking off and tumbling with dream-like slowness into the street. A man rose up in front of him, his opaque glasses reflecting two alternate images of the pock-marked moon. Someone spoke, someone near at hand, someone whose mouth was stopped with rags. Reaching out blindly, Lee's hand disappeared into the ambiance, stumbling up against a face with cracked lips and massy eyebrows.

He crossed at hazard, plunging again into the crowd and then coming out in front of a theater enshrined in almost more neon than one could bear to look upon. The girl looked at him with a vexation turning to outright hostility after he produced one of his free passes.

"The film's almost over," she described.

"I don't care."

He went in, but then had to wait for his eyes to adapt. Someone had left a foot out in the aisle where he could hardly fail to trod upon it. And yet, instead of screaming, she merely gasped and made a face that, in the dark, looked like a mask of woe. He went on, turning finally into a crowded row while holding his suitcase aloft. Here the smell was mostly of insecticide, deodorant and popcorn.

The show itself was nothing; even so, it gave him some relief to be inside at a time when the night and society in general seemed to him excessively weird. Undoubtedly, it would be in just such surroundings as these that he must expire someday, aged twenty-three. He hoped for a good person, someone to prop him up discretely till everyone else had filed outside.

FORTY

SHE HAD BEEN CRYING — the page showed numerous evidences of it. He saw where one full word had floated away. Now, tenderly, he folded the letter and put it away.

This year, spring was proving unduly thin, a mere few weeks squeezed in between a very broad winter (now ended) and the immense summer season yet to come. Lee gathered his blanket, his book and cigarettes and then stepped out into what might once have been a "yard," but now was simply a closed-in area cluttered with garbage tossed down from the upper stories. For ten minutes, he lay looking up hopefully into the somewhat promising face of the sun. Not since Alabama, had he experienced a single day of adequate warmth. Today was bright enough certainly, perhaps too bright, but as for *force* and for *power*… Great was his contempt for the northern sun; he could feel his gorge rising. He had expected to hear flesh sizzling; here, one could all but reach up and fondle the thing without so much as endangering his fingertips.

He did sleep. He almost hated to come awake, knowing that he must again go back mentally over the years and bring himself up-to-date as to where he was and why. This time, however, there were two persons watching him — he could see them — two of them sitting on the steps and studying him bemusedly. Lee jumped up.

"Oh!"

They grinned.

"What are *you* doing here?"

They went inside, all of them jabbering at the same time.

"This, then, is the 'bed,'" said Lee. He pulled back the mattress that they might view the bottle, the tire, and the unsteady column of books that it rested upon. They marveled, Phyllis getting down on one knee to check the titles.

"And here," Lee went on, "is where I keep my suit."

"Christ."

"Where do you do your writing?"

He pointed to the dresser, a green one with a doily on top. He had not done any writing.

"So, you actually live in here then?"

"Certainly. As a matter of fact, I've probably done more suffering here than in any other place in the world."

Phyllis smiled.

"Raskolnikov, he …"

"We know about him. Are you going to show us Toledo, or not?"

They went down. The evening was warm, mild, mellow, the fireflies showing an unnatural interest in Luke's weed-like hair. To the west was unexplored territory, "bourgeois land," Lee had always assumed. Instead, he led them down straightway to the neon district in which, tonight, lavender and red were the predominant colors. They had to go two full blocks before running into their first vomiting drunk.

"I do a lot of suffering in this particular area."

"Yes!" said Phyllis. "And then there's always the chance of getting killed." She grinned. In her long purple dress and high yellow socks, she looked like a stork marching on gaily apace. Two soldiers stopped short in order to stare at her.

"Phyl's supposed to be at school," said Luke. "But I managed to free her. Through the window, if you know what I mean."

"But what about you? Aren't you supposed to be in the Army this session?"

"It's not a good situation, Lee. They teach us how to gouge out eyeballs. It's a whole different philosophy from Antioch's."

"You went AWOL?"

"I snap my fingers at 'em."

The restaurant came up, Lee ushering them into the darkness and to his own special booth.

"Yes, yes, this looks like you," said Phyllis.

"A person could die in here, and no one would know about it for weeks."

"Wonderful. But tell us about Judy."

"She cries a lot. However, I gave her a list of books to read."

"I can just imagine. How considerate."

"Hey!" said Luke. "Why don't we go visit her?"

They looked at each other wildly. The jukebox was playing *I Only Have Eyes for You*, wherefore Lee now particularly hated to be without his lady. Taking a cigarette, he made a brief yellow flame that revealed Lucien's starved face. He found it wonderful in their presence, Lee, surrounded as they were by attentive shadows bending in their direction.

"Very well, tomorrow we go to Chicago. Judy will be pleased." And then: "I suppose your parents know about me?"

They nodded, Luke and Phyllis.

"They hate me, I suppose."

"A little bit. Hey! did I tell you that Phyl is writing a play?"

Lee looked at her. He did not like people of his own age doing any extent of writing while he himself was doing none.

"Good. What's it about?"

"Oh, God. It's not 'about' anything. It's a reply."

They waited.

"A reply to Eliot, if you must know."

"Sounds good."

"Sure, you could make mincemeat out of Eliot."

"No, no, no; I just want to take it to its logical conclusion."

"Well sure. I mean! if he can't do it for himself… "

Came now the waitress with their meal, a heavy one comprised of chicken, slaw, coffee, and browned rolls with butter enough to get them to Chicago and through the trials to come. They jumped to it, wolfing it down.

"Hold it!" said Lee. "I think this is the time to make an agreement — that we'll meet again, right here, thirty years from now."

"Oh, God!"

"No, it's for the best," said Luke.

"But we need a signal. In case one of us is dead."

"We could signal on my harmonica."

"And Tweedy. Tweedy needs a signal, too."

"Poor Tweedy."

"What's it going to be like, Lee, in thirty years from now?"

"Well…" He smoked. "It sure can't go on like this forever."

"Things will be quieter?"

"No question about it."

"Do you think there might be other people like us?"

"Doubt it. No, we're the last of this kind. But we'll have a lot more great writers."

"More than now?"

"Certainly. In thirty years from now, no one's going to care about television, things like that. Shoot, we'll be like the Greeks by that time."

"Really, Lee?"

"Absolutely. Beyond your wildest dreams. And the architecture! Buildings will be built in the shape of great men's heads."

They nodded. Luke, he saw, had taken a piece of his napkin and was writing it down.

They went outside and turned down the block. The "gorge," neon-bestrewn, was perilous at this hour, with sinister-looking individuals popping up on all sides. Phyllis, who had never done anything nor gone anywhere, was taking it in brightly while wearing a clenched smile that seemed to say that reality was pretty much what she had expected, based upon the poetry she had read. The pawnshop came up, the three of them drawn helplessly to the window.

"What's the story behind that guitar, Lee?"

"Farm boy. Trying to break into the music business."

"And where is he now?"

"Killed himself."

"And that suitcase?"

"Ventriloquist. Dummy inside."

"No, no," said Phyl. "There's a letter in there."

"What does it say?"

"That's not for us to know."

"Aw, come on Phyl, read it!"

Instead, that moment, the proprietor stepped into view and stood smiling down at them falsely.

"Jesus!"

They moved off, crossing at the intersection and then passing through a knot of youths who turned and looked grinningly after Phyllis. The burlesque was next, out front a line of old men shuffling nervously. Lee pointed to the poster of a wild-looking stripper dressed like Queen Elizabeth. To Lee's infinite regret, Evelyn West had already come and gone, granting the people a one-night performance only.

"Christ, look at that one! Just hope you never meet a person as vicious as that."

Phyllis came up to judge the picture. "No, actually she's very nice."

"Nice! She'll cut your throat for you!" said the derelict standing with them.

"You have to look at the eyes."

"She's right, Lee."

They got in line behind an elderly man chewing on a substance of some kind. Lee offered his money, but only to get the same baleful stare that the woman seemed to hold in reserve just for him. To Phyllis she was indifferent; she had no objection to people who wouldn't too much enjoy what was going on inside. Luke came up.

"How old are you?"

"Eighteen."

"No. No, I know your type; you're seventeen, aren't you? Alright, take your money, right now, and get away from here where you don't belong." (She snatched back the ticket and began pushing away the money as well, some of the coins actually dropping off onto the pavement. They had to scramble for it, Lee fighting to get the half-dollar piece out from under someone's shoe.)

"Jesus!"

"No, that's the way it is in this town."

"What a bitch! Write about it, Lee."

Phyllis had a way of particularly enjoying herself just when everyone else was angry. Now, with a breeze coming off the lake, she was listening keenly, head tilted, her ancient tune again intimating in her ear of far-off meadows of loveliness and rest.

They went twenty blocks, down to the lake itself and then out onto a wooden pier rising and falling slightly with the tide. Tonight, the water was black, but also of an exceeding thinness; Lee could hear it lapping at the piles. Further down, a foundry of some sort was blazing up now and again, sometimes shooting up flares that raced across the lake.

"Tomorrow, Chicago."

"Poor Tweedy."

For a while, no one spoke. From the factory a glow went up, lingered, and then died away. Later he would be able to recall it perfectly, even to the number of ripples slapping at the posts.

"Tweedy's pregnant."

Silence. Five ripples, each the length of his own heartbeat, passed beneath the pier.

"Oh, you poor children!"

"Christ!" (He put his hand helpfully on Lee's shoulder.)

"She wants to go away, take care of things by herself."

"Don't let her, Lee."

"No."

"Because you'd regret it the rest of your life. Hey! you could come live in Rhode Island. They got a bay there so big; you could feed your whole family out of it."

"God! No, they have to get married."

"Married? You know very well they'd never let her in the dorm with us."

"Oh, God!"

"Hey! we could rent a house, all four of us."

"Yeah!" He loved it. And yet, somehow, over the hills and far away, he knew it would never happen.

"Sure. We could even let Martin come visit us, see how happy we are."

They stood and began climbing back, passing slowly in front of dilapidated warehouses and here and there a tavern doing good business at this hour. Phyllis, in her long-embroidered dress and taut hair, was quite oblivious to the people who slowed and then turned in their tracks to watch her. Luke slumped along behind, piping intermittently into his harmonica. And if the girl appeared to have just stepped forth from out of an abbey, Luke looked as though he had been sleeping in a hill of straw.

Lee had to smuggle them upstairs, lest it be seen in 1957, that two boys and one girl were sharing the same room. For a long time, they sat on the edge of the "bed," each of them thinking somberly about the future and tomorrow, about Judy and Chicago. Phyllis was reading.

"Life is strange," said Luke. "I'm not going back, Lee, not if I have to gouge out eyes. What kind of thing is that, for someone who wants to be a doctor?"

Phyllis grinned.

"Me, I've only got a few years," said Lee, "and *then* where will Judy be?"

"Hey! maybe she'll have twins."

"God!"

"They'd have to be real small, of course — two little small ones walking around in red ribbons. No, you've got to come to Rhode Island Lee; it's small, too."

"Naw, hell, you'll be dead by then. No point in coming to Rhode Island if you aren't there."

"How do you figure, Lee? That I'll be dead?"

"Well! You're a deserter, aren't you? They shoot deserters."

"He's right."

There was a long, deep, remorseful silence, interrupted only by the sound of a page turning in Phyllis' book. From the building opposite, a neon advertisement was casting pools of blood on the floor of the tiny apartment. Lee lit a cigarette and passed it down to Luke. Phyl had stretched out sideways across the "bed" and was smiling up at the ceiling in an aesthetic swoon, strains of poetry circulating through her head. Fated to die a virgin, she had a boy on either side. Lee turned off the lamp. He had the horrible feeling that the others were about to drop off to sleep without him.

"Let me be the first to go to sleep, O. K.?"

"This is a terrible bed."

"See that mirror? Sometimes I can see things going on in there."

Someone shuddered violently.

"Is Phyl asleep?"

"No, no. God."

"And when we awake, ten billion years will have gone by."

"Again, with that? I have to say it, Lee, that kind of stuff makes me want to vomit."

"We need to have a signal. So as to communicate when we're dead."

"Three knocks on wood?"

That moment, by the strangest of things, they heard the next-door tenant (whom Lee had never actually seen), heard him roll over in his creaky bed and then pound three times precisely on the fragile wall. They roared with laughter, even Phyllis as well, who produced a high-pitched sound that Lee was hearing for only the second or perhaps third time.

"We're dead already!"

Outside, a car drove past, throwing a long, yawning shadow that bent and twisted and somersaulted until it had touched all four walls and eight windows. A faint blue mote rose to the surface of the mirror, where it scintillated briefly and disappeared.

"I'll be the first to die probably."

"No, you'll be the last. And that will be your punishment for thinking about it all the time."

"Poor Judy."

"You can't think about life, if you don't think about death."

"That's not good, Lee; I don't like that kind of thing."

"Is Phyl asleep?"

"No, no."

Silence. He heard Luke blow one last note, a tiny one, followed by the sound of a barking dog from far away. A cry like that could come from nowhere else — the burnt ruined hills of Alabama.

FORTY-ONE

HE WOKE IN A PUDDLE OF SUNLIGHT. Using his Will, he was able to force himself back down again.

It was upon his second awakening that he found Phyllis at the window with her hands hanging down. Luke had stationed himself at the other window where he was waiting with infinite patience for the girl's grey mood to go away. Under these circumstances, Lee went back to bed.

He awoke for the third time at shortly after ten to find Luke and Phyllis watching him with amusement.

"Is it O.K. now?"

"Yes, yes, I'm perfectly alright. God!"

"You talk in your sleep, Lee; I thought you ought to know. Here, I tried to jot some of it down."

"Poor Tweedy."

They hit the street in bright season (clouds seething overhead), and then fell by habit into the single-file formation made necessary by their numbers. It was a fine sun, full of optimism, and he saw that each and every green yard had a gardener in it. To such an extent had the American character deteriorated, everywhere he looked there were adults crawling on all fours in a life-long search for weeds.

"It's a bourgeois town, Lee."

"Not at night."

"Look at that one."

It was a middle-age gardener with a watering hose. Lee had no doubt but that he really would spray them if they stepped across the line.

"Hasn't read a book in twenty years."

It was true. Any one of the three of them could have outrun him and outjumped him, while as for the things of the mind…! But it was he and his who owned the American land.

They hastened on, anxious to get back to the blighted area. Phyllis had the lead and was stepping forth stork-like at a pace that Lee couldn't match. They passed a car still smoldering from one of last night's collisions and then, rarest of things, a pile of cats sleeping in the gutter.

Another block further, they turned in at the bus station and formed up in line in front of one of the ticket-sellers whose face, as acidulous and narrow as a dime, suggested he was suffering from bad odors. Lee turned to Phyllis. She had recovered from her mood and now, instead of plaster, her face was cool, placid, and intelligent to a degree. Indeed, he could see clean through the spheroid of her pale green eye, even to being able to read the clock on the wall. This, then, was what Time looked like to Phyllis.

"Don't tell Judy she's pregnant," said Lee. "No! I mean don't tell her that I said that we know that…"

"*Bien entendu.*"

Lee thanked her. In her good moods, she seemed to prefigure that editor or poetess or art curator that was to have been her destiny. Luke came up.

"Hey Lee, there's a person here who thought he was going to Cincinnati." (He pointed to a squatty little man in boots and glasses storming about with a face splotched with anger.) Impossible not to laugh, even Luke, too, who had a way of giving two or three short chuckles and then carrying around a faint smile for a long time afterward. The boy had a vocation for hapless people, especially for the myriads of humpback old ladies with their parcels and worn-out shoes; he was forever darting off to get into conversations with one or another of them.

"Time-travelers, Lee. End of the world. Hey! now *there's* a good face."

In truth, there was an unusually large contingent of them on this day, all of them sitting quite motionless so as not to call attention to themselves.

They moved up for the tickets. The man's fingers were long, very long, his ring worn down to a mere wire from so much erosion with coins. They waited while he analyzed them shrewdly and at great length through the peephole in his eyeshade.

"The 10:12 for Chicago?"

"Yes, sir."

The man sniffed but said no more. Suddenly, understanding what these delaying tactics portended, Lee turned and raced for it. The bus was thirty yards ahead; nevertheless, with Phyllis galloping at his side, he was able to run it down and begin pounding on it with noise, the eighth time he had had to do so since leaving Alabama.

The back bench was taken. Lee cursed. Traveling by sunlight — to Lee, such a procedure was unpleasant at the best of times. Now, in addition to everything else, he found a businessman in a suit who, even as Lee sat looking at him, tacked sharply to one side, revealing yet another just like him sitting just behind. He could feel his gorge rising. At night, with the three of them in the extreme rear, this might have ranked as one of the best rides in his whole career; instead, he found himself pinioned to the window by a fat woman with the steely sun shining direct into his face. He did so loathe it, sun, light, and this geo-economic convention that put such curtails upon the gorgeous night. He wished that Alexander really had done what he had threatened, namely to use his sword upon the sun and slice it into a batch of tiny white shiny stars.

He snoozed briefly, coming awake when the twelve-year-old in front of him turned in her seat and spoke to him. Lee groaned. Behind him were three, not just two, business types wearing suits.

They arrived in Gary, loveliest of cities. The driver was a simple man, qualified for daylight driving only; Lee watched as he stood and smiled and began reciting the prescribed warnings about this town. The passengers listened courteously at first, but soon got to their feet and began pouring down the aisle. Lee had a glimpse of Phyllis swept along in the crowd, a look of desperation on her face.

The station was jammed. A bearded man was waving enthusiastically at Lee, until he recognized his mistake. Luke, who had gone into the men's room, came out wearing an appalled expression.

"It's not good in there Lee."

"Where's Phyl?"

They looked for her, at last finding her sitting off by herself at one of the benches.

"Looks bad. Better talk to her."

"No, you talk to her."

"I can't talk to her!"

"But Lee...!"

"This is *your* woman we're talking about. It's Judy that's mine."

That was true. The boy took up his harmonica finally and made a faint sound on it before heading off toward the girl. Lee's thoughts were upon Judy, and the thought of her lying in the enormous bed with her feet pointing toward the ceiling. Not yet would she have picked them up on her telepathy, no inkling as yet that he was even now homing in on her across two states. Meantime, Luke and Phyllis were kissing emotionally, bringing a great deal of unfavorable attention to themselves. A policeman came by, slowing when he saw them. Luke was in his suit, but the suit was falling apart. For her part, Phyllis had a sore on her leg and the sore was bleeding. Lee had time enough, barely, to report to the men's room, wash his hands, look in the mirror, ignite a cigarette, and then go chasing after the bus until the driver consented to stop.

The back seat could have been entirely free, but for a withered old man with a hearing aid. However, this one seemed content to stay in his own corner and hew to the scenery hurrying by. Unobtrusive as he was, Lee made no attempt to shut down his hearing aid. Already, Chicago had them in its pull. He looked for the high buildings and unblinking searchlights scanning the region to a certain distance. It was still a matter of magic to him, how that out of all the immensity of space and great cities, how it was possible for people to come together again. He wanted to sleep in Judy's arms and when he died, to lie in the same box with her, wherefore everything depended upon the driver now.

How odd, summer was. They passed a dilapidated farm house from the last century, the disembodied souls of those who once had lived there now swarming overhead like a school of flies. The countryside had exhausted its usefulness, leaving only a green and yellow smear in which a few old people could be seen standing about in the fields. And the sun — Lee's opinion had improved. It produced a hum so familiar to everyone by now that no one could even hear it anymore.

They drove straightway to the city gates and demanded to be let inside. The town was somnolent in daylight, a few listless mild-eyed lotus-eaters shuffling down the walk. The bus dipped sharply and dove down into the ground. Today, the crowd was large, the majority of them wearing forced smiles.

The bus parked, groaned, shuddered, and then poured them out onto the platform. He must link up with Luke and Phyllis at once, or risk losing them forever. Never would he accustom himself to it, crowds as large as this. Just then, he heard Luke calling from afar and turned in time to see him vanishing up the escalator.

They gathered in the rotunda. Phyllis was smiling cheerfully, auguring well for the next hour or so.

"So. Here we are."

"I was conceived in a town like this." He took the harmonica but then put it back again. Inexhaustible numbers of people were flowing past on all sides, each of them representing an interesting story that was slipping away.

"Lee! Now *there's* a tough face. Look at it."

"Yeah." (He thought the boy was about to go off in pursuit of it.) "But first, we must find Judy."

They hit the sidewalk, the three of them falling into single-file formation. On this day, the city was yet more littered than on his previous visits. He saw a leaf of newspaper scuttling crab-wise in the wind, no one bothering to pick it up. The bridge came up. Leland turned and addressed himself to the others.

"The bridge. And once we've crossed it, we'll be in risky territory."

"Not good Lee. And you say that Judy's in there?"

He pointed to the slum-cake, now closer than ever to sliding off into the canal. Phyllis was smiling. She did not believe in danger, she for whom the material world had no authenticity in the first place.

"It's grim, Lee. A person could disappear in there and then come out years later full of wisdom."

"That's what happened to me."

Phyllis laughed.

They went forward, crossing into the slum proper. They passed a collapsed building with a bathtub lying belly-up in the rubble. In this place, two boys were selling custards, unclean ones on which green flies were pacing nervously in circles. Luke slowed and was in process of digging out his money — until Lee forced him to put it back. Phyllis had moved out in front and was marching gaily into the worst of the ghetto. They called her, whereon she stopped and came gaily back again.

At Judy's place, they climbed past the woman with the foot in her lap and thence into the building itself where, luckily, the landlady was not on sentry. Phyllis was coming on strongly, her masculine hands finding irregularities in what at first sight seemed a featureless wall. Lee never forgot that they were drawing nigher and nigher to Judy, whom he envisioned lying on her bed, blinking, paying heed to the indications of sound coming from below. She had left her puffy shoes just outside her door, as if in hopes of someone leaving a gift in them. Lee rapped loudly at her door, a massy thing with more than enough space between the bottom and the floor for insects to come in and out.

"Come along, dearie," he said, employing the falsetto voice of death. "It's time."

"No!" Her voice was distant; she had retreated down into the dark part of her room. Impossible not to laugh. They could hear her scrambling wildly, possibly in an effort to force open the window.

"Tweedy!"

No answer.

"Tweedy, it's *me*!"

Still no answer.

"Tweedy!"

Further silence.

"Tweedy! Phyl is here. She wants you to open the door."

"Phyl?"

"Right."

"Tell her to say something."

"Yes, yes, it's me. God! It's alright."

"Is Lee out there?"

"Yes, yes. Yes."

"You're sure?"

"I'm looking at him right now! Even as I speak."

The door opened an inch, and then another before suddenly closing up again. He had to take hold, pulling her out into the hall.

"Lee!" (She hurled herself about his neck.) "Lee!"

He grinned; all his life he had wanted to be greeted in this way. They kissed emotionally, Luke and Phyllis looking on proudly. He lifted and carried her inside where she had definitely been lying with her feet pointing toward the ceiling—almost the first thing he noticed was her short impression in the quilt. Luke came in, saw the size of the place, and marveled. As to Judy, she was wearing trousers and an old shirt of his own that he had believed to be lost. Her hair was in an upheaval and made her look as if she had grown two enormous ears.

"Oh baby, I thought I was going to die."

"Me, too. I thought I was going to die, too."

"Oh, baby."

"Oh!"

"Luke and Phyl are here."

"I know."

Luke, who had wandered down into the dark part, turned and waved. And now at last, with all four of them in one location, it seemed to Lee that nothing very awful could happen, not even if there were tornadoes or a world depression. In fact, he actively craved such things.

Late afternoon having come, they piled out into the hall and, with Phyllis speaking of poets and poetry, began the perilous descent. Below, two disheveled-looking women were arguing hotly in a foreign tongue. Lee had a dread of meeting up with the landlady and having to explain how it was that four persons now inhabited Judy's room.

Outside, the day itself was sinking fast. He saw some half-dozen men slinking homeward with empty lunch boxes, their numbers suggesting how few were those still carrying on any kind of effort in the ghetto. A lamp came on in the top story across the road—this was the moment he loved, with daylight rotting in front of him. Judy, on the other hand, was younger than ever; looking at her, he saw two bright eyes and one dark broach.

"Judy, Judy."

"I know, I know."

They flew into one another's arms. Years later, he was to remember the deranged woman with the foot in her lap, how she was cheering, as it seemed, and urging them on. Luke played the harmonica.

At the corner they turned and began to push into the even more authentic slum. Judy, clutching his hand, also held him by the belt. He saw a woman of Mexican appearance, saw her come out onto her balcony to watch them pass.

"What a lot of poverty!" said Luke. "The government ought to do something."

"Naw, I like 'em better this way. It's when they aren't poor that…"

"That's not a good thing to say, Lee."

They had to stop, the four of them bouncing up against a high wall with a culvert in it that was so low and of such small caliber that it looked as if it had been put in for the use of mice.

"Let's go back," Judy recommended.

"No."

Phyllis grinned.

Luke played his harmonica.

A tight space yes, but not impossibly so. They came out into a festive region where great numbers were standing about aimlessly in a haze of mist and fireworks. The usual people had set up little booths and pavilions, each with a knot of customers shifting nervously as they gazed into the merchandise. Others were vending hot-air balloons bearing the portraits of baseball players. At the next stall, a refined-looking woman, delicate and with a tragic face, was trading small odds and ends of turquoise, tiny glass animals, and playing cards with obscene pictures on them. Even as Lee stood by, a mournful-looking child reached up slowly to purloin a porcelain giraffe.

There was more. The next stall was full of wire cages that held, each of them, two or three brilliantly colored birds, ordinary wrens dipped in paint. He need only purchase a single bird and set it free to enjoy Judy's love throughout eternity; instead, that moment, Luke came up.

"We have to find a hotel, Lee. Quick. It's the crowd."

Phyllis was in a bad state, her face beginning to "flake," so to tell, and to reveal the concrete beneath.

They had to hurry back to Dearborn Street before hitting upon a hotel, the most dilapidated and at the same time most evil-looking such institution that Lee had ever yet set eyes upon. He spied a fat man, his breasts configured like a woman's, sitting in one of the upper windows while picking slowly at his nose.

They went in (the place stank of linoleum and burnt urine) to find a small man seated on the staircase with a sandwich and glass of milk.

"Is there a room?"

"Four of you?"

"Two of us."

"We're just friends," said Lee. "My wife and I."

"Two of you then?"

"Right. Those two."

He looked closely at Phyllis and then, after thinking about it, took another swig of milk. "Well, you'd best talk to Corky. Me, I don't work here." He drank. "And I *sure* don't live here, God no."

"'Corky'?"

He pointed. Corky was sitting across the room in an armchair, hearing everything.

"We need a room, Corky. It's bad."

"Bad?"

Luke nodded. Lee saw there were several others seated in the dim, some of them asleep and some not, and one man wearing pajama trousers and nothing else.

"'Bad,' he says. Alright, I got a room. Dollar an hour."

"How about all night?"

"All night? You make it last that long, boy, and you can have it for free!"

There was widespread laughter from the various chairs. Silence restored, the man handed over two enormous keys held together on a shoestring. "Just keep on going till you find it. You'll find it." And then as an afterthought: "And keep away from Room 204, you read me?"

They climbed, all four, up into a dim region in which the odor grew only the more astringent the higher they went. A woman came out and then, seeing them, ran back in and slammed the door. Their own room, once they had found it, had nothing to do with the keys. Luke nudged it open gently with his foot.

One single cot, eighteen inches in breadth and covered with nothing, stood next to a window blackened over with paint. An abandoned shoe lay in the corner; except for that, there was nothing in the room whatsoever, not so much as a lamp or curtain or a blanket on the cot.

"You can't stay here."

Luke shrugged. Already Phyllis was on the cot, her face to the wall, lying in the embryonic position.

Once more back at Judy's place, that was when the rain began to fall. She lit a candle, the sight of it reducing both of them to silence as they sat across from each other staring into the flame.

"Marry me."

"No. You're too young."

"I'm old as you!"

"I'm a girl."

"But…!"

"I'll go away for a while."

"What!"

"And come back later."

He got up and stormed about the room. "*We are going to get married* — are you listening? *Married*. You and me."

"No. You're too young." Then, more brightly: "We could write to each other."

She drifted into the dark but then then came back a moment later with two cups not much larger than doll-house equipment.

"Will you have tea with me? Now that we are…"

"Lovers?"

They drank in sadness. Looking at her across the table, more than ever he felt as though they were suspended in space, miles above the glittering city. The rain had turned ferocious and had found an entry into the remote part of the room where it was pattering on the floor.

"Will you Lee? Write to me?"

"No! If you leave, my life is finished."

"Oh, it is not. You're going to live a long time and do all kinds of things."

"No, no, no, no, no, I don't want to live 'a long time,' as you call it, and do things. I just want Judy."

"You said everything that happens, it happens over and over again? For all eternity?"

"Yes." (He could see where she was leading — she was smart.) "Yes, I said that."

"Well then! We'll see each other again. Over and over again."

"Goddamn it!" He got up and stormed about the room. "We'll get married."

"No, you're too young." She rose and went off, coming back with her curlers and pins. He did so love to watch while she slowly combed out her long brown hair with the immemorial strokes that dated back to his grandmother, and from thence to *her* grandmother, and so on and so forth even to the Greeks. Later, he would take consolation from having recognized love when he held it in his grasp, from having seized upon it when he could, those few moments permitted in a lifetime.

"I love thee, Judy." (She had freckles on her shoulder, very like those he had seen on certain types of thrushes' eggs.)

"And I love thee."

Came morning, they rolled out and ran downstairs. It was a bright day, the weather made yet more ideal for having so recently been washed by rain. With all these variables of light, temperature, and refraction, he felt that he had been through this day before, down to the last detail, a moment of gold in that twentieth-century of ten billion years ago.

At the corner, they turned into a broad street full of thousands of pedestrians who, because they did not seem to be moving, made Lee think at first that they had stumbled into a wax museum of a late-modern street scene. They hastened. Judy, he was to remember — and he could see her tiny square shoes kicking wildly in and out of view — had to hop and skip in her effort to keep even with him.

"Lee!"

"Hurry."

They entered and then went up at once into the upper room of their second-favorite restaurant. Here they waited, the girl glancing about nervously, as if she expected one of the waiters (lofty types!) to come and order them from the building. At the same time, she had by no means forgotten her red beret, which she wore at a pert angle to drive him insane. Sometimes, she wearied of pretending that she was not as startlingly pretty as in fact she was.

"Did you ever think you'd be here? Having coffee with the boy you love?"

"Yes. But I didn't know it would be in Chicago."

"You thought it would be in 'Queens,' so-called?"

She nodded.

"But you knew it would be me?"

"Of course."

"And how many of those" — he pointed to the street — "will find whom they're looking for?"

She looked, plucking nervously at her hands. "Not many?"

"Right. In fact, they're probably passing each other by at this very moment." (He was watching one girl in particular, who seemed to be moving forward blindly, as if in a forest by night.) "For most people," said Lee, "life is a long blundering through a forest by night."

"We went to a forest once. My father took us."

But Lee, who had heard it before, held up his hand to stop her. Phyllis, looking worrisomely cheerful, had just made her appearance on the stairs. She smiled and waved and summoned Luke who, to Lee's amazement, appeared to have shaved and combed. Seeing the coffee and doughnuts, the boy came forward eagerly.

"No, I have to say it, Lee: this is good. A person can see for miles from up here. But the waiters, Lee, they're not good." Then: "Look at Phyl."

They looked. The girl was in the best of moods. Moreover, in her white blouse (buttoned to the neck), she looked more pristine and bright than he could remember having ever seen her before. And now that all of them were rested and for no particular reason all of them happy… It was the only time that such a coincidence was ever to come about. He looked to Judy, Judy of the wondering eyes, her block-like shoes not quite touching the ground. Deep was she, deep and still and vivid, too, the very nature of her own scarlet hat.

Next, Luke — there was something there that made Lee think of *green*.… Mildness? Endurance? His role was to give back to life more by far than ever life was to give to him.

Phyllis (he caught her listening happily, head tilted to one side, giving heed to far-away music), Phyllis was a tenuous silver, it seemed to him, like the dust that accrues in spring on butterfly wings. Civilization owed her a magazine to edit, or a position in an art gallery — otherwise, she would be the first to disappear.

In his blue diagonally zippered shirt, Lee went on droning in the background, the two girls laughing happily at what he had to say. Why was it? Why that Lee could never see nor hear without hearing and seeing as if from a window in the sky whence he had seen and heard all things so many times before?

FORTY-TWO

THEY ARRIVED AT THE STATION in good time for Lee to go chasing after the bus. To come away without a kiss — it weighed upon him heavily. He was given one last glimpse of three unusual personalities waving sadly to him. Outside, Chicago rolled past slowly, a grey accretion of calcium and spackle.

This time, as so often before, he went straight to the newspaper. And if on this occasion, as so very often before, he arrived late, nevertheless he tried to atone for it by wearing a conscientious expression. But had not been there ten minutes before a fight broke out among the compositors, two of the men having actually begun to square off against each other. For one shining moment, it seemed possible that an expanding chaos might impede the two-star edition; instead, Arbuthnot stepped in at the last moment, putting a stop to it.

Lee gave it another few minutes, his conscientious expression wearing thin. Finally, at eighteen past the hour, he darted into the men's room. It might not be the best location for taking his coffee and sweet-rolls; it was, however, a place where he could repair to one of the cells and enjoy a brief nap.

The days were growing longer — it made him mad — and the sun stronger. Here in the North, one was given a choice between unspeakable cold on the one hand or endless light on the other. He liked his days to end at 5:00 pm; instead, with May coming on, he must some-times lie a full three and four hours moving in and out of conscious-ness in the cruciform depression of his amazing "bed." Finally, toward 8:00, he rose again, dressed, and then crept out into the semi-dark.

Peace and quiet he could admire, but never this dead quality af-fected by the homes in his own immediate vicinity. Nothing more angered him, nothing more decidedly turned him away from the recommended life than the way in which these people had permitted the limited number of hours to be packaged-up, as it were, and doled out according to whether or not it were bright outside — it made his gorge rise.

He went straight to his favorite booth in his own personal restau-rant, but only to find it taken already by two corrupt-looking youths capable of defending it. Lee glared at them, but came away without doing anything. He spent the next twenty minutes striding back and forth in front of the shops. In the lower slum, a red and yellow haze was rising and falling, mixed with the sound of pistol shots and women wailing in the mews.

At the restaurant, he found his booth still in the possession of the same rotten youths. *These* were the reasons he had not eaten in twenty-four hours. But what bothered him more than that, far more, was the letter in his pocket that told of the adventures being had by Luke, Phyllis and Judy, Chicago adventures, and how the three of them were at that moment lying crosswise in the enormous bed while Phyllis read them to sleep from her most recent prose.

He tried once more, but the booth was still occupied and the pawn-shop closed. These days, Monique was performing in Philadelphia and with no assurance she'd ever come back again. He trudged home, finding that his books, at least, were still in place. He passed a few minutes tidying them up in his fastidious way, until his heart could settle. He had his way and he would have tidied the entire world. As to the "bed," he longer complained so much. He had learned to avail himself of it by lying in the lower part while using the upper as a prop for his books, his letters, cigarettes, his knife and radio.

He had only just rolled off to sleep (as he believed) and was dreaming bitterly when something, an animal of some sort (so he imagined) leapt into bed with him and began digging with its paws. He must take action at once. And yet, the only part of him that would function was the part registering alarm!

"Goddamn it!"

The thing burrowed yet closer; he could see two brown eyes.

"Tweedy!"

"I'm here." It was a deep voice, for one so short.

"Tweedy!"

"Luke is here."

"Where?"

"There."

He looked, squinting into the dim. "There?"

"No, that's Phyl."

"Good Lord! But how did you get here, that's what I want to know."

"Maybe you should put on some clothes. We hitch-hiked."

"Hitch-hiked, I see." (This, too, they had done without him.) Now Luke came forward.

"Sure. But one of the drivers got mad. He said: 'Look, you've got two girls. You ought to let me have one.'"

"You didn't, did you?"

They laughed, making him feel yet more ignorant and bewildered.

"We had to leave Chicago, Lee. They think Phyl and Judy are whores."

"What!"

"Sure. But the guy downstairs came to our defense; he said they had every right to be whores."

"And the landlady…?"

"She doesn't want any whores there." He plucked out his harmonica and tested it. After so many nights in the same suit, his hair in an uproar, he looked as if he had just returned from an appalling expedition to the edge of the world.

"Does anybody know you're here?"

"Nope." (They grinned.) "Phyl's supposed to be at school and I'm supposed to be at Fort Franklin. Theoretically. And Judy's supposed to be at work."

Lee dressed. He could feel his strength returning. "Hey! why don't we all just disappear somewhere and not come back? Go to some other country?"

"It's a thought."

"Certainly! And someday, a whole generation will be like us. They just won't know who started it."

They listened, reflecting seriously on what he had to say.

"Maybe. You might be right, Lee. But now, we have to sleep."

He pointed them to the bed and, while they prepared themselves, took Judy aside to talk to her more privately. "And so, you actually hitch-hiked from Chicago for my benefit, I see. And the child, too."

She beamed at him in pride and enthusiasm and then came forward and fitted the top of her head under his chin.

They read and slept and came awake, all save Judy, with the sun. She was speaking lowly, Judy, speaking in her sleep while as for the other girl… Lee came nearer. He had not imagined that her sickness would feed upon her even in sleep; now, looking at her, he saw that she was staring up at the ceiling, her eyes aghast, as if she were lying on the bottom of a sea.

He dressed and sallied out onto the porch to have a cigarette. Dawn was threatening; he could see the birds fleeing from it in wild distress. And that was when the woman of the adjoining apartment stepped out onto the porch with him. She, too, was wild-looking, wilder than the birds, and dressed in a blue-green robe belted at neck and waist.

"Ah! I know you're not married," she said, a look of glittering excitement in her eyes. "You're too young."

"What?"

"Oh, I know alright. You've got a girl in there, two girls! And you're not married, either. I know."

"Aw, for Christ's sake. They could be my sisters!"

"Are they?"

They glared.

"And I know where you work, too. At that newspaper!"

"So what?"

"Ah, 'so what' — I'll tell you 'so what'!" Instead, she turned and fled inside and went immediately around to the blinds and peeped out at him.

He worked away the morning in usual fashion, which is to say by running up and down the stairs and then escaping into the men's room whenever the sound of telephones and the middle-aged faces became too much for him. Sometimes, he could fall off to sleep at his work station, until the journalists learned where to find him. And then, too, between the sound of the press, the stink of ink, the telephones, and his diet of jelly rolls… He could sense himself day by day falling deeper and deeper into the state called "pre-journalism."

Come noon, he flew downstairs and raced across town to share the hour with his friends. They were in good form, most of them, but especially Phyllis, who had taken up at a table in the corner of the diner where she sat speaking excitedly and waving one arm around. She had also managed to spill the catsup with the result that, in addition to her archaic clothes and woolen socks, she now had a gory stain running down her dress.

"Phyl's telling about her play," Luke explained, evidently very pleased that she was feeling as well as she was, and never mind that the remaining fifteen or twenty customers were listening in growing annoyance. "She's going to model it on the *Analects*."

"Good."

"Tell him, Phyl."

"No! God. I just got through telling."

A man got up slowly, taking his food with him. Lee waited a moment before asking his question:

"Good. Now are we all agreed about what I said?"

"You mean…?"

"Right."

"Disappear?"

Lee nodded. "Go to Europe, for example?"

There was a pause, enough to let him know that they had settled upon some smaller course than the one he had recommended.

"We're going back to Antioch, Lee."

"I see."

"Phyl has to finish her work."

"I see. Whereas you…"

"I've got to go back Lee. They could shoot me."

"Aw, for God's sake. They can't *shoot* you if they can't *find* you!"

"It's not good, Lee."

"Knew it. No, I knew it! Every goddamn time I'm ready to actually do something, that's when everybody else starts puking out on me. Every goddamn time! Alright, Tweedy and me, we'll do it by ourselves."

"Don't let him, Judy."

"Will you? If I ask?"

"If I have to."

"See!"

"Well, we'll be waiting for you. If you ever change your mind."

He looked at them. Only then did it occur to him that they were on the verge of separating, possibly for weeks or even months.

"When are you leaving?"

The boy examined his watch, removed it, and slapped it twice across the table.

"Nine minutes."

"I see."

They ate in silence, the three of them checking up at his face from time to time for signs of continuing anger.

"We'll do it next year, Lee."

"Ha."

"We'll go to Mexico."

"Seriously?"

"Oh sure."

"That might be even better — Mexico."

"Much better. You'll see."

He remembered bidding them good-bye and shaking hands all around.

"We'll see each other again."

He had to hasten, racing back to work before the teletype machines had produced a new international crisis with bells going off. This time he had stayed away too long with the result that the sports editor, a primitive man with a nose notoriously like a penis, stood waiting for him.

"You want to know something? You aren't worth a shit — did you know that? Not one little shit!" (He had a way of making his eyes go red, until they resembled two little far-away stars of the class called "pink dwarfs.")

"I'm entitled to go to lunch."

"You got no titles, nothing!"

How Lee yearned to kick him in the belly, a taut artifact that hung out over his belt like a skein full of glycerin.

"Look, I never even wanted to work here in the first place!"

"Can't pay taxes, if you don't work. And now, would you please get your valuable butt to the teletype room and do what we're paying you to do?"

How Lee yearned to kick him in the belly, a great taut affair that hung out over his belt like a skein of glycerin. He could not but notice how the other journalists, no friends of his, were grinning in his direction. It was not permitted to smoke in this location; nevertheless, Lee got into his bored expression and took out a cigarette. That was when the dying journalist, his only friend, called him to the phone.

It was Judy. He could not make out what she was saying.

"Where are you?"

"Jail!"

He flew downstairs and out into the street. This "jail" was nearby, the same edifice he had often enough visited in the past in order to collect the arrest reports and daily obits. Here before, it had always been for him a place of fascination, whereas now his one remaining hope was to find where his love was being held before they strapped her into a chair and put her to sleep forever.

A woman, the hardest-looking in the world, was at the desk.

"I'm looking for three people who…"

She studied him, trying to determine whether he ought not be arrested as well. "Room 101," she said finally.

He raced the distance, coming out into a lobby where half-a-dozen uniformed men were watching a game on television.

"I'm looking for three people…"

"Those college kids? They're back there."

He went through and then into a small room without furniture (years later, he would still recall perfectly the odor of it, so much like a veterinary clinic in which surgery was performed), where Phyllis, Luke, and Judy were being lectured by a tall man who kept jabbing into the air with his finger of indignation. This scene burned into his mind: Phyllis smiling brightly, Luke toying with, but not actually playing, his larger harmonica, and the eighteen-inch-tall Tweedy, her shirt tail hanging out, a ruffian with two tiny fists in the fighting position.

"Lee!"

"They called Antioch, Lee; we're in trouble."

"Why?"

"Why? Look at 'em!"

"But what did they *do*?"

"Well now, that's just exactly what we're looking into."

"We missed the bus, that's all."

"Vagrancy," spoke the man.

"Oh, for God's sakes. That's pure shit!"

"Hey! Watch out how you talk here, buster!"

"That's why they called Antioch — to see if we're vagrants."

"Oh, good Lord. And what about Van Gogh? Was he a vagrant, too?"

"They don't care about stuff like that Lee."

"A jury might."

He ended up having to show his library card and driver's license and then sign a form that he was not allowed to read. He remembered the four of them being herded down to the hard woman who returned their possessions — two thin books with notes on the jackets, a small harmonica, normally kept in reserve (which the woman handled with distaste), and finally, a beautiful broach made of butterfly wing.

"Do they know you're mixed up with people like this, over at the paper?"

"No. But I guess you'll be telling them, won't you?"

She raised both eyebrows.

At last, they hit the street, falling quite naturally into single file.

"It was grim, Lee. You could hear them beating up people in the next room."

"But what did you *do*?"

"Oh, you don't have to *do* anything. They can tell just by looking at you."

"See? We should have disappeared, like I said."

"Phyl was reciting to them. They couldn't cope with it."

"Oh, God. It was only *Thanatopsis*!"

"Judy kicked the tall one."

"He deserved it," she said grimly.

"I see. Well maybe we ought to just go back right now and have it out with them once and for all!"

"Don't let him, Judy."

The station was crowded, a new wave of elderly women with bags and worn suitcases having just blown into town.

"That's the one who called the police," Luke said, pointing out the thin-faced ticket-seller in cage two. "Look at him. Probably the greatest thing that ever happened to him."

"He's looking at us right now!"

They sat quietly, faces forward.

"You've got to write about this Lee."

"Oh, I will, you can count upon it."

"Tell 'em we weren't doing anything."

"Yeah. And tell about Phyl."

He stayed with them, watching while they climbed aboard the correct bus and then waiting until their faces appeared in the window.

"Explain it to them," Lee commanded. "At Antioch, I mean."

"Don't worry."

"We'll see each other soon."

And then they were gone, the bus rolling off into the sun exactly as on that day his late beloved grandmother had traveled away in just such weather as this, never to come back again.

"They'll be alright," Judy mooted.

"I doubt it."

"And what about you — aren't you supposed to be at work?"

"To hell with 'em."

"You better, Lee."

"And just leave you here, right? Ha."

"I'll take the next bus."

"Absolutely not! Wait for me and then at five, we can just disappear, like we've always said."

"No, Lee, it's best. Before we get into even more trouble."

(He could see the ticket-seller counting eagerly, measuring the moments before he could call the police again.)

"It's best, Lee."

"Wait." He took her around the corner, out of sight of man and world. They flew into one another's arms. "Oh, baby." (He had to absorb enough of her perfume and analgesic hair to suffice him for the next weeks, or eternity, should it come to that.)

"It's not fair!"

"Think of me."

FORTY-THREE

YEARS NOW PASSED, or rather a few days in which his spiritual development was that of years. More and more, he spent his life in cafeterias, or dozing in the men's room, or dallying around the elevator for the hour of departure. How he did so loathe it, business, busyness, commerce, enterprise, and all the other barbiturates of the panic-stricken North. Sometimes, he wished he were back in Alabama again, a home of one's own filled to overflowing with canned fruits and the divine Judy glowing in the door. And that, of course, was when the dying journalist, his sole remaining friend, called him to the telephone.

Luke: "We've been excommunicated Lee."

"What?"

"Antioch. They've expelled us."

"Can't be."

"They did. Write about it Lee."

"Did you explain it to them?"

"Oh, sure. I said:

'Fools and harlots have pleasures of their own,

the vulgar herd can never understand.'"

"Good! What did they say?"

"They couldn't cope with it."

"Maybe I should talk to them."

"They know about the baby."

"What!"

"Phyl told 'em."

"Can't be."

"She did, Lee."

"Let me talk to her."

"She's gone, Lee."

"Gone! Back to North Carolina?"

"Sure. She was expelled, too."

"Can't be. What's happening, Luke?"

"I don't know. I'm about ready to snap my fingers at the whole thing."

"What are you going to do?"

"I don't know. Start over from scratch, I guess."

"What about Phyl?"

"She doesn't want to see us anymore."

"What! Can't be."

"It's true."

"Goddamn it! Well, what about Mexico — we're still going, aren't we?"

"Oh sure. I wouldn't miss it for the world." (Lee could hear a small tweeting, one single note on the larger harmonica.) Then: "Don't worry — we'll see each other again."

Lee trudged home, his head full of bees. Things were coming to a conclusion, no doubt about it, and these things were moving faster than he liked. There was a letter from Judy, or rather one letter and one postcard, both full of kisses, also an evil-looking telegram on yellow paper. He knew what it was, nothing surprised him anymore. And yet, he *was* surprised to find himself summoned to a hotel downtown, there to discuss matters with one of Antioch's higher officials flying up for just that purpose. His first thought (which later on he put out of mind) was that they were rushing someone up to apologize to him. It was a strange thing, that whereas he loved the college still, yet he had hardly ever felt more elated than when they were sending him away. He could see it, his face etched over with corruption and perceptions, and himself returning forty years later to a reduced campus putting up a cheerful front with a residue of low-grade students shuffling across the yard. (And in fact, seeing later on what the next generation had had to settle for, he gave thanks to the moon for having brought him on when it did, instead of when it might.)

He slept, Lee rising from his "bed" at the same moment as, after so many weeks and months, the bed finally crashed down under him with terrific noise. His first concern was for the well-being of the books used to support it, his second that the woman next door would most probably be hoping that he had shot himself at last.

He put on his lavender shirt with the steel buttons. Balmy weather it was, southern in smell and texture, a dangerous combination for anyone electing to go up against him on a night like this. one. The pawnshop came up, the bookstore and mission, the burlesque, bus station, and his second-favorite restaurant with the district's third-loveliest whore positioned out front. The hotel itself was wedged-in between the best and worst best parts of town.

He entered the lobby, his face quite bored, but then had to wait around for a while before anyone acknowledged him.

"Are you Leland?"

Not only had they sent a woman, not only was she fat, they had sent a fat woman wearing a hat.

"I'm being expelled, right?"

"I don't see that we have any choice."

"Me neither, I didn't have any choice either."

They looked at each other and then, slowly, sank into the chairs. She had a portmanteau in which he could immediately verify the same dossier (running over with papers) that his counselor used to maintain.

"So," she said. "How have you been keeping? Apart from this, I mean."

Lee looked at her. It didn't matter what he said, he knew it and she knew it, too. He was so tired of adults. Finally, taking a cigarette: "I did what I wanted to do. I always do."

"I believe that. And what you wanted was to have a girl in your apartment. Spend the night with her."

"That happens all the time at Antioch! We just happen to be in love — that's the only difference."

"Love!" She laughed bitterly. "Pregnant, is what you mean. Oh yes! we know about that, too."

"Well, what about Luke and Phyllis? They aren't pregnant."

"They're being processed for other reasons."

"'Processed.'" Suddenly he stood and began looking for the exit. It occurred to him that, in a sense, he had been set at liberty and could rise now and do whatever he wanted, provided only that he actually do it.

"Just a moment! What about your job?"

He looked at her in disbelief. "I'm being expelled and you want me to finish out my job?"

"Someone has to."

"And what about my things? May I go pick them up?"

"No, no; we'll see that you get them."

He got outside, took a breath, and then headed off quickly toward the neon section. He had done about as well as he could expect of himself, considering how much larger and more corrupted the woman was than himself. Perhaps he might really be a writer after all, the more so as time went on and he himself was expelled from larger and larger institutions. Antioch had claimed to be a haven for such as himself, until faced with the reality. Then they had coughed and blinked and, finally, had regurgitated him back into the world.

He lit a cigarette and tossed the hair out of his eyes. The theater came up, the huge poster beaming down on him with approval from the post-mortem world. Lee stopped. He had eleven free passes and James Dean was back in town.

FORTY-FOUR

SUMMER NOW — he had seen it before — warms days and nights full of rain. Arising late, he would come out into the yard and watch where the downtown factories sent up tendrils of smoke that lifted to a certain distance, and then stopped and stayed.

He went back and seized off two more hours of sleep. Three letters were waiting for him, a morose one from Luke (no mention of Mexico) and two that were cheerful in Judy's lucid hand. She was coming that very day, leaving directly after work and running all the way (she said) to the bus station. He could see it — the slum dwellers turning to stare at the red ribbon streaming out behind and her blistered suitcase bumping over the cobbles.

He spent the afternoon cleaning and sweeping, a pleasant task in consideration of the divine visitor he had in prospect. Finally, he pulled out even the carpet, too, and was thrashing at it vehemently, until he caught the neighboring bourgeois woman watching with approval.

He bathed and combed and checked his money. He was depending upon it that she would bring further quarters and dimes and even green bills; as for himself, it was amazing how little he had after all his suffering — a few bank notes with the usual portraits on them, not of philosophers and composers, but Indian killers and land surveyors risen to high position.

Three times he went out to check on the climate. He was quite serene, knowing, as he did, that his love had broken out of Chicago by this time and even now was rushing on toward him at a speed mid-point between that of light and sound. No doubt about it, there was a stillness this night. Across the road, the woman came out in her apron and, never knowing that he was watching, stood gazing up resentfully at Lee's own special star.

He knew this much about himself, that by having given up on institutions, whether of church, school, or place of work, that he was on the threshold of a mode of life that most men could not endure. Great was his arrogance, and growing; he had been right about the world and everyone else wrong—the best things had nothing to do with what most people were spending their time upon. Moreover, he had been receiving inklings lately, not so much about this or that, life on other planets, "eternal recurrence," etc., etc., no, but even stranger than that.

He went back and got into his purple shirt. It would be a struggle, a fight and an ordeal, when came the time to give up on being young. Again, he checked himself in the mirror, pausing only to toss the hair out of his eyes.

He set out much too early for the station and after four blocks of it (talking to himself), turned and came back. That was when the inspiration hit him to go out into the yard with a flashlight and gather as many flowers as he could.

The station was crowded, a ripple of excitement running through the room in anticipation of Tweedy. At the counter, two emaciated ticker-sellers were perched side by side, one of them gazing out the window toward the future and the other looking into the past. Lee stood harkening off toward that western road whence the cars and trucks were coming and going so thickly that he had no hope of identifying the one bringing Judy. He closed his eyes, but the only transmission he could pick up (and it was faint) seemed to emanate from one of his long-ago-departed dogs. Five minutes went by, this signal also falling away gradually. Now it was Judy coming on, a deep and steady hum like unto a motor or a bee. He prepared himself. An airplane drove overhead.

In fact, the bus came in and berthed before he realized he had been watching in the wrong direction. He ran for it, but then halted and came back and lit a cigarette and lounged up against the column. It was forever the same — they had been through it a thousand times, and yet he could never be apart from her for any length without extreme nervousness and worry over whether she was still the same. Now the door sprang open, letting out an elderly man, his hat held courteously in one hand. Lee felt a sympathy for all such people, people like himself enslaved to night travel and constant relocation. One man, his addiction far advanced, came off carrying a pillow and wearing sunglasses.

Judy. It was her shortness that gave her away. Lee ran forward. She had halted in the doorway and was probing with one foot, as if about to step down into a flood of indeterminate depth. Somehow, she had fallen into a struggle with her suitcase.

"Good grief!"

Lee ran up. "Hi."

"Hi."

(She had not changed, not at all; he could see that it was she.)

"Oh, baby. Did I ever miss you!"

"Oh!"

They fell into one another's arms.

"Did you have the back seat?"

She nodded proudly. "And I finished another book."

He hugged her, the first time in weeks, her brown hair with its rich odors going straight to the dream centers of his mind.

"Come on, let's get out of here before we get arrested."

He took her suitcase, at the same time handing over the immense bouquet of flowers that she took in both arms.

"Oh! Where did you get these Lee?"

"Took 'em off a little boy."

"Oh, you did not."

She looked good, with her cheery smile. He always felt that he had but moments only in which to commit her to memory before she turned, first, into but another adult, and secondly, vanished off the earth.

"I'd almost forgotten how beautiful you are."

"You shouldn't forget."

"Oh, baby."

He wanted to consume her, but instead merely began to walk a little faster. The neon district was coming up quickly, at least one drunk floundering in their path.

"I have to leave tomorrow."

He stopped. "No!"

"I have to."

"Why! Why!"

"I have to, Lee. They want me to."

"Your parents, you mean?"

"They want to see me. They said you'd come get me, if you really cared."

"New York?"

"You always wanted to."

"Why can't we just stay here? Besides, parents hate me."

"It's not right, Lee. You can't stay here forever."

"I don't mind."

They went on in silence, the girl checking up at his face every two minutes.

"Don't be mad."

"I thought you'd stay with me."

"I want to."

"First Phyl, and then Luke. Now you."

"Lee!"

"I even cleaned the room."

They stepped into the light and moved past a row of derelicts grinning in such a way as to show off their rotted teeth. Formerly, Lee had been able to traverse the slum within minutes, but not now, not since it had put on such a burst of expansion. The journalist's house came up. Lee would have loved to go up and knock and show off his girl, except that the place was dark and empty now, the man himself having recently dropped out of sight.

He had left the lamp burning, a warm and welcoming sight as they hastened up to the porch. The woman next door had been waiting for them apparently, but now had fallen asleep with her forehead pasted to the window pane. No doubt she had observed him running off to town with flowers.

"Good Lord!" He got down and took a look at her at close range, impressed in spite of himself at the grimness in her face. "Shall we wake her?"

"Don't, Lee."

He opened slowly, needing a full ten seconds with the key. Her suitcase was surprisingly heavy; he carried it straightway to the room and, while she sought about for something to put the flowers in, opened the thing to find it full of books, a blouse, a pair of square brown shoes and a few bits and pieces of underwear that she had tried to put out of sight.

"Judy."

She came to him, beaming in her warm and enthusiastic way. That such a thing must someday die, and with nothing between that day and this except a thin and tenuous stretch of water-colored Time…

"I love thee, Judy."

"I love thee. Darling."

He had forgotten how wretched he had been, all the days he didn't have Judy in his arms.

"You are the ocean itself."

"I thought it was the forest."

"That, too."

"And the sun?"

"And stars."

He woke in the night, lay for a moment, and then disentangled himself and went downstairs. They were in a stronghold surrounded by danger and it was his duty to rise at certain hours and make the rounds. Just now it was quiet, but with moonlight splashing on the ground. In the doorway, he stood facing off in the direction of the city and buildings whose lights had finally burned out. To his thinking, nothing could be more exquisite than to live in times of catastrophe, the world reduced to a tiny number of privacy-adoring survivors. Stepping down into the yard, he spent a minute looking up at her window and knowing that although he was young yet also was he formidable, and that no living person could do any slightest harm to her without having first to face up to him. Night was *his* element, he had been born for it, night and standing vigil for long periods — the true preparation for when catastrophes come.

He went back and stood looking down at her for some while before he recognized that she had come awake.

"You should be sleeping," she said.

"You, too."

Outside, a car went past.

"Would you like to go down to Antioch tomorrow and take one last look? No one has to see us."

"I can't, Lee."

"Just think: we'll never, never see it again." He grinned and then, to his embarrassment, found that he was near to crying.

"Lee! There are other places besides Antioch."

"No there aren't."

"Lots. And you'll see all of them. And Antioch will go into decline for what they did."

He remembered helping her get her things together and then pacing nervously while she put on lipstick and make-up. He wanted the minutes to pass slowly, that it might seem she had stayed with him a long time. In fact, the time was fleeing and he could think of nothing to say.

They walked toward town, Lee stealing glimpses of her when it was safe. As a measure of cruelty, she had put on the same white sweater and red collar she had been wearing the night they met. And now, she was bobbing along at his side.

They passed into the slum, finding at so early an hour only one single sleepy-looking individual who had come out to sweep the walk. The restaurant came up, the same in which he used to spend his time with thoughts glued on Judy. He had spent so much time, had suffered so much, and now it seemed that he had been consigned to the place, had perhaps been so consigned from the beginning, and was never to go away.

He waited while she bought her ticket, purchasing it by irony and without either of them realizing it, from the same man who had sent her to jail. Outside, the sun was bright, a few languorous clouds coasting overhead.

"Are you still going to read the books on my list?"

She turned, laughing at him. "Of course. I have to now — to finish my education." Her face was close, tilted up at him. "What will happen to you, Lee?"

"I don't know."

"Who will love you?"

She was looking at him in the way he adored, her two brown eyes friendly and warm. He remembered thinking that this was how great Hector must have felt, his time having come around. And he, too, knowing that he must spend eternity in the aftermath of something that happened one time.

OTHER BOOKS PUBLISHED BY ARKTOS

OTHER BOOKS PUBLISHED BY ARKTOS

OTHER BOOKS PUBLISHED BY ARKTOS

OTHER BOOKS PUBLISHED BY ARKTOS

	Wildest Dreams
ERNST VON SALOMON	*It Cannot Be Stormed*
	The Outlaws
SRI SRI RAVI SHANKAR	*Celebrating Silence*
	Know Your Child
	Management Mantras
	Patanjali Yoga Sutras
	Secrets of Relationships
GEORGE T. SHAW (ED.)	*A Fair Hearing*
FENEK SOLÈRE	*Kraal*
OSWALD SPENGLER	*Man and Technics*
RICHARD STOREY	*The Uniqueness of Western Law*
TOMISLAV SUNIC	*Against Democracy and Equality*
	Homo Americanus
	Postmortem Report
	Titans are in Town
HANS-JÜRGEN SYBERBERG	*On the Fortunes and Misfortunes of Art in Post-War Germany*
ABIR TAHA	*Defining Terrorism*
	The Epic of Arya (2nd ed.)
	Nietzsche's Coming God, or the Redemption of the Divine
	Verses of Light
BAL GANGADHAR TILAK	*The Arctic Home in the Vedas*
DOMINIQUE VENNER	*For a Positive Critique*
	The Shock of History
MARKUS WILLINGER	*A Europe of Nations*
	Generation Identity
ALEXANDER WOLFHEZE	*Alba Rosa*

CPSIA information can be obtained
at www.ICGtesting.com
Printed in the USA
BVHW081921250919
559383BV00001B/62/P

9 781912 975389